Car

Hamel, The Obeah Man

Anonymous

With a new introduction by
Amon Saba Saakana
and notes by John Gilmore

MACMILLAN
CARIBBEAN

Macmillan Education
Between Towns Road, Oxford, OX4 3PP
A division of Macmillan Publishers Limited
Companies and representatives throughout the world

www.macmillan-caribbean.com

ISBN: 978-0-333-91938-5

Design © Macmillan Publishers Limited 2008

Typeset by EXPO Holdings, Malaysia
Cover design by Gary Fielder
Cover Image: The British Library Board
All Rights Reserved. Shelf Mark K.123.59

Printed and bound in Hong Kong

2012   2011   2010   2009   2008
10   9   8   7   6   5   4   3   2   1

CONTENTS

CARIBBEAN CLASSICS

Series Editor: John Gilmore

Titles already published:

SERIES EDITOR'S PREFACE

I FIRST read *Hamel, The Obeah Man,* many years ago in a photo-copy of the original edition in the library of the University of the West Indies at Mona. It was a book I had long known of, through Kamau Brathwaite's important essay on 'Creative Literature of the British West Indies during the period of Slavery' (*Savacou,* Vol. 1, No. 1, June 1970, 46–73; reprinted in the author's collected essays, *Roots* [Ann Arbor: University of Michigan Press, 1993], 127–70). While Brathwaite pointed out that '*Hamel* is a deeply race-conscious and colour-prejudiced book', he also described it as 'such a surprise' in contrast to much of the rest of the literature of the period, because 'it has as its central character, a black man'. More than this, Hamel is a black man of eloquence and intelli-gence, whom Brathwaite credits with 'what is probably the first Black Power speech in our literature' (the reference is to what is 319–20 in this edition). I had read some of the poetry and prose fiction produced in the Caribbean in the eighteenth and early nineteenth centuries which was discussed by Brathwaite, and be-lieved that, in spite of its very real limitations, this literature had much to offer anyone with an interest in the history of Caribbean culture. From what Brathwaite said, however, *Hamel, The Obeah Man* was clearly in a class of its own. Unfortunately, there seemed to be no copy of the novel available in Barbados, where I was then living, and the bulk of the work—over 600 pages in the original edition—made the idea of ordering a photocopy from some over-seas library seem prohibitively expensive.

However, the wait proved worthwhile, for when I finally came to be sitting in the library at Mona, with a copy of *Hamel* in front of me, I had just come from spending a few days in the parish of Portland, on Jamaica's north coast, the very area where the novel is set. I had been on the Rio Grande, I had passed through the mountains between Portland and Kingston, and from the opening pages of the novel I was convinced that the scenery was described by a writer who had known the area at first hand.

It has to be admitted that Brathwaite is more cautious: he expresses some scepticism as to whether the author of the novel had even been in the Caribbean, and draws attention to Hamel's 'South American poncho' (18) as an example of an implausible detail. The geographical references in the passage at 90 also seem as though they might be rather confused. Nevertheless, the novel clearly shows, as Dr. Amon Saba Saakana indicates in his perceptive introduction to this edition, a thorough understanding of the workings of class and race in a Caribbean society based on colonialism, the plantation system, and the enslavement of Africans for the benefit of the mainly white land-owning class. The author's identity remains unknown, though a prolonged search of the Jamaican and British periodical press of the period might turn up some clues. Some comments may, however, be ventured as to what type of person he or she was. To begin with, our author was almost certainly male—the open discussion of sexual matters is quite alien to the delicacy and restraint which would have been expected of female writers at the time. He is aware of some of the injustices and suffering caused by slavery, but argues that any rapid transition to freedom for the enslaved would be contrary to their own best interests and dangerous to society as a whole. His main concern is for the safety of the owners of land and slaves in the Caribbean colonies—the safety of both their persons and the property rights which they enjoyed under the existing system. In spite of the way in which he makes Hamel himself an impressive figure, and presents some white characters (particularly Roland and Fillbeer) in a less than flattering light, the author is clearly a believer in white racial superiority. Combah is portrayed, not as the heroic leader of a revolutionary struggle for the freedom of his people, but as little better than a buffoon whose main motivation is lust for a white woman, and the generality of his followers are treated in the same manner.

But the author's greatest scorn is reserved for Roland, the missionary, whose religious hypocrisy and sexual depravity make him a sort of Protestant counterpart to Ambrosio, the villainous title-character of M. G. Lewis's celebrated Gothic novel *The Monk* (first published 1796). Indeed, with its skilful use of the dramatic possibilities of the wilder parts of the Jamaican landscape, of the ignorance and fear with which most contemporary readers would have viewed obeah—described by the author, like many other white writers, as essentially fraudulent, but nevertheless having real power over believers and therefore deservedly feared even by white people—and of the almost blasphemous titillation produced by the association of criminal lustfulness with the representative of what is portrayed as debased form of true religion in the person of Roland, *Hamel, The Obeah Man* is essentially a Caribbean representative of the genre of the Gothic novel which was so popular in Europe at the time. Were it not for the fact that references in the novel to specific historical events indicate that it was written, or at least completed, no more than two years or so before its original publication in 1827, one might almost be tempted to suggest that the author was M. G. Lewis himself, who owned plantations in Jamaica which he visited on two occasions. But Lewis died in 1818, and his well-known *Journal of a West India Proprietor* (published posthumously in 1834) shows that he had rather more reservations about slavery as an institution than are apparent in *Hamel.*

Viewed simply as a Gothic novel, *Hamel* can be read for entertainment as a skilful and successful example of a genre in which we do not expect realism. However, the modern reader who approaches the novel with a desire to see what it might reveal about the history of Caribbean culture will soon realize that the parallel is not exact. While Lewis does deliberately play upon the Protestant prejudices and misunderstanding of Catholicism which he could have expected to find among most of the British reading public at the time *The Monk* was published, the lustful, murderous Ambrosio, who goes so far as to make a pact with the Devil in an ultimately unsuccessful attempt to escape the punishment he so richly deserves, can hardly be taken seriously as a typical representative of monasticism. The author of *Hamel,* on the other hand, does want his readers to take Roland seriously as a type of Protestant missionary (though he is careful to distinguish such missionaries from the priests of the Church of England which was the established church in Jamaica and other British

colonies in the Caribbean). The alleged religious motivation of
such missionaries, our author would have us believe, was only a
hypocritical cover for their activities as agents of the movement
against colonial slavery which was then growing in importance in
British political life. The novelist, and others like him, claimed
(and, in some cases, perhaps sincerely believed) that, were it not
for the interference of missionaries and other anti-slavery agita-
tors sent out from Britain, the slaves in the colonies would have
remained contented with their lot and no unrest would occur—
hence the importance given to Roland's support of Combah and
the novelist's need to portray it as entirely self-interested. A few
years later, this sort of attitude led to the brutal persecution of
Baptist and other missionaries and their followers during the slave
rebellion in Jamaica in 1831–2 known as the Baptist War—a persecution which was entirely counter-productive, as it helped to
hasten the passage by the British parliament in 1833 of the act
which abolished slavery in the colonies.

The strength of the hostility to the anti-slavery movement
shown in the way in which Roland is characterised suggests that
the author was either a British person who had lived in Jamaica for
some time, or possibly a white Jamaican Creole. If the author did
write the novel on the British side of the Atlantic, inspired presumably by personal or family ownership of Jamaican property,
for the level of local detail shown in its pages to have been acquired entirely at second hand would have demanded considerable effort. The language used in the novel also suggests personal
knowledge. In one passage (185) he gives what is supposed to be
a song sung in Jamaican Creole in what is (apart from the use of
'buckras' for 'white people') entirely Standard English prose, saying that he could not reproduce the song 'in its native simplicity,
inasmuch as the lingo (I must not call it language) would be utterly
unintelligible to all my uncreolized countrymen'. This claim for
the cultural superiority of one form of language over another
could be being used simply as a literary device—any writer of
fiction can pretend to be fluent in any language if allowed to offer
only what purports to be a translation into their own language.
Similarly, the way in which Caribbean English terms such as

'great house' are explained for the benefit of British readers (see, for example, 14) is an obvious means of adding local colour through the use of information which could have been obtained at second-hand. However, some specifically Jamaican terms, such as 'contoo' (11), 'John-crows' (44), 'puntees' (94), 'macau-cas' (266), 'cutacoo' (316), and 'nyam-nyam' (390), are intro-duced without explanation, and without their meaning being clear from the context. Since the novel is, at least on one level, a work of anti-abolitionist propaganda addressed to a mainly British readership, this suggests a personal familiarity with such vocabulary on the part of the author and a failure to realize that some (if not most) British readers would not understand it. While modern Caribbean writers are often determined to preserve cul-tural authenticity in their use of language even if it means their mainly extra-regional readership has to work a bit harder (and, sometimes, in spite of pressures from European or North American publishers to assimilate their language to the expecta-tions of potential markets), it seems anachronistic to assume such a motive here.

It is true that the author's cultural background is heavily influenced by European models. He does quote from Bryan Edward's 'Jamaica, A Descriptive and Didactic Poem', but most of his quotations come from British writers such as Shakespeare and Milton (with several drawn from relatively obscure plays for-merly attributed to Shakespeare but now known to be by other writers). Mr. Guthrie, the white Creole planter in the novel who has never left the shores of Jamaica except for his brief experience of being kidnapped by pirates, and who must therefore have re-ceived whatever education he had in the island, displays a fond-ness for peppering his conversation with bits of Latin. These are sometimes (though not always) used with considerable appropri-ateness to the situation in which they are introduced, but they are drawn mainly from Virgil and Horace, authors with whom anyone with a basic classical education would have been expected to be familiar. From what we know from other sources of the type of education which was available in the Caribbean colonies to the children of the upper classes in this period, there is nothing implausible about Mr. Guthrie having this sort of knowledge, even if he does display it in a somewhat idiosyncratic manner. Similarly, the author's references to the mythology and history of ancient Greece and Rome are by no means unusual for writers of the time, though we should note (as Saakana points out) how they are used to emphasize the idea of white superiority and devalue or deny African cultural achievements.

Michal is an excellent example of the 'tragic mulata' figure who has a long history in Caribbean literature, and Saakana draws our attention to the 'ring of authenticity' in the author's description of her reaction to the kiss of the disguised 'Sebastian' and, later, to her discovery of his true identity. The whole sorry history of the complexities of race and class in a slave society is against her.

But it is Hamel himself who holds our attention. He is part of the tradition of the 'noble savage', long established in European literature, the outsider who criticises the society in which he finds himself. He helps to foment the rebellion of the slaves and ensure that Combah's followers believe he has supernatural support, yet he ensures the safety of the Guthries and Fairfax's ultimate recovery of both Joanna and his inheritance, thus bringing about the failure of the rebellion. Is he simply, as Saakana puts it, a Judas-figure, a traitor who betrays his people? In a throwaway line in a footnote, Brathwaite suggests that 'There is ... an element of Anansi in Hamel.' Such an interpretation makes him a much more complex figure, for Anansi, the African trickster, part spider, part man, familiar to generations of Caribbean storytellers and their audiences, is more than a cheerful amoralist whose concern for self-preservation overrides everything else, including his none the less real devotion to his wife and children. Anansi is not just a survivor, he is the ultimate anti-establishment figure. Our novelist appears to have created Hamel, the black obeah-man, as a means of counteracting the white obeah of Roland, of missionaries and abolitionists. However, while *Hamel, The Obeah Man*, the novel, is intended to prop up the system of slavery and white racial supremacy, Hamel, the character, takes on a life of his own, becoming an eloquent critic of the system he so ambiguously defends. He can easily be read in ways which are quite independent of whatever the novelist's intentions may have been. Hamel's survival, and the way in which he retains his dignity, and his air of mysterious power, to the very end, is a serious challenge to notions of white superiority, a subversion of any concept of a racial monopoly of virtue or tragic grandeur. Everyone will have their own interpretation of *Hamel*, and we hope that the publication of this new edition will bring new readers to this major example of early Caribbean fiction and encourage new critical approaches and comparisons with the other early novels in the Macmillan Caribbean Classics series.

John Gilmore
Centre for Caribbean Studies
and
Centre for Translation and Comparative Cultural Studies
University of Warwick

GENERAL NOTE

While a few minor misprints have been silently corrected, the text of the novel in this edition follows the spelling, capitalization, punctuation and paragraphing of the original.

INTRODUCTION

IT IS usually difficult, if not impossible, to judge a work of art outside its time, centuries after it is created. But it is possible to understand its aesthetic and political values by contextualising the events, attitudes and proclivities of individuals and groups within a given society. This is what substantiates an evaluation in retrospect: what was the dominant position of the society, what were the conditions under which the majority of people lived, what were the relations between the different classes in society, what were the outside influences to which the society reacted in transforming itself? These are the considerations which ignite the world of the critic if s/he is to understand and do justice to the work under scrutiny.

The introductory chapter of *Hamel, The Obeah Man*, casts an illusory spell: it enthrals the reader into a world of tropical beauty and describes two opposite characters, a European who may have seen better days and a slave boy, Cuffy (in Asante, Kofi). The anonymous novelist informs us that the 'youngster's features scarcely harmonised with those of his very demure and melancholy-looking master' (2). Thus in the first three pages of the novel one is made aware of the inhabitants of two different worlds locked in the same geographical space. This illustration of difference, though subtle, establishes the fundamental clashes of world view, the disharmonious relations between slave-master and slave. Certainly in this case the author does not tell us that the European is a slave-master but he does crystallise that he is a master, delineating that though there may have been good intentions on the part of some Europeans, the conflicting conditions of the master/slave syndrome is symptomatic of its very nature.

There is something of the adventure tale, of the adventurer, of the moral rogue, of the thinly-veiled lecher in the description of the late afternoon European rider on the Jamaican mountainside at the approach of sunset. Despite his malodorous state, his 'countenance brightened very visibly at sight of some young negro girls…' (3). The author thus, again, very subtly hints at a sexual prowl, a sexual advantage which was not unknown to the British adventurer at home and abroad. Because of an entrenched class society, the adventurer with an assumed superiority of position, whether true or false, could safeguard his interest in the choice of women, whether by flattery, bribery or force. This undercurrent is only hinted at (there is no development of this theme at this point), but it does weave itself back into the novel at a later stage.

The poetic inclination of the prose is part of weaving a spell so that the reader is fascinated by the flora and fauna, the landscape that is permanently beautiful and which late Victorians would up-root and transplant to Britain to furnish exotic and unique gardens. The sky becomes 'the canopy of heaven' (5), and the wind, 'as if it had still reserved some of its power for an effort of desperation, burst on them with such exasperated fury …' (7), and such-like descriptions abound throughout the book, though they are most prominent in the first few pages. The prose cascades from straight descriptions to the poetic. Throughout, the anonymous author is representing the world of the European mind, its sensuality at the sight of young 'negro' women, pleasure at and fear of the environment: the lush vegetation, the roar of the wind, the life-threatening flashes of lightning, and the social, real world which he must encounter, symbolically interact with and release his anxieties, traumas and predetermination upon. His encounter with the frightening side of this tropical haven forces him to cry, at his weakness, at his perilous experience of near-fatal accidents.

Thus reaching the only safe haven from the crushing world of nature in its frightening self, the stranger explores the cavern of his retreat where he partakes of food, now confronting his worst fears: 'A human skull … from which the teeth were missing; but on turning it up, the traveller found them with a quantity of broken glass crammed into the cerebellum, and covered up with a wad of silk cotton … There were several other skulls in a second recess …' (12). These contained gunpowder, bullets mixed with nails, and pieces of rags in which a live black snake lay. These experiences and accoutrements have already alerted us to the vicinity of an obeah man and the fear that is evoked in the description is certainly meant to alarm the reader and induce a feeling of apprehension and distance. Our anonymous author is now describing the nature of a phobia which the reader is lulled into by projecting both the gentle and terrifying sides of an exotic landscape, the nimble young 'negro' women and the beastliness of the 'negro' necromancer. The skull provokes devilish images and the Adamic snake, in the culture of the Judeo-Christian tradition, certainly unleashes a foretaste of corruption. By contrast the snake is represented as a protector and sometimes divinised from Kemet (ancient Egypt) to modern Africa in terms of religion and royalty.

Elsewhere in the novel the author shows his comparative knowledge of African traditions by exposing the rituals of oath-taking (77–8), and later he describes the nature of obeah itself in a way which is quite revolutionary: 'The influence of the Obeah man was not limited: *he possessed knowledge—the secrets of all ranks, and of all sorts of transactions* (80, emphasis added). If we compare the nature of the Obeah man in a traditional African society, we shall see immediate remarkable congruence: amongst the Igbo of Nigeria the word for the equivalent of *obeah man* is *dibia*, a compound word, *di* meaning master, and *abia* meaning knowledge. Thus a *dibia* or *obeah* man is *master of knowledge*. How is this acquired? By years of formal training and induction. (See John Umeh, *After God is Dibia*.)

But the reader is also taken aback when the European intruder finally meets he whom he perceives to be the owner of the contents of the cave, the necromancer, the obeah man. This collision is one of the intelligences, and the obeah man comes out as a 'smart man', a learned man, and his rejoinder to the intruder's question about his knowledge of his entrance to the cave is a classic: '… the Negroes say that none but the devil himself can pass, or one whom the devil leads; and that in the dark' (17). He adds that only once before did any white man try to enter this place, and it was one who was fleeing from 'the punishment of crimes and misdeeds', but fell to his death. Is this a prophetic comment on Roland's fate?

To say our anonymous author was familiar with African peoples would not be unfair, for he keenly chronicles even the tipple of libation poured to departed ancestors before a drink is taken. And this is shown in his description of Hamel, who is not only a necromancer ('dealer in magic', 18) but who appears to hold a strong philosophical position even during the time of slavery. For he held 'no feeling hostile to his fellow-creatures, [was not] at war with human nature, or dissatisfied with himself' (18). In spite of the writer's keenest observations, however, he makes Hamel confess that though many slaves were Christians they did not fast. This point is made to appear as though fasting were equated with denial, which in turn was a Christian phenomenon. This, of course, is far from the truth, for traditional African religion from the most ancient of times advocated fasting as an act of purification, of getting closer to God, and thus accomplishing one's goal. Obviously, the intruder, a Protestant missionary, and the writer who placed the words in Hamel's mouth, were totally unaware of this fact.

This superiorising of the European quickly takes another turn, when Roland, the missionary, attacks the African for being unable to look after himself 'without white men, who shall teach your children to read, to write, to pray to the only true God …'(19). These encounters and interactions can be seen as outlining the parameters of the entire novel: on the one hand the beauty of the landscape and the innocence of the people, and on the other the savagery of nature and the barbarian state of the African slave, who is helpless without European intervention. Thus the interaction between European and African throughout the novel is one of either benign sympathy or savage condemnation. There is no middle ground: as the DJ says, 'take no prisoners'. We are all condemned! Either to serve the European or to be hunted, jailed or murdered.

And yet this popular notion of illiteracy as a sign of barbarian ignorance is a ploy of the dominant culture in self-cultivating/projecting itself as the summit of the cultural paradigm, and has to be seen in its true historical context. All African societies had sacred learning and writing traditions, but these, like in early Europe, were open only to the few. The colonial conquest of territories and the institutionalisation of the colonial model, legalised forced labour, jail, abductions, imposed hut taxes, political exile and mur-

der, destroyed these traditions through the introduction of
Christianity. Just as the local steel-smelting traditions were destroyed by the introduction of foreign manufactured tools, so too
did the introduction of the Christian school and its propaganda
and cruel enforcements decimate or near-decimate African intellectual traditions.

At this point it is important to state that *Hamel* has already de-
veloped themes which would resonate in novels centred in the
Caribbean by Caribbean authors such as H. G. De Lisser, Jean
Rhys, Edgar Mittelholzer, George Lamming, V. S. Naipaul, Roy
Heath, and Jamaica Kincaid, all of whom make use of images of
alienation, the outsider, mental illness, the impostor, mixed
race/nationality, colour/race and sexuality.

The repartee (15–22) between Roland and Hamel is a deliber-
ate ploy by the author to let the reader feel the intelligence of the
latter and the prejudices of the former, but it is also an opportunity
to work out publicly some of the predetermined positions which
Europeans had taken in relation to their African slaves. Roland is
exposed as a tyrant, while Hamel appears to epitomise the noble
savage. Convicted of murder by Hamel, and convinced that he has
been morally and intellectually defeated, Roland now plots to rid
himself of Hamel: 'The point once gained, the rebellion in vigour,
Hamel might be outwitted, anyhow disposed of; it were no sin to
slay an accomplice of the devil ...' (30). But Roland's personal
emotional viciousness cannot be immediately acted on because
he needs Combah, the so-called monarch of the African slaves of
the island, in his plot to seize a white Creole young lady who has
scoffed at him and rejected his love.

This novel, symptomatic of its period, is replete with plots and
sub-plots too numerous to mention. However, the main thrust of
the story is the exposing of the missionary Roland as a debaucher,
a rapist, a murderer, while Hamel and Combah betray each other
over the planned abduction of Joanna Guthrie, the whimsically
beautiful white Creole model of gracefulness and virtue. Combah
reins in Hamel to capture her for him, while Hamel desires her
for himself, as does Roland. Simultaneously, the mysterious,
Dionysian figure of the 'coloured' (mixed race) gentleman who

assists the Guthries on a stormy night metamorphoses into
Fairfax, the man whom Joanna has always loved, the disinherited
white Creole who returns to claim his Jamaican property.

A significant contribution to our understanding of the psychol-
ogy of the 'coloured' underclass (since they served in the capacity
of servants and were given a semblance of education) is the way in
which the author has handled the persona of Michal, the female
servant to Joanna Guthrie. In modern times this has been dealt
with resolutely and thoroughly by Frantz Fanon in *Black Skin,
White Masks,* and by Calvin Hernton, to a lesser but no less force-
ful degree, in *Sex and Racism in America.* But for 1827 this novel
is a revelation. Michal is very taken by the mannerisms and language of the 'coloured' gentleman, but when he dares to impugn
her sobriety and standards by kissing her lips, the vituperative,
distancing, insulted persona takes over. The longish extract which
follows is so witty, so intelligently portrayed that it should be
heard in its entirety:

> Quadroon damsels do not look for beauty in the youth of their own
> colour; their first ideas of admiration or love are devoted to the gen-
> uine white breed ... Therefore, however natural the desire she might
> have to appear to advantage, even before a young Mulatto-man, noth-
> ing was farther from her thoughts than to inspire him with anything
> like that confidence which prompted him, after he had tenderly
> squeezed the hand unconsciously held out to him, to imprint a kiss
> upon her lips. Nothing was more unexpected, and few things had
> more astonished her. She snatched away her hand, and tore herself
> from his embrace ... and though her tongue refused to express the
> feelings which this insult had roused, her black eyes flashed with so
> much anger and indignation ... (47)

Apart from the Adamic reappearance of the serpent figure as
metaphor (not quoted), the specificity of this emotional trauma
has a ring of authenticity about it. The author reinforces Michal's
consternation at being considered embraceable by a man of her
own race by describing her as thinking of 'the touch of the
Negroes' as a 'contamination' (334). This does not mean, however, that women of colour in all cases favoured a European, but

the effects of colonialism meant that this was generally true. An African-Jamaican working-class female in De Lisser's *Jane's Career* made it known that she would rather marry an ordinary 'white' man than an educated 'black' man. In 1993 I was walking in downtown Port of Spain with a highly educated woman who was at the top of her profession. She had the appearance of several ethnic groups in her, with her brown straightish hair and light complexion (like a Greek or southern Italian). Then I came upon a 'black' school-friend of mine from childhood; he was wearing working shorts and dressed shabbily due to the nature of his job. The moment I began talking to him, the woman I was with immediately turned red and became inarticulate with embarrassment and hurried away. Since then she has avoided me like the plague!

The author of *Hamel*, therefore, was perfectly aware of these abnormalities in a slave society and exposes them quite well. Another facet of the novel's oscillating authenticity is the belief that the European adventurer was probably also an adventurer at home, and that a criminal or even a murderer could leave Europe and pretend to the highest positions of colonial society in the Caribbean. This was also a major theme in Jean Rhys's *Wide Sargasso Sea*, where the embattled young heroine, wholly dependent on a tropical environment for emotional/psychological stability, is confronted by a penurious European who wants to marry her in order to seize control of her money. Colonialism thus malevolently informs the lives of the exploited and reduces human worth to sheer emotional stress, ambivalence and self-loathing. In a short story by V. S. Naipaul, 'Tell Me Who To Kill', the young Indo-Trinidadian who comes to London, ostensibly to study, finds himself precariously cast as an outsider, afraid of the young Teddy boys, ashamed of his own historical past, and longing to assume the supposed stability of his English friend, Harry, who appears to be at one with his environment. In Jamaica Kincaid's *Annie John*, the schoolgirl, Annie, brought up by parents who believed in nature and a father who constructed both his house and furniture himself, experiences, like C. L. R. James and V. S. Naipaul in real life, the wonders of a colonial education which alienates her from her own parents to such an extent that she experiences, like Naipaul, a nervous breakdown (albeit not explicitly referred to as such in the novel). In all these instances, one is confronted with the nightmare of colonialism in which one's birthplace becomes small, trivial, irrelevant, and the bigness of Europe, of England, with its assumed monopoly of language and power, becomes the model for aspiration. Michal is such a victim. Roland is also a victim of his superiority, his racism, in a universe in which the Africans are unintelligent. By each vector assuming a victimised intentionality in his/her psychological matrix, each becomes a victim in real life. But there is a twist.

It appears our anonymous author demonstrates greater understanding and sympathy for those who circulate in an almost exclusively European world. Hamel is the author's pet creation as he juxtaposes one type of priest with another, European with African, Christian with Pagan; and, as Kamau Brathwaite has pointed out, our novelist was perhaps a free-thinker, and thus felt contempt for the contradictions of a Christianity which supposedly set an example of morality and religion, but whose ministers were in practice sometimes immoral and debauched. On the level of intellectual weighting, therefore, Hamel has to possess the ability to speak. Michal, as already pointed out, becomes the example of the woman of colour, almost 'white' (a 'quadroon', a person of one fourth African blood) who apes the cultural mores of her employers. Amongst this class of people, regardless of degree of colour, being articulate in the English language is of normative value. But as our author turns his attention to the masses, he inevitably betrays any lingering idea we may have had of him as 'fair' or balanced, as can be seen in the following excerpt:

> The summons of the king was repeated by half the voices in attendance, and by all the echoes, until there seemed an almost *Babel-like confusion of tongues,* vociferating nothing that could be clearly understood, amid this *chaotic gabbling,* but the word Brutchie, bandied about until one might have thought the very rocks were deafened with the *barbarous sound,* and nature herself grown weary of so *odious* a name … The moon shed a flood of light … on the darker [figure] of Combah … whom the addition of a pair of horns would have qualified for the personification of the *fiend* so frequently represented by the painters of yore … (66–7, emphasis added)

The earlier reading of the author's predisposition to portraying sympathetically the articulate is here contrasted with his own voice and also with the role he designs for Hamel who is made to refer to the masses as '... almost *brutal idiots*, engaged in sensualities solely, *without mind, spirit, worth, courage, or discretion* ... Come, master Roland, from this *nasty* place...' (82–3, emphasis added). And there are occasional reminders that this vestige of traditional African society seen in Jamaica reminds the author of the ancient Greek and Roman life, whose literature is frequently referred to in the novel. Thus, on the one hand, there is a classicising of African traditions, and on the other a brutalising of it. Where Graeco-Roman myth or history is seen as a romanticised past, the African is seen as a brutal present.

Another theme which underpins the novel's thrust is the role of revolutionary upheaval. Here it is obvious that Haiti is the model (the author himself alludes to this) and some of the characteristics of the Haitian Revolution in the late eighteenth and early nineteenth centuries are played out as undercurrents in this novel. Toussaint L'Ouverture, the leader of the revolution in its main stage, had a strong appetite for European women, and his snuff-box, according to C. L. R. James and others, contained hairs snipped from their private parts. Combah dreams of abducting Joanna and making her his wife, and of having Europeans work as servants for him, which parallels the desires of Dessalines and Henri Christophe, who later became successive monarchs in Haiti! This theme is also in both James's book, *Black Jacobins,* and his play of the same name, produced in 1938 in London, with Paul Robeson in the lead. One of the figures in our author's 'revolution' is made to advocate the destruction of Europeans and the burial of Roland himself, whom he sees as a betrayer (77); this position, which sees the role of the European priest as predominantly treacherous, was also advocated during the Haitian Revolution by Moise, whose uncle, Toussaint, had him shot. This contextualising of the social and political location of some of the action makes us realize that the author was well aware of the significance of the Haitian Revolution to the Jamaica of 1827. None of these themes are central, but they are nevertheless important.

But our author's treatment of the revolutionary plotters exposes his fundamental bias against the masses in his characterisation of them:

> No Triumph of Bacchus or Silenus, the living monuments of Titian, Poussin, Rubens, or any other artist, would give my readers an idea of this *absurdest of all absurd processions;* although, as in those masterpieces of art, which many will call to their recollections, the chief part of the performers are represented drunk. *But theirs is the mirth of drunkenness, hilarity and joy;* whereas our sable satyrs, *wanting the cloven hoofs and the tails, were no less sleepy than intoxicated, and staggered along like wounded and fainting soldiers in a retreat* ... and some seemed to have *fallen into their last sleep, and could not be roused even by pinching or slapping* ... [In relation to their songs, our author continues:] the whole produced *a confusion of words and noises,* from which it was as difficult as useless to draw any meaning ... but of harmony the nymphs who sang them had no notion ... [The men who joined in were] some laughing, some almost crying, solemn, lyrical, and *ludicrous* ... (97–9, emphasis added)

These lines are the narrator's and they direct the reader's attention to the historical comparison he constantly makes between the events he is describing and their Graeco-Roman parallels. The African slaves themselves are compared with historical personae of Greece and Rome in a way in which the former are seen as lacking. This attempt at classicising and relating to a moment in history turns the reader away from finding any moral meaning in the present revolutionary situation and distances him from a chaotic, disorganised, drunken *rabble* (the author's own words) who do not celebrate with joy and hilarity, but with stupidity and drunken stupor. Thus the entirety of human effort and the aims the narrator places on the 'revolution' are reduced to the level of irresponsibility and imbecility. Interestingly enough, these same descriptions abound in a descendant of these Africans, Vic Reid, in whose novel *New Day* the masses likewise become a rabble and have their aims reduced to irresponsible violence. That this is not an isolated incident can be judged by the narrator of *Hamel* also using the language of condemnation and prejudice by referring to the Africans' rituals as being 'filthy rites' and by claiming that the 'Negro race' had an 'ingenuity' for lying (106). This is further compounded and reinforced elsewhere when the narrator shifts suddenly from the third person to the first: 'The fire was soon kindled by some hocus-pocus of *mine* host...' (126) '*My* countrymen will treat with scorn ...' (128); '*I* regret *I* must not give the story in its native simplicity...' (185). This appears to be a critical slip in which we recognise the writer has actually witnessed some of these events, but his perception of what he has seen actually impairs the novel's worth. There is no rational reason for the shift from the third to the first person, thus causing us to identify the writer as personally manipulating characters and events according to his own preferences and prejudices.

Later, after we have first been introduced to him, Hamel becomes the spokesman of reaction (109–10) and one wonders why Hamel was presented with such a flourish, such intelligence, such likeableness—presumably because the writer wanted the reader to empathise with Hamel as an individual (as distinct from the rabble) so that when he begins to betray the revolution he would be seen as taking an intelligent position. This is the same course Davie takes in Reid's novel; his descendants become integrated into the Jamaican upper class by betraying the masses and supporting the planter class. Hamel is even made to condemn the British king for planning freedom for the slaves!

Narratively, this novel is essentially about the mysterious mulatto who becomes the person, Fairfax, whom Joanna has always loved. When Michal discovers that the mulatto Sebastian is really the white Creole Fairfax, she falls to her knees in tearful apologies. Joanna's mother, who suffered mental illness as a result of having been raped by Roland, is totally against the intended marriage of her daughter to Fairfax, but the author kills her off and the happy couple claim each other.

In the second volume, most of the themes of the first are replayed: Roland argues against the claims of the white Creole planter, Mr. Guthrie, that England is a land of 'moral depravity ... that the metropolis swarms with prostitutes ...' by saying that the Society for the Suppression of Vice has reformed them (214).

There is, of course, only one reason why Roland would pursue such an argument: to defend his own immorality and vice. It is to be noted that Roland's double-consciousness, his righteousness and his crassness, his moral idealism and his practical immorality and villainy are characteristics of the 'pork-knocker', the man who wants to uplift himself by any means necessary. Thus on the one hand he plots with Combah, the king of the African masses, to capture Joanna, even though he had already plotted to secure Joanna for himself and hand Combah over to the colonial authorities. When Combah combatively pronounces that he would have Joanna for himself, this engenders such rage in Roland that he screams, 'To you, a miserable Black!' (235). Combah attacks him but is himself injured in the eyes and body by Roland's discharged pistols.

Interestingly, the author depicts the Africans' armed struggle against slavery as being motivated by the beauty of the mixed-race woman (337)! The fairer the woman, the greater the prize. Yet in the next paragraph he is able to have Combah define these spoils of war as an aftermath of '... the possession of the country, of the destruction ... of the white male inhabitants, and of the annihilation of the buckra soldiers' (338). But these conflicting positions only amplify problems of plotting. Our author was so desirous of including all the themes he had digested of the Haitian Revolution that he places them side by side in an illogical, incongruous alignment. These thematic threads which linked to Haiti are directly commented on by the rebelling Africans themselves.

Some of the incongruities or ironies of revolution are beautifully illustrated by the author. He allows Combah to hand over his cutlass (the surrender of one's sword, in European terms) to Fairfax who, despite being deprived of his rightful inheritance and being aided by some Africans in his regaining of it, is nevertheless linked with the forces of reaction. This incident can be linked to Toussaint L'Ouverture giving himself over to the French at the height of the revolution. Thus these symbolic gestures take on specific meanings when contrasted with the historical records.

After the revolutionary struggle is defeated, Hamel confesses that he could not bring himself to act against the disinherited

Fairfax and the lovely Joanna, and knowingly accepts the fact that
he has betrayed his companions. The author brings Hamel's betrayal to a biblical climax when Fairfax, having secured his own
life and that of Joanna through Hamel's treachery, gives the latter
a sack of gold (388). This clear-cut allusion to Judas expresses the
cynical vision which permeates the plot throughout. The poetry
employed in celebrating Hamel's treachery reverses the tyranny
of his actions as:

> [Hamel was] ... gazing on the deep blue waves that heaved around
> him. The wind freshened, and the sky became overcast ... They
> watched him without regarding the time they so misapplied, until his
> little boat had diminished to a speck. The sun declined; the twilight
> sank into darkness; and although the moon arose in splendour, they
> saw no more of Hamel or his bark ... (396)

Our understanding of this novel is affected by our knowledge of
real historical events, the records of which exist with numerous
examples of individuals and their causes. Unfortunately, the novel
is unique, as Brathwaite has written, but only for the reason that it
sets in train a view of history which successive Caribbean novelists
would imitate whether consciously or not. This imitation, limita-
tion of vision, ridiculing of the poverty of misery, represents an essential middle-class sensibility in which the impact of colonialism
has removed from view the real uniqueness of what was taking
place outside the historical European imagination, with its ro-
manticising, classicising mentality, distanced from events in the
ancient past which became a celebration of mythology and of
comparison for the African slaves and the Caribbean setting. This
colonial cocoon, this psychological brainwashing which is
achieved through British education and values, severely limits not
the creative imagination but the formalities of organised thinking
to go beyond the limited structures of consciousness. In the end,
however, our anonymous author should be congratulated on his
honesty: that the irrepressibility of onerous patronising, of
Christian/imperial pandering, and all the ramifications that these
imply, are ably articulated in their various contradictory stances,

at once praising and damning. These are the psychopathological conflicts that define colonialism, and they are most beautifully dramatised in this novel.

Amon Saba Saakana, Ph.D.

BIBLIOGRAPHY

FICTION

De Boissierre, Ralph, *Crown Jewel* (London: Picador, 1981)

De Lisser, H. G., *Jane's Career* (London: Heinemann, 1972)

Heath, Roy, *Genetha* (London: Allison & Busby, 1981)

Kincaid, Jamaica, *Annie John* (London: Plume, 1988)

Lamming, George, *Season of Adventure* (London: Michael Joseph, 1960)

Mittelholzer, Edgar, *The Kaywana Quartet* (London: Secker & Warburg, 1976)

Naipaul, V. S., 'Tell Me Who To Kill', in *In A Free State* (Harmondsworth: Penguin, 1973)

Reid, V. S., *New Day* (London: Heinemann, 1973)

Rhys, Jean, *Wide Sargasso Sea* (Harmondsworth: Penguin, 1968)

NON-FICTION

Fanon, Frantz, *Black Skin, White Masks* (London: MacGibbon & Kee, 1968)

Hernton, Calvin C., *Sex and Racism in America* (New York: Grove Press, 1966)

James, C. L. R., *The Black Jacobins* (New York: Vintage Books, 1963)
—————————, *Beyond a Boundary* (London: Hutchinson, 1963)

Naipaul, V. S., *Finding the Centre* (London: Andre Deutsch, 1984)

Parkinson, Wenda, *'This Gilded African': Toussaint L'Ouverture* (London: Quartet Books, 1980)

Umeh, John Anenechukwu, *After God is Dibia* (2 vols., London: Karnak House, 1997–9)

HAMEL,

THE OBEAH MAN.

—— I apprehend and do attach thee
For an abuser of the world, a practiser
Of arts inhibited and out of warrant.

OTHELLO.

[First published in two volumes, London, 1827]

HAMEL.

VOLUME ONE

CHAPTER 1.

Yet hold! for oh! this prologue lets me in
To a most fatal tragedy to come.   RICHARD III.

AT the close of a sultry day in the month of October, in the year
one thousand eight hundred and twenty-two; or rather at the moment when the sun (whose fiery ardour had not been moderated
in any part of his course by the least zephyr of the sea breeze) had
just sunk behind the emerald summits of the Blue Mountain, and
relieved from his scorching rays those Europeans who toil on the
northern shores of Jamaica; a person who (from some circumstances about to be explained) appeared to be a stranger was seen
riding along the western bank of the Rio Grande, that clear and
beautiful stream which, hurrying down from the wildernesses of
the island, carries the torrents of its highest mountains to the
Atlantic. The stranger seemed to be seeking a ford, and strove
from time to time to prevail on a sulky-looking Spanish horse,
which bore him without manifesting any satisfaction at his burthen, to venture through the deep and rapid current; but it was evident that the rider and his steed were of two minds on the point,
and that the pertinacity of the latter was more than a match for the
hesitating and undecided anxiety of the former; whose timidity,
arising from inexperience of the river, induced him not to press
his beast into the flood against that instinct to which he preferred
to trust his fortune on the present occasion.

The rider was accoutred in a black coat, cut straight, or it might
be of a dingy grey, with black cloth buttons, and a waistcoat of the
same. His trowsers were of brown holland, tucked into a huge pair

1

of spatterdashes, buttoned above his knee, as a defence against the bites of musquitos. He wore a large brimmed hat, slouched by many a tropical shower, and rendered rusty by constant exposure to the tropical sun, although at present he carried an umbrella secured in the straps of a portmanteau mounted behind him on his horse's crupper; and his great-coat, of the same sombre hue as his other vestments, was fastened upon his saddle bow. He was attended by a bare-legged negro boy on foot, dressed in an Osnaburgh frock and drawers, which, with a glazed hat on his head, formed the whole of his costume. The boy hung on sometimes to his master's stirrup, that he might keep pace with the horse; and sometimes, falling into the rear, brought himself up by grasping the animal's long tail; a liberty the beast admitted with an occasional affectation of elevating his croupe and lowering his ears,— intimations that he had a right to kick (though he did not at present) as well understood by young Cuffy as expressed by the horse.

This youngster's features scarcely harmonized with those of his very demure and melancholy-looking master, whose pale and cadaverous countenance indicated something more than bodily mortification and fatigue. His eyes, black and penetrating, were shadowed by brows that had once been dark as the skin of his follower, but now, with the locks that strayed in right lines from under his huge castor, exhibited the mingled hues of black and grey; his nose was sharp and aquiline; and his mouth, though rather of the largest, by no means badly formed, was furnished with a set of short but regular teeth, as white as those of Cuffy, whose happy physiognomy bespoke the innocence and kindness of his heart, and relieved that of the spectator from the sympathy of sadness inspired by the looks of the white-faced traveller. Yet the gloom on the cheek of this last was not attributable perhaps to any dignified grief or sentimentality of disposition—at least his features did not augur any such feeling; nor to age, for he was by some years short of forty. Anxiety of mind, as well as fatigue of body, natural irritability, and pecuniary cares, will impress even on a more juvenile countenance those lines which, visible there only, are channelled by time and memory on the invisible and wasted heart. Whether this were the case in the present instance, will be seen in the course of our narrative.

The stranger and his footman continued their route for some distance beside the river, halting again and again to compare notes as to the fordability of several spots, where the latter declared he could see the tracks of mules and horses, which he thought had crossed from the other side; but his master imagined them to be only indications of the cattle having been there to drink or cool themselves, and referred the point invariably to his horse, who, however anxious to drink or roll in the stream, always manifested the same unwillingness to traverse it. The evening was closing in rapidly, and the traveller, impatient at last of his beast's fears or obstinacy, had directed his valet to strip and try a ford, which, as he could distinguish by marks on the opposite side, was certainly used at times; when Cuffy, who was already half across the river, called to his master that he could see some Negroes coming down the hills from the interior towards a row of stones or rocks placed a little farther up the winding current, for the convenience of foot passengers, which had been hidden from their view by the trees growing on its banks.

To this rudest of rude bridges the traveller and his boy advanced without delay, being anxious no doubt to leave the river behind them, and hurry to their quarters, yet at some miles distance beyond it, if possible before nightfall; and they had just gained the bridge in question, when they were saluted by the Negroes, who were coming down from their provision grounds with yams, cocos, and various fruits for the next day's market on their heads. There was an excellent ford just above the stepping stones, which the cantancrous horse was compelled to pass, Cuffy still leading the way; and the Negroes furnished them with abundant directions to the settlement for which the traveller inquired, though accompanied with a piece of intelligence not altogether so welcome, as they intimated a report that the said settlement had been deserted since the death of its proprietor, whose widow had gone down to Port Antonio, while his slaves, some eighteen or twenty, had run away into the woods.

Notwithstanding this information, the traveller's countenance brightened very visibly at sight of some young negro girls of the party, to each of whom he had something agreeable to say—some compliment to their persons, attended with a cavalier and rather equivocal expression of his eyes, which raised a smile on the lips of the sable beauties, and elicited some rather diverting remarks from them on the discrepancy between his language and his looks. One of them, who said she was handmaid to her mistress, observed that he smelt sweet like her lady's washball; and most of them remarked on the perfumed state of his person, to which it must be avowed he was not inattentive: and whether they were cosmetics, or preparations for the hair, or essences to gratify his own olfactory nerves, which he breathed, he was, in fact, 'perfumed like a milliner.'

Yet in the midst of these odours he asked the young girls whether they were married; and if married, whether the ceremony had been performed by a priest or a missionary, or whether they were married after the African fashion. He enquired too about their soul's grace, their work, profits, punishments:— whether they expected to be free, and how many Mulatto and Quadroon girls there were on their master's estate, and if his daughter were handsome; and then relapsed into some rather spiritual advice, mingled with a few allusions to the worm which dieth not, and the fire which is not quenched.

The girls began to think him an unaccountable buckra, and rather affected with insanity; more especially as he persisted in his intention of proceeding to the settlement of which they had given him such an unfavourable account, and refused their assurance, on the part of their master or the overseer, of good quarters and hospitable entertainment for the night. Cuffy would fain have seconded their arguments, but his master silenced him with a gloomy frown; and after a few more desultory observations to the women, with some of whom he chose to shake hands, the head of the Spanish steed was turned toward the mountains; and Cuffy again seizing its tail, master and man resumed their course. The short twilight expired, and the shadows of night rendered still more sombre the forlorn and unfrequented path along which they journeyed.

CHAPTER 2.

The hurricane shall rave, the thunder roll,
And ocean whelm them in its deepest tide,
Or leave them fix'd on the hard pointed rock,
The sport of howling winds.
BRYAN EDWARDS'S JAMAICA.

IT WAS soon as dark as midnight, and the wind, which had withheld its accustomed influence during the whole of the day, began to sigh among the trees, and mingle its distant murmurs with those of the rills and waterfalls which, with the exception of the screams of the crickets, are almost the only sounds that are wont to break even the midday silence of the solitudes which Cuffy and his master were now exploring. A zig-zag path, only wide enough for one horseman, led them round the sides of the hills, now mounting, now descending into the depths of ravines ploughed by torrents which, peaceably insignificant at present, yet manifested, by the ruin and confusion along their channels, the headlong passion to which they were sometimes subject, being strewn with disjointed rocks and fallen trees, which the horse and rider were sorely puzzled to evade or traverse. The interminable forest generally overshadowed their road; but when from time to time, emerging from its shelter, the latter looked, as if for some assurance, to the canopy of heaven, he failed not to remark the violence with which the increasing vapours were hurried across it, and the flashes of fire which seemed to flit along the summits of the Blue Mountain. These were, after some time, accompanied with a sort of stifled thunder, not bursting, as it is wont to do, during a tornado, with a crash that threatens to rend heaven and earth, but rumbling and confused, as if its echoes were overpowered by the wind, which became every moment more clamorous and contentious.

Poor Cuffy's heart trembled in its sanctuary, and even his master could not repress an involuntary shudder as the lightning blazed around him, and the rain, beginning to drive in his face with persevering and accumulating force, caused him perhaps to

5

think with some regret of the hospitable assurances he had ne-
glected, and with some apprehensions as to those he might or
might not receive before his eyes should behold the sun. The
horse too, by no means enamoured of its situation, or the elementary confusion which triumphed around, manifested a very
sincere desire to retrace his steps towards the habitable country
he had left, and lingered onwards most reluctantly, in spite of
sundry kicks bestowed on his ribs by his fractious master, whose
impatience increased with the storm which already penetrated
through his garments. A tropical wetting is but too often the pre-
cursor and cause of those baleful fevers which are almost the
only curse upon the otherwise blissful climate of the Antilles,—
blissful in the idea of the inhabitants; and our traveller, already
initiated in the miseries of this scourge, was but too full of
apprehensions and forebodings, as he felt the tempest invade
him to the skin.

The thoughts of a sick bed, or sickness without a bed, without
medicine, in an abandoned dwelling in the midst of the jungle, as
it was represented to him, crowded fast on his perturbed imagination, which now first reproached him for the expedition he had
undertaken, although the feeling was purely selfish: however, it
was of short duration; the uproar of the elements increased so
rapidly and violently, that all apprehensions for the past or the future quickly yielded to more immediate fears for his present personal safety. They had been for some time ascending, and had now
gained the summit of a steep hill, whence the road began to descend as abruptly into another dingle, through which they could
discover, by the occasional flashes of lightning, a river of more importance than the many petty streams they had already crossed.
This was indeed the Rio Grande again, but little inferior in magnitude to the volume of water it had presented to them some miles
below; and how were they to pass it? or how indeed were they to
reach it? The road, scarcely three feet wide, wound along the side
of a precipice, against which the wind raged with such fury, and
the rain beat so spitefully, that the horse for a long time refused to
face either of them, and was at last driven down into the valley by
master and man on foot, urging him with sticks, and preventing

him from turning round in the narrow path, so slippery and precipitous that he slid down the last portion of it on his hind quarters, and rolled over and over into the narrow plain below, bursting his girths and scattering abroad his harness and the portmanteau, umbrella, and great coat. These were, however, readjusted with a promptitude inspired by the occasion, and with a resolution which was little else than the effect of despair; the river was passed in comparative safety; Cuffy, who led the horse, only stumbling occasionally over the loose rocks which strewed its channel. But scarcely had they reached the terra firma on the other side, when the terrified boy cried out that the earth shook beneath him, and ran up the path which they had found, as if he expected the river to rise and arrest him, or hurry him with its waters down its impetuous current. The horse, no less alarmed, or afraid of losing his negro guide and friend, hastened after him. Another eminence was gained, from whence a track of fire was distinguishable through the storm, driving apparently at a great distance before the wind. 'Earthquakes are not uncommon,' thought the traveller; 'but fire—this must be produced by human means.' Cuffy thought otherwise; more especially when he descried other fires in different directions, and one or two now and then flashing into view at no very great apparent distance. The earth shook again; and the wind, as if it had still reserved some of its power for an effort of desperation, burst on them with such exasperated fury, that it seemed impossible to make farther progress against it. Cuffy clung to the boughs and the rocks beside him; and his master being fain to follow his example, the steed, with his equipage, was left to the mercy of the elements, from which they saw him gradually recede to the distance of fifty or sixty yards, like a ship driving at her anchors and going bodily to leeward, until he was lost in the darkness. Cuffy, true to his trust, abandoned his hold to keep sight of his master's baggage; while his master, encumbered with his spatterdashes, and fearful of following the fate of his Bucephalus, encouraged his valet to stand by the horse, and took a firmer grasp of the rocks from which he sought protection. Often and often was his voice lost in the tumult of the storm, as he shouted to his boy for some assurance of his safety. No answer reached his ears—no sound but that of the elements raging as if to produce a second chaos, thunder and wind, the roaring of the augmented waterfalls, the rumbling of the rocks which they loosed from their beds, the creaking and crashing of falling trees. It was in vain that the lightning at every other instant illuminated the scene with its partial flashes, now here, now there: it gleamed only on mountains uncultivated and uninhabited, (except perhaps by a few outlawed runaways who lived by a predatory warfare on the wild hogs and pigeons of the desart,) on naked precipices and foaming torrents, or on the giant trees of the forest quivering beneath the blast of the hurricane. Then came down the rain, not as in the temperate zone even in its most weeping seasons, when the spectator would fain imagine a second deluge; but torrents, sheets of water, seemed to rush from the clouds, and threaten the annihilation of all life beneath the sky. The forlorn and dispirited traveller, still clinging to the rocks which yielded him a partial and precarious kind of security, had groped his way along them to a chink, in whose recesses he flattered himself with an idea of weathering the storm till daylight, drenched—nay, almost drowned—as he was by this time; but even here the elementary war pursued him; a stream of water began to ripple down the chink, soon swelling to a torrent, augmented by another which found its way through the chasms of the precipice as if it had burst from some subterranean reservoir. The traveller's situation became insupportable; he must remove or perish; yet not daring to quit the crags to which he clung, and availing himself of the partial lee they afforded, he essayed to clamber up the face of the precipice, and with much difficulty and struggling reached the edge of the chink whence the torrent fell. Here he found himself comparatively safe in a long narrow passage or natural alley, in which he was at least secured from the wind by the high and inaccessible rocks on either side of it. Yet as the torrent still flowed over his feet and half way up his legs, he waded onwards to find a spot of higher ground, or an insulated piece of rock that might elevate him above the stream, and with this hope pursued the course of it for above a hundred yards, till he came to a chasm that opened on it from another mass of rocks, between which and his present station another brawling cataract, at the depth of fifty feet beneath him, found its way towards the streams which united in the Rio Grande below. A fallen tree formed a bridge across this fissure, on the opposite side of which the mouth of a cave might be distinguished by the glare of the lightning, sufficient in appearance to ensure our traveller shelter and safety for the night—shelter from the rain, and security from the wind. It was a most perilous undertaking to pass this bridge; but prompted by hope, and urged by misery and fear, he ventured on its uncertain surface, keeping his balance by means of a branch that hung from the opposite side, which, with much ado, he reached at last without accident. Here he found what appeared to him steps cut by human art for some height in the face of the rock: he ascended them, and walked into the cave.

CHAPTER 3.

Let me wipe off this honorable dew.

SHAKSPEARE.

As soon as the traveller found himself safe from the storm, he sat down on the floor of the cave, and burst into a flood of tears; and something like an acknowledgment of heaven's mercy passed his lips. His next thought was for his boy and his equipage, the horse and the portmanteau; nor was he long in adverting to the deplorable condition in which he yet found himself, drenched with rain, and exhausted with the fatigue of having borne up against the passion of the hurricane. To sit still might be fatal to him in this state, and he had even thoughts of stripping off his wet garments, and parading the cave, as far as he could see into it, till daylight; but was checked by the idea which he could not dismiss of stepping on scorpions or centipedes, or becoming an easier prey to the musquitos which like himself had here found a refuge from the weather. While he yet mused on the manner in which he was to pass the hours till morning, his olfactory nerves became sensible of a smell of fire,—the smoke of burning wood, which evidently came from the interior of the cave; and hastily concluding it to be owing to one of the wandering fires he had seen abroad, he explored his way through the cavern towards the smell, expecting to find an outlet on the other side of the mountain, through which he calculated the smoke was driven perhaps from a distance. The odour and its vapour increased as he proceeded; and he had not made a very long or very painful march, before he began to perceive a glimmering of light, by which he attained an inner apartment as it were of the cave, filled it is true with smoke, but in some measure illuminated by the fire from which it exhaled; not one of the wandering fires of the wilderness, but a fire of burning brands laid on the floor of the apartment too evidently by human hands. 'This,' thought he, 'is at least the abode of man: runaway slave, Maroon, or robber, I will yet claim his hospitality; my situation cannot be worse, and what have I to lose? But where is the tenant of the dwelling? Here are plantains too, not long roasted, and rum; and what are these?' he added, taking up some garments that lay on the floor, a contoo, and an instrument of music, a bonjaw. 'Let us at least summon the master of the cave. What ho! hilloh!' The voice died away unheeded, and the traveller listened to its echoes until he felt almost afraid and ashamed to disturb the silence again. Yet he mustered courage to exert his voice a second and a third time, though as at first ineffectually. Sufficiently removed from the storm without, to hear no more of it than an occasional murmur which stole along the vault he had penetrated, too faint to cause him any farther concern, his own voice was reverberated on his ears with a force from which he shrank within himself, so painful was it to his oppressed and agitated nerves. He called no more; but conforming himself with a philosophical moderation to the hour and the scene in which he found himself, he trimmed the fire; took off his wet clothes, which he wrung and disposed around it; attired himself in the contoo of his invisible host; and wrapping his feet in a blanket which lay beside it, helped himself from the calabash of rum, and put some of the plantains on the fire again to warm. He had seated himself on a bundle of sticks, and as he took a second taste of the rum calabash, surveyed at his leisure, by the cheerful blaze he had made, the extent and furniture of his apartment.

It was a lofty cavern hewn by the hand of nature in the otherwise solid lime-stone rock, from the roof of which hung many stalactites, whose points were blackened by the smoke from the fire beneath. Besides the opening by which the traveller had entered, there were four other apertures, each leading, as it seemed from the glimpse he had taken of them, to other recesses in the rock, and so much resembling each other that he could not now distinctly ascertain that which had admitted him. Alarmed for a moment at this discovery, he arose from his seat, and taking a firebrand from the blazing pile, would fain have explored these vomitories, into each of which he walked a few paces, without however deriving the information he required, or gaining any but a conviction that they extended farther than he was disposed at present to penetrate. He next surveyed the precincts of the cave itself, and its rather curious contents. In a recess stood a couple of spears, one solely of hard wood, whose point was rendered still harder by fire; the other was shod with iron and rusted apparently with blood; a bamboo rod, ten feet in length and about an inch in thickness, leaned against the rock beside them, carved or tattoed from end to end. In another angle of the vault was a calabash filled with various sorts of hair, among which it was easy to discriminate that of white men, horses, and dogs. These were huddled together, and crowded with feathers of various birds, especially those of domestic poultry and wild parrots, with one or two of the spoils of a macaw. A human skull was placed beside this calabash, from which the teeth were missing; but on turning it up, the traveller found them with a quantity of broken glass crammed into the cerebellum, and covered up with a wad of silk cotton, to prevent them from falling out. There were several other skulls in a second recess, some perfect, some which had been broken apparently with a sharp pointed instrument, and many of them serving as calabashes or boxes to hold the strange property of the master of the cave; one was a receptacle for gunpowder, which the inquisitive traveller narrowly escaped inflaming; a second contained bullets and shot of various sizes, mixed with old nails and pieces of rag; and from a third he saw with no little horror a black snake uncoil itself the moment he touched it. There were three muskets, all old and out of order; a pistol and two cutlasses, disposed on different ledges of the rock; a large conch-shell fitted with a belt of mahoe bark, to be worn over the shoulder, hung from a projection, with several other pieces of rope made of similar materials, to which were attached rings of wood and hollowed stones, perhaps intended for amulets or charms. A lamp of clay at last arrested his attention; it had carved on it some rude figures, and was filled with oil of the Palma Christi, having a wick formed of the fibres of the plantain stalk. This the intruder took the liberty of illuming, to assist him more conveniently than did his flickering firebrand in the farther search he seemed disposed to prosecute. By the help of this he espied a pair of shoepatters, a sort of coarse sandal, and a red cloak resembling the South-American poncho. Some salted fish was suspended from a part of the roof, with a

ing with a malignant fury, by a threatening action command him
into silence, and trace on his forehead, in burning characters, the
fearful syllable death. The only sound which escaped the lips of
the demon was that of his own name—Roland! Roland!—articulated in a voice of mingled triumph and revenge—Roland!

The traveller started from his dream as if he had been roused by
the sting of a scorpion. He sat upright for an instant, and stared
wildly around, scarce recollecting his own identity or situation;
but what was his amazement, not to say horror, on perceiving before him the very figure of the demon of his dream, or a figure
which his fancy so quickly substituted for him, that the idea of the
first was as if by magic resolved and condensed into that which he
beheld?

This figure stood before the lamp, whose rays served to define
the outline of his person with the greatest accuracy. Of his features little or nothing could be seen, except the light gleaming
from his eyeballs. He stood in an attitude which the dreamer's
fears quickly determined to be the menacing posture of the
demon from which he had shrunk; the forefinger of his right hand
elevated, the left hand leaning on a bamboo staff. 'In the name of
God or Devil,' cried Roland impatiently, 'who or what art thou?'

The figure relaxed from its position, lowered its right hand, advanced a step forward with a gentle inclination of the head, and
replied in a mild and almost musical tone of voice—'Master—
what you will.' A less experienced person than Roland might have
entertained a momentary supposition that the being before him,
who had first excited his fears to give him courage, was no other
than the evil spirit himself, thus come to tempt him; but our traveller was too much *au fait* on the affairs of this world to expect a
bow from the Enemy of mankind; though scared as he had been
from his terrific dream, it was some moments before he could
thoroughly collect himself. 'What you please,—a Negro,' repeated the figure, as if to give the white man time to reassure himself.

'What I please, and a Negro'—rejoined Roland, as if unconscious of what he heard.—'But what may be your business, and
what want you here? Is this your cave?'

'My business,' replied the black man, 'is sometimes to go round the lines of my master's estate, sometimes to look after runaway Negroes, to watch the provision grounds, to hunt wild hogs.'

'Whose cave then is this,' said the other, 'so well provided with food and necessaries, and—if I mistake not—with evidences of an illicit calling? The owner of the cave, methinks, must be a wizard—is he not?'

'The cave, master,' replied the Negro, 'has harboured, as I have heard for long times past, many runaway Negroes; they have their provisions here.'

'They have,' interrupted the other. 'I found a fire, and roasted plantains and rum, all ready for entertainment: though I fancied from what I have seen, that Obeah spells were rather the business of those who frequent this cavern.'

'You are at least fortunate,' answered the Negro, seeming to pay no attention to the remark of Roland about Obeah, 'in having found shelter from the storm, and food; and those to whom the cave belongs, were they here, would still respect the laws of hospitality, and make you welcome, be what they may, to all you can require at their hands. But if you have satisfied your hunger, be not offended that I do the same. My presence shall be no annoyance to you. Sleep again, if you feel disposed. I will eat in silence, and at a distance from you.'

'Sit down, sit down,' resumed the white man, as he arose himself; 'eat and be happy. I have no farther disposition to sleep: my mind is too much harassed with what I have encountered this night; my boy, and my horse, and my baggage, are lost in the storm. And where were you?' added he, looking inquisitively in the face of the Negro; 'your dress is untouched by the rain.'

'I had taken shelter,' replied the Negro, 'in another part of these caverns, which extend through to the other side of the mountain, before the rain began.'

'To the other side of the mountain!' interrupted Roland. 'Aye! you know by what entrance I arrived here then?'

'I know,' replied the Negro unmoved, 'that you must have entered from the side of Rio Grande, a fearful pass across the devil's gully; over which' (he added with a submissive and respectful smile) 'the Negroes say that none but the devil himself can pass, or one whom the devil leads; and that in the dark.'

'Ha!' cried Roland, a little moved by the observation; 'but you have passed it?'

'It was never passed by a white man before,' replied the Negro, as if he had not adverted to the question. 'There was once one who fled towards it for refuge, not from a hurricane, but from the punishment of crimes and misdeeds.'

'What had he committed?' said Roland.

'It was told of him, but I know not how truly,' replied the other, 'that he had set fire to a gentleman's estate, and attempted to kill his daughter in a fit of jealousy. He galloped from his pursuers, and scrambled up the pass you found, where they could not follow him; and halting at the bridge, invoked the white man's God to help him over; but he slipped, and tumbled down the gully.'

While this conversation took place, the Negro had renewed the fire, taken a piece of salted pork from the jar, put it into an iron pot with some water in it, which Roland had overlooked in his examination of the premises, and set it on the fire to boil. He produced some water also from one of the recesses, with which he mixed himself some rum in a small calabash; and after the libation of a little on the earth, drank to the health of the white man. Roland was neither pleased nor surprised to see him find the food and materials he required with so much ease and familiarity; not doubting that he was at least one of the proprietors of the cave, according to his account of them. But though be felt a confidence in the hospitality of one who could, had he been so disposed, have taken his life while he was sleeping, still he could not regard him without a suspicious feeling, and watched him as he moved about the cave with the same anxious scrutiny as that with which an alarmed cat keeps sight of a terrier dog who has invaded the stable or loft where her offspring are concealed. He had full time to remark the singularity of his dress and appearance, of which it may not be improper to give the reader some idea; as Hamel (by which name he was known) will probably take a principal part in the scenes and events hereafter to be described.

This dealer in magic, for he was no less a personage, was of a slight and elegant make, though very small of stature, being considerably under the middle size. His age was at least sixty; but the lines which that had traced on his features indicated, notwithstanding his profession, no feeling hostile to his fellow-creatures, at war with human nature, or dissatisfied with himself. He was attired in a South American poncho, which had once been of a bright scarlet colour, fastened round his waist by a thin leathern girdle; and his head was decorated with a red silk handkerchief, tied in the fashion of a turban. He was barefooted, and without any offensive weapon; for such the bamboo wand on which he had leaned could hardly he denominated. He moved with an elasticity uncommon for his years; and his manner indicated on his part perfect confidence, wholly unsuspicious of his guest or his purpose. Yet it was but too evident to Roland, that the Negro had evaded his questions as to the magic talents or qualities of some one who frequented the cave; but as the use of Obeah is denounced by law, however despised by white men, he could not attach any particular consequence to such evasion, nor justify himself in expecting any confession on a subject of such importance to the professors or participators in this blind sort of necromancy, if it may be so called.

'Whether conjuror or not,' thought Roland, 'he does justice to his food;' for in fact the Obeah man had seated himself to his meal at a respectful distance from his guest, and feasted on his humble viands with a perseverance worthy of any high priest, not excepting those who presided at the slaughter of hecatombs. 'I have not eaten,' said he to his guest, 'for twenty hours.'

'Why so?' demanded Roland: 'have you penances in your religion—fasts, mortifications?'

The Negro shook his head and smiled. 'Have *you*, master? Do you think fasting or reading prayers will compensate for injuries done to man? Not that I mean to imply anything as relative to yourself,' he added; remarking that his question rather affected the white man. 'Your religion is now become that of almost all the slaves and free people of colour; yet I never knew them fast or mortify themselves.'

'Then wherefore have you abstained from eating so long?' interrupted Roland.

'I have been some distance hence,' replied Hamel, 'to a plantation that had been deserted. The owner is dead; his wife, afraid to remain among her Negroes, had taken her children to the Bay at Port Antonio; and a white man, a missionary preaching man, was expected to come there, to try if he could persuade the Negroes to go down to the same place to be sold.'

'You think he would not have succeeded?' said Roland. 'Those who have once shaken off their bonds are not likely to offer themselves again as willing prisoners; besides, there is such a stir making in England for the emancipation of the slaves, that—and it is so much against the religion which the slave owners at least affect to profess, that perhaps few people just now would venture to purchase them; and they would be more apt to increase their numbers from other estates, which will follow their example, than tamely to surrender themselves again to whips and chains; nay, might they not in turn apply the whips and chains to their oppressors?'

'Whips and chains!' said the Obeah man, with a seemingly innocent smile. 'Have you not whips and chains in your country yonder too? How do you punish violence, incendiaries, murderers, ravishers, traitors, and rebels? Can you govern white men with prayers and talking? You have happiness and plenty there, and no man works but when he likes; why do not the white men stay in their own country, and leave the Negroes to themselves here?'

'Ah!' replied Roland, 'you can never be happy, at least for some years, without white men, who shall teach your children to read, to write, to pray to the only true God; the knowledge of the only means of salvation. Would you wish your little ones to become the prey of hell-fire? What ideas will they have of a crucified Saviour? You have among you, it is true, freemen and slaves who can read and write, and some who have made even a little progress in religion; but unfortunately those who are most instructed seem to hold their religion lightest. In my country yonder, as you call it, we are obliged to have priests and ministers of religion, and bishops or elders over them, to keep them from doing wrong; and without some such system here you will relapse into anarchy and in-fidelity.'

'Is your religion a science then,' said Hamel, 'that it must be taught and learned? and are your chief men in it in danger of doing wrong? We know our duty here already; and it were better to leave us to the God who has guarded us hitherto.'

'Your God,' interrupted Roland, 'has left you slaves; the Christian's God will make you free.'

'Ah!' cried the wizard, 'is it so? Will your God make the Negroes free?' (He looked the white man steadily in the face.) 'Will he leave us unencumbered with white parsons? What security can you give us of that? It were better I belonged still to a tyrannical master, than that I was subjected to a tyrannical white priest, who should take from me one of my ten fingers.'

'Your master,' cried Roland rather exultingly, 'takes the labour of all your ten fingers.'

'Not so,' rejoined Hamel: 'we work, it is true, for our masters; but they feed us, clothe us, give us land and houses, attend us in sickness and old age, and leave our minds, our thoughts, to ourselves.'

'They leave you to the Devil,' said the white man. 'If you had a spark of courage, you would emancipate yourselves; if you had one glimmering of the greatness of our God, you would take up the cross, and devote yourselves to his service.'

'You are a bold man,' replied Hamel again, 'to talk so to me; or a cunning man, and wish to make me think you can and will serve my countrymen.'

'I both can and will,' rejoined the other, 'if you are disposed to profit by the opportunity that is about to occur; I am the Missionary that was expected at your abandoned plantation.'

'I know it,' answered the Obeah man, with a polite and significant nod.

'You know it!' cried Roland.

'Yes, master.'

'But how?'

'Ah! master,' said the Obeah man, 'there is nothing in these mountains, in this island, which is concealed from me. I boast not of my secrets; my business is to use them with advantage.'

'Know you then the real purpose for which I was travelling to the forsaken settlement?'

'I know it, my kind master.'

The Missionary was a little amazed; but thinking that Hamel's intention might be only to impose on him, he demanded of him to explain what it was.

'It is for you to explain,' replied the other; 'my explanation will not profit you; I could give you evidences of greater knowledge than you dream of; I could tell you who and what you are.'

'Tell me,' exclaimed the Missionary with impatience: 'give me some proof of your intelligence.'

'Here is a powder,' said the Obeah man, calmly taking a little phial from his girdle, 'which will satisfy many men. Will you please to hold forth your hand? See—it is white as the snows of Mount Atlas.' (The Missionary stared again with amazement.) 'I once placed some of it in the palm of a white man, who called upon his God in my presence to avouch his innocence: he was accused of murder. I bid him close his hand as I now close yours;—grasp it tight, press your fingers to your palm;—I told him his God would vouch for him: that if he were innocent, the powder would still be white; if guilty, his fingers would be crimsoned as with blood. Have you pressed your fingers with violence?' The Missionary's heart palpitated, his teeth almost chattered, and his hand trembled as he re-opened it; but the powder was still white as before. 'Hah!' cried the wizard, 'you dared not close your hand; my charm is ineffectual, or you stand self-convicted.'

The Missionary breathed again; if a mountain had been moved from his breast, he could not have felt a greater relief. He held forth his hand with the white powder in it, exclaiming, 'False—jugglery.'

'Is it false?' cried Hamel; 'should it have taken the hue of fire? Yet is it neither falsehood nor jugglery. Let me touch your fingers;—if this hand'—(he looked on the Missionary with an inquisitive smile)—'has never shed innocent blood, let this powder remain unchanged; but if it has shed innocent blood'—(he rubbed the powder firmly with his own finger)—'Lo now! look you there! crimson as the sun-setting in a storm! Are you satisfied? See where it flows like blood even to your arm! deep—deep!'

'Damnation!' cried the Methodist, shuddering at the sight, and shrinking from the touch of his host. 'Thou art in league with the fiends of hell. What trick is this? Am I a man to tremble beneath the gaze of a Negro? Thou hast divined aright—No—no,—'tis falsehood all; thy knowledge is a trick;—yet how hast thou divined? or who has known me? Perdition! Dost thou not tremble for the consequences of thy indiscretion? Think'st thou my arm could not annihilate thee?'

'I fear you not,' modestly replied the wizard, who had watched his emotion as a boa constrictor may be supposed to watch the unhappy deer he means to spring upon: 'I fear you not. You have eaten of my food, and drank from my own calabash; you cannot harm me, nor do I meditate any evil to you; your secret is in safe keeping.'

'If it were confined to me,' thought Roland, 'it were better. Whence does he derive his knowledge? Oh God! what scorpions has he awakened in my bosom! Shall I be outwitted, circumvented, made subservient to a dealer in sorcery and incantations? and for what? Yes—I will submit.' A thousand fancies mingled in his mind, which resolved themselves at last into one paramount idea; namely, to mould, if he could, the conjuror to his own purposes. 'An arduous task, it is true,' thought he; 'but weightier matters have been brought to bear.' He dreamed not that perhaps the wizard entertained similar views with respect to himself. He looked towards him, and saw him leaning against the rock at one of the entrances, absorbed in a profound contemplation, which seemed to abstract him from all conviction of the scene before him; his arms folded under his poncho, his eyes fixed on the floor of the cave. The lamp gleaming on his forehead shewed that his features at least betrayed nothing of what was passing in a mind of which he was so much the master; yet as it lighted up his crimson head-dress and his ruddy garment, whose shadows were deepened by the gloom behind them, it gave to his appearance something of the demon with which Roland was yet fain to associate him; it is true he could not avoid the idea. In a few moments he moved from his position, put himself for an instant in the attitude of one listening to catch a distant sound, and suddenly hurried from the cave.

CHAPTER 5.

Apparel vice like virtue's harbinger;
Bear a fair presence, though your heart be tainted;
Teach sin the carriage of a holy saint:
Be secret—false.

COMEDY OF ERRORS.

THE blast of a conch, a faint and but just audible sound, moaned through the rocky galleries that opened into the cave where the Obeah man, Hamel, had just left his agitated and disconcerted guest. He paced the cave with an irritation almost amounting to frenzy; now cursing his own untoward fortune, now venting imprecations on the wizard whose singular penetration had unravelled at least one circumstance of his (the Missionary's) life. Yet gloomy and melancholy as the event to which the spell seemed to relate, it was perhaps one which his recollection had almost represented as venial, in comparison with other deeds which preyed on his memory. Misfortune and guilt might have claimed an equal share in that: passion and remorse had been the cause and consequence of these, which had as yet escaped detection; as had indeed the first alluded to—known, as Roland had imagined, to himself alone. Yet Hamel had only charged him with shedding blood. The particulars of the circumstance might be a mystery to him still; or he might have made a vague charge on the suggestion solely of his own fancy, taking the chance of getting credit for displaying a supernatural power, to acquire a natural one over the mind of a white man, whose business at any rate he seemed to understand; whose business, if discovered to the authorities of the island, would be death. Death! The Missionary's mind glowed with the thought, and his heart died almost within him, as the conviction sank upon it. 'Death! an ignominious death!' Yet what assurance had he that this vile Negro knew his business? He had said nought of it. The Missionary's feelings had betrayed him into an avowal of guilt of some kind, an avowal of which the wizard would not fail to profit: and then—and then!—'These Negroes

23

are not such dolts as the white men give out to one another, but cunning and secret. Who would have dreamed of such a cave as this, so tenanted, in such a wilderness? Let it be Roland's business at least to try if he cannot make it and its tenant useful to his own purposes.'

While these reflections, half muttered to himself, half mental, allowed the agitation of his mind to subside, like a boisterous ocean rocking itself into repose after a storm, the Missionary had laid aside the Negro's blanket and contoo, in which he had been enveloped, and resumed his own more appropriate dress. He trimmed the lamp, and fed the fire, as if not altogether in charity with darkness; and seeing by his watch that it must needs be daylight abroad, began to explore the passage from the cave by which Hamel had so suddenly disappeared: for he could by no recollections divine that by which he had made his own ingress; nor is to be supposed that he was ambitious of again passing over that awful gully, by the bridge which, according to the Obeah man's account, the Enemy of mankind had constructed, and reserved for his own particular friends. However, his fortune did not favour him here; a few yards in darkness brought him to a spot whence he could feel two or three currents of air, evidently issuing from as many passages in the rock; and the sounds of his feet, now equipped with his iron-heeled boots, echoed along these galleries in so many directions, that he became afraid of trusting himself beyond the extent of the spot at which he had halted. The lamp was portable, and might assist him in unravelling the labyrinth; without it he must, as he thought, be lost. He returned to possess himself of it; and as he re-entered the cave by the same aperture as that by which he had quitted it, he saw the Obeah man likewise re-entering it by another of the passages, followed by a tall athletic Negro, in whose presence the other seemed to dwindle almost into insignificance. The light flashed on his face, and exhibited his features to the gaze of the Missionary, as he stepped into the chief apartment of the cavern; features which were but too well known to him, although the sight of them here, and under such circumstances, was anything but welcome to Roland.

'What do you here?' cried he to the Negro. 'Merciful heaven! are you a confederate with this juggling wizard, and have you betrayed —'

The Negro drew himself up to his full height with a resolved and haughty dignity, and answered instantly—'I have betrayed nothing, no man's business, no man's name. Hamel has a power as well as yourself—a greater power than yours; I should be a fool to overlook it.'

'What!' cried the Methodist, with an amazement bordering on horror, 'are you too leagued with the Prince of Darkness? Is it for this you have been baptized, and made a member of the church of Christ? Have you redeemed your soul from hell, to cast it headlong into the bottomless pit again? And have you faith even in Obeah spells, philtres, and charms? Or are these to be the medicaments of your weak and sickly power in its infancy? Perish the thought! The curse of God shall wait upon your hopes, annihilate your schemes, and bring down death and ruin on your devoted head—on all your followers. I quit you; I renounce you; lead me from the cave; let me leap into one of your abysses; hurl me down the rocks; kill, murder me. My soul shall never testify to such abominations, nor my efforts for your temporal and eternal salvation be blasted by the breath of those who tamper with the Devil.'

'We do not tamper with the Devil,' said the Obeah man, very modestly interrupting him; 'we know no Devil with whom we have any power: it were well if we did.'

'How!' cried the Missionary again; 'it were well—well to prostrate your souls at the feet of Moloch? But you are nought. Combah!' (The tall Negro made a sign of acknowledgment as to his name.) 'Combah! you have taken the cross of God; you have sworn to renounce the devil and his works; keep to your oath, so shall God prosper you: fail in it, and the care of heaven shall fail you too.'

'Master Roland;' said Hamel, interposing, 'we say nothing against your religion, nor your God; we had a religion before we knew yours; such as it was, it is. You have had proof of the knowledge we possess, and even I may help to further the scheme you have in view.'

'Said you not,' replied Roland, addressing himself to Combah, 'that you had not betrayed me? He that is false to his God, does not long keep his faith with man.'

'He has not betrayed you,' rejoined the Obeah man: 'his secrets, like yours, are no mysteries to me. Have not I vowed to make him king? You too have promised your aid; but I have vowed.'

'What are your vows?' cried the Missionary, with some little amazement.

'My vows,' said the other, 'are his destiny; I have read that in his face, in his forehead, in the stars; it is his spell—I know it, I have divined it, seen it!'

'And mine too, have you read that in your visions?'

'Master Roland,' replied the wizard again, 'if I knew your fate, you would still doubt me, though I told you what it might be; nor would you believe that my art could make manifest what is in the womb of time, independent of me, and of the power which you say I derive from a being inimical to your God who rules all things.'

Notwithstanding this remark, the Missionary would have been curious to hear his supposed destiny, even from the lips of a man he affected to despise: the specimen he had seen of the wizard's influence and knowledge, doubtful and suspicious as it yet seemed, had made no trifling impression on the superstitious mind of a man bewildered with crimes and intrigues; and he would have been contented to submit himself to the guidance of Hamel in any other case wherein his own reputation was not at stake, as in this. For he would do all religiously; and with that feeling consigned in his own mind the wizard and all his influence to the devil, whenever the conviction of it crossed his recollection. In the midst of this debate, if such it may be called, the other Negro, Combah, interposed his good offices, to make peace between his two friends, whom he naturally enough wished to make the stepping-stones to a power which he had the hardihood to covet—no less than the office of king.

'Master Roland,' he said, 'the white men believe in you, the Mulattos and Quadroons too; but the Negroes fear Hamel. When we shall have made them free, they will be also free to choose what prayers they like; and if you can shew them such wondrous things as Hamel has shewn to me, you will have the same chance, at least, of succeeding with them.'

The Obeah man smiled; but the Missionary's features expressed only rage and mortification at this suggestion, heightened by the recollection of the wizard's trick just practised on himself, and the conviction of the mean figure he must cut in the eyes of both, if Combah should have been made acquainted with that circumstance. Heated with this indignant feeling, he traversed the cave with an impatient step, as if intent on quitting it, and looking alternately into the various openings which led from it, as if determined to try his fortune, and explore a way though one of them even in the dark. It was in vain that Combah tried to pacify him; his passion seemed to augment with the concessions of the others; and he continued to denounce the wizard as an agent of hell, while he blundered along one of the galleries, until he was scared back again by the bats flying about him as they returned from the light of the still to pass their holidays here. Ashamed of his fears, and amazed at the tranquillity he observed on the features of the two Negroes, he caught up a machet, and made another sally through a different opening, along which the tenants of the cave could hear him groping and stumbling, now shouting, then grumbling again; hacking the rock as he cut at the bats, and cursing these as fiends who inhabited this den of his evil genius, if such a being could exist. His mental and secret determination was to denounce the Obeah man, whom he was resolved to bring to justice; but of this nought escaped his lips even in murmurs. Thus blundering on, he reached at last the daylight, and beheld the chasm which he had entered the previous night.

CHAPTER 6.

Come on, sir; here's the place. Stand still: how fearful
And dizzy 'tis to cast one's eyes so low!
SHAKSPEARE.

THE way was long enough and close enough, with the exercise
of slashing at the bats, to cover the person of the Missionary
with a good tropical perspiration, by the time he arrived at the
exit from this cave of abomination, as he had sirnamed it in his
mind; so that he stood for some time at the mouth of the gallery,
inhaling the fresh breeze, and feasting his eyes with the light of
heaven, before he adverted to his particular situation, or to
the consideration of any means by which he could descend
from that which, had he been covered with feathers, (having
only two legs,) might have been called his Alpine perch. A spectator from below would have imagined that nothing less than
feathers, or the leathery wings usually and fancifully given to
personifications of Satan, could have elevated any animated
thing to such a pinnacle as that on which master Roland stood
surveying the scene before him,—not of course like the Devil
looking over Lincoln, nor as a black carrion crow vulture elongating his telescopic vision to assure himself of the spot from
which his dilated nostril snuffed the carcass;—but as what he really was, a pious adventurer at a stand-still from necessity, inhaling the breath of life to give him strength and confidence to
proceed in his vocation.

The illuminated azure of the sky above him was yet stained with
fleecy clouds sailing gently to the westward. They might be compared to wounded stragglers in the rear of a victorious army; the
followers of the storm; harmless, impotent indications of the violence which had preceded them. The distant sea sparkled in the
sun, while its huge waves still retained the elasticity which the
hurricane had imparted to them, their summits flashing with
white spray, hurried along by the wind, like tears chased from the
sunny cheeks of youth by hope:—but let us leave metaphors. A

considerable plain lay beneath the eyes of the Methodist, between the sea and the woods which he immediately overlooked to
the eastward. It was here that he could trace the progress of the
fires which had alarmed him the previous night. They had raged
through a great extent of long grass, withered by the dry season,
and kindled by the negligence of runaway Negroes; and although
the rain had now quenched their flames, it was very apparent, by
the blackened acres they had left, and the smoke yet reeking from
them, that their fury must have been uncontrollable except by nature's own efforts; and that, once within their influence, all escape
from them would have been impossible to any human being. The
Missionary's course lay across a part of this plain, as he thought,
where he contemplated only dust and ashes; and willing to see
everything that related to himself in the best light possible, he was
fain to attribute the storm he had weathered to the providence of
heaven interposing to save the life of one so valuable to the
unchristian Negroes whom he yet meant to enlighten metaphysically and spiritually. Every stream was yet swollen, and the Rio
Grande rolled among a mass of foam which marked its course
high above its usual and natural banks; while fragments of rock
and broken trees, to the enthusiast's imagination, rose and fell as
the waves hurled and tossed them about, like condemned spirits
tossing on the restless billows of Hades. He felt a sort of pride in
the idea, and looked around, bewildered for a moment, in search
of some more or less pious fellow-creature who might applaud or
envy him for the conceit: but his own safety diverted his attention
to other objects. He stood at the mouth of the gallery, as we have
stated, where the face of the perpendicular rock beneath was cut
into some shallow steps leading to a narrow ledge, whence a tree
hung over that frightful chasm called the Devil's Gully; a chasm
not more than fifteen feet across, but apparently of an immense
profundity; for, owing to his present position, the Missionary
could not see down to the current of water which had perhaps
formed and now occupied it as its channel to the Rio Grande.
Another tree lay across the gully; but though he had passed this
bridge in the dark, it was too awful to be encountered in the light,
which served only to make manifest the danger he had escaped;

nay, so terrible did the very descent to it appear down the face of
the rock, that he had not hardihood enough to attempt it, urged as
he was by horror and disgust of the abominations he had seen in
the wizard's cavern, by his ambition to denounce the Obeah man,
and his anxiety to regain the habitations of civilized life, for more
than one purpose which he had at heart. It was in vain that he
strained his neck in every direction, to spy out some hope for effecting his escape, some human being who might come to his
assistance; in vain he searched with his eyes every bush beneath
him for his boy Cuffy, and his Spanish horse, and all his moveables. The mountain path was not visible from his eyrie, and the
jungle concealed everything that could have consoled him, encouraged him, or given him a hope of emancipation from the
Obeah man's abode and power. Hour after hour elapsed as the
Missionary still contemplated the scene before him; and he began
to feel again the calls of hunger, as well as to entertain some little
surprise that neither Hamel nor Combah interfered with or even
followed him. What could be their motive for thus neglecting
him? Did they calculate on starving him into submission to their
plans, knowing the almost insurmountable difficulties he must
encounter, in attempting to descend the rocks? His life was in
their power, but that was not worth their taking; moreover
Combah depended much on him for his influence with the
Christian part of the population; and Combah was a Christian. If
he could be prevailed on, the wizard might be kept in check; nay,
was it not prudent after all to give or appear to give way to the
Obeah man, who had such a strange and perverse power over the
minds of the Blacks? The point once gained, the rebellion in
vigour, Hamel might be outwitted, anyhow disposed of; it were no
sin to slay an accomplice of the devil, or to launch him from his
fastness into the dingles below. 'Indeed,' thought he, as the reflection gained on him, 'it were perhaps an act of piety and just retri-
bution, and one which Combah himself might be induced to put
in force.'

Roland determined to return into the cavern; in fact, any longer
stay in his present position was evidently absurd, as he was utterly
afraid to attempt a descent; and happen what might, he must re-

turn through the Obeah man's apartment, before he could regain
the abodes of white men. There was a lady too in the case; a young
person on whom he had set his affections, whom he desired ar-
dently to revisit, as soon as he should have effected the purpose
for which he had undertaken his journey to the abandoned settlement noticed in a previous part of this narrative. Without the help
of Combah, he knew not how to assure himself of any success with
this young person; for she had not as yet returned his love, nor any
acknowledgment of it or for it. She would neither listen to nor
even look on him, if she could avoid it; and she had been heard to
express no less horror of him and his misplaced affection, than
that which the Missionary himself had felt for Hamel and his
office. This feeling had incensed the Methodist without at all diminishing his love, which was of a nature more passionate perhaps
than refined. It wounded him besides in the tenderest part of his
spirituality, his vanity; for he knew that she preferred another one,
whom he was accustomed to regard as a worthless, irreligious,
profane, and at the same time daring adventurer; who had scoffed
at him and his *religion*, and denounced him publicly as a cheat and
an impostor. To circumvent this youth, and to gain possession of
the lady, had been the first motives for his league with Combah. In
the confusion of a revolt, successful or unsuccessful, an opportunity would be contrived by the would-be king and his followers for
the Missionary to seize and carry off his prize; at least he had so
bargained with his majesty. Once his, forever his, thought he;
fraud, violence, would be compensated by the offer of his hand;
and his character was in too high esteem among all ranks who
knew him by name and by his preaching, to suffer anything from
the breath of slander. This was his idea, supposing the revolt to
fail. If it succeeded, he became the right-hand man of the king,
viceroy over him, as Trinculo happily observes; the keeper of his
conscience, high priest, pope protestant of the island, with a beautiful girl for his wife. The enthusiast's ambition was not so immod-
erate as to extend farther than a desire for dominion over the
consciences of all the inhabitants and their monarch; but the
monarch, it seemed, had already revolted from his spiritual pros-
tration, in listening to and expressing his wish to profit by the

spells of an infidel dabbler in magic, or a pretended dabbler; for
Roland was undecided as to the opinion he ought to adopt about
him, not being altogether persuaded of the possibility of enlisting
fiends and demons into human service.

'Well,' thought he, turning round to retrace his steps, 'something must be done; I shall not be the first who has held a candle
to the D—.' The very thought made him shudder. 'If argument
fail, cunning, manoeuvring, may do it; at any rate I must get out of
this infernal abode, cost what it will; inquire for my servant and my
horse; and if the rivers admit of it, pursue my course to that plantation of misery where the revolted Negroes await me.'

With this idea he recomposed his features, and recommenced
his battle with the bats, returning with much deliberation and
more confidence to the interior of the cave. Here let us for the
present leave him, and adjourn to a different scene and subject, of
no less importance, to the reader at least, than the trio of persons
whom we quit for the purpose of introducing the young and beautiful, the amiable and innocent Joanna.

CHAPTER 7.

_____ Cytherea,
How bravely thou becom'st thy bed, fresh lily!
And whiter than the sheets—that I might touch!
But kiss; one kiss!

SHAKSPEARE.

THE storm of the preceding night, whose violence we have commemorated, had wrecked, no doubt, many a gallant vessel and many a wayworn bark, whose crews, sinking into the waves which ingulphed them, sank likewise into oblivion, as far at least as all knowledge or certainty of their fate has been rendered evident. Others, dead in nature, may yet live in history for a year or two; and vice versa, the survivors in nature are all dead in history, with the exception of a few miserables whom fortune rescued from the deep to be recorded in these pages.

It was near midnight, and the storm was at its height, and every house in the island which had such means of defence barricadoed to resist it, when a rather motley group of persons, eight or ten in number, knocked at the house of a gentleman in the parish of St Mary, and demanded the rights of hospitality. This house was situated within half a mile of the sea, at _____ Bay, and the strangers said they had been wrecked in a large canoe, with which they had crossed from Cuba; where, as they farther stated, they had been detained as prisoners by a party of pirates. The inhabitants of the house were more surprised at their being able to reach it, although to leeward of the spot where they had been cast on shore, than at their request to be received and entertained in it; an indulgence to which all persons in the island, in case of need at least, would have fancied themselves entitled under any circumstances; I should say all _white_ persons. A window of the piazza was opened, and the party reconnoitred, with the help of a lanthorn, by an old gentleman from within; for being strangers and from another island, they were liable to a little suspicion; and the mention of the word pirates perhaps gave birth to an idea of the possibility of

33

their being themselves of that calling. They presented themselves
to the old gentleman's gaze in succession; and the opened window
being on the lee side of the house, he could examine their features
with some little attention, and make what enquiries he thought fit
to put to them, so as to be heard and answered; but the violence of
the storm threatening to burst in the shutters on the weather-side
of the piazza, it became necessary, as a security in case of such an
accident, to shut the aforesaid window; for if the gale should once
gain passage through the house, the building would inevitably go
to pieces, and its inhabitants might be blown away with the rest of
its contents; a circumstance that has occurred more than once in
this part of the globe. The shipwrecked men were therefore admitted, after a mutilated set of interrogatories through the piazza
window, which was closed and again barricadoed, for fear the
wind might shift; and all hands immediately repaired, as if by instinct, to that portion of the building which was more directly
threatened. Here the owner of the mansion resumed the labours
he had evidently left but a few minutes before, which consisted in
pulling to pieces a bedstead, with the materials of which he was
adding to his stauncheons and barricadoes; almost heedless of his
guests, whom he had commended to the care of a Negro butler,
desiring he would furnish them from the beaufet with rum or any
liqueurs they might like: food was for the present out of the question, all the offices of the house being detached, and consequently
unattainable except by quitting the mansion. But the new guests,
too sensible of the danger which menaced them, repaired at once
to his assistance, and secured the bed-posts against the shutters
and doors, before they attended to any of the other directions of
their host, or adverted to the rest of the inmates of the dwelling,
whose situation seemed yet to require some attention, after all
measures of security had been completed. It was then that one of
the party, looking into a chamber whose window opened upon the
piazza, beheld a lady pale and almost insensible, supported in an
arm chair by a Quadroon soubrette; who applied a smelling bottle
of some essence to her nostrils with one hand, while with the
other she chafed her mistress's temples. It was but a momentary
glance in which the stranger indulged—a feeling of delicacy pre-

vented him from gazing with too much curiosity; but it sufficed to convince him that the soubrette was a very beautiful girl, and that the lady herself was no ordinary person; she looked but little turned of thirty years of age, for her complexion was smooth; clear, and bright, as if she had never known a tropical climate; but it was the whiteness almost of alabaster, without a tinge of blood in her cheek; and as she lay in the arm chair so languid and pale, her dark hair disheveled a little on her brows, assumed a deeper hue, perhaps by so glaring a contrast. She opened her eyes at the moment that this stranger removed from his position; and seeing a man in the piazza whom she neither knew nor recollected to have seen before, uttered a faint and half-stifled cry as she clung to the arms of the Quadroon.

'Leave me not, Michal,' she said; 'leave me not. What man is that? Is the house on fire? Where is Joanna?'

The stranger looked round on hearing this exclamation, which did not escape the notice of his comrades, who crowded towards the window; and at the same moment Joanna herself appeared, in answer to her mother's interrogatory, from a contiguous apartment; but as she approached the arm chair, she started at the sight of so many black and brown faces staring into the chamber, and would have retired again, in evident alarm, had not the stranger who had first beheld her mother, called to her in a gentle and assuring voice, that she had nothing to fear. The lord of the mansion had left his barricades for an instant; but the howling of the storm recalled him quickly to his post, whither the stranger directed his companions to attend him again, while he himself, fixed by the appearance of the young lady, delayed for a moment or two joining them.

'Who and what are you?' said Joanna, in a timid voice.

'We are shipwrecked men,' replied the stranger; 'profiting by your hospitality.'

If the young lady was startled in the first instance, she was even yet surprised to hear a man with a mulatto skin speak in a dialect so very far removed from that of the Negroes; and *he* appeared to be a little confounded at the sight of this beautiful creature. Her complexion was nearly similar to that of her mother, pale and delicate; but her figure was firm and elastic, not withstanding her alarm; and the scanty portion of clothes in which she was clad, concealed but little of its elegant outline. Her paleness might be attributed to her apprehensions, for the colour had even fled from her lips, or at least there was but enough of the rose left there to characterize her as an animated creature of this earth, who might otherwise have been almost fancied a being of another world. She was as fair as pale, with large blue eyes, from which her terror had but just chased her tears, as was but too evident from the expression of grief still upon her features; and with her hair partly bound round her head in braids, partly disordered on her shoulders, and waiving in the current of the wind, she wanted only the chaplet of flowers which the painter has given to Proserpine, to have formed the type, if not the model, for that beautiful production of the pencil of Schiavoni, where Pluto, with the air and hue of a stout Sambo, is carrying off his prize from her pastoral diversions to the realms of Tartarus. But the figure of Pluto would not correspond with that of the spectator, who still fixed his eyes on her as by a kind of fascination; for the king of Erebus, according to the artist, is short, thick, and clumsy; whereas this sambo-coloured man was tall and well proportioned, of a most dignified and commanding manner, open and undisguised, with nothing in his appearance indicative of the robber or ravisher. He sighed as he looked at her again, and quickly removed his gaze to his companions, who were yet labouring for their host to secure the very spars of the roof, lest the hurricane should tear that shelter from their heads. The young lady turned to her mother with a view to assist the soubrette in her attentions; and the old gentleman, working like a Hercules, from time to time thanked his guests for their assistance, without which his house and household would have been, as he said, in but a very indifferent plight; for the Negroes belonging to the estate, in confirmation of the truth that charity begins at home, had all abandoned their master's abode, to guard each his own dwelling. At any other time, at least upon a less serious occasion, his costume and appearance would have excited a smile even on the negro faces which were now turned on him; for both almost bordered on the ludicrous. In the hurry of quitting his chamber at the commencement of the storm, he had put on a long dressing gown of chintz or dark-figured cotton, two-thirds of which had been since torn off by his efforts and struggles in contending against the elements, so that it had become a sort of spencer, which gave to view a pair of black silk breeches, with large Spanish silver knee-buckles, matched, though scarcely surpassed, by another pair of the same metal on his shoes. He was some fifty years of age; and his hair, a mixture of brown and grey, was combed from off his face with such accuracy and perseverance to form a queue, tied close up to his occiput, that it seemed to drag with it all the muscular part and power of his cheeks, forehead, nose, and mouth; so that many of his acquaintance were accustomed to fancy he never could shut his eyes without letting go his pigtail. Indeed by the same rule he could never open them to their full capability of extension; for the corners were drawn forcibly towards his temples, resembling in figure and effect those of the cayman; and all he could do as to motion with these his half opened window-lights, was to wink them once or twice a day. Superadded to this rather droll part of his physiognomy, one of the aforesaid eyes was gifted with a most ominous cast in its vision, and appeared to the spectator on whom it was intended to be turned (under the influence of any passion) to be contemplating the stars, or reading calculations, (written by the imagination of which it was the light,) in the penetralia of the brains behind it. With all this singularity in his materiel, he displayed a most pompous though inoffensive solemnity in his march, manners, deportment, and address, which extended to the language in which he sometimes buried rather than clothed his thoughts. He had likewise a taste for ornamenting his discourse with quotations from the Latin authors; and though he understood or appeared to understand the application and translation of these elegancies, his hearers were not always so fortunate, owing to some peculiarities to which he was attached of now and then altering the cases and genders of adjectives and articles. Things are not expected to be exactly similar in the old and new world. Mr Guthrie knew nothing but by hear-say of the first, having never been off the island of Jamaica but once in his life, and that only a few years back, when he was taken by a boat's crew

from a log of mahogany of which he was making prize in the ocean
(having seen it with a glass from his piazza window.) He had no
sooner seen than he desired to possess it; ordered out his boats
and Negroes, came up with and was himself securing it, when a
strange sail, which had been skulking under the rocks, sprung out
upon him like a lion on his prey; and before his Negroes could disengage him from the log, he was a prisoner. Indeed he bid them
seek their own safety, for (his presence of mind not forsaking him)
he calculated on the expense of redeeming half a dozen slaves as
well as himself, and had nearly lost his life for his prudence or par-
simony; the pirates threatening to fling him into the sea, until he
persuaded them that the Negroes had rowed off from their own
fears. However, they carried him away; but being happily taken
into Guadaloupe by a French cruizer, they were disposed of according to law; and he, having proved his innocence, was dismissed with great courtesy, and sent home. Upon his arrival
however, he found he had cause to regret his absence; some of his
buildings had been burnt, it was supposed maliciously; and he had
found his wife in a state of melancholy and ill health, owing, as was
said, to her alarm respecting him, in the first place; and in the second, to her terrors occasioned by the fire, from which to this hour
she had not recovered. These terrors were revived on the present
occasion. The combustion of the elements, the earthquake which
had convulsed the house, the wind and the lightning, however frequent in the island, all raging in unison, had filled her with physical alarm, as well as superstitious apprehensions, to which her
state of mind had left her but too subject. It was to no purpose that
her husband argued with her on the folly of such fancies; in vain
that her daughter sought and practised every means of consoling
her. Though not insensible, she appeared to be indifferent to
both, to everything that had hitherto given her any sort of consolation or interest. She even preferred, or seemed to prefer, the absence of her daughter, as if the sight of this her only child
increased her agitations, and as if those attentions which Joanna
too fondly paid her, excited only painful recollections. So, in the
midst of her present alarms, she had in a manner banished her
daughter to her own chamber, and accepted the services of the

soubrette; and hence the tears and distress of the former, for whose presence she had only called at the sight of the strange guests with whom the storm had accommodated them, and then only from an apprehension for her personal safety.

CHAPTER 8.

This tempest will not give me leave to ponder
On things would hurt me more.

SHAKSPEARE.

WE left Mr Guthrie, and his black and brown guests, still engaged
in the defence of his chateau against the attacks of the hurricane.
Their arrival had been extremely àpropos, and their services actually saved the dwelling from being blown to pieces; but as they had
come with a very different purpose from that which they had executed, it may not be amiss to acquaint the reader with the actual
primary intention of this band of worthies, which was no less than
robbery.

It was no less than robbery; but that was to have been the sec-
ondary object at which they aimed; the first being to make prize of
the fair Joanna—for her advancement, it is true, as the royal-
minded Combah designed to make her queen of the island. His
majesty had rightly calculated that it would be too late to make any
attempt on this his bride elect, after the island should have been
alarmed; as many would take to the ships, and all who did not
would crowd into the towns for security in such an event; and it
would be a business of great difficulty to get possession of her
under the circumstances that would attend the latter case; and
next to impossible, if her parents should once get her off the island. It were better to take time by the forelock, and secure the
young lady before a fear or suspicion of a revolt should affect the
minds of the inhabitants. With this feeling a canoe had been provided, whose crew were to hover on the coast, sometimes at sea,
sometimes on shore, as occasion might require. They were to
watch to windward for a certain signal, at the sight of which they
were, if necessary, to attack the house of Mr Guthrie; at any rate to
seize the young lady, hurry her away to the canoe, and bring her,
not to the abandoned settlement behind Port Antonio, but to the
cave of the Obeah man. This signal was to be the kindling of three
fires on one of the ridges of the Blue Mountain; and we have seen

how it happened that on the night in question Roland and his boy
Cuffy had looked with no little terror on as many if not more of
these wandering flames; which, although they had been accidentally kindled by runaway Negroes, had carried a conviction to the
minds of Combah's delegates, that this was their signal, and that
now was the moment for going to work. But the storm had run
their canoe on the rocks, damaged it, and, as they feared, almost
beaten it to pieces. It was not without difficulty that they saved
their lives; and to escape from the hurricane, they had ultimately
been obliged to ask hospitality at the very dwelling against whose
inmates they had meditated such horrible violence. Their plan
therefore (at least for the present) was suspended, if not frus-
trated; for although they might have carried off Joanna by sea, it
would be worse than madness to attempt such a scheme by land;
nay, it would be impossible, except the whole country were in
open revolt; and even then it would be no easy matter to persuade
Mr Guthrie's Negroes to suffer such violence to be done to him on
any pretence. These were ideas which had been communicated
among the party as they groped their way in the storm to the mansion where we have introduced them. Once within it, they had little opportunity of comparing notes or hatching any fresh
schemes, or even of mutual converse: they were occupied with
the master of the house in counteracting the fury of the wind; and
although they had had a sight of the fair creature who had been
marked for their prey, there was but one of them who had been allowed more than a momentary look at her; and he, strange to say,
had turned them aside from the contemplation of a person whom
they had in some sort hired him to steal, or to assist in stealing.
This stranger they had brought from the south side of Cuba,
where he described himself to have fled from the cruelty and oppression of a white man who wished to make a property of him.
His story might be true or false; but at any rate he had ingratiated
himself so far in their good opinion, as to have learnt the purpose
for which they were bound to Jamaica; and on the plea of avenging himself on the tyrant who had oppressed him, he had been
permitted, and finally encouraged, to take part with them in their
enterprise; more particularly, as he gave them reason to see that

he was acquainted with the part of the island in which the scene of
their affair was to be laid, and with the house in question; although
he owned no knowledge of its inmates. *He* was to assist in carrying
off the young lady; *they* to further his views of vengeance on the
unjust and inhuman tyrant who had practised against his liberty
and independence. But let us return to Mr Guthrie.

This unsuspecting gentleman, occupied more with the danger
which had threatened his mansion from the fury of the elements,
than with the fears and fancies of his wife, to which time had a little hardened him, succeeded eventually, with the assistance of his
guests, in securing his doors and windows, and the spars of his
house; and, in short, enabled it to weather the gale, which abated,
as we have seen, towards morning, and had so far subsided by daylight, as to admit of the defences being withdrawn for the purposes of ingress and egress.

The old gentleman's gratitude, as well as hospitality, began now
to manifest themselves more visibly in his wishes and offers of rewards and refreshments, for the services he had received from his
strange guests; offers which he, with apparent difficulty only,
could prevail on them to accept—that is, as to the rewards. The
refreshments they declined; not thinking it advisable perhaps to
continue under the roof of one to whom they had meditated so
deep an injury, especially as his Negroes began to assemble about
the premises, and learnt with some feeling of shame and surprise,
that their master owed the preservation of his house to a band of
strange people of colour. Nay, Mr Guthrie spared no pains to encrease their shame, in vaunting to them the noble and disinterested endeavours of these good men, as he called them, who had
so fortunately come to his assistance, when his own Negroes had
left him to the mercy of the storm.

'I tell you,' cried he, (feeling for the skirts of his dressing gown,)
'that you have entailed a lasting disgrace on yourselves and your
posterity; you are as bad as the white people in England; you left
your master and mistress, and your young mistress—your bene-
factors—your natural lord, myself—to perish in the wind: what
could the white varlets in England do worse? You think yourselves
better than they are; Mr Roland tells you that you are, and I used

to think he was right. I only wonder you did not profit by the occasion to thieve; but I suppose you were too busy with your own cocks and hens, and your pigs, your plantains, your furniture, your houses, your fine clothes, your doubloons, and your dollars; and now perhaps you are only come to see whether the storm has not left something for you to plunder, or blown something away from the stores of which you may make prize. Are not you ashamed that I should owe my safety to strangers? Why, I suppose it would have been the same if we had been attacked by pirates or runaway Negroes. You would have left us to our fate; we might have been robbed, murdered, and flung in the sea, before you would have come to our help.'

This harangue was made from the steps of the piazza, where Mr Guthrie, heated, exhausted, indignant, and enraged, gave vent to his passion in thus stigmatizing the feelings of his slaves for attending to their own affairs in the late emergency, instead of sacrificing them to their concern for his. If his figure and appearance were ludicrous by the lamp light of the preceding night, they were scarcely less than diverting even to his Negroes by day. In feeling for the skirts of his dressing gown, which had now been restored to him by the soubrette, he had discovered a woful gash in his silk breeches, over which he hung the fragments he had received, in the manner of a petticoat. His features were disfigured with perspiration, dust, and dirt; and his hands, which he displayed in suiting the action to the word, were as black nearly as those of the sable gentry he addressed. So laughable indeed was his appearance altogether, that the brown stranger in whose praise he was speaking (the person who had appeared to possess an influence over his comrades) could scarcely retain his gravity, in spite of the more serious ideas which we may suppose were fermenting in his brains, whenever the sinister eye of his host was diverted from him to the multitude he anathematized. As for the rest of the chosen few who had merited the eulogy of Mr Guthrie, they had begun some time since to effect a retreat towards the shore, on pretence of examining their boat, and securing what effects the sea might have spared them from it;—not altogether a pretence, although there was perhaps a no less

important consideration which affected them in thus withdraw-
ing themselves; namely, the apprehension of being suspected,
recognized by any of the multitude, detected, and secured. Nay,
one of them had overheard an old black woman, surnamed the
White Fairy, (because she was as black as pitch,) muttering beneath the piazza window, that her master need not brag so much
of his new friends, who, bad as they looked, ('fit only for the John-
crows,') still looked better than they were in reality; and, as the lis-
tener seemed to wince a little on hearing her oracular innuendo,
she had begun to assume a bolder tone, and called out for the
sailor's paper, a word significative of passport. The paper, sure
enough, had been prepared; but there was no immediate occasion, according to their ideas, of submitting it to inspection and
scrutiny; and they judged it better to remove to the sea-shore, for
the purposes above-mentioned. Thither they proceeded without
delay; leaving their comrade with the master of the house, to answer all interrogatories, and make any reconnoissance he should
think proper for the furthering of the scheme which was the subject of their expedition.

Mr Guthrie saw them depart, without making any remark, supposing their intention to be such as they represented; but as soon
as his passion thus vented on his slaves had in some measure
abated, he began to pay a little attention to this more important-
looking personage; of whom, considering his colour, he felt au-
thorized to ask his name and lineage, at the same time that he
begged his acceptance of a doubloon, in testimony of the services
he wished to acknowledge. This the Mulatto-man decidedly renounced, as well as all claim to it; declaring, that he and his comrades were no less indebted to Mr Guthrie, than he to them; but if
there were to be obligation on either part, it would be of a nature
very different from any hitherto thought or spoken of; and perhaps he might have it in his power, without however claiming any
acknowledgment for it, to render his liberal host some really essential benefit.

'Halt!' cried the lord of the house, with a most solemn inclination of his head, at the same time stretching his dirty face, to ex-
pand his eyeballs; 'an essential benefit! This is an enigma in which

you are pleased to indulge, friend. What may be your means of serving one who certainly had as little title as expectation to receive assistance already at your hands? But I have no right to ask questions, whether you may or may not be disposed to gratify my curiosity. Still are your words the words of mystery; and we know we have much to fear just now from the abominably impudent and shameless opinions about liberty, forsooth, which our transatlantic cousins, in the old stupid world, are foisting upon the better-informed, better-educated, more liberal and enlightened people of the great Antilles. Are we to have a revolt? Come, you may be in the secret?'

'God forbid,' replied the Mulatto, 'that you should fear even a revolt. Nor can I detail the ideas which I may entertain of being useful to you; you would not credit *me*, a stranger, and a man of colour.'

'Why, faith!' rejoined Mr Guthrie, 'you are a man of a common colour, but of no common speech; nor can I think that you have African blood in your veins, despite your colour. Let me see, you told us last night that you came from Cuba, where you had been detained by pirates. Are you a free man? Yes,' he continued, 'I think I may answer that question myself.'

The Mulatto bowed.

'And your comrades?'

'Those who brought me from Cuba,' replied he, 'assured me that they were free; that they keep or kept a canoe, with which they carried passengers, and sometimes goods, from Montego bay to St Lucie.'

'And you believe their story?' demanded the other.

'I do not.'

'But you can see their tale is true, as to the mischief they have suffered.'

'Yonder is their bark, which they have hauled beyond the reach of the waves and spray; and, as you may distinguish, even without your glass, they are endeavouring to repair it.'

'I will at least send them tools and assistance,' observed Mr Guthrie, looking at them through his telescope; 'and a carpenter or two, and anything else you think they may be in need of.'

'At your pleasure, sir,' replied the Mulatto; 'and it is time that I should also retire to them.'

'No! no!' interrupted Mr Guthrie; 'sit you down here; you shall be taken care of, at least. The Negroes will give your companions wherewithal to make a breakfast. You shall be entertained here, while I go to dress myself. Sit down.'

It was in vain that the Mulatto protested against such an honour as breakfasting in the piazza of the white man: his bows either were not sufficiently disqualifying, or there was something in his physiognomy which excited the pertinacity of the buckra. At any rate, he allowed himself to be prevailed on, and took his station, as desired: while Mr Guthrie, having given the orders he had proposed, and sent down the assistance and provisions he designed for his late guests, betook himself to his own room, to depurate his person, as he termed the act of ablution; and left the Mulatto-man alone in the hall of his mansion.

The hall opened into the piazza, and several bed-chambers communicated with the hall. The Mulatto had not been doomed to his own company many minutes before he saw one of the doors gently open, and a pair of black eyes peep on him from a face, the rest of which was concealed behind the door. There could be nothing repulsive in his exterior; for the aforesaid eyes, as far as he divined, expressed an increasing curiosity; and the face, after a sufficient stare, gradually elongating itself from its concealment, displayed the pretty features of the soubrette. This young beauty had not failed to take notice of the stranger's figure and appearance the previous night; and if she was pleased, or rather not displeased, with them under the circumstances of that time, and the calamity that attended it, there was no reason why she should not indulge herself with a second, a daylight perusal of them. So, having heard the finale of the dialogue in the piazza, and her young mistress being by this time attired, and after having made the above-mentioned observation of the premises, she stepped fearlessly out of the chamber, and shutting the door behind her, beckoned with a familiar smile to the stranger to follow her to the further end of the piazza; where she made a halt, and turning round upon him suddenly, took advantage of the full

glare of the daylight to examine his features to her heart's
content.

We have before remarked, in mentioning the picture of
Schiavoni, that this Mulatto was a tall, athletic, personable man.
Michal the soubrette, surveying him from head to foot, was
speedily convinced of this; and had his skin been white instead of
tawny, she had taken him to be a very handsome buckra.
Quadroon damsels do not look for beauty in the youth of their
own colour; their first ideas of admiration or love are devoted to
the genuine white breed, either native or imported, to which they
are themselves indebted, as they think, for the charms of their
own persons, and all the favour they find in the eyes of those who
sigh for their affections. Therefore, however natural the desire
she might have to appear to advantage, even before a young
Mulatto-man, nothing was farther from her thoughts than to inspire him with anything like that confidence which prompted
him, after he had tenderly squeezed the hand unconsciously held
out to him, to imprint a kiss upon her lips. Nothing was more unexpected, and few things had more astonished her. She snatched
away her hand, and tore herself from his embrace as if she had
been in the folds of such a serpent as that which stopped the
march of the Roman army; and though her tongue refused to express the feelings which this insult had roused, her black eyes
flashed with so much anger and indignation, that the heart of the
Mulatto for a moment sunk within him, and he felt the necessity,
by looks as well as words of supplication, to apologize for the liberty he had taken. There is a natural grace in the manners or persons of colour (nay, even in those of Negroes;) so that the apology
to which she listened, however elegantly worded and delivered,
seemed only what she might have expected; but the tone of voice
was in no wise creole; and Michal, as she set him down in her mind
for an impudent fellow, concluded he had acquired his gentility
with his free and easy manners in other countries, and in pursuit
of his business, whatever it might be. However, as her resentment
began to abate with the manifestation of his repentance, she gave
way to the more natural kindness of her disposition, and told him
with a smile, that he was no guest for her master and mistress, but

must come and breakfast at her house, not twenty yards from the
back piazza; where her mother would give him plenty of coffee
and roasted plantains, which were now waiting his pleasure. As
she spoke this, she descended the piazza steps; and the Mulatto,
convinced by her expression, and his own reflections, that she was
in the right, followed her not unwillingly to the abode which she
had pointed out, where he was indulged with the seat of honour,
and regaled with an excellent breakfast: while at the same time he
feasted his eyes with gazing on those, and the many other charms,
of the pretty and amiable soubrette.

CHAPTER 9.

The purest treasure mortal times afford,
Is spotless reputation;—that away,
Men are but gilded loam or painted clay.
SHAKSPEARE.

THE mother of Michal, a mulatto woman of some forty years of age, had no sooner supplied her daughter's guest with all he desired, than she left him to attend her sick mistress, who was too unwell to quit her bed; she left him however with her daughter; and this latter took the first opportunity of her mother's absence to ask by what name she was to call him, and why he had not given Mr Guthrie an answer to his question on the same subject.

'Why, my pretty mistress,' said he, 'did *you* listen to all we talked of?' (A nod admitted the fact.) 'My name is, at least my companions called me, Sebastian or Sebastiano; but you shall call me what you please; I should like that you would find me a name, so it gave me a title to your kind thoughts.'

'No, no,' replied the soubrette; 'you are too rude and too bold; I shall give you no name; you are as impudent as if you were a white man, and an old ugly one too—for such are always the first to take liberties. I have seen now and then a young gentleman modest and timid, and almost afraid to speak to the Mulatto and Quadroon girls; but an old fellow no sooner comes into the house, than he begins winking his eyes at us almost before my mistress's face; and if her back is turned for a moment, he has some impertinent thing to say, if he has not the rudeness to lay his hands on us.'

'Well, pretty mistress,' rejoined the Mulatto, looking steadily in her face, 'there is some motive for their presumption, if no excuse; and you ought not to grieve on such occasions, where even the insolence of white men is still a tribute of admiration, in some shape or other, to the charms of your face and person.'

'Indeed! indeed!' cried the Quadroon, looking more and more earnestly at him. 'Why, Mr Sebastian, you have a fine smooth tongue, and you talk indeed quite like—I know not what—like the parson on a Sunday, or like Mr Roland the missionary, who preaches every day.'

'Does Mr Roland preach every day then?' replied Sebastian. 'Where is he?'

'He went to windward yesterday,' said the soubrette, a little surprised to hear her guest speak of Mr Roland as if he knew him.

'And for what purpose?' rejoined the other.

'Oh, for no good!' said the Quadroon; 'but for what he only knows himself. I am sure I wish he may never come back; but how do you happen to know him, Mr Sebastian? I thought you came from Cuba with those ill-looking Negroes that you brought here. Where did you ever see Mr Roland?'

'Ah, Michal! Miss Michal!' replied the Mulatto; 'I have seen him in this island, and I have too much cause to know him; but tell me, why does he come here every day to preach? Is it your master, or your mistress, or your young mistress, that encourages him?'

'My master!' answered the girl with a smile, 'my master! he detests him; and my mistress—poor mistress!—she can hardly bear the sight of him; and Miss Joanna won't have him for a husband, although he teazes her and poor mistress every day.'

'And why will not your young lady marry him?'

'Oh!' said Michal, 'he is nothing—a poor preacher; and Miss Joanna likes somebody else better—a fine young gentleman she saw in England or France.'

'And does Roland know of this?'

'Yes, yes; Mr Roland knows it, because mistress told him.'

'And what said he?'

'What said he?' repeated the soubrette. 'He said that Mr Fairfax was a villain; one who believed in neither God nor devil; that he had committed a murder, and that he robbed upon the sea.'

'Indeed! indeed!' ejaculated the Mulatto. 'Bravo, my prince of missionaries!'

'But do not imagine that Miss Joanna believes it all,' continued Michal.

'Not all of it, I dare say,' replied the other.

'No, no, Mr Sebastian; she told her father—for I heard her— that Mr Fairfax was an honourable young gentleman, and never

could be guilty of such crimes; but yet my master hates the name
of Fairfax, and told her that this very young gentleman would be
his bitterest enemy, and laughed at all she had to say of him, and
told her never to think about him again; for she never would perhaps see him, or if she did, it would be in the character of a robber,
come to despoil *him* of all he had yet to lose in this world. This is
no secret here,' continued the soubrette; 'and as you know Mr
Roland, I do not mind telling you everything about him; and my
master, who cannot bear him for preaching to the Negroes, would
send him away from here whenever he comes; but my mistress
begs he may allowed to stay; yet she is so unhappy when he does
come, that it makes my heart almost break to see her; and there is
some mystery between them that nobody else knows. Now tell
me, Mr Sebastian,'—(the maid looked at him with a mingled expression of archness and tenderness)—'what you are thinking
about, that you do not seem to attend to me? Some pretty girl you
have left in Cuba? You are the captain of your canoe, are you not?'

The Mulatto smiled, or forced a smile for her in return, and assured her that the only pretty girl he was thinking of was herself;
and he regretted his dark skin must lower him so much in her
eyes, that he could gain nothing in her esteem by expressing the
kind feelings with which she inspired him. The Quadroon smiled
in earnest at this parade of words, which after all seemed yet in
character with the manners of the speaker; but it was a smile of
unaffected goodnature and simplicity; and she told her guest with
a very ingenuous air, and in a no less ingenuous tone of voice, that
notwithstanding his dark skin, she had never before seen such a
Mulatto-man as himself; and she could not but wonder where he,
who was so young, had learned to talk so prettily, and so like what
she fancied of a fine gentleman. She thought he must have been
educated in England; perhaps by Mr W——? He shook his head.

'Indeed, my pretty mistress, I was educated in England, and
have been in France; and what is more, I have been acquainted
with the gentleman you speak of. Mr Fairfax is not unknown to
me; I have attended, I may say served him.'

'Have you, really?' demanded the soubrette. 'Why did not
you tell me so before? How happy will Miss Joanna be to hear

something of him! But is he what Mr Roland calls him? He is not a buccaneer, is he? nor one who will not believe in God? I know he is a handsome young man, and brave, and rich, and honourable. Well! well! one day he must marry my young mistress, and then perhaps, Mr Sebastian, I may see you again sometimes.'

'Ah Michal!' replied he; 'the sight of your pretty face will always cheer my heart; I could love you for having been always near the object which Mr Fairfax so much prizes.'

'You could love me, Mr Sebastian?' interrupted the Quadroon; 'you could love me! If we were in England perhaps. Who knows what may be our fate one of these days, by and bye? Indeed you may deserve a more honourable love than mine; you are a free man, and I am a slave.'

'You shall be free, Michal, if you will be faithful.'

Michal shook her head. 'What would my mistress say, and my mother?' she added laughing. 'No, no; do not talk about love to me; come and tell Miss Joanna about Mr Fairfax, or tell me something for her, if you please; for Mr Guthrie will be too much on his guard, or too fanciful, to give you an opportunity of speaking with her alone; and we shall have Mr Roland coming here again by and bye. Yonder is his house, by the coco-nut trees, half way down to the bay. I have seen him sometimes for an hour together spying into the piazza at my master's with his glass.'

'Spying here also I should think sometimes—does he not, Michal? *I* should, I fear, if I dwelt yonder; or what would you think of me if I did not? At least since you allow me to fancy there may be something in my brown face that is not altogether horrible to you. You would find me, Michal—you *will* find me, I hope, a faithful—'

'A faithful what? A faithful how much, Mr Sailor? By the virtue of my conscience, and Miss Michal's too, making love to the Quadroon! Why, thou naughty flirt! It was for this that you took away Mr What's-his-name to breakfast with you. Why did you not,' continued Mr Guthrie, addressing himself to the Mulatto, 'why did you not stay to breakfast with me, where I had left you?'

The Mulatto bowed, and expressed his sense of the honour his host had intended him; adding, 'that he could not consider himself entitled to it; that he knew, or thought he knew, his proper place, which was here, at Miss Michal's invitation; not that he had presumed to speak to her in any terms of gallantry.'

'Why, what was it then,' said the white gentleman, 'that I heard? Mister—Mister—'

'Sebastian is his name,' interrupted Michal.

'Mister Sebastian! a fine Spanish title or designation indeed! Mr Sebastian,' continued he, 'you are a very extraordinary personage, to say the least of you: did you acquire that nomenclature in Cuba? Your language and manners have nothing in common with those of your associates, and little in common with those of persons of your colour in general. I can with difficulty persuade myself that I have understood aright all you have told me of yourself.'

'There will be little cause for suspicion at my language or manners,' replied the Mulatto, 'when you are informed, that although I have a brown complexion, I have spent the chief part of my life in Europe—in England, in France, in Italy, and in other countries; where I have had an opportunity of improving myself, by which I might have profited to a much greater extent than my appearance indicates.'

'He has been with Mr Fairfax,' said the pretty Quadroon, interposing.

'With Fairfax!' echoed Mr Guthrie, opening his eyes to their widest; 'with Fairfax! What do I hear?' A crowd of ideas seemed to rush into his mind, as far at least as the incarcerated muscles of his face allowed his auditors to divine from the little motion of which it was capable. 'You the companion of Mr Fairfax? What could have brought you here? By heaven, you are spies! No fortune can have led you to this spot, it must have been design, a scheme concerted, premeditation; yet what had you to gain? Does my daughter know that this man comes from Mr Fairfax? Michal, speak.'

'How can she know?' replied the maid. 'She has not seen him; and it is not five minutes since I learned it myself.'

'What do you know of him?' said Mr Guthrie, again addressing the Mulatto. 'Describe me his person—but stay; come with me to the house: I wish even *that* vermin Roland were here. Let Miss

Guthrie see you, and hear from you what sort of a being is this Fairfax who is to chase us from our inheritance, at least from a great part of it, as he threatens, and yet has the assurance (or has had) to think of aspiring to her affections. If we may believe Roland (which heaven forbid!) Mr Fairfax is a very singular person, and one who does not stick at trifles: indeed this very argument is proof of it; and Roland says he makes nothing of cutting throats either by land or water.'

'How should Mr Roland know this?' observed the Mulatto. 'Has he witnessed any of his exploits? But let me tell you, Mr Guthrie, once for all, *I* am no spy at least, and have no design against your peace or happiness.'

'No, I'll be sworn!' replied the white man. 'I can trust your features, and believe you are nought but what you appear. Nay, never flinch, man: Roland has denounced your Mr Fairfax as a pirate, and waits his coming to the island to cause his arrest. He says he has half a dozen Negroes to prove what he asserts, if their evidence were to be admitted. But come: Michal, go call Joanna. Sebastian, or whatever may be your name, I shall forget neither the services you have rendered me, nor what the laws of hospitality demand of me in your behalf. I ask as a favour only, that you return with me to the house, and let my daughter question you, if she has any such desire, about your friend, or master, or companion, or whatever else he may be, Mr Oliver Fairfax.'

CHAPTER 10.

I do mistake my person all this while.
Upon my life she finds, altho' I cannot,
Myself to be a marvellous proper man.

SHAKSPEARE.

THERE was nothing that could be called prepossessing in the costume of the Mulatto-man; which consisted of a large pair of loose Osnaburgh trowsers, over a pair of brown leathern boots; a check shirt, buttoned up close to the neck; and a waistcoat with loose sleeves, of drab-coloured cloth, braided in front, and at the seams, but much the worse for the service it had done. He carried a Spanish sword, slung from his right shoulder by a brass or copper chain, consisting of oblong links, bright with friction; and his head was graced with a huge white sombrero beaver. He followed his host with a firm and undaunted step into the piazza which he had last quitted with the Quadroon, and doffed his castor with a courteous and sufficiently submissive air to the fair maiden who advanced along the piazza to receive him; the timid, the beautiful Joanna. She returned his salutation with a natural grace, and with little effort, although her features, pale with grief and watching, indicated considerable agitation, anxiety, and irresolution: yet still regarding him only as an inferior, she scarcely examined his features, and indeed paid little attention to his figure; but she turned her eyes in some confusion on the floor, when her father signified that the person before her, calling himself Sebastian, was acquainted with Mr Oliver Fairfax, of whom he would be kind enough to give her some information, various reports of a most odious description respecting him having found their way to the country. Besides which, he had other reasons to inquire particularly concerning him, as he was the last in an entail that would devolve on himself in the event of Mr Fairfax's death—a circumstance bruited abroad, among the other reports. 'Now, Mr Sebastian,' he added, 'do you know if this last be true?'

As he said this, Mr Guthrie, who had used the privilege of his vision during his speech, of looking right and left at the same time, now turned, or endeavoured to turn, the gaze of both eyes on the Mulatto; an effort in which he succeeded without being detected; as no one unacquainted with him could have imagined, from the obliquity of his scrutinizing glance, that it was directed where it was intended. The Mulatto almost laughed unconsciously, as he replied, looking steadfastly at the lady while he spoke, that Mr Fairfax was certainly alive. A half-suppressed sigh escaped the lips of Joanna at this piece of news; and her face, which was previously pale as marble, assumed for a moment the hue of crimson. She seated herself on a sofa, as she said—venturing at last to open her lips—'You have never heard him mention my father's name?'

'Often.'

'And you attended him in France? You have seen me—you remember me?'

She smiled as she put this question, notwithstanding that her blushes spread by this time over the whole of her neck; and the Mulatto, as if inspired by the beauties he fancied her smile disclosed, answered, not without something bordering on emotion—'I have seen you, lady; I remember you; I can never, never forget you.'

'Never, never forget you!' cried the father, taking up the words of his brown acquaintance, and ogling him with a more and more inquisitive squint. 'Never forget you! Why, what does all this portend, Mr Sebastian? Where is this same Fairfax, then? Is he here, or is he coming to the island?'

'That,' replied the Mulatto, 'is a question I dare not resolve, considering the reports about him which you have mentioned: his life might not be safe, if he were here.'

'Oh fie! oh fie!' said the planter, interrupting him: 'the law cannot hurt him, if he be innocent.'

'But he may have great difficulty in proving his innocence; and this may be, or might be, a still more difficult moment. Has this young lady any farther questions to propose to me?'

He said this with a slight inclination of the head, which she returned with a languid smile; for her rosy colour had faded faster, if possible, than it had appeared: she sat, as at first, pale and melancholy; and the Mulatto thought he saw a tear steal down her cheek, as she replied to his question with the monosyllable 'None.'

'What commands then,' he continued, 'has Mr Guthrie for me? Or may I now retire to the sea-shore, to my ship, and my black companions?'

'Your black companions!' repeated his host. 'Why, you are none so white yourself, though you speak as if you had lived only with white people. You are a very mysterious personage, Mr Sebastian, and have set my wits at defiance with the most absolute success. I really know no more of you, your black companions, as you call them, your business, or what you may be at, than if I had never exchanged a word with you. I shall really despair of my intellectual faculties henceforth: I must be an idiot, a nincompoop, a noncompos: I have lost all my common sense even. The world is a riddle to me: my wife, all mystery, tears, and fits; my daughter in—no matter. A strange man says he is wrecked on my estate; helps me (thank God for all things) in a storm; I catch him saying soft things to my Quadroon servant; and he tells my daughter, before my face, that he will never—no, never—forget her:—a brown man in the sublime! Pray, sir, excuse my curiosity; and let me ask again the meaning of that high-flown sentiment, "never forget you." What had my daughter done to merit so much distinction? Had she overwhelmed you with obligations, when you were in France or England?'

'There is nothing so remarkable,' replied the Mulatto, 'in my observation. I will apply the same words to yourself: I shall not easily forget *you;* and really, I never contemplated anything like gallantry to your servant. Now, sir, let me recommend you to dismiss me. I have other business in hand, which demands my immediate presence and attention. Let me be gone.'

'Shall we ever see you again?' said Joanna in a faint voice, as he turned to depart, having already made his receding bow, while

Mr Guthrie pursued him with one of his eyes: 'shall we ever see
you again?'

The Mulatto stopped to say, 'most certainly, madam;' which his
host as immediately repeated, as he had done many other of his
expressions.

'Most certainly, madam! There again!'

But the stranger was gone before he could articulate the rest of
the exclamations which were crowding into his throat for utterance. Sebastian strode along the piazza and down the steps,
placed his sombrero on his head, and walked deliberately to the
sea-shore; leaving Mr Guthrie with his mouth wide open, and the
young lady still seated on the sofa; her heart beating with agitation, and her eyes dimmed with tears, for which her father at least
knew not how to account.

He had hardly reached the shore, whither the mortified
planter watched him, (without exactly defining to himself the
feelings that chagrined him,) when the sable dame, before mentioned as the White Fairy, came up to the great house with an important air, to tell her master that she knew the canoe Negroes
were rogues and thieves: she had been down to the beach with
plantains and cocoes for them, and spoke to one of the party,
whom she knew to have belonged once to the estate of Mr
Fairfax. He had been a runaway for several years; and there was
a second, whom she had seen the day after her master's trash-
house had been set on fire, long, long ago, talking to Mr Roland,
who sent him away with a paper; but after he was gone, her master's Negroes said they had seen him at their houses the night before, and accused him of having set fire to the building. She said,
she was sure he was the man; and that they had now mended
their canoe, and only waited for the Mulatto, who was just gone
away, to put to sea again and *him* she believed to be only a
buccaneer.

'Why so?' demanded her master with amazement, while the
countenance of Joanna expressed no little surprise. 'Why so, you
old fool? Your head is always full of the marvellous and the prodi-
gious; and I have been often tempted to think you were half a
witch in your heart. You should have had an Obeah-man for your

husband, and a broomstick for your steed. Why do you fancy that
brown swaggering fellow to be a buccaneer?'

'Swaggering indeed!' muttered Ariel. 'He is no good, no worth.'

'But why, Beelzebub?' cried her master in a passion. 'Have you
found him out by inspiration, as Michal has done? Here, Michal!
what has he been saying to you?'

Michal was coming up to the window, from which Mr Guthrie
had seen her in close conversation with Sebastian; but the black
Ariel was determined to be beforehand with her, and told her
master that he *swaggered*, and bid her go say to her mistress, to
put her house in order for him; for he should come at night and
marry her.

'Ah! you old fool; so that is what he told you, is it? He knows
what a simpleton you are. Michal, what said Mr Sebastian to you?'

'Master,' replied the soubrette in an undertone of voice; 'he
tells you to be on your guard; yes, really, to-night and every night;
and if he should come again, not to open the piazza windows for
him or his companions, except you have people ready to seize
them and bind them, or put them all in the stocks; and to have the
shore watched, and arms ready in the house.'

'And what reason, in the name of heaven, did he assign for
telling you all this? Is it to ensure your affections, and your love,
and all your favours?'

'No, sir,' said the slave, with a deep blush, (for Quadroons blush
like angels, who have anything to blush for;) 'he told me that he
had eaten salt with me who am your slave; and he would be cut in
pieces before a hair of your head, or of Miss Joanna's head, should
be hurt.'

The old gentleman could not help putting his hand to his head
as he looked at his daughter's shining braids; and his breath came
thick for a moment, while he told her to go and see her mother,
but not to alarm her. And having cautioned the White Fairy to
keep her secret, or at least to say nothing more to any one else of
her buccaneer friend, whom he could see with his glass already
seated in the canoe; he beckoned Michal into the piazza, which he
paraded for half an hour, stopping at intervals to consult her, or at
least to extract from her every word of the Mulatto's conversation,

and every thought that her mind had conceived respecting him. When he had made himself master of all she had to communicate, and sufficiently arranged his own ideas on the subject, he ordered his horse to the door, and rode off, to put in execution the scheme he had planned for the security of his house and family, in case the recommendations of his late guest should turn out to be worthy of his attention.

CHAPTER 11.

A fairy world
I tread; a land of genii! Airy shapes,
Oft visible to contemplation's eye,
Roam in the midnight hour these sacred shades.

WE left the adventurous Roland, who is doomed to cut such a respectable figure in our narrative, recommencing his skirmish with
the bats, as he began to retrace his steps from the brink of the
Devil's Gully into the interior of the Obeah man's cave. We must
use a little expedition with him on the present occasion, and beg
the reader to imagine the facility with which his black allies conducted him, on no other terms than being blindfolded, through
the caverns which he had himself essayed in vain to explore: how
they consoled him with assurances of his boy's safety, and the recovery of his Spanish horse; and how, leading him higher up in the
mountains, to cross the swollen rivulets nearer their sources, they
finally introduced him at nightfall to the slaves at the forsaken settlement, to which he was journeying on the previous night, when
the storm overtook him, and our history began.

Behold him then, after rather a tedious journey on foot, standing beside the ruins of a house which had been all but destroyed
by the hurricane; the roof totally demolished, and the spars of it
scattered about the small surrounding plain, part of which had
formerly served as a barbicue to dry the coffee which the deceased planter had been used to cultivate. The walls were partly
standing, being built of stone; and within them a narrow staircase
of the same materials led to a cellar, which he intended to visit as
soon as he should have had an opportunity of conversing with the
Liberals whom he expected to meet on this occasion. There were
two gigantic palms to the eastward of the building, waving their
feathery summits most gracefully, as the land-wind sighed its
spicy breath through their plumes; and their long shadows
seemed to float upon the whitened walls whenever the shafts of
these noble trees traversed the rays of the moon, whose brilliant

orb lighted up the surrounding scenery with a splendour but little inferior to that of the sun in more northern climes. But for the ruined mansion before him, Mr Roland, or a spectator more alive to the impressions of nature, might have almost fancied this a fairy scene, if not the very abode of romance. It was a plain of about three or four acres, like an amphitheatre, environed by huge masses of perpendicular rocks crowned with the everlasting forest of the island, and watered by a considerable rivulet which tumbled from among them, and after flowing nearly round their bases, precipitated itself into a deep ravine, so clothed with the rank foliage of the overhanging trees, that even by daylight its further course could hardly be discriminated. There were many other little rills produced by the late rains, some of which seemed as it were to leap from their rocky precipices into the streams below, whilst others murmured unseen beneath or behind the fragments which their temporary currents had heaped in the courses through which they disembogued themselves. The air was filled with these accumulated and soothing sounds, so moderated by the night-wind, that they ought to have inspired in a more virtuous bosom none but the most pleasing recollections or ideas; feelings sacred perhaps to melancholy, but in no wise at war with humanity.

So thought, so felt, the Missionary; but he quickly reassured himself by calling to mind the purpose for which he had travelled to this sequestered spot. Meanwhile the Obeah man was employed in clearing a passage to the cellar among the dismantled fragments which encumbered the floor of the house; and Combah, who had been for some time assisting him, while Roland was thus musing to little purpose, began to hack the fallen spars and rafters with a billhook, which he had brought with him to cut them into junks for making a fire; when their ears were saluted with a whistle, which rang round the amphitheatre with such an echo, in spite of the waterfalls, that it was impossible to tell from what particular spot it emanated. However, Combah replied to it, as soon as the echoes had died away, by four distinct repetitions of the same sound, waiting at every interval, that the listeners might be enabled to discriminate the number beyond the possibility of mistake. The fourth was replied to by a fifth from the unseen tenant of the wilderness; and a sixth, from the sable monarch elect, appeared to rouse the very rocks to language; for a score of voices, as it seemed, shouted in all directions to answer it, as clamorous as the yell of demons might be supposed, and scarcely less startling to the ears and nerves of the Missionary: 'This,' thought he, ' is not my signal.' But the voices shouted again a second hideous and discordant yell; and ' Brutchie, Brutchie,' as the watchword, was reverberated from mouth to mouth, as well as from precipice to precipice.

'Brutchie, Brutchie,' repeated the monarch.

'Brutchie! what is Brutchie?' said the Missionary, half afraid it was some signal which boded him no good.

'You forget,' replied Combah, ' that you should have been here last night; but see, here comes your servant Cuffy, and your horse: let these be a signal for your safety.'

'For heaven's sake,' cried Roland, seeing it was his boy advancing, 'send away my boy! I will have no witness to my presence here, but yourselves. I will have no spies to misinterpret me to the authorities of the island, or denounce me to the enemies of liberty and emancipation. Cuffy, begone! Who brought you here? Who directed you?'

'Peace, peace!' said Combah, interposing: 'do you forget that you asked your way to this very settlement? And did not your boy attend to your questions? Did he not hear the account which you received of the plantation; and knew he not that you were determined to come here? But ask him still, if you choose, how he found his way.'

'Come hither, Cuffy,' cried his master; 'who was it guided your steps?'

'A brown man,' replied the boy.

'How! a brown man?'

'Yes; a Mulatto man, with a large Spanish hat, and a gold chain to his sword, and a musket. He rode the horse here himself, and said that he was coming to hear you preach.'

'To hear me preach!' repeated the Missionary in some amazement. 'A Mulatto man; who can this be? And where is he?'

'He got off the horse,' said the boy, 'at the bottom of the rocks below, and went over the river by some other pass; a nearer way, he said; and he bid me tell you to expect him in this Mr M'L——'s house; but the house is tumbled down; and so, if he was here before me, which he might be, perhaps he is gone away again.'

'This is some mischief,' said the preacher, after a pause. 'A Mulatto man, and a Spanish hat, and a gold chain! I know of none such. Be on your guard, Combah! But here come your friends. I must speak to them, as I promised; for there is no law to prevent my preaching, even by night. Go, Cuffy, down the rocks again, where you parted with the brown man. If you see him, bring him here; if not, stay till I come down to you.'

'And if any one,' added Combah, 'speaks to you in the way, say you are waiting for Brutchie.'

The boy and the horse jogged off towards the winding path by which the Missionary had arrived at this amphitheatre; while the Negroes he had come to visit saluted him and Combah with all imaginable politeness; each of them shaking hands with himself, although they did not presume to such familiarity with the Brutchie, by which they understand a king or prince.

Combah had indeed been no less in his own country; as a token of which, the skin of his forehead had been torn off in his youth, from the setting-on of his woolly hair to within a narrow space of his eye-brows, over which the edge of the skin which had been so mutilated, obtruded itself a little; sufficiently, by darkening the expression of his eyes, to give his countenance a character of additional ghastliness, in the opinion of some of the Whites: otherwise, he had regular and not unhandsome features. He received his new subjects, who were to swear allegiance to him, with a fine affectation of royalty; and bid them go down into the cellar, to his friend who was busy there making a fire. But he presently called one of them back by name; and stepping a pace or two from the Missionary, bid him take a hoe and a calabash, and fill the latter with some dirt from the grave of a child which his late master had buried about eighteen months ago. This command was intended to be a secret from Roland; but he, having had more than one misgiving regarding his personal safety, was too much on the alert to allow any sound to escape him, which his senses could by possibility arrive at. He held his breath, strained forward his neck, opened his mouth, and tried to swallow every whisper of the monarch's speech; but as he heard it only in part, the words ' hoe' and ' grave' were all he could distinguish. They were, however, more than sufficient to renew his alarm; fearing that some scheme was to be played off on him, if he should prove refractory with the Obeah man, whose magic rites he had predetermined to denounce publicly, should he see anything which in his ideas militated against his duty to his God, or the rights of the Christian religion. Thus shrinking within himself at the mention of the word 'grave,' which he fancied could only be intended for himself, he called his majesty to him, as a pope's legate in ancient days would have summoned a sovereign of Europe; and assuming a courage which he had not, would have told him that his plans were wicked, and that he was forsaken by the angels of heaven. But the monarch put his finger on the preacher's lips, and himself burst into a loud laugh, as if to drown the words and feelings which oppressed the other for want of utterance. Still the Missionary was obstinate; and it required some assurance on the part of Combah, to prevent him quitting the assembly, which began to increase—Negroes pouring in from all quarters of this strange amphitheatre; some from the path which Cuffy had taken, others by a road which wound up higher into the mountains, and others apparently from the chinks and crannies in the precipices. The Missionary looked round in some astonishment at the increase of his congregation; and yet beheld others on the tops of the rocks, moving along like demons or black ghosts (to which he compared them in his mind) across the sky radiant with the beams of the moon, seeking a passage by which they might descend into the arena below.

So little precaution seemed now to be used, that although the word 'Brutchie' was from time to time echoed about, the Missionary felt satisfied that any one who pleased might have joined the assembly unnoticed, for any purpose of participation, or for the sake of obtaining evidence against him or his coadjutors, in case anything should be said or done contrary to the regulations and institutions of the island. Under this impression, his eyes were

in perpetual search of the brown man with the Spanish hat, of
whom Cuffy had given him the above-mentioned account; a character of some interest to the Missionary's mind, inasmuch as it
baffled all his conjectures, and kept his fears and fancies constantly and painfully alive. But he had scarcely time enough to
give way to these thoughts, or to experience the intensity of anxiety they would have caused him; for his companion Combah, having already convened the audience, who now amounted to at least
a hundred, in front of the dilapidated mansion, and invited his
vicar elect to ascend the ruined walls, called to them in a stentorian voice to be silent, and to listen to the Missionary's prayers and
preaching.

It would ill become us, in detailing the scene which followed, to
trust to paper the whole of the preacher's oration. Many, if not
most, of our readers would be more than scandalized at what must
appear on such an occasion a profanation, at least, of terms and of
ideas which they hold nearest their hearts. For all such feelings we
have a proper respect; and if an expression should escape from the
ink-horn (as Cervantes would say) which might involve a suspicion of the narrator's attention to the delicacy of his readers' feelings, we beg to observe on the meaning of the word *suspicion,* that
it but 'implies a doubt, an indecision between two or more be-
liefs;' and we beg our readers to select for us the more charitable
conclusion which they can extract from this indecision.

The summons of the king was repeated by half the voices in attendance, and by all the echoes, until there seemed an almost
Babel-like confusion of tongues, vociferating nothing that could
be clearly understood, amid this chaotic gabbling, but the word
Brutchie, bandied about until one might have thought the very
rocks were deafened with the barbarous sound, and nature herself grown weary of so odious a name. It might have been fancied
at last that this was almost literally the case; for the voices and the
echoes at length subsiding, silence was gradually restored, with
the expectations of the audience, until for a time no sound was
heard but that of the waterfalls, and the waving of the trees; every
mind being as it were bound up in suspense, and every ear impatient to receive the glad tidings which the spiritual comforter had

promised. The moon shed a flood of light on his dark figure, and on the darker one of Combah, who stood at his elbow, and whom the addition of a pair of horns would have qualified for the personification of the fiend so frequently represented by the painters of yore as attendant tempter on holy monks and ascetics. Roland began his business, as his rivals in Great Britain are wont to do, by a private hiding of his face in his hands for a time, while he leaned against the broken wall for support, the Brutchie having taken charge of his hat; and when this had been followed by audible prayers, also usual with the orthodox, he spread open his arms, and began as follows.

CHAPTER 12.

Good friends, sweet friends, let me not stir you up
To any sudden flood of mutiny;
For I have neither wit, nor words, nor worth,
Action or utterance, nor the power of speech
To stir men's blood; I only speak right on;
I tell you that which you yourselves do know.
JULIUS CÆSAR, ACT 3.

'BRETHREN,—You know, many of you, how I have laboured in your service; what perils, what fatigues, I have undergone; how I have hungered and thirsted, been broiled in the sun, and drenched in the rivers and the rains; how I have been threatened by your cruel masters and the unjust magistrates in different towns: (one of them has sworn to put me in the stocks.) Why have I endured all this? For your good; to spread among you the true light, to preach the cross of God, and the value and power of faith, to save your souls from everlasting damnation. It required no common courage to tell you, which I do from my conscience, that the Christian religion, of which you may all become members, acknowledges no such distinction as that of master and slave: it makes all men equal; I say, it makes all men equal, all brothers.' This piece of information was received with murmurs of approbation, augmenting at last into a general hurrah which lasted several minutes, so as to have drowned the language of the preacher, had he not paused. It gave almost universal satisfaction, the black gentleman at Roland's elbow being the only individual dissentient; and he with some reason, as it disqualified him in one word for the office and the rights of king. He pulled the preacher gently by the flap of his coat, during the tumult of congratulation below, and reminded him of his private and royal necessities. But Roland bid him fear nothing; and as soon as silence was again secured, resumed his oratory aloud.

'Brethren, you know the white people well. They brought you or your fathers from Africa; they *bought* you, they say; which means, they hired people to steal you and bring you on board their ships. They brought you here, and made you work, and flogged you. Then they took your wives and your daughters for their mistresses, to live with them; and you know they flog *them*, if they like. Now these white men call themselves Christians; but they are *not* Christians; they are more heathens than any of your ancestors were, as some of you have before heard from myself and other zealous men, who come here to show you your rights. You will perhaps say I am a white man. So I am outwardly—my skin is white; but my heart is like yours; and if that is black as your skins, so is mine. I am an exception to the white men; I have never flogged you, nor ravished your daughters.' Here a loud demoniac sort of laugh was heard from the cellar below, where, as Roland at the sound recollected, his Obeah rival was at work. However he continued his speech; for the moonlight could not betray the expression pourtrayed on his writhing features, except to his own mind's eye; yet he faultered out again the words 'ravished your daughters. Let me tell you,' he continued, 'how the first people calling themselves Christians treated the inhabitants of this island, when they conquered it. They said that they had a right from heaven to burn them, if they would not be true Christians; and I have told you that true Christianity makes all men equal; that is, it does away at once with slavery. They burned them, they hung them, they cut their throats, they strangled them, they hunted them with dogs, until they killed them every one. There is not one of their descendants now alive, not one. Those conquerors knew it was impossible to trust people who had it in their power to revenge themselves. Need I repeat that? I do not say that the white people here will serve *you* so: no—but had you all come with them when they first conquered the country, they would have made you do all this for them: yes, they would have put swords and guns in your hands, and told you to fire upon and to stab those who were masters of the lands; they would have told you to show no mercy, to spare nobody, to drive the men into the sea or fling them down the precipices, and to destroy them every one, that they and you might have the houses and the lands, and their daughters and wives, for themselves and yourselves, without any fear of their being taken away from you: for if any of the people had been left alive, they might have risen again and overpowered you, or got men to come from other countries to fight for them and conquer you again; when they would have killed you every one without mercy. But if you had left nobody alive except your friends; I say, except your friends, those who toil for you, sweat for you, travel for you, all to save your souls from damnation,—you would have been perfectly safe; you, and your sons, and your grandsons, from generation to generation. Now, my friends and brethren, there are many of you who are true Christians; and such you may all become, if you will—'

'Shed blood enough,' cried a voice in the vault below. This cellar was immediately underneath the preacher, who, except his royal companion, was perhaps the only person near enough to distinguish accurately the stray words which from time to time escaped to the upper air. Combah looked down in a little alarm; and the preacher muttered 'Perdition!' as he resumed. 'The white people here are none of them true Christians, because they believe in slavery; and there is no such thing as slavery in the religion which I profess. You know that the white people in England want to make you free: there are many true believers there; one of them, a great man, rich, and a lord, says that the white men here are receivers of stolen goods, or inheritors, which is the same thing: he means that *you* are the stolen goods. Now, he is a fine, great, wise, brave man: one of his ancestors helped to conquer England itself a long, long time ago; and got for his share four great parishes in one county, with all the slaves upon it, who were called villains; and another of his ancestors went round the world in a ship, and beat the Spaniards in America, and stole all their money, almost a million of dollars; more than you can count; besides silks, and satins, and musks, and all sorts of things. He came upon them unawares, and killed a great many of them. So you see he too was a great brave man; and he has had many more rich and great ancestors and relations, whose money he has inherited, besides all this; and he has lands and slaves—no, not slaves, poor men—to work for them and for him, in England and Ireland. He gives them no clothes, and nothing to eat; but he is a great, wise man, and very religious and virtuous; and what he says must in this instance be as true as the Gospel itself.

'What is the use of your masters giving you houses, and clothes, and fish, and grounds to cultivate? It is that you may work for them. Why do you tell me that your mistresses attend to you in sickness and old age; that they are kind to you and your children? Pshaw! it is that you may slave for them, and that the children may take heart, and hope to pass *their* old age in the same way. But remember what I said about slavery and true Christianity; if you will be true Christians, you cannot be slaves. Slaves! Did not those of St Domingo make themselves free? *They* were brave men: they had white wives when they were free; for they loved their mistresses, and shed only the blood of their oppressors. But if you were free, as the English nation wants to make you—remember—choose your own schoolmasters and preachers; do not let them send you parsons and bishops to enslave your very hearts, to eat you and drink you, and make you work for them, for fear of the Devil. No; think of those who have taught you religion, as I have done; who have laboured night and day to instruct you; who have pointed out to you the road to freedom; who have saved you from hell. Do you know that in England every man works one day in the week for a parson, who is as wicked as your masters? and every man pays his corn, and his milk, and his fruit, and his vegetables, his honey, and his pigs and calves, to him? And these parsons are among the people who want to keep you slaves; you must hear only missionaries. The parsons will not let anybody there speak against them; not a word: they catch them up, and put them in the stocks and in gaol for two or three years or more. You had better remain as you are, than have such as these for your masters. You have a right to be free; but still remember the light I have shewn you, the true religion. If you forsake your God, he will forsake you; and hell has room for millions yet unborn, your children and your children's children; do not entail an everlasting curse on them! Beware of the fire which is not quenched; beware—beware!'

The Missionary was here startled and confounded, as well as interrupted in his unaccountable career, by an explosion in the vault below; the smoke of which, finding its way to his nostrils and those of the Brutchie, caused the last to shift his quarters, and the first to jump headlong down. He could not spring towards the multitude who stood with their mouths open devouring his discourse, for they occupied all the spare place as far as the ruins of the walls and beams would allow. To the outside of the ruin consequently he was obliged to turn about, and spring down into the area of the building, where, as fortune had ordained, his weight broke through the rotten boards that had formed the floor of the hall, and he fell, amidst the cockroaches and rubbish which he carried with him, into the vault below, in which Hamel and a chosen few were celebrating some orgies of a very different nature from those which constituted the externals of Roland's faith. Meanwhile, his sudden disappearance from above disconcerted some of his audience, as it did not fail to amuse others, who would have compared this his exit with that of Empedocles, had they ever heard of him or of mount Etna; or with the secession of Lycurgus, after he had favoured the Spartans with his very moral and salutary laws, not inferior in interest or humanity to the doctrine they had just heard. But knowing nothing of these ancient worthies, their admiration was limited to the descent, unexpected and unaccountable except to those who were near enough to smell the smoke and witness the accident of this modern apostle, who found anything but a welcome among the crew which his evil genius had thus doomed him to encounter in the cellar. As soon as he had a little recovered from the confusion caused by his downfall, he heard exclamations of 'Turn him out—fool—mule—what does he want here?'—and Brutchie was appealed to from below, to come and take away his preaching man. The consternation of Roland was not inferior to the indignation of those he had disturbed; for he found himself among a dozen or more of wild-looking negroes, most of them naked to the waist; or if they had garments, they were more or less stained with blood. There was likewise a human skull on a table in the midst of them, filled with earth; and a calabash, containing a filthy-looking mixture, placed beside a small iron pot which flamed with burning rum, whose blue and ghastly light, sufficient to illuminate the cellar, cast a glare of deeper hideousness on the faces and persons of these practitioners.

A cow's horn tipped with brass, in all probability once the magazine of a rifleman, promised to hold more of the compound which had caused the explosion, as it had not received any damage; and although the cellar was still reeking with smoke, the combustion had not been of any importance, except that it had brought down to them this troublesome and unwelcome guest.

Roland remained in some confusion, while all eyes were turned on him, fancying that Combah had thus betrayed him; for which his imagination quickly apprehended a sufficient cause in his having preached, or rather harangued, solely for himself, omitting to mention Mr Brutchie, much less to recommend him as a monarch to the assembled multitude, who had heard from him only a doctrine of equality and republican emancipation. Meanwhile the company still glared on him, now in silence; and he heard with additional alarm his friend Combah above, dismissing the crowd from before the house, and telling them to dance and be happy, for there was plenty of rum, and women, and music; and they had only to enjoy themselves for an hour, while he went to talk with the Missionary, who was gone down to eat some supper below. They gave the chief a hurrah, and withdrew farther into the arena, as he desired.

CHAPTER 13.

Look round about;
And when thou find'st a man that's like thyself,
Good Murder, stab him; he's a murderer.
Go thou with him; and when it is thy hap
To find another that is like to thee,
Good Rapine, stab him; he's a ravisher.

TITUS ANDRONICUS.

BEFORE the king elect of the island descended to the relief of his apostolic friend, he took the precaution to station a sufficient guard round the house to prevent surprise, as far at least as concerned the forbidden ceremonies about to be transacted below. The dancing and other diversions, although discountenanced, if not interdicted, by the legislature of the island and the proprietors of the adjoining lands, would not subject the partakers or the spectators of the performance to anything beyond a simple flagellation; but the celebration of Obeah rights, or the circumstance of being present at such celebration without immediately giving information of it, would render all concerned in or about it liable to a much heavier punishment, banishment or death. To prevent such discovery, half a dozen Negroes were stationed about the ruins, with orders to let no one approach the building before due notice was given to those engaged in it. These were some of the initiated, persons who had already taken an oath which, like that of the Eleusinian mysteries, they dared not reveal, on pain of being instantly assassinated by their comrades, besides the curse which they would entail on themselves and their posterity by such a backsliding.

Combah felt a perfect security in thus disposing them; and having heard the eboe drum strike up in the arena, and seen the black fairies begin to flit about in the moonlight, he descended to the cellar, where all rose to receive him from the floor on which they were seated round the low table furnished with the materials before enumerated; Roland standing in the midst of them, sweating with heat, fright, and horror. They made an opening for him to enter the circle, then re-seated themselves, all except Hamel, who asked of Brutchie what was to be done with Roland. The king told him without hesitation that the Missionary had not kept his word; for that he had promised to make the people believe him to be sent by heaven for their king,—he had engaged to anoint his head with holy coco-nut oil, to put a crown upon it, and then to cry out 'Long live Combah, king of Jamaica!' as he said the white people did yonder on the other side of the water: after which he was to have persuaded all the Negroes to come and kiss his (Combah's) right hand, and swear to obey him, and follow him to war upon the Whites all over the island. 'Now, master Missionary,' he continued, 'why have you only spoken for yourself? And what is worse, why have you preached that the Negroes are all to be free alike, and have no king to lead them to fight or make laws to keep them in order? Master Missionary! the Negroes must work, some of them, or how are they to live? You do not preach like a wise man: you tell the Negroes only to kill the white people.'

'No, no,' cried the other, interrupting him: 'God forbid that I should ever counsel them to do anything so wicked.'

'So wicked!' replied Combah: 'so wicked? Why, what else did you mean? Hamel, Cudjoe, Caesar, Jupiter, Pluto, and you, all of you, did you not hear what master Roland said? Did not he tell the Negroes to kill the white men, to take their wives and daughters, and to make him schoolmaster, parson, and bishop of the island?'

'He did—he did,' was echoed around.

'Roland! you are not a man. These are wiser and braver than you; and to them I shall leave you, to be dealt with as they please; for in them I put my trust, and not in you, nor in your religion, nor in any of those who belong to it. There is no truth nor reality in you, for what you promise to day you are afraid of tomorrow; and you want only to set the people of the island fighting and quarrelling, that you may get their money and some of the white women for your share. These men are ready to swear that they will never forsake me, nor flinch from killing the Whites; and I to swear I will never forsake them, and while I live never cease to revenge the death of any one of them a hundredfold, if he dies by the hands of the Whites, until there shall not be a white man left in the island. Come, Hamel, let me hear and give the oath!'

'Oh no, for mercy's sake!' exclaimed the terrified Missionary, 'let me not be a witness to anything so horrible; spare me the sight of such atrocities, which your religion may justify, but mine contemplates as a sacrifice to the Devil, an acknowledgment of the power of Satan.'

'You are premature,' answered Combah. 'What atrocities do you speak of? What have you seen or done? We are speaking of an oath: our ceremonies are awful, but not atrocious. There have been some who shed the blood of a child to swear by, and cared not that the infant bled to death, because it was a white man's child; but we shed only our own. But, Roland, you must also take the oath, or—.'

'Or what?' cried the trembling Missionary.

'— Or here they dig your grave.'

'Gracious heaven! my grave! And must I drink blood?'

'Is it not so?' continued the king, looking round him. 'You have witnessed the rights of Obeah, the mysteries of the enslaved Coromantins: you must swear to keep them inviolate.'

'I swear—I swear,' said the Missionary; 'on my knees I swear.'

'Aye,' replied the Brutchie; 'but you must swear as we do. You have violated the sanctuary of the Obeah man; you have visited his dwelling; you volunteered to preach to these runaways above, and to all the slaves, that they were free from the power of the Whites, and that I was their king.'

'I will still do so,' cried Roland; 'put me to the proof. Let me out of this dreadful place: I will put the crown upon your head, if you have one, and swear that you are sanctified by heaven to be their king.'

'You are right, master Roland,' replied the king: 'you shall do all this; and had you done it, you had before now departed in peace. You must swear to do it, and swear by your God, which is ours, to keep our oaths and our secrets; and you must swear as we do. Look at this skull!'

'I swear—I swear by my God! Let that suffice,' cried Roland.

'No!' replied a voice from the circle; 'he is not afraid to swear by his God; he will not keep that oath: he must take the skull in his hand.'

'Why,' exclaimed another, 'do you trifle with this foolish man? If you cannot trust him, let us dig his grave—bury him. What does he here? and what do we want with white preachers, or with white men at all? Master Brutchie, he will certainly betray us, if he goes alive from here: we only waste time and words; make him take the oath, or I am ready to kill him on the spot.'

'What is there then in the oath,' said Combah, 'that you should not take it? What! would you not do more for Miss Jo—?'

'Hush!' cried the Missionary: 'it is for her that I shall sell my soul, and yet shall be unrewarded with her love. I say to you, Brutchie—Combah—I came here by accident; I sought not to penetrate your mysteries; I was wrong, I was unfortunate; I will do anything but this;—Oh, stay that cruel man's hand! kill me not; let me not be murdered, Combah! I will do all; I will swear anything; what—how—you please.'

The Missionary was on the ground, thrown down by the un-feeling Negro who had offered to kill him, and who now stood over him with a sharpened billhook in his hand, ready to hew him to death. The blue flames of the only light by which the vault was illuminated, exhibited the horrid passion of the assassin in colours still more frightful than those with which nature had depicted it. He was of the race called Mocos, a people known on some occa-sions to be cannibals, who file their teeth so as to make them re-semble those of a cat, and render them narrow and sharp as needles. He gnashed these in the face of his shuddering suppliant; and his brawny arm was already raised to strike, when Combah ar-rested it, and bid him let the Missionary take the oath. Upon this, the skull was handed to him by Hamel; and be repeated without delay the words dictated to him; imprecating curses on his own head, that it might speedily become like that which he held in his hand, filled with dirt, if he ever mentioned to any man, woman, or child, of any colour, what he had seen this night, or at any other time, of Obeah. The skull was then deposited again on the table; and Hamel, taking the calabash containing, as was related, a filthy-looking mixture, held it close to the Missionary's face, and bid him see that it was blood—blood drawn from their own veins, and mixed with gunpowder and with the grave-dirt of the skull. He dipped his finger in the mess, and crossed the face and the breast of Roland; finally holding it to his lips, and commanding him to taste and swallow a portion, and then to say after him as follows:—'If I lie, if I am treacherous, if I mean to deceive in any way those whose blood I have tasted, may the grave-dirt make my heart rot, till it bursts and tumbles out before my face! May I die, and never awake in the grave, or awake to everlasting pain and torment, and become the slave of the white man's devil for ever and ever!' Having repeated this, the mixture was again put to his lips: he tasted it, and sunk to the ground in an agony created by his horror and disgust.

Meanwhile, the dancing and festivity were carried on above with an increasing energy, as the rum inspired the minds and accelerated the motions of the performers. A calabash of it was handed to the Missionary below; and he learnt from Combah, that his being a Christian alone excused him from having been obliged to contribute some of his own blood to the execrable mess which he had tasted; that the same indulgence had been granted to himself, (for Roland had formerly christened him;) and that he too had taken the oath, and had been followed by all the others, while the Missionary lay in a state of insensibility. Combah added, that now, if he were willing, Roland should tell the multitude that they must have a king, and that as they knew him (Combah) to have been a prince in his own country, there was none more worthy to be called so than himself.

The Missionary groaned with horror, but dared not hesitate; yet, as he arose from the earth, his mind was again convulsed with the recollection of what he had seen and done, and with the conviction of what he had yet to go through, in recommending and anointing as a delegate from heaven, and as a monarch, one whom he found to be an apostate from the faith which he had once sworn to maintain; one linked with dealers in necromancy, bound together by oaths of a nature so diabolical, as to bar all communion, all possibility of amalgamation, with Christian society; one, in

short, at whose conduct even the miserable conscience of the
Missionary revolted, after all his political aversions to any farther
intercourse with him had been silenced, as they were, only by necessity, compulsion, and the fear of immediate death. Yet
Combah had promised him not only his assistance, but his whole
power, all the influence he should acquire, to get possession of the
beautiful and unsuspecting girl, against whose peace he had practised; the gentle, the amiable Joanna. Nothing less than a revolution, he felt assured, could make him master of her person; and
this revolution he could only effect, as he thought, by means similar at least to those he had already employed in perverting the
minds of the Negroes. Combah had been his friend, his favourite,
his disciple; and until he found him in the cave of the Obeah man,
his heart had been set on making him a sovereign, for his own purposes. But by seeing him with that mystical personage, his suspicions and apprehensions were influenced to a degree bordering
almost on frenzy. He felt that Hamel was his rival; and from the
knowledge which he appeared to possess, and which must make a
greater impression on the minds of the Negroes than on his own,
he felt that his rival was a formidable one. Indeed it was but too evident, that Hamel had introduced the Brutchie to him in his cave,
to disconcert the hopes of the Missionary, and display his own pre-
eminence; for he might have allowed him to depart unknown, unseen, as he had come, betrayed to the wizard solely by his conch,
for which the latter might have accounted to Roland as he
pleased, or not at all. But Hamel, already jealous of the Christian's
influence, and well acquainted with some particulars of his life,
contrived to impress his enemy with even a superior notion of his
own capability, and rendered him almost contemptible in the eyes
of Combah. This was a triumph too dear to the Obeah man, to be
renounced or trifled with: he had acquired, and hoped to retain,
all the influence he could desire over the mind of the Brutchie.
The Missionary he could have destroyed in his cave; but Roland
might be made to serve his purposes. There was a pride, an additional triumph, which he contemplated, in enslaving a white man,
the enslaver of free men's minds; of making a Christian preacher,
this man whom the Negroes worshipped, and the white men

deprecated for the influence he had obtained, work for him; of bending the very soul of the apostle, as he called himself, to his own service, to do his drudgery, to dictate to the credulous Negroes what he should, by his invisible means, compel him to dictate; and then to sink this very man to the lowest possible degradation of human nature; to make him participate in rites and ceremonies which he loathed, abhorred, and execrated; to damn his very soul, in his own estimation, by submission to such participation; and for what? To save his vile ignoble carcass from the grave, to writhe a little longer beneath *his* lash, to crawl under a heavier load of years and cares: 'his soul disdained him for so mean a thought.'

It was Hamel, in fact, who had first put the Brutchie upon the scheme of compromising with Roland for the delivery of Joanna. When he discovered his information to the Missionary in his cave, it was not a mere affectation. The influence of the Obeah man was not limited: he possessed knowledge—the secrets of all ranks, and of all sorts of transactions; he knew of Roland's passion and practices, and he taught the Brutchie how to profit by his rival's weaknesses. But we have seen that Combah had himself intentions with respect to the person of Joanna: even *he* was indisposed to keep his faith, where a woman, a beautiful woman, was concerned; and he meant, it seems, to disappoint the hopes of his pious minister on this his fondest, his tenderest expectation. His scheme had been detailed only to the worthies who had passed the previous night at Mr Guthrie's; and he might have had his reasons for assigning such an intention respecting her as that which we have related. Hamel had his suspicions of it, however, and was fully bent on thwarting it, if such should appear to be the Brutchie's real intention: nay, he had hopes of securing the young lady himself, (though for what purpose it might be improper here to explain,) in the event of a revolt which should effect any permanent revolution. On such a revolution his own soul was bent: his arts, his influence, his every energy, were devoted to the extermination of the Whites, or to their expulsion from the island. It is not enough to say he detested them: his hatred was charged with the recollection of the outrages he had himself endured. An

African, torn from his country, chained, trampled on, herded with the rabble of his own and other nations, sold to a black tyrant— black as himself—compelled to work in irons, and whipped into desperation by his brutal master; his vengeance was yet directed against the Whites who had enslaved and thus degraded him; for he had found means long since to revenge himself, though without taking his life, on the sable tyrant who had purchased him from the ship in which he had been imported; free Negroes having the same right to buy slaves as that claimed by the Europeans themselves. He had, in fact, become the property of this black master, having shewn so daring a spirit on his arrival, that no white merchant would be concerned with him; and he had fallen in consequence, at a very low price, to the lot of one who had not the white man's plea of superiority to boast as an argument for more exalted rights. But for this purchaser, he would have gone to the Spanish mines.

Let us, however, return to Mr Roland.

CHAPTER 14.

Some devil whisper curses in my ear,
And prompt me, that my tongue may utter forth
The venomous malice of my swelling heart.
TITUS ANDRONICUS.

IT may be supposed that the wretchedness of Roland's mind and person, the latter disfigured with the dirt in which he had been rolled, excited little sympathy in the bosoms of his negro associates in the horrible ceremony detailed in the last chapter. Yet Hamel, who had still farther designs on him, affected a kind of condolence, wiped his clothes officiously, and assured him he knew that he (the Missionary) meant to have urged the propriety of Combah being publicly acknowledged by the multitude as their king, if he had not been prevented by the accident which had thus hurried him so unintentionally and unexpectedly into the cellar where those only who did not choose to be Christians were engaged in preparing the oath they were bound to take to their Brutchie. 'You know, brother,' continued he, while Roland shrunk from the appellation, and the touch which accompanied it,—'you know, brother, all men are not of one mind: there are more religions than one; and ours at least has the advantage of yours in being older. For I remember a white man telling me in my own country, in Coromantin,—a good man, but not a Christian,—that my religion was as old as the deluge, when people worshipped serpents. But you, none of you know anything of it; *you* only have seen and taken our oath, an oath which makes us brothers; would it not have been the same, if we had taken your oath?' The Obeah man said this, feeling the compunction and disgust which his language and his grasp produced in his hearer. 'We call you brother from your participating in *our* mysteries, as you so name those initiated in *yours*. You called the mob of Negroes dancing yonder, half or more of them drunk, almost brutal idiots, engaged in sensualities solely, without mind, spirit, worth, courage, or discretion—brothers; you said "brethren" to them, and told them that

82

your religion made you all alike. That is the best part of your religion; but as I could not deserve the title by the means you have recommended to them, I have reason to rejoice at having had an opportunity of calling myself your brother, from a cause unconnected with that which binds you to the drunken and dancing rabble yonder. Come, master Roland, from this nasty place; come with me up the stairs of the cellar. Let us breathe the sweet air, and see what more we are to do with these people before they have drowned the rest of their reason. They know me not; or if they distinguish me with you, they will take me for your convert; will they not, Roland? They will know nothing of your supper. There is Brutchie has leaped through the hole you made in your descent—he has *as*cended by it. This should be a good omen to you, as you without intending it have found him, made him, a way to mount at once above the heads of his countrymen, while they are waiting to follow one another up the steps in succession. You made this observation, brother Roland? I know that nothing is lost to the wise man. But shall you be the last to ascend the stairs in the rear of all your new brethren?—No; let me at least imitate the meekness of your example; I will follow you—I will be the last.'

Roland, staggering with heat and exhaustion, and the fatigues he had endured in his terrible ordeal, mounted the steps with a beating heart, cursing his folly, treachery, cruelty, and all the bad passions which had swayed him to this, as he now fancied it, mad enterprise. Yet he was fully sensible to the insulting irony of the Obeah man's conversation; and in spite of his oath, which had indeed been crammed down his throat, he would have denounced the leader and his crew, in his fever of rage, had he possessed the present means; or stabbed the wizard to the heart, if he could have done so without a certainty of discovery and punishment. 'Call me not brother,' he said; 'I neither claim nor indeed merit the title; I have no brother, sister, parent or friend; I am alone; and better had it been for me to die beneath the weapon of that butcher who threatened me, than to have saved my life by——'

'Hush—hush!' said the Obeah man in a gentle voice, degenerating at last into a whisper; 'that skull—you remember—it was a child's: that child, Roland, was a victim; it came to an untimely death—I have seen the hand that killed it.' (The Missionary's fingers were convulsed, and his heart knocked against his ribs.) 'It was killed by mistake; yet the hand that smote it was raised to shed blood, though not the blood of that child.'

'Peace—peace!' sighed the Missionary, in a stifled and half-murmured tone, fearing to be overheard; 'in the name of your God, be silent.'

'Of my God!' said the Obeah man. 'I have done. Here, Brutchie, is your great ally. Your multitude are half intoxicated by this time; and your friends are gone among them, to set their minds at rest on many points. I shall still wait here, and watch the stars a little longer. Do you as you like: your Missionary will say all you please.'

'Ah!' thought the Missionary, as he turned from him; 'I had not calculated on what has happened. These fiends in human shape are not the fools I took them for. I reckoned indeed on bewildering the minds of my hearers, and of reserving the power I should acquire to make my own terms with Combah. I have outwitted myself, and been still more outwitted by that juggling and treacherous Hamel; and so degraded am I, that if they but tell my story here among this crew, I am undone for ever, even with them. And of what value shall I be to Combah? Yet—yet,' (and he ground his teeth together, as the idea burned through his mind) 'I may have vengeance. Thanks to the white man's laws, these wretches cannot give evidence against me; nay, could they, who shall believe them? I have trusted no white man, woman, or child; my dearest victim knows me not still, and she yet thinks me what I seem to these. I can denounce them; and spurn their execrable oath; and then—what am I? How shall I gain Joanna? Must I see her the wife of another? And must I for ever be the slave of those who refused to send me here? Must I do their work, to gain their approbation?—A set of hypocrites!'—

But here his reverie was interrupted by his companion Combah inquiring if he was still able to address the Negroes a second time, according to his promise; and if he would argue them into a belief that they must have a king. 'For they are already so disposed,' said he; 'you heard them call me Brutchie. They have kings in their own country; and they will be nothing without a king.'

'Combah,' replied the Missionary in a melancholy tone, 'you have ruined and undone me. I must do what you expect of me, what I have promised; though I think it better that you should put off, till the next Saturday night, the business of placing a crown upon your head. Besides, they do not crown their kings in their own country; and after the indignities I have endured, my strength fails me. Yet if it must be so, let the drum be stopped, and that profane dancing; and call the attention of those who can attend. But I will mount no more upon that ruined building; let us walk into the midst.'

A shout from Combah awakened the curiosity of the multitude, and a second silenced the drum. The word Brutchie, again bawled and howled around in acknowledgment, and in token of respect, produced an effect like that of the lyre of Orpheus, when he visited the abodes of Pluto and his bride, suspending all the operations of the Pandemonium. Even the demons of the Obeah cup relaxed from their exertions in poisoning, as it were with the breath of pestilence, the minds of every coterie which they could get at; the furies of the rum calabash allowed at last their victims to sink upon their grassy beds; and all was enchanted into silence, except the streams which ever flow, and the fragrant winds that blow. Mr Missionary had raised his head and cleared his voice, and the word 'Brethren' was on his lips, when a sable orator from the crowd interrupted his words by roaring out with stentorian might,—'Brutchie! Combah! I long to see you king,—so you send away the parson.'

'Why so, you drunken fool?' replied his majesty. 'Hold your tongue, and let master Roland speak.'

'No more, if you please, master Brutchie; I long to see you king, because then I shall work no more, no more be flogged, no more be preached; I shall have my wives to work for me and find me my plantains; and I can sit on a rock or on the soft grass, and cry *swish*, and whistle. Oh, master Brutchie, be king: don't have a white parson; he will want all the women and young girls for himself, and be preaching hell fire and duppie to make us work for himself and all his little ones; for he will want fine clothes, and money, and horses, and sheep, and pigs, and cocks and hens, and all other things besides, and a fine house; and we must all work to give him these. But you will have your own wives to work for you; and you will want nothing from us but to fight sometimes for you, and go to war for other people's plantains and cocoes, if there should be no rain here, or if these hurricanes come too often and sweep everything away from this part of the island. And then, Brutchie, when you get strong, we can make war on the white men, and catch king George's ships when they come into Port Antonio, and Kingston, and Annotto Bay, and more bays down to leeward, and make them pay salt fish and herrings, and osnaburghs and pennistons. Oh, Brutchie, Brutchie, take away the missionaries! If you must have people to preach, why can't the Negroes preach as well? as well as the white skin man, who only preaches for the women, that every one must have a white husband, and must not work for him, but the man must slave for her; a pretty thing! I know I'll *wallop* my three wives if they don't work for me.'

'You wallop your wife!' cried another, a female voice. 'I hope Brutchie will wallop your back. Hold your tongue, you drunken fellow; I am ashamed of you. Master Brutchie, please make the Missionary speak again; he is a good man, and preaches the true Gospel for black women as well as Quadroon misses and white fine ladies, that turn sick if the sun shines in their green cat's eyes. We have no more business to work than they have; and I hope to see the time come when the white men shall work for us, and bring us silk gowns, and muslin, and umbrellas to keep the sun from burning our complexions as well as theirs; and when we shall have horses, and sumpter mules, and kittereens, and Madeira wine, and porter; and wear white nice pretty shoes, and white kid gloves, and pink handkerchiefs; and play the music in the buckras' houses, and dance with the parson and all the fine young gentlemen that come from England and America. Please to make master Roland speak again; I love to hear him preach.'

This speaker had the misfortune to be interrupted, as well as the last, (although she had pretty well exhausted the topics of her eloquence,) but in a different way from that in which the honorable *gentleman* had been cut short. A mutilated shout was heard from the bottom of the rocks, where Cuffy, having watched till he was tired, had long since fallen asleep, in spite of the temptations of the drum, which only served at last to lull him into repose. The horse had been allowed to wander at liberty in search of pasture, which he found among the rocks on the river's brink, without straying to any great distance, Cuffy having only taken the bit out of his mouth, and tied the bridle about his neck for security. In this state the animal now made his appearance, followed by two men who had in vain attempted to secure him, and by Cuffy, awaked from his almost Lethean sleep, roaring out in the rear to the multitude to catch his horse. The beast ran headlong into the crowd, as if he were pleased to shew the sweetness of his disposition, and put every human being he came near to the rout, until he entangled himself among some rocks, and was secured, much to the satisfaction of Roland, who would gladly have remounted him and rode away; but ere he could do this, the two men who had surprised the horse and the sleeper below, having found out the Brutchie in the moonlight, came to tell the cause of their pursuing them; which was no other than a suspicion that they belonged to some white man who was watching the Negro performances.

'Give back the horse to the boy,' said the king rather impatiently; 'and tell me who you are—what—how—wherefore—and whence you came to this place;—what has happened, Quamina? And who is the other—Quao? Diego?'

'Master Brutchie,' replied the first of the Negroes whom he had recognised, 'the canoe broke upon the rocks at —— bay last night in the storm, and we could not mend it till this morning: we saw the fires, and we got into master Guthrie's house.'

'Ah! hah!' cried the Missionary, overhearing what was said, though in only a half whisper. 'Master Guthrie's house! What had they to do there?'

The Negroes looked anxiously at Roland, of whom they had some previous knowledge, a little startled at his white face; and wondered in their turn how he came there, and what he had to do at such a place. But Combah, without expressing any apprehension for the consequence, demanded, in a sufficiently loud and

imperious tone, 'What news of the buckra woman?' adding, before he had given time for an answer, 'You were wrong—we made
no fires; but what have you done with her?'

'We left her where we found her,' replied Quamina; 'for a
brown man whom we brought from Cuba advised us to put to sea
again next day, and made us believe that master Guthrie suspected us, and was prepared to seize us or kill us, if we attempted
anything more to-night.'

'A brown man!' said the king in some surprise.

'Yes, master Brutchie, a tall brown man with a large Spanish
hat.'

'Why—this,' said the Missionary, 'must be the same who came
hither on my horse.'

'Is he here then?' said Quamina in a low tone of voice. 'Hush!
catch him, master Brutchie, if he is here: for he is no good man; he
is a deep rogue, a most powerful desperate villain: he ran the
canoe a second time upon the rocks on purpose to day, and
laughed at us when he saw the water come in at two great holes in
its bottom.'

'Laughed at you!' repeated Combah: 'laughed at you! I think indeed you deserve to be laughed at; how many were you?'

'We were eight men,' replied the Negro, quite abashed; 'but
one man was of Sebastian's side, and two more were of neither
side, and would not help us; and so he beat us, and flung us about,
and tossed Diego and myself into the sea; for we had no arms
loaded but what were so wet that the gunpowder would not go off;
and our machets, which lay in the bottom of the canoe while we
rowed to windward, he threw into the sea before we thought of
using them.'

'He had a sword?' enquired Combah, looking at the Missionary.

'Yes, he had a sword,' replied the Negro, 'with a gold chain; but
he did not draw his sword. We had saved him from Cuba, where
he was a prisoner, and had escaped from pirates; he knew the bay
where we were to land—so he told us—and Mr Guthrie's house,
and all the country round about: and so he did; but when he ran
our boat a second time on the rocks, he told us he would not betray us, because we had assisted him in his necessity; nor would he

injure us, except we offered violence to him: he bid us begone to
our masters and surrender ourselves, or mend the canoe again,
and take ourselves off the island, if we pleased; but he threatened,
if we dared to attempt anything against Mr Guthrie or his wife—'

'His wife!' cried the Missionary, interrupting the Negro's
speech. 'What would you attempt against his wife?'

'His wife was sick in bed,' replied Quamina.

'I know it—at least I thought so,' said the Missionary: 'but had
she been well, what meant you to have done?'

'Roland, hear me,' said Combah, intending to answer for his
delegate. 'It was Joanna they were to bring away.'

'Joanna!' repeated the Missionary, half choked with the various passions inspired by the sound of her name, and the idea of
the fate which she had escaped. 'Gracious heaven! Combah, is
this your faith to me? Is it for this that I have sunk myself to a level
with the beasts of the field, or the more brute beasts who are
preached up as the best part of humanity.' (Then turning aside.)
'Villain! infamous villain! May the curse of his own God and mine
rend asunder his black and marble heart!'

The latter part of this speech was inaudible to those with whom
he was conversing, being more in the nature of a soliloquy than
belonging to the dialogue. Combah heard only an indistinct and
grumbling murmur; but though he suspected what was passing in
the mind of his devout friend, he was perfectly unabashed, and
addressing himself again to Roland with the greatest ease and indifference, merely told him that it was part of their bargain that
he, Combah, should deliver up Joanna to be the wife of his friend;
and how could he do so until he had got her into his possession?
'But these men,' he continued, 'have been too soon, too rash—we
were not ready. They would have brought me the white woman,
and I should have had the glory of giving her to you. But now, if we
have not alarmed Mr Guthrie, some new plan must be devised:
for the canoe is spoiled, and this brown man has perhaps gone to
make the governor acquainted with the scheme we had in view.'

'The brown man,' replied the Missionary, still trembling with
rage and mortification, 'is here—so Cuffy says; but Combah—
Combah!—how can you persuade your conscience it was right to

send these men in secret, without my knowledge or concurrence, to steal the woman you had sworn should be my wife?'

'She shall be your wife: we wanted only more men to go down to leeward—to Hanover and Westmoreland—to fix the day for rising; and the first signal for it here was to be the seizure of Miss Joanna, and the fires on Portland Ridge and the Carrion-crow Hills. But, Quamina, what did your brown man threaten, in case you attempted anything against Mr Guthrie?'

'He threatened,' replied the other, 'to have us every one hanged, and said that Mr Guthrie was on his guard; that he would watch us, and send notice to the governor.'

'Fools!' cried the monarch again, 'why did you not seize him, and hurl him into the sea, or bring him here?'

'Here!' said the Negro, as if surprised: 'why here? We might have brought him to Hamel's cave: we knew only of the meeting here from an old blind man whom we found sitting at the mouth of it; and when you call us fools, Brutchie, for not seizing this Sebastian, I can only tell you, you do not know what you say: if you were to meddle with him yourself, you would find him a match for you, and more. Diego and myself closed with him, to get his sword from him; but he seized us, and knocked our heads together as if we had been two cats, and then flung us, one with his right hand, and the other with his left, into the sea, as if we had been two rotten coco-nuts. Quao and another had got hold of Nimrod, the black man we call Drybones, who took Sebastian's part; but he came to his help as soon as he had flung us into the water, and threw Quao down on the rocks with such force that he lay there for dead; and the other man he took up in his arms, and almost squeezed the breath out of him, holding him in the air like a parrot, while he bawled and prayed for his life until he could speak no more.'

'And what then?' said Combah, looking inquisitively at the narrator of Sebastian's feats: 'what then? Was this brown man the master of you all?'

'He ran away then,' answered the Negro, 'with Nimrod into the woods, and we followed them; but they escaped us. We got to the cave where Hamel sometimes lives, and there we found an old black man sitting on the rock, who said he was waiting for him (Hamel) to come and cure his eyes; but it would be long first; for a boy with a horse had told him, that he for whom he waited had gone into the woods and across the rivers with a white parson, to make him preach to the Negroes here. We came by the Negro path, not by the horse road; and so, as this white man says, Sebastian may have got here before us, and may be now concealed among the crowd, listening to what is going on.'

During this explanation the drum had been resumed with the rest of the festivities; and Combah, unwilling that the communication respecting Sebastian's conduct and escape should be imparted to his followers, had gradually led the Missionary, and his own delegate Quamina, to the edge of the rocks, where the river, and the road winding beside it, began to descend into the ravine before described, away from the rest of the party. The conspirators now danced and drank, and again tampered with the miserable wretches whose passions had been first inflamed by Roland's harangue, stirring them up with mad and vain speculations about liberty and revenge, to undertake or promise to undertake adventures for which they were utterly unfitted in every respect save in having the power, the manual capability, of cutting throats, or otherwise putting to death those of their supposed enemies who should have the ill-fortune to fall into their clutches. But Combah was affected with a very different feeling: the tale he had heard of Sebastian, his having wormed himself into the secret of his companions, his conflict with them, his threats and his escape, led him to apprehend a discovery: an event that would not only be fatal to his hopes of royalty, but deprive him of all the chance he might ever have possessed of obtaining the white lady for his wife.

Roland likewise was not much less tormented with fears and anticipations which, crowding on his mind, chased away for a time even the bitter recollections of the horrors and indignities he had this night endured. Thus harassed in mind, he was totally useless as a counsellor to the monarch elect, and even incapable of forming any plan for his own safety, in case the treasonous practices in which he had taken but too important an interest, should come to the knowledge of the authorities of the island. Recourse must be

had to Hamel—to a Negro conjuror! 'Death and misery!' said the
preacher to himself; humiliated more deeply at the thought: 'must
I owe my safety from the *white* men to this abortion from human
society? this devil, fiend, juggler, who cannot fail, if he have the
power, to expose me, mortify me, deliver me up as an offering,
when he shall find occasion and need, wherewith to ensure his
own reprieve or escape from justice. I am indeed undone, and
wish that my career of vanity might here be closed for ever. Yet I
was not born wicked, nor have I crimes to answer for, unless those
actions are crimes, which love of beauty, idolatry of women, drives
us all in turn to venture on. Then, who sees not that all is treachery, selfishness, hypocrisy, in this execrable world? Power—interest—wealth—women! Ah! master W——, S——, B——, and the
whole tribe of you,—I know you—I know you and all your *secret*
motives. *Secret?*—perdition! glaring as the sun: the whole world
knows you, loathes you, despises you, as I do from my heart; and
your mob screens itself beneath the mask you first invented for
yourselves, from the confession, from subjecting itself to the exchange, the reciprocity of the mutual curse you breathe for one
another. Wretches! you but deceive yourselves; you are all an ab-
horrence. Yet I will not despair. Can not I turn you to account?—
But whither am I wandering? Yet guide me, Spirit of Heav— '
—Heaven, he would have said; but Combah having sent for the
Obeah man as his fittest counsellor, that black gentleman interrupted the farther soliloquy of the Missionary with the remarks
which will be found in the next chapter.

CHAPTER 15.

How shall we laugh
When the pale coward slaves, to us, remote,
Direct th' uplifted hand, th' imploring eye!
Their conscious groans shall feed our great revenge;
Their endless woes our wond'rous wrongs repay.
BRYAN EDWARDS.

'DOES Roland faulter?' said the wizard: 'the holy and virtuous minister of God! Fear not for yourself; there are too many of your religious people in your own country to take up your cause. Though you were stained with ten thousand crimes, and all the treasons ever told of the Coromantins and of all the other Negroes whose bones lie under this soil, far from their native land, there is no one here dare punish you, while you give away or sell your Bible-books, and preach the Methodist religion. Though you were convicted of rebellion and murder, of rape, incest—hear me if you please, master Roland—though you combined with thieves and assassins, preached murder to them, and drank blood from an Obeah cup in token of your contract with them; and though all the inhabitants of this island knew it, believed it, and could prove it,— aha! none dare prosecute you; or if they did, and proved you guilty, they dare not punish you. They would condemn you, and send to England for advice, or let you escape; and if they sent to England, are there not thousands like yourself to vindicate you, to prove you innocent, to swear your crimes are imputations, lies, inventions; and that you are, were, and must be, a holy, virtuous, man—a martyr, at the worst? Ah, Roland! yours is a fine religion; but what will become of *me*?—The very mention of mine damns me, with your great friends, to everlasting fire and torment—to a level lake of Scotch brimstone. I should be hung and quartered, and my head stuck on a pole, or on the top of a mill-house—the Christians one and all would gibbet *me*—although I had never committed one crime beyond that (if it be a crime) of selling or giving away puntees, feathers, or glass bottles, to scare thieves from the orange or shaddock trees. Would the white men in the island believe I could be innocent of deeper crimes?—I tell you, master Roland, when you preach the mortifications, the perils, the hardships of your religion, you preach what is anything but true. You have the finest religion in the world, as far as I have heard; for you eat and drink all day, and make love to all the women yourselves, and to all the Quadroons and Mulatto girls here, if you like; you have got (at least the parsons here have got) houses and lands, and slaves, and wives, and everything the other white men have, without working for them. They give them to you as long as you live, for going to church on a Sunday, and preaching out of a big book. And what do I get, master Roland? Curses, execrations, hanging, quartering, and the like; and yet I preach no crimes, no murder, no violence, no rape. My own wrongs I have a right to revenge, because the law will not do me justice. I was stolen by Christians; the very man who stole me became a Methodist; I asked him, when he wanted me to go to a church, if he would buy my freedom for me? He offered me his blessing!— Now, master Roland, fear not for yourself: no white man knows of your being here. Go down again to your house; learn from Mr Guthrie all he has to tell; or from his wife, who has no secrets from you; or from his daughter, if she will —'

'No more, no more,' interrupted Roland. 'If you have any knowledge, as you once boasted, superior to that of your companions, or of the Whites, tell me, tell Combah, who is this Mulatto man with the Spanish hat?—this Sebastian, who seems to have the strength of three or four men, and throws your countrymen about as if they were dogs. Tell us, where is he, and what does he, and how dared he to take my horse to bring him here? Do you know him?'

'Aye,' said the Obeah man; 'I know him well; and I warn you to beware of him. Tempt him not, touch him not, provoke him not: he is your bitterest, your most dangerous enemy.'

'And why?'

'Because you have injured him.'

'I never injured a Mulatto man,' said the Missionary; 'why should I fear him? Does Combah know the man?'

'If Combah knows him,' said the wizard, 'he will mind my caution. This Mulatto, as you say—for I have not heard of him except from your boy and from yourself—is no ordinary person, it seems; but a brave and desperate fellow. Keep clear of him; avoid all intercourse with him; and you are safe. Let not your vanity interfere to solicit for you any connexion with him, however trifling.—But see, Combah! the stars are beginning to look pale; the daylight must be fast approaching. If Roland will say anything more to your assembly here, it must be done at once. These men should be sent down to leeward—this Quamina and Diego; for though they were not a match for Sebastian, they are faithful. There is no time to lose: the governor will be alarmed, the soldiers sent among us, and martial law proclaimed. Roland must seize his bride at once, or let you seize her, before another day passes by. Seize her, Brutchie, but use her well.'

'No, no;' said Roland, interposing; 'leave that business to me. If she is to be mine, let me at least win her. Hamel knows that I shall never be suspected; I have admission to the house at all hours; I can sleep there.'

'Yes, yes,' said Hamel, 'on pretence of being at hand to give assistance in case of an attempt. These holy men know how to value the laws of hospitality!'

This latter sentence was of course not intended for the Missionary: he neither heard it, nor felt any compunction for harbouring so horrible an intention. Brutchie admitted the propriety of the scheme; for he too had his own private views. But he was resolved that the crowd should yet acknowledge him as king in the presence and by the address of Roland; and Hamel, feeling an interest also in seeing his own prediction respecting him fulfilled, had adopted a similar resolution. The prediction had in fact been already fulfilled, for the rabble had saluted him as Brutchie; but the crown was to be placed on his head, and the coco-nut oil poured on it, and the people were to kiss his hand and cry 'God save him;'—a farce that tickled the fancy of the Obeah man, and the vanity of the would-be king; the first being delighted at the idea of seeing a white man, a Missionary too, a preacher of the religion by which he was denounced, doing the first of all honours to a black African, and crowning him king over the island, the Whites, the Christians, and himself; and the latter participating perhaps in these feelings, and being swollen besides with the conceit of being restored from slavery to royalty by his own exertions, and of having acquired a power of revenging himself on the robbers of Europe who had dragged him from his native soil. Natural ambition, and the prospect of sensual gratifications, combined with these feelings, and led to the performance of the scene we are about to describe.

The day had fairly begun to dawn, and the stars had faded in the blue sky, which now assumed a rosy tinge, rendering the pale moon still paler; and the pigeons were already winging their way, as well as the parrots, across the amphitheatre among the rocks, the scene of all the noise and bustle we have related; the crickets were even clearing their throats; the land wind still breathed its fragrance at intervals, and shook the dew drops (with every one of the sighs it seemed to heave) from the feathery branches of the gigantic palms already noticed, beneath which it was the royal pleasure of Brutchie Combah to be dubbed a true king. It must be confessed that his majesty's loyal subjects were not in the very finest trim or costume for the occasion;—but men are men; and subjects, though lords and dukes, are no more. Besides, his majesty meant to create a batch or two of these on the spot, in the fashion of him of Hayti; and would have made a due selection for the occasion, if it had not occurred to him that many of those he most valued were too drunk at the moment to appreciate or even to understand the nature of the honours which were to be thrust upon them: some were also ingloriously asleep, lolling their heads in the laps of the sable nymphs in whose honour they had been dancing all night; others sprawling on the grass or on the white barbicue; two or three couple quarrelling or scolding; and a few merely seated as spectators of those who still kept up an eternal jigging to the monotony of the eternal drum. The rum was all expended, not a drop even being left to drink to the long life of the new monarch, as soon as Roland should have consecrated him: but they had saluted him already in that fashion during the night, and a draught of the river might suit the occasion as well as rum—

the latter, as Roland observed, not being usually drank at the courts in Europe; and water might in some sort revive and restore the senses of the company. A crown had been prepared, made by a Negro blacksmith, in the fashion of that of Lombardy, every alternate spike being gilded, and the whole surrounded by a cincture of alternate blue and white glass beads. The holy oil too was produced by Hamel, from whose hands the Missionary refused to take it, intimating that he had received enough from his unchristian fingers. It was contained in a small glass phial, and was handed round among those who might perhaps be denominated the king's courtiers, and who in turn peeped into it like so many parrots into a marrow-bone, and then applied it to their flat noses for farther information as to its sacred or divine qualities. However it came back, without having caused any audible remark, to the hands which had first produced it, every Quashie being sensible that silence would at least save him from exposing himself on a point of which be was as profoundly ignorant as the high priest who was about to perform the ceremony.

The wizard was however rather incensed at the objection started by the Missionary, and said to him in an under tone—'Brother! there is nothing in the colour of this; take it; it is not red, nor need you put it to your lips.'

Roland gave him a look of horror, and waved to him to keep it for himself; for they were on their march across the little plain, from the brow or the dingle where the river disembogued, towards the palm-trees which stood (and which yet stand) to the eastward of the ruined house. No Triumph of Bacchus or Silenus, the living monuments of Titian, Poussin, Rubens, or any other artist, would give my readers an idea of this absurdest of all absurd processions; although, as in those master-pieces of art, which many will call to their recollections, the chief part of the performers are represented drunk. But theirs is the mirth of drunkenness, hilarity, and joy; whereas our sable satyrs, wanting the cloven hoofs and the tails, were no less sleepy than intoxicated, and staggered along like wounded and fainting soldiers in a retreat, now and then tumbling against one another, now and then tumbling down altogether. Silence had been proclaimed, and all had been summoned to attend; but the first was not so easily obtained as it had been over night; and some seemed to have fallen into their last sleep, and could not be roused even by pinching or slapping. The drummer too, as if he had been smitten with the *chorea sancti viti,* and bewildered between drowsiness and drink, could not pay that implicit attention to the royal orders which they deserved, but kept up a most persevering though less fractious rub-a-dub, as it were in spite of himself, or because his hands continued to wriggle, whilst his brains were entranced by the goodly vision before him and the o'ermastering rum within him. He sat drumming in his *sotto voce,* with his mouth wide open, and his eyes about half open, except during those intervals when he could raise them into a stare, while the procession past by him. First came half a dozen women, dancing for a few yards at a time, then walking as many, but in their walk knocking their elbows against their hips, which they wrenched forward with a grace which none but Hottentots could surpass, to render the contact more elegant and insinuating as well as more easy. At the same time they sang extemporaneous songs in praise of the new king and the Missionary, which, all adapted to the same tune, and all delivered in unison, consisted of various and distinct effusions, each of the prophetic beauties giving vent to her own particular inspirations; so that the whole produced a confusion of words and noises, from which it was as difficult as useless to draw any meaning. To give some idea of their poetry however,—one, for instance, exclaimed 'No more fum-fum*—oh, oh!'—while another sang, 'King George will send for me, oh! for me, oh!':—and another warbled—

'The soldier Buckra fight for we,
The sailor Buckra too—o;
The Buckra Parson make we free,
And drive the Scotchman in de sea—
       Oh, oh!—oh, oh!
       Brutchie, Brutchie, oh, oh!
       Broder to king Georgy—oh!'

* Flogging

But it would require the subtlety of an alchemist to analyse more than one of these Pindarics out of the six—that is from end to end. They were linked into one another with some attention to melody; but of harmony the nymphs who sang them had no notion. After these came about a dozen men, clapping their hands in time with the singers, and sometimes dancing a step or two, and yelling out 'Brutchie Combah!' These were all drunk in different degrees, and all variously affected,—some laughing, some almost crying, solemn, lyrical, and ludicrous; some hiccupping; and one or two with uplifted eyes and dilated nostrils attempting a psalm. One of them carried the diadem, and would have placed it on his own skull more than once, if Hamel, who walked behind him, had not rapped his knuckles with a bamboo-staff, as often as he observed him guilty of such impiety and profanation. The king was by the side of the Obeah man; and Roland, disfigured and dirty, with his hat crumpled, and his hair sticking out in all wrong directions, walked on the other side of his majesty, with a small bible in his hand, which he had drawn from his pocket. He was wofully cast down; and yet his majesty, walking between his two confessors, looked perhaps more like a culprit tramping to the gallows than himself, and much more so in fact than a monarch marching to a throne. The rear of the procession was brought up by the rest of the Obeah conspirators; some smoking short pipes, some laughing and floundering about, romping with the women, and singing songs (none of the chastest,) and it closed by forty or fifty rabble in Osnaburgh frocks, being all who could be awaked or brought to service.

They reached the palm-trees; and having faced about, the Obeah man spread his arms towards the east, from which the day was glimmering. But Roland, already scandalized, called out to him to forbear; and the black ladies, always inclining to his side, told the wizard it was not for him to preach when the white parson was there; a remark that only excited a smile from Hamel, who surrendered his claims (if claims they were) most courteously to his rival, and begged him to make haste, and finish before the sun should rise. The Missionary began a prayer, in which his own feelings, getting almost the better of his discretion, led him away from the subject he had undertaken, to invocate peace and tranquillity for himself—for he could still pray; but quickly resuming the recollection of his work, he asked his drunken audience whether they would like to have a king, if they were free, as soon as the governor should go away: because, if they would, Brutchie Combah was the man for them, as he was brave and wise—he would fain have been able to add, religious. The Missionary repeated the question more than once, without receiving any answer; and as the audience, collectively at least, seemed on this occasion deaf or dumb, or both, he bethought himself of asking them individually whether they approved of his proposition. The first he appealed to, having heard him verbatim and seriatim, replied only with a wild stare, and the monosyllable 'sa,' (sir.) Roland gave him up for a fool, and attacked the next, whose answer could not be made to extend beyond a hiccup. A third whispered—'Yes, if master Roland please.' But Combah, becoming impatient, snatched the tin crown from the knight or squire who had squeezed it out of shape in his drunken efforts to place it on his own head, and tried, though with very moderate success, to ram his own woolly skull into it. But it had become so bent into salient and re-entering angles, that although the king pricked his fingers with the spikes till they bled, he could not set it perpendicularly or horizontally on his head; he could not render the *tiara recta.* On the contrary, it stuck on the right side of his cerebellum, like a dragoon's foraging cap, of which the glass beads, escaping from the magic crown that ought to have rounded his royal temples, formed the queue, that elegant appendage which fashion has taken from the head of the tom-fool to put on that of the hero. But the king had no sooner impressed the crown on his mortal brows, than Hamel reminded him of the necessity of the unction, and again offered the phial to the Missionary, who shrunk from his rival, and the holy oil he tendered, as if it were a scorpion he was to handle. Still it was necessary to take it, and to go through the ceremony he had commenced, although the gracious monarch had already set the example to his subjects of crying out 'God save the king!' and was engaged in saluting each of those around him with a royal kiss, while this little coquetry between the Obeah man and the

Missionary continued. But the Obeah man would not resign the point: he was determined, though in the politest manner, to make his rival administer the oil, and kept urging it so pertinaciously, while the mob were hiccupping out 'God save king Brutchie—king Combah!' that Roland was at last obliged to take it.

The drunken shouts echoed around the amphitheatre, while the increasing daylight had already warned some of his majesty's less intoxicated subjects to retire from his gracious presence, to handle the hoe or the bill for the less dignified, though not less arbitrary, cudjoes in the plains below—the drivers; whose whips (the mortal badge of power and servitude) cracked till the very mountains repeated the sound. On some estates this signal has been commuted for the ringing of a bell, or the blast of a conch shell (sounds in every respect more agreeable,) and such was the stillness of the air and the serenity of the morning, that many of these were heard to mingle with the echoes of the whips, though at the distance of many miles, when the intoxicated bawlers, suspending their screams in order to take breath, allowed any echoes to be heard less hateful than those of their own bellowings. These various and to them unwelcome intimations insensibly thinned the ranks of the multitude, awakening, more effectually than the charms of the coronation could have done, even some of the heaviest sleepers, who resumed their legs to slink away through the passes among the rocks, or by one of the two main roads, each to his own master's domain. Some were however disposed to play the truant; and others remained as decided runaways, scorning to move from the scene, except as occasion or choice might direct them to the fastnesses in the interior. The sun was above the horizon, and his upward rays began to gild the summits of the rocks of this romantic amphitheatre: the vapours of the night, rising from the surrounding forest into a visible existence, now flitted along the edges of the precipices, obscuring sometimes the giant trees which grew among and above their grey pinnacles—sometimes the pinnacles themselves, while their feathered plumes were still discernible above the mist—sometimes both pinnacles and trees at once; and then again wreathing themselves into wild and fantastic forms, as they mounted into the upper air. These clouds reflected the sunbeams for a few moments, and melted away to leave a space, as it appeared, for others to succeed them in the same creation, progress, and decay.

The Missionary had taken the phial of coco-nut oil from the hands of his enemy; and as the king objected to have his crown removed to receive his unction, Roland prepared to pour the contents of the bottle, over which he had muttered a sort of prayer, upon the sacred head it encircled. The oil was white, or colourless, as he received it; but having drawn the cork, and held it for a moment at arm's length as high as he could reach, for the gratification of the bystanders, he with no little astonishment saw it assume a dye of the deepest crimson. This change was effected so rapidly, that Roland had not time to reason upon it, his agitation at the sight getting the better of his presence of mind; and instead of emptying the bottle on the head of the sovereign, he threw it with horror away from him, over the heads of the crowd, into the arena beyond.

Combah, surprized at the action, which he deemed an insult and a tergiversation, seized the Missionary by the throat; while Hamel exclaimed that it was not blood, and begged the Brutchie to forbear. But the monarch was too enraged to listen to him, and held the preacher in his gripe with a ferocious vigour, in spite of Hamel's intercession; while the mob, not knowing precisely what ought to have been done with the bottle, called to one another in amazement for some explanation, thinking that master Roland was going to be put to death, as a part of the ceremony. Hamel still talked of patience and forbearance, exclaiming—'Spare my friend, my friend, my brother Roland, the Christian Missionary.' Roland, already half strangled by the black king whom he had been about to sanctify, was yet sensible to the insulting intercession of his rival. Life however is not to be surrendered in extremities of violence without a struggle: the Missionary grappled with the monarch, closed, tripped him up, and rolled with him on the sand. But the king had not loosed his grasp, though he was undermost; and notwithstanding Roland had in turn fastened his fingers on the neck of his antagonist, his own weazand was in very especial jeopardy.

Fate has prevented us from declaring what would have been the result, had things remained in this state a few moments longer: for a very unexpected circumstance intervened to put an end to the royal and religious fracas, and to this chapter at the same time.

CHAPTER 16.

Run, run, Bonduca—not the quick race swifter,
The virgin from the hated ravisher
Not half so fearful: not a flight drawn home,
A round stone from a sling, a lover's wish,
E'er made that haste that they have.

BONDUCA.

A SHOUT from the top of the precipice to the eastward of the palm
trees between them and the eastern sky, called off the attention of
all those, his majesty's new subjects, who remained to witness his
royal scuffle with the parson. The shout was repeated; but the
clouds, hanging before the towering crag from which the sound
proceeded, enveloped the voice and the speaker in mystery. His
words however were sufficiently articulate; and when the
Negroes heard the voice say distinctly 'Maroons!' a cry of consternation issued from every mouth below; the drunken became
sober, the sleepers awakened, the brave became cowards, and
nine out of every ten ran away as fast as their legs could carry
them. Even Brutchie relaxed his hold; and Roland, gasping for
breath, gave his royal antagonist half-a-dozen hearty English
punches with his fist in the bread-basket and elsewhere, before he
turned up his strained and starting eyeballs to inform himself of
the person from whom the voice proceeded. At the same moment
the clouds, clearing partially away, left only a sort of filmy mist, re-
splendent with the beams of the sun, between the rock and the
spectators. It was more than half transparent; and while it betrayed the speaker whose clamorous voice had alarmed the fraternity, the illuminated vapour served to magnify his form into
that of a giant of no common dimensions—to the eyes of Roland,
as well as Combah, a demon of the first magnitude, with a sword
hanging by his side, a monstrous musket in his left hand, and on
his head the huge Spanish sombrero which had excited the
amazement and apprehensions of Roland, even by the mention
made of it. The figure, looking down into the arena, and waving his

104

right arm as a signal, exclaimed again—'Begone—the Maroons
are upon you—away!'

At this, every tenth man fled: the king, in as great distress as his
subjects, forgetting his dignity and his crown (his crown and dignity) moved off with all possible celerity. Hamel was already gone;
and Roland, fancying a black marshal at his heels in the shape of a
Maroon, caught up his hat, ran after Cuffy, who was already on his
march, mounted his Spanish nag, and galloped across the plain,
and down the rocky road beside the waterfall, at the risk of every
bone in his own and his horse's body.

Indeed, Cuffy would have been but little disappointed, had the
horse and rider been brought up by a downfall of some kind; for
his master's apprehensions rendering speed to his own heels at
least, he had kicked his beast into a pace by which the poor boy
was distanced and unable to continue his hold upon the tail of the
steed. He would have been left completely in the lurch, but for
the day-light which enabled him to discriminate the road by its
various angles, long after they had descended to the base of the
rocks where he had dreamed away three parts of the night. This
being all on the descent, Cuffy did not hesitate to quit the only
practicable horse-road, and scrambled with facility from rock to
rock, and from gully to gully, so that he was soon even with, and
shortly after in advance of, his master; with whom he then jogged
on unceremoniously and expeditiously for at least half-a-dozen
miles, until they reached the Devil's Gully, as it was called—the
spot where the hurricane had stopped them in their march towards the settlement from which they had just made so ignoble a
retreat.

What a crowd of miserable ideas and recollections oppressed
the mind of the forlorn voyager, as he passed this ominous, this
fearful chasm! whence, as he now learned from him, his boy had
been blown fairly away to leeward, even as far as the river where
he had shaken hands with the black girls, from whom he afterwards found protection during the night. They were soon at the
same spot again, and having passed about a mile, arrived at
Belmont, where the boy was dispatched to the house to beg a
breakfast for his master; while Roland, heated, feverish, and

broken-down in mind and body, indulged himself with the re-
freshment of a bath in the river.—Let us here take leave of him for
the present, and attend to the gentleman with the sombrero hat,
whom we left on the summit of the rock.

No *coup-de-théâtre* was ever brought about with more facility
or better effect, than the dispersion of the crowd by the hand-
waving and the awful summons of Sebastian. Enveloped as he was
in the mist, it was but a passing glance which he had taken of the
fracas below; the fog again gathering round him with so much
celerity that he had not time to assure himself of the retreat of the
rabble. Nor was it until the clouds finally cleared away, that he
could persuade himself he stood alone, the only figure in the landscape, the master in fact of the theatre of the late struggle. He descended from the rocks with his gun on his shoulder, and walked
deliberately about the little plain, looking into the ruined mansion, and into its cellar, from which all evidences had been withdrawn that could have testified to the filthy rites practised there
over night, except it were signs of the fire. The grass was trampled
with the dancing; and there had been a shuffling upon the barbicue as well as in many other places, where the sand was rumpled
with the feats and the frolics of this band of worthies. A few broken pipes, and a stray calabash or two, were all the insignia of their
drunken festivities.

But although the coast was clear, and Sebastian might have fancied he had the field to himself, yet (as the reader must suppose)
he could not be altogether uninformed of the purpose for which
the meeting had been held; at least he could not but guess that it
was held for some illegal purpose, however the ingenuity of the
Negro race in lying, and their perseverance in standing out in a lie,
might have led him to believe, if it had come to the question, that
it was all an innocent frolic, a merry-making; and that the scuffle
which he had in part witnessed, between the king and his vicar,
was all in the way of such frolics. As a brown man, he would have
been told that the parson got drunk and quarrelled with Combah,
whom they commonly called Brutchie. But the Mulatto, for want
of such an assurance, believed, as he could not avoid doing, that all
was not right; more especially as he had put their assembly to

flight by the bare mention of the Maroons. Moreover, he had heard, during his cruise in the canoe, that a revolt was intended as the sequel to the attack on Mr Guthrie's house, although the mode of effecting it was a mystery to his companions, as well as himself. He knew also that such attempts at rebellion are generally reserved for Christmas-time, when the holidays allow of the Negroes extending their communications over the island with more facility and certainty than at other seasons. He had not ventured into the crowd, to hear the harangue of Roland—that is, to distinguish the purport of his speech; and the brawling of the cataracts had prevented his discovering what was said from a distance: but he divined too well the arguments of the preacher, and had waited till daylight to assure himself, not only of the presence of that gentleman, but of his taking at least some interest in the events of the night, whatever they might be. He had beheld him indeed sufficiently interested in the matter; and it appeared almost probable that but for his interference Roland would have hardly escaped strangulation.

Sebastian walked around the arena of this natural amphitheatre, with his gun apparently ready in case of a surprise, searching into the chinks of the rocks, and looking under the trees and bushes, lest any one should have concealed himself there, to take advantage of his being alone, and revenge the crowd for having been alarmed by a name. But all was solitude: he heard only the roaring of water, and the screaming of crickets, with the occasional gabbling of the parrots as they flew across the plain. There were doubtless some of the Negro crew eying the Mulatto from their eyries; but they were all invisible to him, ensconced among the rocks on high, perched perhaps on trees, or laid flat on the summits of the crags which overhung the plain: there was nothing human visible but himself. He sat down by the ruins of the house under the shade of a shaddock tree; and, laying his gun by his side, began to ruminate on his peculiar, and as he thought unhappy, situation; but before he could give vent to any of the griefs which preyed on his mind, his reverie was startled by the report of a gun, and a black man rushed suddenly into the arena, as if in pursuit of some game at which he had fired. ' This,' thought he, 'must be a

hog-hunter, a Maroon, a pigeon shooter, or—No: it is my man, my
individual Hamel!' He rose from his position; and the Obeah man,
with an activity and celerity beyond his years, ran joyfully, as it
seemed, towards him, and welcomed him to the island.

Sebastian raised himself to his full height, and said to him in a
serious and rather mysterious tone of voice—'Fairfax will be here
tomorrow, if he does not land to-day. He has not forgotten Hamel,
nor his services; but what have you been doing here? There is
treason and rebellion on foot. Hamel! keep yourself free from suspicion; remember what a white man has done for you; do not *you*
disgrace the generosity of your benefactor. Here has been a plot
to carry off a young lady by rascals and runaways—a crew of villains who designed to rob old Guthrie's house. I owed to them my
safety, perhaps my life, at any rate my liberty and the means of returning to my native land; else I had delivered them up to the
magistrates, the instant they set foot in Jamaica. You must know of
this plot, Hamel. A man named Combah was their employer; and
they told me that a parson was to make him king. Surely this parson is not Roland.'

The Obeah man hesitated.

'I know that Roland was here: I saw him, or my eyes deceived
me; though it is long since they beheld him before.'

'Well, master,' said the wizard; 'Roland *was* here, and quarrelled with the Negroes, as you saw; but we are not safe here:
there are eyes on us that we can neither see nor evade: a gang of
runaways who frequent this ruined abode, who belonged to it, are
probably even now within shot of you: not that I apprehend anything for your safety; but come—let us decamp.'

'Hark ye, Hamel!'' said the other, as they walked across the
plain to the river's brink; 'I warn you again to be prudent. I have
sent a slave to tell the governor of this Combah and the gang of
rascals who brought me from Cuba. I gave them notice; I beat it
into their sheep's heads; I bid them return to their masters, or take
themselves off the island. I cautioned or caused to be cautioned
Mr Guthrie; I will alarm the country; I came to your house—to
your little cave among the rocks.'

'Who told you where to find me?'

'Ask me not, Hamel: there were too many knew that there was mischief plotting. I learnt at the ford above Golden Vale estate, that a man, who by the description must have been this Roland, had passed to windward, intending a journey to this very spot; I saw the fires the previous night; I am satisfied there is a plot on foot; and I command—I entreat you to tell me all. You may save the island—you may save yourself. I count upon your fidelity; I will not believe you capable of deceiving or betraying the son of your benefactor, him to whom you vowed you would repay the services his family had conferred upon you.'

'I remember the oath—I remember the occasion,' replied the Obeah man. 'I never can forget the services, the favours, I have received; I was redeemed from the fangs of a tyrant, from the basest slavery, from the dominion of one who was a slave in my own country, when I was the possessor of flocks and herds—aye, and of slaves too. But you must give me time, master, to think what I must do. Fear not for yourself: not a hair of your head shall be hurt.'

'I fear for you more than for myself,' replied the brown man. 'I have taken precautions to alarm the magistracy; and if need be, I will alarm the island;—but that were better avoided: our friends in England despair of us already; and if they hear of an insurrection, what shall we expect? What shall they do who are in debt to their merchants? And all are in debt: foreclosures here and there, judgments, levyings, vendues,—we shall have a revolution of property first, and then be hunted into the sea, or murdered by the Negroes: the island will be worthless to the Whites, worthless to the Blacks. If freedom be any object to you —'

'No, no,' rejoined the wizard with a sigh. 'Freedom! I am free enough, except the white men quit the island. I never thought to see you back again; yet I wish now I had been free. But give me time: there shall be no harm. You have done well: your plan, your discovery, has been your own. Hamel is innocent of all that may happen to either party, black or white. Why do your friends in England send Missionaries to preach here? Are the merchants and mortgagees there the slaves of the Methodists? And why does king George want to make the slaves free for nothing, after the white men have paid for them? You know, master, there must be something wicked here, if the king says we should be free; but what will be our freedom? What are we to do—the ignorant, nasty, drunken Negroes, who were born slaves in Congo, and Coromantin, and Houssa, and Mundingo. Some will make the others work: there will be slaves for ever, unless the white men stay with soldiers and cannons to keep the strong ones from beating the weak ones, and making the women do all the work. Some of the slaves who won't work must die: and what is to become of those, the black men and the brown men, who have now got a few slaves to work for them,—some one, some two or three? Ah! your great men in England must be very silly or very wicked, or all must be wrong here: for they will make Jamaica ten times worse than my own country was ever made by war, and fighting, and robbery, and murder.'

While this dialogue was taking place, Sebastian and Hamel had turned their backs on the scene of the nocturnal orgies, festivities, and broils; and were walking slowly down the rocky dingle which formed the channel of the rivulet, and the narrow road beside it, covered with the umbrageous canopy of trees, whose interwoven boughs were still closer bound together by the numerous parasitical plants of the wilderness.

'Here are the tracks of Roland's horse,' said the Obeah man. 'He has gone with expedition home. You should have heard his speech:—no wonder he was in a hurry to escape.'

'The noise of the waterfall prevented me,' replied Sebastian. 'I knew him always subtle and intriguing.'

'You know him not,' said Hamel; 'or at least you know but half of him. It shall be my business to make you fully acquainted with him: but that must not be yet. I never thought to have seen you back again—no, never; but when I heard how you had beaten the sailors, and flung them in the sea, I knew it must be yourself—I knew of none other who had the strength or the dexterity to do so.'

'They saved me, and were entitled at least to some consideration. But tell me, Hamel—though I denounce *them* not, what must I say of yourself? There are stories abroad of you that will endanger your existence here. The man I sent to Spanish Town declared that you have the reputation of being a practitioner of Obeah; and that, although you do your duty as a watchman and a hog-hunter, you have some secret hiding-place, some cave, which I know not, among the rocks, where runaways come to hear their fortunes and to buy charms of you for the purpose of tormenting and destroying one another:—nay, when I entered your cave— the one that I remember—I saw a person there who came for you, to lay your hands, as he said, upon his eyes; for he was blind. It was he told me what was to be done here, about making a preaching.'

'I have some secrets, sir,' replied the Obeah man, 'by which Sebastian himself has not disdained to profit; but I have not used them hitherto to the prejudice of any man—that is, my secrets. For the rest I have no fear. I know how cheaply a Negro's life is valued here, if he is even suspected of what you allude to; and my life is of little value to myself even. If I cannot employ it to your advantage, the sooner I lay it down, the better; but I *have* the power to serve you, and that most effectually.'

'Not by any illicit means, Hamel. What would be said of me, if I were to employ an Obeah man? Deny it—tell me the tale is groundless. Where is this cave? and who was the blind man?'

'I have no cave but that you know of,' replied the wizard. 'You have not seen the extent of it, and must not.'

'Must not, Hamel!'

'You must not, you cannot:—you would be lost among the windings; and there is a spell upon it, and upon him that shall enter it to explore its secrets.'

'Nonsense!' replied Sebastian. 'We have no faith in spells. But how happens it, that I, who have so often sat in the cave in my youth, spent whole days in it, clambered among its rocks and upon the trees around its mouth, should yet have been ignorant that it extended beyond the little chamber which alone it seems to contain? Have I not stood on every pinnacle above it and about it, to wait for a shot at the pigeons? And what is the spell you talk of?'

'Your father,' said the Obeah man, 'believed in the spell: he told it me; he said the words were Spanish, and had belonged to the cave ever since the conquest of the island.'

'But what did they portend—these words?'

'Ah!' cried Hamel, 'you will find them on your father's papers: I hardly understood them then, and I forget them now; but I know it was bad luck to him that came to search—that he should find blood who came to look for it, and shed blood before he could get out again.'

'Well,' rejoined the other, 'I should not have looked for blood. I can remember once in years past Joanna and myself, in my father's life, having mounted to the top of one of those pinnacles about your rocks, looked down into a little lake environed with impassable crags. We would have descended, but could not; or we thought it impossible to re-ascend. There was a large yellow snake coiled up on its brink: we pelted it with pieces of the rock; and before we struck it, it only hissed at us for our pains: but at last Joanna threw a stone which hit some part of it, and rebounded into the lake; and then—'

'It followed you?' said the Obeah man.

'It darted into the water, as if it were enraged by the blow, and then sprang again to the shore, and glided rapidly into a small cavity at the base of the rock; and while we stood and gazed in expectation of seeing it return to the lake, we heard it, or it might have been another, hissing among the bushes beneath us at the foot of the pinnacle on which we stood. Joanna was alarmed; and we fled in haste from the spot. We have never been there since together; and though I searched alone for the place many a time, I could not find it again.'

'I have found it,' said Hamel: 'I have seen the snake.'

'*The* snake!' repeated the other. 'Is there then but one, and always one? Years have passed away since the time at which I looked upon the lake and the serpent beside it.'

'I have known it for years,' rejoined the wizard; 'and there has been a snake there always. In my country they would say it guarded something—a treasure—a mine of gold perhaps, or of precious stones.'

Sebastian smiled. 'In other countries,' said he, 'it would be accused of guarding something more valuable—a pretty maiden, for instance.'

'Even that may be,' replied the wizard. 'Master, I am glad to see you; I wish you had come sooner; but—I must repeat it—I never thought to behold you again among these mountains, nor in this island. Whither will you go?'

'I go to Belmont as the attendant of Fairfax. I have a part to act, and want your help and testimony; but you must first tell me about this meeting, and who were at it, and what is intended to be done by this Combah. I must have him secured: the insurrection must be suppressed before I can attempt anything for myself. I should have gone at once to the governor; but I must have betrayed my own purpose; and that betrayal would have defeated me perhaps for ever. You will have martial law: many will be apprehended, and some one will impeach you, Hamel, if you have done aught amiss. Do you think these creatures, who ran away at the mention of the Maroons, will hesitate to sacrifice you, if by so doing they can themselves escape from the penalty of rebellion or conspiracy?'

'I have done nothing that they know of,' replied the Obeah man. 'They will lie no doubt, if they are taken, and tell of one another to get clear themselves. But you shall know all tomorrow; give me a night to think of it; and be assured there shall be no more meetings. I have influence with all who can do harm—influence enough to make them give up their dearest hopes: these they shall resign. I must have an eye on master Roland too.—But here, sir, we are arrived at my mountain grounds, and my cave—the cave with which you are acquainted; and yonder sits a figure by the side of the lagoon before it.'

'The blind man,' said the other; 'is it not? Yet he sees us, and sees his way into the cave too without stepping into the water. Your presence, Hamel, has already cured him of his affliction.'

'I shall know him before long,' replied the Obeah man; ' who and what he is. Your gun is loaded, master; but stay! use it not—is it some treachery?—I have heard often that such a figure has been seen by the lagoon; and many Negroes have reported there is a duppie haunts the rocks and even the cave itself; yet strange to say, (if such a spirit does frequent the spot) I never met with him before. I that have made the cave my own, as I may say, have looked in vain for the goblin which others cannot fail to espy in my

absence. They say it is myself—my own duppie. Let us take a circuit, sir, to the other side of the lagoon, and look into the cave from
a distance; I have a glass; there are no means of concealment
where the figure entered, and you can keep your musket ready in
case of any attempt at violence.'

'Nay, Hamel,' said Sebastian, taking the Obeah man's gun, 'give
me your arms rather. Mine is a Spanish piece. I took it from the
robbers in the canoe, and it was wet.'

'Trust not to mine,' rejoined the other; 'it is uncertain. Stay,
draw your charge—I have fresh ammunition: here is a horn half
filled with powder, and I have bullets or small shot, which you
please. Let us ensure every chance in our favour: we know not
whom we have to encounter.'

The Spanish piece was unloaded, and Hamel drew from under
his frock the cow's horn tipped with brass, which had been used
in the cellar; undertaking to recharge the gun, while Sebastian,
with the other musket and the spyglass, stole softly among the
bushes to the farther side of the lake; and lying down on the
grass, began to reconnoitre the mouth of the cave, not a little surprised that Hamel should profess his ignorance respecting this
mysterious personage, who had the reputation of haunting the
spot where the Obeah man was accustomed to pass so many of
his hours.

'A most strange and unaccountable creature is this Hamel,'
thought he; 'yet I believe he would not harm me:—but what is
this? Neither a blind man nor a duppie, nor a black man, nor—
what in the name of fortune is it that I see?' The mouth of the cave
opened full upon the little lagoon before it, which reflected its
vaulty cove, and the mass of foliage and flowers that hung from the
rock above it and screened its interior from the glare of the sun.
There were two benches within it, one of which was altogether vacant, but on the other a figure seemed to repose, a youthful figure,
neither Negro nor Mulatto, but a white boy.

'Who can this be?' said he to Hamel, who had crept close to
him. 'Take the glass and examine. This is not your duppie, whatever the other may have been: this is a buckra young gentleman.'

'It is a buckra girl, sir, or I am much mistaken.'

'A girl, Hamel!' said the other; 'and for what purpose does she come here?'

'That you may ask her, if she is a girl; but she has the garments of a man—of a boy at least—has she not?'

'And what has become of the blind Negro? Can you discover him?' said Sebastian. 'Or has he converted his clumsy and decrepid figure into that which looks so amiable?'

'The figure sleeps sound,' replied the conjuror. 'I can see how deep she breathes; for it is certainly a woman: the outline of her bosom too is evident, if I mistake not. But where the man has vanished, you see my skill cannot yet discover. I shall begin to think it is a duppie.'

'Or your genius, Hamel,' said the other,—'good or bad; who takes his turn in your absence; for it seems it is invisible while you are here. There is something unaccountable in it; but it must be unsubstantial, or whither is it gone? Put up the glass, and let us walk towards the cave. We can go silently and softly enough to avoid disturbing the sleeping figure, if it sleeps in reality; or to discover if the sleep be feigned, or if it be a mere change of character. There can be no deception in that figure, I should think, which can forebode us any harm: youth is sincere, at least.'

'I have no fear, master,' said the Obeah man. 'Take you one side of the lagoon, and I will pass by the other; so that escape from one of us shall be impossible. The figure moves not.'

There was a pass by which the duppie, or blind Negro, or whatever he might be, could have retired from their sight; and this was by a sort of steps hollowed in the rock behind the foliage that hung from the crags above, to which the steps led. But Hamel dared not trust his friend, for such he seemed to consider him, with even this secret of his dwelling in the wilderness. Having been once stolen from his own country; having experienced all the bitterness, all the extremes of misery, which slavery inflicts on a free mind, he was too wary, too suspicious, to trifle for a moment with his own security, as far as his abode at least could ensure it to him. We have seen how he was provisioned; we shall hereafter see how he was fortified. After all, he probably had some inkling of the figure which had disappeared, however he chose by his observations to

encrease the mystery of that disappearance in the imagination of
Sebastian.

They measured their steps so accurately, the Obeah man and
the Mulatto, that they arrived at the mouth of the cave together,
without having made noise sufficient to have alarmed the most
vigilant dragon that ever figured in romance, had he been here
guarding golden fleece, or golden apples, or maiden with golden
locks. The figure they beheld in the cave had no gold about it; and
as there was no dragon to alarm, we may proceed at once to give
some account of the sleeper.

CHAPTER 17.

You do impeach your modesty too much
To leave the city, and commit yourself
Into the hands of one that loves you not;
To trust the opportunity of night,
And the ill counsel of a desert place,
With the rich worth of your virginity.
                    MIDSUMMER NIGHT'S DREAM.

THE figure which lay before the admiring eyes of the Obeah man
and his brown-faced companion was really in a deep sleep. Her
skin (for it certainly was a woman) was nearly as white as that of
any European, of a clear and animated hue, the roses glowing
upon her cheeks—a blush no doubt occasioned by her sleep; and
her forehead was shaded by some of the prettiest brown curls that
ever graced the brows of a Quadroon damsel. Her eyes were
closed of course; but the long black eyelashes which like
portcullises guarded those portals of her heart, or mind, or genius,
or whatever it may hereafter appear to be, that the portals betrayed when they were open,—had been designed by nature with
such attention to symmetry, and to what we have learned from our
ancestors to consider beautiful, that even Hamel, with all his
mountain of arcana on his mind, could not look on them altogether unmoved, or insensible to the charms which the younger
of the spectators contemplated with a more fervid, a more passionate feeling. Her eyebrows were also black as ebony, thin, and
arched with a precision that art can seldom imitate, at least on living subjects. Her lips were twice as rosy as her cheeks, like two
pieces of polished coral; and the *ensemble* of her face was certainly as engaging as anything that had ever fixed the attention of
the Obeah man on this side of the great Atlantic. The damsel was
dressed in male attire; videlicet, a blue jacket of woollen cloth,
with a waistcoat and trowsers of white jean, which with her shirt
were white as snow; a pink handkerchief, tied loosely round the
collar of the latter, was tucked through a button hole into her

117

bosom. Her head was bare; but a straw hat which she had worn lay on the ground beside her, appearing to have fallen off in her sleep. Her feet were also naked, as if she had shaken off a pair of shoes with which they had been encumbered; but they were as round, as neat, and as exquisitely modelled, as any that Sebastian had ever yet beheld. So also were her hands, in one of the fingers of which she wore a ring by which that brown gentleman would have recognised her, if he had not already divined from her physiognomy that she was Michal, the pretty soubrette from the mansion of his late host Mr Guthrie. This discovery he kept however to himself; and when the Obeah man said with a sigh, 'What a pretty creature!'—(it was said in a whisper)—Sebastian replied only by another, a longer, deeper-drawn, and rather impassioned sigh, and a slight inclination of his head, as if to express his perfect accordance with the remark of the conjuror. He was not so old as Hamel by at least thirty years.

'What can be her business here?' thought the younger of the spectators. 'And what a poor disguise! Or rather, why has she assumed this masculine attire, for it is no disguise?'

'There is love at the bottom of all this,' said the Obeah man in a whisper. 'These Mulattos and Mestees think of nothing else, from the hour in which they are weaned from their mothers' breast until time has wasted away every trace of their beauty; and then they console themselves with the recollection of all the transports they have enjoyed.'

'From the mother's breast?'

'Yes, master, yes: their mothers breathe it into their very souls with every kiss which they impart to them, and fill their heads with the anticipation of the charms they will possess, and the conquests they will make, and the riches they will acquire, by their connexion with some great buckra planter. Yet avarice is not their ruling passion, even in old age. My life upon it, this young girl is in love with some white gentleman—for they always aspire: ambition goes at least hand in hand with love—ambition of distinction, of being above the pity at least of all their friends and rivals, if not of being an object of their envy. How sound she sleeps, poor child!— Shall I leave her to your care?'

Sebastian could not help smiling at this courtesy of his companion; for as such he considered it. 'I do not know,' he replied, 'which of us should take charge of her, or whether either of us should meddle with her.'

'Let me go,' rejoined the Obeah man: 'I will prepare you some food. Yonder is my house; you must be hungry and exhausted; I will make you a fire here before the cave, and get you some cocoes, and send down if you please to the great house for a bottle of wine.'

'Not for the world—not for the world,' said the other. 'Bring me some of your own mess—your pepper-pot, so there be no rats in it, nor dog nor cat flesh; some cocoes or plantains, and some fruit. But what am I to think of the blind Negro? Is this duppie of yours to be a spy upon me?'

'You have a better one in your thoughts and recollections, sir,' said the wizard. 'I do not think you have anything to fear. If you should see this man, you may force him to tell who and what he is. Ghosts cannot harm you.'

'Well, begone; and let us see the result.'

The Obeah man took him at his word, and descended towards a Negro house at the distance of about half a mile. The brown man then stepped gently into the cave, and sat down on the vacant bench, taking care to make no noise that could disturb the sleeping beauty who occupied the other. He kept his eyes for some time on Hamel, until he saw him dive as it were into a plantain walk, a part of the estate to which these rocks and caves belonged; when he turned his attention again to the pretty girl, whose features he re-perused with no less admiration than he had conceived before, and with rather more scrutiny than he had felt at sufficient ease to employ in the presence of the wizard. 'What a sweet face!' said he to himself. 'Can the Eastern Houris surpass its loveliness—or even the beauties of Great Britain? And what a form! Praxiteles himself could not have desired a more enchanting model. How beautiful is the blush upon her cheek! It is almost as deep as the rose-colour of her silk handkerchief. And her skin—how smooth and delicate, and how fair!—Who would suppose her to be the descendant of an African black—of one whose skin was as sooty as that of Hamel? And where are the thick lips, and the flat nose, and the woolly hair? Not even Joanna herself could surpass her in any of the externals of beauty. Whither does she wander alone, unguarded, unattended? What has she done, and what does she design?'—These ideas were succeeded by many others for which the reader will easily give credit to the Mulatto, if he will fancy himself in a similar situation. Youth, beauty, and clean linen,—according to Archer's Catechism,—are the incentives to love; and the beauties of the tropics are not more inexorable than those of the temperate zone. Here were the lips (like Romeo's two blushing pilgrims) which he had already had the impudence to salute, and for so doing had been already reproved. He was tempted however to repeat the offence; for, as he drew near, and leaned over the back of the bench on which the sleeper lay, to take a more perfect view of her, there was something so attractive in her person and condition, 'so redolent of youth' and love, something so sweet and fragrant in the breath which he inhaled as he hung over her, something so fascinating in the smile which seemed to play about her mouth,—that he forgot, absolutely forgot, the colour of his skin, and the aversion which it would excite in the eyes of the beauty, if he should rouse her, and she should detect him presuming upon her defenceless situation. He hesitated some time before he could muster sufficient hardihood; but at last the charms of the pretty creature persuaded him that he was in some sort excusable, when, kneeling by her side, he imprinted a kiss on her rosy lips. She awoke not with the first, nor yet with the second; but the third—(we may suppose that the adventurer had become bolder)—disturbed her repose. She opened her black eyes very gently; and seeing the brown man on his knee by her side, sprang rapidly on her feet, exclaiming—'Oh heaven! Sebastian, is it you?—I was dreaming of you.'

'Of me?' replied the Mulatto, somewhat ashamed of himself. 'Why of me?'

His looks expressed some contrition for the liberty he had taken, which the girl heeded not, merely remarking that she had watched the stars all night, and had been overwhelmed at length with sleep. 'But where have you been?' she continued. 'Not, I hope, with those wretches in the canoe: they are villains and robbers.'

''Twas I that told you so, my pretty maid. Did I not warn you, and bid you warn old Guthrie, of their intentions? Did I not send Drybones Nimrod to you again? You are still dreaming.'

'Yes, yes,' replied she, recollecting herself; 'I remember—forgive me, Sebastian. That Nimrod told me I might find you here; or at least that I should find a man, a black man, who would or could tell me much about you.'

'About me, Michal?' rejoined Sebastian. 'What has made you curious about me? Did your mistress bid you make inquiries?'

'My mistress,' said the Quadroon, rather interrupting him, 'is somewhat anxious respecting you, and is not displeased that I expressed a desire to learn some farther news of you. I had her permission to go to Belmont.'

'But why in this disguise?'

'Ah, sir,' replied the Quadroon, 'do not you be too curious. As I have already told you, I watched the stars last night in this cave: my business was to find you; or to find the man who dwells here. I came alone, unprotected; yet my disguise was of no avail, at least with you: it might have served me with others.'

'Well, Michal,' said the Mulatto in return; 'whom saw you here?'

'I have seen no one distinctly; I sat here all night, and thought once or twice that I heard footsteps, and fancied too that I could see a figure walking beside the lagoon; but I was mistaken; for when I went out to look, I could discover no one.'

'Still,' interrupted Sebastian, 'you have at length found him you sought. Here am I, the unworthy person for whom it seems you have undertaken this pilgrimage: what are your wishes now? Is it some message, or some token, from your mistress—a letter?'

'No, indeed,' replied the soubrette, with a smile which relieved the little confusion under which she appeared to labour; 'my mistress had no message for the captain of the canoe: it was not her fancy that led me to seek you.'

'Whose fancy was it then?' rejoined Sebastian. 'There can be no guile, no treachery, in that bosom: my enemy could not employ such an instrument to injure me; he could not, I am sure, prevail on such an emissary to attempt even to deceive me.'

'Your enemies,' said the Quadroon, 'if you have any, must be the companions of your canoe; for they are bad men. Alas! I know not how to tell you—I have hardly told to myself—why I have sought you; but I believe it was because I feared some mischief might happen to you. There was a mystery in what you said to me before you joined your comrades; and you seemed unhappy and cast down. I was standing on the rocks by the sea side, straining my eyes in search of your canoe, when I was accosted by him you call Nimrod, whom I knew again. He begged me to take your message to my master, to whom I told that your canoe was again broken, and its crew gone a shore; and that Nimrod was to set off for Spanish Town, to put the governor on his guard, for the slaves were going to rise. To own the truth, I feared they had killed you, and thrown you into the sea.'

'And it was to satisfy yourself on this point that you came to the watchman's cave for news of me? Nimrod was right;—but your mistress had surely some concern in your enterprise?'

'Not the least, I assure you,' replied Michal. 'I was perhaps impertinent and foolish to come here; but I had—you will despise me for owning it—a wish to serve you.'

'How, Michal?'

The eyes of the Quadroon were cast down; but the Mulatto had taken her hand, as if to encourage her. 'I have deserved nothing of you,' said he: 'what service could you render me? I own with pleasure the gratification which my vanity derives from such a confession on the part of a pretty girl; but I am at a loss to imagine from your own account in what way I could be benefited by your concern.'

'I am vain, and bold, and foolish,' said the soubrette, with a look of apprehension. 'I suppose it was my fate to come hither: I thought I might save you from the company of bad men—rebels, pirates; that I might prevail on you to renounce this terrible life, and caution you even against being too intimate with the man who dwells in yonder hut and in this cave; for he is suspected of being an Obeah man, and when Mr Fairfax comes home, he will be taken up and perhaps transported.'

'I am but too much indebted to you,' replied the Mulatto, considerably flattered with the benevolent expressions of the soubrette: 'I know not how to thank you.'

'I shall be sufficiently thanked,' said Michal, 'if you will assure me that you are not a pirate nor a buccaneer. But own to me fairly who and what you are. For my own part, I feel assured that you are a good and honest man, and not a robber.'

'What if I *were*, Michal?' rejoined the Mulatto. 'Suppose I were really in league with him whom you call an Obeah man; that I were the captain of the crew I brought to your master's house; that I came here to aid rebellion; but finding myself suspected and likely to be betrayed, that I should summon my companions to my assistance, and make at least a prize of you? The buccaneers were as fond of women as of cash; nay, they loved money only as the means of pleasure; and were I to search the island—the Carribbean sea, Michal—where should I find a more glorious prize than the pretty girl that stands beside me?'

The Quadroon smiled. 'If it were so,' she replied, 'I should be deeply and sincerely grieved; but you are jesting, and I feel convinced you are an honest man.'

The Mulatto saw but too clearly that the pretty damsel had taken a fancy to his dingy face; and had he been at all the character which he had just represented, he would no doubt have taken advantage of the disposition she had betrayed towards him. Sebastian was but a young man—the Quadroon was young and beautiful; and it requires perhaps considerable fortitude to steer clear of such temptations as these, which Fortune, or the Enemy of Mankind, lays in the way of men of honour, to lead them into mischief. He could not but reflect on the danger of the charming girl, unsuspicious, confiding, generous, and open-hearted; yet he could not approve of her derogating from the pride of her sex in descending, although in his own favour, to one beneath her in the scale of colour; nor could he entertain or endure the thought of her exposing herself to a similar peril in any future case. This feeling has effected the ruin of many a pretty creature, and the disgrace of many a worthy man, at the very moment in which they both perhaps entertained some of the noblest sentiments of which the human mind is capable. As there is allowed to be but one step from the throne to the scaffold, so there is in matters of the heart but one step from heroism to the meanest capitulation.

'Michal,' said Sebastian, 'you deserve the love of any man, be his colour what it may; but you should look upwards, as the rest of your sex do.'

'To what?' replied the damsel: 'to what? To the love of some white gentleman who will be pleased with me and proud of me, till he goes home to England to spend his fortune; and then I shall hear no more of him! If I should ever love such a person, I should be most unhappy.'

'And you would rather love some one of your own caste, with whom you could hope to spend the whole of your life? Some one fairer than me, provided he would be sincere, faithful, and affectionate.'

'You mock me, Sebastian,' answered the soubrette; 'but if you will not tell me who you are, I shall console myself that I have seen you in safety. Perhaps you will come back again to Mr Guthrie's, if you were sincere in your advice about guarding us against the Negroes.'

'I dare not, Michal; but you may stay with me to-day. Are you a slave?'

'I am, sir,' replied the girl; 'but for my freedom—my master has provided for that in his will; and my mistress, my young mistress, would make me free to-morrow, if I were to ask her.'

'Why do you not?'

'I have no want of freedom: what should I do with myself? A time may come when such a change may make me happier; but now it would be useless to me.'

'Stay with me yet to-day, my pretty mistress. There is something in your voice and speech, and your manner, and your kind looks, that charms my heart, and cheats me out of the recollections that oppress me. Yonder comes Hamel with provisions: I have been *your* guest—you shall now be mine: the old man shall wait upon us—or we will wait on one another—or I will wait on you, Michal. Be seated: it is a happiness to be with you, near you—to look on you; and it would be a happiness to love you.'

The Quadroon girl looked wistfully in his face, as she seated herself again on the bench; and as the youth returned her placid

and affectionate smile, he construed the expression of her features to mean, as a corollary to his last words—'it would be also a
happiness to myself.' 'I must not love you,' thought he; 'I must not
adore you; but I must and will like you—aye, and love you too, if I
cannot help it:—but I will not wrong you, nor deceive you, nor
take any advantage of you—no, by my hopes of happiness!' He
went from the cave, to meet the Obeah man on the bank of the lagoon; but not before he had tenderly pressed the fair hand of the
black-eyed damsel in his own—in both his own—and then—
(God of Negro love!)—with his lips.

CHAPTER 18.

Look thou be true; do not give dalliance
Too much the rein; the strongest oaths are straw
To the fire in the blood: be more abstemious;
Or else, good night your vow.

TEMPEST.

THE Obeah man arrived on the instant with his provisions in a basket; and having set them down in the cave, began to collect a few sticks for a fire. There was a smile upon his features, by which Michal suspected that he had been a witness to the gallantry of Sebastian. He made her however a profound bow, and congratulated her, with the politeness of a courtier, on the happy sleep she had enjoyed. The fire was soon kindled by some hocus-pocus of mine host, and the plantains and cocoes put beside it to roast; while Sebastian drew from the basket two or three pine apples, and a wooden bottle of fermented sugar-cane juice; and the Quadroon, not to be idle, went with a calabash to fetch some water from a little fountain which gushed from the rock at the distance of a few yards, and trickled into the lagoon. While she was gone, the Obeah man found an opportunity to tell Sebastian that there had been an alarm at the great house respecting the expected appearance of Mr Fairfax, who was to come to take possession of his estate, and drive out the trustee attorney, with the help of a brown man and the crew of a privateer ship which had been wrecked in the storm. 'This story,' added he, 'must come from Mr Guthrie's Negroes.'

'Aye, aye, Hamel, a story loses little in the telling,' said Sebastian; 'but no matter.'

The Quadroon observed them whispering, and with some mortification; for she liked not the looks any more than the character she had heard of the Obeah man; and she would have been as well content, if on this account alone, to have dispensed with his company, although she would thus have been condemned to a *tête-à-tête,* and in the wilderness, with the mysterious personage

whose manners, and language, and figure, and brown face, had so
bewitched, or it may be bewildered, her reason.

Hamel had been liberal in producing his provisions, and prepared with much expedition a substantial mess after the Negro
fashion, consisting of all sorts of good things—(cats, rats, dogs,
and lizards excepted)—mixed up with ochros and peppers. He
did not however presume to eat with the youth and his fair companion, but waited on them as occasion required or when he was
wanted, at other times retiring out of their sight from the cave,
though not out of hearing; and when they had satisfied their appe-
tites, he cleared all away, and retired for the present, as he said, to
take a little sleep, of which he stood so much in need.

Michal and the brown man were thus left alone a second time,
seated as before, side by side, on one of the rude benches, from
whence they could see through the entrance of the little cave over
the distant woods and plains below—the first silent, and un-
tenanted except by wild animals, the latter enlivened with the in-
dustry of busy Negroes, whose songs, as they toiled, were
sometimes wafted upon the wind, in an indistinct murmur, to
their attentive ears. Not that their ears or their attention were directed to catch these particular sounds: a mutual feeling occupied
them occasionally—an idea of being overheard themselves, if not
overlooked; and they listened from time to time to catch any
sounds that might chance to be distinguishable or audible. The
youth listened for the duppie; the damsel listened oftener to the
beating of her own heart, and ran over in her mind, as she listened,
all the possible chances of spending her life—the heyday of it, her
halcyon years—in the company and society of this (as she thought
him) enterprising Mulatto. Old age she thought not of; or if the
idea obtruded itself among the bright prospects which her fancy
conjured up, it was exiled into the background, the remotest distance, where, like deformed mountains in the horizon of a picture, it was so disguised by the aerial hue with which her fancy
clothed it, that it looked still lovely, as flattering as any other portion of the scene. She had easily persuaded herself that Sebastian
at least liked her—loved her. How kindly he had spoken to her—
how affectionately! She thought too of his kisses; and though he

had presumed even on the second occasion, that is, when he awakened her in the cave, still he had treated her with respect and tenderness, and last of all he had kissed even her hand. Who knows not that even yet many of the marriages, if they may be called marriages, of people of colour in Jamaica and the other islands are attended, like those of the patriarchs of old, with little or no ceremony?—There is no intervention, in those cases, of priest or lawyer; no vows, oaths, protestations, of love and obedience; no mention of mysteries, and no invocation of any god or gods. My countrymen will treat with scorn the idea of such being marriages, as the parties do not swear upon the Bible, or at the altar, to keep to one another for life—an oath too often broken among themselves; but they have long sufficed for the society to which they were adapted by nature, and in many, if not in most, cases are considered as binding, and are as *religiously* abided by, as the union of the most devout and virtuous people of Europe.

> 'Love, light as air, at sight of human ties
> Spreads his light wings, and in a moment flies.'

Here are no ties but those of love, mutual regard, and a conscientious feeling of the propriety, if not of the necessity, of treating each other after the Christian recommendation—as each would in turn wish to be treated. The consequence of this facility, as it would be called in England, is that young women are no sooner marriageable than they are married—at that season of life too, when heart and soul are the only gifts desired or offered, and nature is sole mistress; though, as it is usual with her elsewhere, she practises a little coquetry to enhance the value of those gifts, and to increase the sum of happiness at which her votaries arrive. Perhaps an old maid was never heard of in this class of society, any more than among the Turks and Persians. ·

> 'Here love his golden shafts employs, here lights
> His constant lamp, and waves his purple wings—
> Reigns here, and revels.'

This state of things being premised for the advantage of the reader, who will excuse the digression, we must return to the pretty Quadroon, whom we left counting the beats of her own heart, with her mind running upon love, anxious yet fearful to hear some declaration from her companion that would enable herself, though by a look only, by a sigh, by silence even, to assure Sebastian that such avowal was most agreeable to her—that she heard it with pleasure, with gratitude. It never occurred to her till this moment, that he might have a wife already; although, from the kind of liberty he had presumed to take with her, she could not but expect that now, when they were alone together—(and she was sensible that he had taken a fancy to her)—this mark of it might be repeated. She was calculating in her mind how to receive or permit such a liberty, or whether she should not play the coquette—what she should say or do; and while her mind was agitated with these contending influences, her bosom rose and fell, and her rosy lips gave vent to many a sigh that seemed to come laden with grief from her heart, and the colour on her cheeks faded and flushed alternately, like gleams of sunshine chased at intervals by flitting clouds from a lovely landscape, and returning after every little absence with renovated splendour and beauty. She leaned on the back of the rude bench, resting her head on one of her hands, whose taper, ivory-looking fingers were buried (some of them at least) in her brown curls; and whenever the eyes of Sebastian were turned towards them, they encountered hers, dark, full, glowing with the kind feelings of her heart, and glistening—not with tears; for why should she weep?—Yet what else but tears could render them so brilliant, so fascinating? Then every glance was the harbinger of a smile, tender and delicate, replete with grace and affection, yet moderated with an expression of timidity, if not of bashfulness. 'Heaven and earth!' thought the Mulatto, as he gazed upon her. 'An angel! or a devil come to tempt me from my duty, from my fidelity!—Can such things be? She is more beautiful at every glimpse, at every glance that my eyes dare take of her. She that discouraged me, and rebuked my cavalier impertinence, yet now fears—heeds me not.' 'What are you thinking of, Michal?' said he at length, aloud.

'I am thinking,' she replied, with a blush which preceded her speech, 'I am thinking of this same strange man, this Hamel, who is supposed to deal in spells and incantations, to hold conversations with spirits, and to bring about anything he chooses to undertake by invisible means. Know you not that this very cave in which we sit is said to be enchanted?'

'I could almost believe so,' replied Sebastian, in a subdued tone of voice, as if indifferent whether Michal should fully understand him or not; 'I feel I am myself enchanted; but it cannot be by Hamel, nor by his agency: if I am enchanted, it is by yourself.'

The poor girl's face and throat were suffused with crimson. 'By me? Sebastian—by *me?*' She started from her position. 'No, no—not by me; I have no such power; and if I had, I would not use it against you. Do not think so of me. No, Sebastian, I wish to see you happy; and if it depended on me, your days should be as happy—'

'Sit down again, Michal,' said the Mulatto, interrupting her, and taking her hand, to which he felt it indispensable that he should communicate some gentle pressure, in return for her courteous assurance: 'sit down, Michal. I have no right to expect anything from you—no claim to your affection in any way. Would you lower yourself by attaching your destiny to that of a man darker than yourself?'

'If you say this,' answered Michal, 'to mean you do not like me, I shall hear it with patience, and bear it; but your skin is no objection to me. Perhaps you have been married in England.'

He shook his head *negatively*.

'You have no wife?'

'None.'

'Well, Sebastian, I ask not to be your wife; but if you do not like me, why did you kiss me?'

'I *do* like you—I cannot help myself; but, Michal, I am wrong; I have no business to love you; I am engaged to another.'

'And who is that other?' said the soubrette. 'She may be prettier than I am; but will she love you faithfully? Will she be your slave? My mistress will make me free: let me be near you, wait upon you, work for you; but do not turn me away from you—But I know not what I say.'

'Ah, Michal,' replied the Mulatto, 'you speak as you look—only what is amiable and affectionate—' (the poor girl's tears chased one another down her cheeks;) 'but why do you weep?'

'I cannot help it—let me go home to my mother—I was foolish to come here. Let me go, Sebastian; do not, do not—pray do not touch me again, if you are engaged to another wife:—do not make sport of me.'

It would certainly have seemed more honourable, and perhaps more humane, to have undeceived the pretty soubrette at once as to the obstacles which prevented her becoming even the creole wife of Sebastian; but he felt a considerable difficulty, as well as delicacy, in trusting her with his secret; and there was besides something of vanity (however hatefully attached to our nature) so gratifying in having made a conquest of such a lovely woman, that he had hardly resolution sufficient to renounce at once the pleasure he derived from it, at the same time that he was making vows internally to take no advantage of her. Many a pretty girl's cheek has faded from the same cause; and there are ladies too of fine feelings, who have trifled in a similar way with men of sense, until both parties have been rendered very miserable, very unfortunate, and very wicked:—from playing the fool they have got to playing the devil, and ended perhaps by playing the fool again.

The Quadroon, not being familiar with her pockets, was some time finding a handkerchief to wipe away her tears; and Sebastian, but too delighted in assisting her, and sufficiently affected at the sight of her grief, produced his own for the purpose; yet he would rather have kissed away those precious drops which, though not quite so large as those of the tender-hearted Pantagruel, had power to melt a more obdurate heart than his own. Indeed it would seem that his heart was but too sensible, at least to the impression made by the many charms of the lovely soubrette; and it was in some measure owing to *her* resolution that he retained his self-possession, and adhered to his vow (if vow it were, as related in the last chapter) of refraining from attempting to take any advantage of her situation or of her predilection for himself. It is better to avoid a precipice altogether; and if to dance on the edge of one be a folly, how vain would it be for the dancer to have his eyes blinded, though by the hand of a pretty girl!

The tears were succeeded by smiles, and the smiles were followed again by tears; but the Mulatto imprinted one kiss only, a kiss of peace, on the forehead of the beauty who now checked herself, to make inquiries about his affianced wife. At last, overcome with a sense of his injustice in trifling with her for a moment, he told Michal that he was engaged to be married to her mistress.

CHAPTER 19.

Turn not away, I am no Æthiop;
No wanton Cressid, nor a changing Helen;
But rather one made wretched by thy loss.
What! turn'st thou still from me?

LONDON PRODIGAL.

HUMBLED and mortified, as the Quadroon could not but feel, yet she was sensible that there was something more than common in the behaviour of her gallant, something more honourable, after all, than she could have expected from any one else. He liked her, if he did not love her, it was sufficiently evident; as evident as it was to him that he was beloved by her. Yet he had put her on her guard; he had owned he was engaged to be married. Another, if he had been white, would have taken advantage of her affection or passion at once, and kept his secret to himself, at least until he chose to get rid of her. Such had been the reflection of the pretty Michal, even while the caresses of Mr Sebastian convinced her that her person, which she imagined was all her fortune, was sufficiently to his taste. She might have thought his general plea of an engagement only an excuse to avoid a serious connection with her; but when he told her that he was affianced to her mistress, she turned aside from him with a smile of incredulity and a feeling of displeasure, thinking of course that he was making a jest of her and her tears. These she dried forthwith, as she arose from the seat, where she left her companion no less mortified than she was, and regretting that the poor soubrette should have reason to think less favourably of him than she had been disposed to do; not a little confused too as to the effect which he saw he had produced by the disclosure of his engagement.

'Well, Mr Sebastian,' said the damsel, 'I shall return back to my mother, and leave you to be happy with her you love, whoever she is. Farewell; you will make a brave husband, for you are as secret and as mysterious as if you were the chief among the rebellious Negroes.'

'Stay, Michal,' replied the Mulatto, 'till the heat of the sun is past: I have a message for your master.'

'For my master?'

'Yes, and another for your mistress;—and I would not part with you in any unkindness. Michal, it is but too plain—But I will not think of what is past, except to cheer my heart with the conviction that you have not despised my dingy complexion. I thank heaven and your own goodness, that I have not thought to abuse your generous, your disinterested kindness towards an unknown unfriended stranger, such as I appear to be: but, Michal, I am not altogether what I seem; and if I delay gratifying your commendable curiosity for a time, it is not that I am ungrateful to you, insensible to your worth and your excellence'—(the Quadroon heaved one more sigh)—'but yourself might be made unhappy, at least uneasy, by the knowledge of the circumstances in which I am involved; and I must not stir till my trusty Nimrod shall have had time to apprise the governor and the council of the danger which threatens the island. I call him trusty, for it is his interest to be true to me, and he can gain nothing by treachery. You little think, Michal, what a tragedy was to have been performed to-night—no less than the massacre of your master, and the violation of his daughter.'

'What!' said the soubrette, turning pale with apprehension, 'how much of your language should I believe? Can it be?'

'Aye—and his house to have been burned: this very Hamel owned it to me, though he will not tell me who are the conspirators.'

'And will it be attempted?

'No: he has promised to prevent it.'

'And why?' said the Quadroon.

'For my sake, Michal. Your master has been already put on his guard—'

'Yes,' answered she, interrupting him: 'but he is not half watchful enough. You may tell me, Mr Sebastian, what you please about it; I will not betray your confidence.'

'I can tell you no more at present,' replied he; 'for see—yonder comes Hamel again, is it not, from the woods? No, it is the strange blind man, who vanished so unaccountably when I arrived here.'

'Vanished!' said the soubrette. 'This is then the black man of whom you spoke to me before. What an ugly monster! And why does he wear that black shirt? I thought at first it was his skin. But he walks as if he were blind—does he not?—so carefully; and although he does not feel his way actually, he seems to measure every step. No wonder the place is bewitched: if such a creature as this is once seen gliding about in this fashion, there cannot long be wanting a story of a duppie. No wonder Hamel has the reputation of dealing with the evil spirit. But see, Sebastian, he comes towards us!'

'Hush!' replied the Mulatto in a whisper, laying his finger on the Quadroon's lips: 'be silent—come farther into the cave; and let us watch him. If he comes near enough, I'll seize him, and find out who he is.'

'Oh, touch him not, Sebastian!' said the timid girl. 'If he is a spirit, he can strike you dead perhaps.'

'He is no spirit, Michal, but a man like me. I can hear the tramp of his feet as he walks along the shore of the lagoon: who ever told of a duppie whose step was audible? Nay, Hamel counselled me to make him tell his purpose, if I should see him again.'

'Hamel is a traitor,' replied the Quadroon in the same whisper: 'trust him not.'

'Hush! hush! he draws near!'

The black man came with a steady pace towards the cave, having been some minutes coasting more than half of the little lagoon; during which the Mulatto and his companion had plenty of time to examine his person and attire. He seemed as old as Hamel, and not unlike him in size and features; but he was clothed in a black frock (fastened with a thin leathern belt, similar to that worn by the Obeah man) which descended to his knees: the rest of his person was naked, as he had nothing on his head, hands, legs, or feet. He stopped at the distance of a few paces from the cave, and raised his head as if he would have looked to the mouth of it; but it seemed as if his eyes were covered with cataracts: and though Sebastian stepped out of the cave towards him, he appeared to be insensible of his approach, until the Mulatto demanded who he was; when he sprang or rather darted into the lagoon, and disappeared. The Quadroon, seeing this, ran also out of the cave, to watch his rising again from the water. There was neither bush nor rock upon its margin, and the lagoon itself was not forty yards across; but although the water continued agitated for a considerable time, while its buoyant circles rolled and sparkled upon the silvery shore, the black man did not rise again.

'These Negroes,' said Sebastian, looking around with a most vigilant eye, 'are almost amphibious, as I have known of old; but he will not surely drown himself to escape our curiosity. I have heard that the pearl fishers can sink for half an hour; but this man, who seemed almost decrepid as he walked, can scarce have practised diving to this extent. But we will give him time.'

'No!' said the Quadroon with a sigh; 'he will come no more.'

'You do not think he is drowned, Michal?'

'I know not what to think. If he were a spirit, such as I have read of, fire, air, the earth, or the water, are alike to him: he can dissolve himself into the elements. No, Sebastian, he resembles yourself—he is a mystery; and when he seemed to be in your very possession, when you thought him yours, he vanished from your sight, as you will from mine.'

'Never!' said he in return.

'Why should you then entertain me with such idle tales as those you tell me? Yes, yes, Sebastian; you are not what you seem: you say so, and I believe you:—but I *am* what I seem—a weak, vain, silly child, who had the presumption to wish to be of value in your eyes.'

The Mulatto laid his hand on her shoulder, leaned on it, and as she turned up her face as if to look on him, whispered in her ear—'You cannot keep a secret: what would you think of me were I to tell you mine? What would others think of me? If I were but what I seem, Michal, I had been yours—yours only—too proud, too happy to be yours. I value you not the less—but I was not born to make you happy, and I will not make you wretched: you would despise and hate me; and that at least I will not deserve. Come what will come, what must come, you shall think of Sebastian, if you ever recall him to your memory, as of one who did nothing to forfeit the kind thoughts you entertained of him.

'Tis strange this animal appears not: he must be surely drowned; and what is become of our host Hamel? Let us try to climb this rock, and see, if it be possible, something more of this enchanted spot, as you call it. Perhaps from an eminence we may descry the duppie beneath the water; for it seems as clear as crystal, though it is so deep and blue. But how shall we ascend? You cannot clamber by the trees: there is a path—there was at least when I was young.'

'There *is* certainly,' said Michal: 'for I have heard my mistress speak of it, and of another little lagoon, less than this, in the midst of some rocks.'

'And a yellow snake beside the lagoon?' said Sebastian.

'Aye, indeed,' replied the damsel, looking at him with surprise; 'there was a yellow snake in the story.'

'Which your mistress struck with a stone.'

The Quadroon was all amazement again, and stopped to reconnoitre her companion, as if to assure herself he was only what he seemed. She ran him over with her black eyes, while the smile of which he could not divest himself was reflected on her pretty face; and then said laughing—'And you are engaged to my mistress—a brown man marry a rich buckra's white daughter, one who is sought after by all the young gentlemen in the country!'

'Whether I shall marry her, Michal,' replied he, 'must in some measure depend on you.'

'On me?' cried the damsel, laughing aloud. 'I shall do well to recommend you who have disdained me: although I must not complain, as I am renounced for a white lady of the first distinction. But if you are already engaged to be married to her, what need have you of my services?'

'Michal, you will take a message for me, for letter I cannot write. I know my letters, siren,'—continued he, after a pause, during which he observed her smiling again; 'but we have nothing to write on, or to write with, in this desart, except it be on the water, or on this sand, or on those—'

'Those what, Sebastian?' said she, interrupting his speech as well as his gaze, which was fixed on her features.

'Those lips of yours, which I must kiss no more.'

'Ah no! no more, Sebastian, except you think your mistress and mine would like your kisses from my lips.'

'We must leave pleasantry, and you shall be the bearer of my message; but let us first return to the cave, and take some little rest. I have not slept for two nights. I found you sleeping, Michal: let me repose awhile on the same bench, and dream.'

'Not of me!' said the Quadroon.

'Well, of your mistress, who resembles you but too much—so much, that in spite of myself I would fain, as I said, write my message to her on your rosy lips.'

'No—rather write it and all your passion, on the water, or on the sands, that it may perish as soon as it is uttered, and nothing may remain to reproach you hereafter, when you shall have forgotten it.'

The Mulatto smiled, as they entered the cave. He laid himself on one of the benches, and soon fell asleep; while the Quadroon seated herself on a stone, and leaned against the rock at the entrance, her head resting on her fair hand, which was supported on her knee; and her dark eyes fixed intently on the object of her affection.

CHAPTER 20.

I might call him
A thing divine, for nothing natural
I ever saw so noble.

TEMPEST.

THE course of our narrative reverts now to the abode of Mr Guthrie and its inmates. We have seen how that gentleman had sallied from his chateau, to effect a plan or plans for its security; having commissioned his daughter to communicate his cause for apprehension to her mother, if possible without alarming her. But this was too difficult an undertaking for such a person as Joanna, already alarmed for herself. Mrs Guthrie was by this time up and dressed, in spite of the agitation she had endured the previous night; although the vigour she had now assumed seemed in a great measure the effect of despair. She listened, without betraying any visible emotion, to the account her daughter gave her of the canoe Negroes, and of Sebastian; and to the story of the hints which the latter had left with Michal about the intended attack on their house and premises. The White Fairy's tale was repeated also. But although the unhappy lady suppressed the exhibition of her feelings, the melancholy news did not the less afflict her.

'My poor Joanna!' she exclaimed at last: 'when will heaven be weary of persecuting us? And what mischief is there yet in store? Does not this come of preaching emancipation? I knew how it must affect the minds of all the Negroes—who knows it not? I have told Mr Roland so, and told him in vain:—would to God that the people in England, who interest themselves so much with our affairs, were but obliged to come here, and know what it is to expose their own lives and fortunes, while they are endangering ours. It would teach them a lesson of humanity at least, a science in which they seem to be almost ignorant, notwithstanding their professions.'

'Why, my dear mother,' replied Joanna, 'are you then so partial to Mr Roland? Every one says he is a most designing, a most

139

dangerous man. He preaches almost murder to the Negroes. There is Michal heard him, not a week ago, preaching in the mill-house at Belmont, telling the Negroes that God Almighty made all men free alike, and that it was the devil who enslaved them; and he bid them shake off the devil. He said the people of England were determined to make them free, if they would take up the cross and follow him; and if the people of Jamaica prevented them, if the work were not done, the Negroes were to do it them-selves; and that the bulk of their fellow-subjects would rejoice that it was done, however deplorable the consequences might be.'

'Good heaven!' exclaimed the elder lady: 'how horrible! I have no predilection for Mr Roland—I shudder when l think of him— I cannot talk of him: when I am dead, which I devoutly hope to be ere long, you will know, at least your father will—for I would not have *you* know, dear Joanna! what would afflict you almost beyond endurance—the cause, the sole cause, why I bear the visits here of that dreadful man. You think it is because he seeks to marry you. He is most anxious to do so, and in my opinion most unworthy; but he has acquired a power over me—how, I can never divulge while I live; and though I will die rather than recommend his suit, I dare not, cannot, discountenance it to his face.'

'What would become of me, if he were to marry me?' said the daughter. 'Would he still preach rebellion, and revolution, and emancipation?'

'Not one of them,' replied Mrs Guthrie. 'He has offered to preach the very reverse, and moreover to hold up his party to ridicule, to unmask those whom he does not hesitate to call igno-rant and fanatical hypocrites.'

'What a hypocrite must he be himself!' said Joanna with a sigh. 'Oh mother! cast him off; let *me* defy him, let me denounce him: I fear him not. And here is a person from Mr Fairfax—the cap-tain of the canoe which was driven on the rocks last night in our bay: he says he was with Oliver in France, though I remember him not.'

'What of him, what of him, Joanna?' said her mother. 'Horror of horrors!—so young and so unprincipled—can such things be? Can heaven permit them?'

'Oh mother, these are falsehoods: Fairfax is the soul of honour.
If you knew his real character, his kindness, his assurances to me!
I have seen much of him in England and in France, where he
travelled with us, and in Italy—always the same, frank, open,
generous—'

'I am lost in wonder,' replied Mrs Guthrie, 'when I think on
his having had the audacity to propose himself to you as a
husband.'

'Why, my dear mother? I have known him from my infancy, and
I have loved him as long. He was the companion of my childish
days and my childish thoughts. I thought, as he has promised, that
our union, if ever it shall take place—'

'Oh never, never!' said the elder lady.

'Well, mother, it never shall, against your consent; but *if* you
should consent, our union would heal every breach between our
families. It might help to soothe your own sorrows, to see me set-
tled with a brave and generous husband; and I should have nothing left to sigh for on this side of the grave.'

'Joanna!' said her mother, in a severe tone of voice, 'it is impossible: you never can be the wife of such a—'

'What mother, what?' cried the alarmed young lady.

'Such a monster. Do you remember the night of our fire,
Joanna? No—I recollect—you were from home.'

Joanna had put her handkerchief to her eyes; and her mother
could hear, though not without the deepest emotion, the convulsive sobs which seemed almost to burst her heart.

'Unhappy fortune!' she continued: 'but I must not excuse him.
No, Joanna! I have told you that your union is forbidden: it would
be horrible in the eyes of God and man.'

'Impossible!' cried the daughter. 'This is more of Roland's
treachery; some circumstance of his invention, as hideous as his
own character. Oh mother, you are imposed on.'

'Would to God I were: with what transport should I see you
give yourself to this young man, if he were unstained with
crimes—at least a crime which bars your union for ever, and renders his very love, though it were now as pure as that of angels, an
utter abomination.'

The grief of the elder lady became here as poignant as that of her daughter; but the consolations of the wretched were denied to her: the fountains of her tears were dried up; and hope had long ceased to present to her view any prospect of tranquillity but in the grave.

'Think not of Fairfax,' she said: 'he cannot make you happy. While you entertain an idea of ever becoming his wife, you only add to the pangs which rend the heart of your unhappy mother. But here comes your father. See, Joanna, what he has done, what measures he has taken for our safety. Let not our own Negroes know our danger, or only those to whom we are to confide our safety.'

CHAPTER 21.

Demand me nothing; what you
Know, you know.   OTHELLO.

MR Guthrie came into the piazza with the Negro whom
Sebastian had sent to give him an account of the canoe being
again stranded and broken—the identical Drybones, otherwise
called Nimrod, by whose assistance he had overpowered all who
had the temerity to contend against him, and finally to make his
escape, as he had felt bound to do, without involving them in any
immediate peril.

'You say your name is Nimrod—do you not?' said the planter as
he entered. 'Some paper, and a pen and ink, Joanna!'

'Yes, master, Nimrod Drybones is my name.'

'Where is your pass?'

'I have no pass: master will please to give me one, if I must have
one to go to Spanish Town, to tell the governor what is going on.'

'And what *is* going on, Mr Drybones?'

'D—d Negroes going to rise, to fight for the white women and
cut the buckras' throats.'

'How do you know this?'

'Sebastian told me, and I know it besides too well: I know why I
came from Cuba. It was lucky for you, master, that there was a
storm last night, and the canoe was broke.'

'Why so, sir? I thought it unlucky, as my house was almost
blown away.'

'Lucky it was not quite blown away. Master must please to
know, we came to thieve a young lady—that young lady, that
pretty mistress—to make her queen of Jamaica, and wife to a man
named Combah.'

'The devil you did!'

'Master, please not to be angry. Sebastian is a brave man: he ran
the canoe upon the rocks, and flung the robbers into the sea.'

'The devil he did! Why he must be a devil himself. Where is he
gone?'

143

'He is gone to a Negro house or a cave among the rocks of Belmont, to see a man who is a watchman to Mr Fairfax; and Mr Fairfax is coming home tomorrow, to take possession of his estate, and turn out the attorney.'

'Where!' said the planter, pursing up his mouth: 'where is he coming from?'

'He is coming from England, or France, or some other country.'

'And he calculates on arriving tomorrow?'

'Sure to come tomorrow—Sebastian says so. He is coming to you, master, to help him to take his estate from the attorney.'

'Well done! I hope he will make himself at home. Send for Roland—to tell him this.'

'Mr Roland,' replied Joanna, 'is gone to windward: he went away yesterday.'

'What the devil!' said the planter, 'does he want to windward? If there is a riot in the country, I warrant him—'

'In it, master?' said Drybones inquisitively.

'Anywhere but in it,' replied Mr Guthrie: 'he is too fearful of his carcass. He is the general; he keeps out of the scuffle; he snuffs the battle from afar. He will be agreeably diverted, on his return, to find Mr Fairfax ready to receive him, and to hear him justify all the libels be has told of him. Poor Oliver! I should indeed like to see him. He was always a gallant fellow; though his cursed trustees have laid claim, as they say, in his behalf to all my aunt's Negroes—but I think they cannot make a good title.—Well, Drybones, how came you to get your neck out of the halter? Was it compunction, honour, gratitude, loyalty, or fear, that put it in to your wise head to let others fling themselves down the precipice, without taking hold of your hand in the leap?'

'Master, I don't know what is punction—I never had my neck in a halter.'

'Very like it, I think,' said the planter. 'But tell me how you got out of the scrape.'

'Master, I never had my neck in the halter.'

'Well, but what induced you to give up the scheme? You say you came from Cuba to steal my only child.'

'Yes, master, but I won't thieve her.'

'*I* must take care of that,' said Mr Guthrie; 'but I wish to know the motive which induced you to give up the project which you had in view of making her queen of Jamaica: tell me that.'

Drybones seemed to listen to the planter's question as if it were a demonstration of Euclid, giving it all his attention, and turning his head in every possible direction, as if to let the argument into his brain by his ears, eyes, nose, or mouth; but without effect: for although he elevated his chin towards the roof of the house, then dropped it on his bosom, looked sideways over his nose to the sky, to the floor, behind him on both sides, at both his hands—raised his eyebrows, and stuck his tongue half out of his squabby lips,— the question of the white man remained as it seemed wholly unintelligible, and he could only reply to it by the monosyllable— 'Sir?'

'Confusion!' said the buckra, in an under tone: 'it is all up with us. Mr Drybones is struck foolish, as stupid as a cunning mule, or an old monkey who knows nothing but what is of no use except to himself.' Then aloud—'You will not tell me, then, why you left your partners, and came here upon a different errand to that with which you set out.'

'Yes, master,' said the Negro, 'I come here twice; the first time to thieve Missy Guthrie, this time to say I won't thieve her.'

'Worse and worse! Did you help Sebastian to throw the Negroes into the sea?'

'Master, the Negroes got out of the sea again; there was nobody drowned: but Sebastian told them they would be hanged if they did not go home to their masters at Falmouth and Lucie.'

'Did you throw anybody in the sea?'

'Yes, master, I threw the blunderbuss and two machets.'

'Well, that is something: why did you do that?'

'Master, I was afraid, and my head lost itself; I did not know what I did.'

'Now, the devil confound you!' exclaimed the planter, losing his temper. 'Are you fit to go to Spanish Town to the governor? I'll have you put into the stocks forthwith, for an obstinate trickified ass.'

'Master, I'm no rickify hass.'

'I tell you you are a—you know what you are. There, go along. Somebody!' (Every Negro answers to that name; and two or three waiting boys came running in.) 'Take this good-for-nothing Negro: put him in the stocks in the hot-house.'

Drybones made a polite bow, and went off, guarded by the servants, only requesting some one else might go to Spanish Town to the governor, instead of him.

'Aye, aye. Where is Michal?' cried the planter, still in a passion. 'Let her set some of the women to talk with this ourang-outang, and see if they can make any sense of him. Drybones, indeed! I am afraid there is nothing to be got out of him excepting by moistening his bones, and his clay too. A pretty thing to send this fish—for he is hardly flesh—to the governor! His grace would think me as great a jackass as the man I sent. This morning I was put down by a Mulatto fine-gentleman, who baffled all my wit, and satire, and cross-examination: now I am defied by a bullet-headed, woolly-headed, ram-headed, old Negro. I should like to see what a jury would make of him. Where is Michal?'

'Michal is gone to Belmont,' said Joanna: 'I gave her leave.'

'What! to go to Belmont? Did not you tell me that brown buccaneering-looking fellow was gone to Belmont? Why, Michal is gone after him, I dare be sworn: I caught them philandering together this morning. These brown girls are the devil incarnate: they fly at a pretty fellow as a parcel of sharks rush at a piece of salt beef. But see; let Rose or Eleanor be sent for; tell them to make this Drybones drunk; give him grog enough; soften Mr Nimrod's heart, and loosen his tongue, and hunt out of him something more consistent than the tale with which he has been trying to bamboozle us. There is some mischief in the wind: I have been to the Custos, and have sent to the barracks; the militia will be called out; and if this proves to be a hoax of our friend Sebastian, Solomon— Solomon Guthrie—am I henceforth and for evermore. Boy! give me out my regimentals, and my cocked hat and sword: this is muster-day, and I must attend it.'

CHAPTER 22A.

There was an ancient sage philosopher,
That had read Alexander Ross over,
And swore the world, as he could prove,
Was made of fighting and of love.

HUDIBRAS.

THE facetious Thomas Brown has observed, that 'upon the report of a war among the princes of the earth, the devils keep holiday below;' and well they may, if there be any such in the region alluded to, which according to Peter Pindar cannot be a bit hotter than Jamaica, nor the long-tailed black gentlemen there a bit more wicked than the inhabitants above. We must suppose he meant the white inhabitants, as the rest of the population, black, brown, yellow, and tawney, are represented now-a-days, by the kind-hearted writers, speakers, and preachers, of Great Britain, who have never seen them, to be angels of various colours; men and women of all virtues—martyrs. But as to the holiday-keeping, these black martyrs make fine work for the devils, with the aid of the climate, and at little expense to themselves, as may be seen from the accounts of the Maroon wars, during the last of which, while the whites died by scores of fatigue or by the guns of their enemies, general Cudjoe lost in killed and wounded one man. We might expatiate on the horrors of the Negro war in St Domingo; but it is perhaps better to confine our attention to this, or rather to the prospect of this, before us.

The regiment of the parish as usual turned out to muster with the dragoons, all in military array. Nothing, as Voltaire says in his *Candide*, was ever gayer, finer, more brilliant, than the disposition of the army: trumpets, drums, cannons, fifes, and hautboys, filled the air with noise and smoke, and the hearts of the spectators with awe and confidence; those of the Blacks with the first, those of the Whites with the last. Both parties were used to similar exhibitions, but they felt nothing the less on that account. Major Guthrie (his exact rank was not ascertained) not being altogether a Mars or a

field-marshal, came at a peaceable pace into the plain, surrounded by several gentlemen, anxious to hear something of this
gang of pirates or robbers, and still farther curious to learn something of the aspiring Mr Combah. But though he was not a son of
Mars, he had assumed a very military air with his red coat; rather
saddened (that is the coat) as to colour, with the many drenchings
it had sustained on the muster-ground for the last few years, and a
little tarnished as to the gold lace and epaulettes. The cocked-hat
too, which he wore fore and aft, had the look of an old campaigner,
being tanned by sun and rain into a good wholesome mahogany
Mulatto-colour: still it was a poor substitute, as to comfort, for the
umbrella beaver which he usually wore, and left his brown
cheeks, and browner tip of the nose, to the mercy of the unmerci-
ful sun which had blistered and peeled them many a time before
in the like manner. This might have been prevented by flapping
the cocked hat; but that would have been considered out of eti-
quette. He wore it very much over his nose, to give room for his little high pigtail, which was a sort of dwarf club, as we have before
related, tied so close to his cranium—or, as a sailor would say,
hauled taught home and belayed—that it gave his companions an
idea of a ship being pooped by a stern sea, and going with her bows
headlong into the trough of the water. His sword was a weapon of
great antiquity, nothing of the modern regimental fashion emanating from the Horse Guards, but a real genuine Toledo, a rapier
with the twelve apostles carved on its blade, which had descended
as an heir-loom from his great ancestor Hugh Guthrie, one of
those brave adventurers who in the time of the commonwealth
shared the fame and fortunes of Penn and Venables, and conquered the island from the Spaniards. This weapon had been one
of his ancestor's trophies, and had been taken by him from a
Spanish colonel at the attack of Rio Nuovo under Doyley. The rest
of his equipage deserved no particular remark, if we except the
Creole steed which carried him, a venerable well-bred horse,
about five and twenty years of age, of a brown colour, with a white
face and tail, and a pair of wall eyes.

The business of the muster was disposed of in the usual very
military fashion, and horse and foot were dismissed with a hint or

two to keep themselves on the alert for the present. But as nothing certain had transpired of the meditated revolt, except from the hints of Sebastian and the unsatisfactory statement of Mr Drybones, many of the militia doubted the existence of any cause for alarm, and cursed old Guthrie in their hearts for putting themselves and the population into any disquietude about what they considered an imaginary danger.

While this gentleman was gone to his parade, at the distance of some few miles from his plantation, Rose and Eleanor, the two brown girls who had their instructions respecting Drybones, repaired alternately to the wooden Bastile in which he was immured by one leg, and tried all their skill to elicit a farther communication from him as to the reasons for his deserting his comrades: but although the hothouse-keeper indulged him with a plentiful dose of grog to console him for the tyrannous impressment of his limb, and the brown beauties played off many of their pretty fascinating arts, he was at first impenetrable to all questioning: and all he could be got to say was—'Please to send to the gubna (governor) or there will be a rebellion;' and 'Master Fairfax comes here tomorrow.' Yet as the spirit of rum began to evaporate, and the spirit of reason to prevail, it occurred to the individual Drybones, that his situation was a perilous one at best, as he subjected himself to the double suspicion of being a spy in the eyes of one party; and a traitor in those of the other; and he thought after all he might as well tell Mr Guthrie the truth, that he had determined to take the white man's side out of respect for Mr Fairfax, to whom his Negroes looked with a feeling of curiosity and affection, as he had been long absent, had been their favourite, and was so immediately expected. Besides, he had received from Sebastian such reasons of weight as those which the representatives of certain boroughs in England communicate to the individuals who find them particularly worthy of a seat in the senate: in short, he had a good understanding with the brown man, whose part he had taken from these and other motives of his own; he knew that Sebastian would have the means of rewarding him very handsomely; and he was overawed by his superiority of mind and personal strength: his *genius* was rebuked by the Mulatto's, as Mark

Antony's was by Cæsar's. Perhaps he would have thought of coming to this explanation with Mr Guthrie at once, if he had had any explanation on the subject with Sebastian; but he was afraid of compromising the character of that person, and knew not what might be elicited from him by cross-examination. He had therefore resolved to say nothing; but now that the blue-eyed Minerva came to his aid in a calabash of rum and water, he determined to let the cat out of the bag, if needs must, and try at the same time to escape from the bilboes, where he was as little at his ease as Asmodeus in his bottle.

With this intention, he sent for Miss Rose, and made her a fine speech about her beauty and good nature, and told her he wanted to talk with master Guthrie about Mr Fairfax; but as that had no effect, he went so far as to say he came from Mr Fairfax, who was in the island, disguised as a sailor, at his own house at Belmont; that it was he who had persuaded Sebastian not to let Miss Joanna be made queen of Jamaica, but to protect her and save her for him; that all this however was a mighty secret, for if it were known, Mr Fillbeer the attorney would prevent his taking possession of his house.

'Mr Fairfax is already at Belmont,' said Rose, peeping into Mrs Guthrie's apartment to communicate the confession of the prisoner in a whisper; 'but it is a secret; he is disguised like a sailor-boy: master will help him to turn out the mortgagee—will he not, mistress?'

The ladies looked on one another with surprise; but Joanna quickly remarked, that it must be an invention of Mr Nimrod's; or why had he not divulged the circumstance before? The elder lady only uttered a deep sigh.

'Mistress had better speak to him,' said the maid, 'and hear if he makes his story good. He says he must go to the governor, or somebody for him; or there will be a rebellion in the island.'

'I hope,' said Joanna, 'my father is not acting unwisely in detaining this man here. But he will return shortly; and then we can send to Belmont to know if it be true as he reports.'

Rose returned to the prisoner; but his impatience could not wait the arrival of Mr Guthrie, and was urging fresh disclosures in a whisper to the other brown girl, Eleanor. 'Mr Fairfax,' he said to her, 'is gone to seize a gang of Negroes belonging to him that ran away into the woods behind Port Antonio. Tell Miss Joanna that master Roland is gone there too, and it can be for no good.'

'No, indeed,' said Eleanor (a frisky damsel;) 'but tell us, Drybones, what's become of that tall brown man with the great hat and the chain to his sword.'

'That is Sebastian,' replied the Negro.

'Yes, but where is he gone to, and where is he to live, and who does he belong to?'

'He belongs to himself,' said Drybones; 'and he says you are really a pretty girl, and he wants to speak to you, at——'

'Where?' said the girl, interrupting him, and pinching his ear till he affected to roar as with pain. 'He never saw me, sir, so tell no lies;—nor did you either.'

'Hi! that is a good joke: did not I see him kiss missy?'

'Kiss me! kiss me, Nimrod!—Drybones! I never let a brown man touch my lips, I assure you: besides, he looked so fierce and terrible, and such a funny colour. Why, he was neither brown nor black, nor Sambo, nor Mestee; I don't know what colour he was. Lord! I would not let him kiss me, if he was a white man; much less since he is a Mulatto (and darker than I am) except I was two or three and twenty years old.'

'Cha! cha!' replied Drybones; 'you all run after him as soon as you see him. I know Miss Michal is run away to have him for herself, and Miss Rose likes him too.'

'I never have seen him,' said Rose; 'therefore I can't be in love with him. But a brown man! Why, you are a fool to talk so about him. Oh, here comes master: now, Drybones, speak the truth—don't lie.'

Mr Guthrie came into the hothouse with two gentlemen, and having turned out the girls, interrogated the prisoner again with more success than before. He had had time to collect himself, and told a sufficiently connected story to induce the planter to set him at liberty, or rather to despatch him with two trusty Negroes to Spanish Town, according to his wish. The matter of Fairfax's disguise rather puzzled him, though he knew the difficulties his neighbour would have to contend against in getting possession of his property from a rapacious and unprincipled puritan, who had, in conjunction with Roland, plotted to keep it for ever from the real owner. No wonder Peter Pindar should say the people were as wicked as devils:—but of this anon.

Mr Guthrie returned to the house with his friends, set his guards, prepared his arms, and ate a hearty dinner; as every man of sense would do, who expects an attack of anything but apoplexy; seeing that valour, which is next in rank to discretion, depends principally on the food of the body, at least much more so than on the food of the mind, for the time being. 'Roast beef against terrors.' According to Mr Gill—

> 'He that would fortify his mind,
> His stomach first should fill.'

A libation of Madeira wine is not a bad addition to the flesh of bulls and goats, and would have been quite as acceptable to the immortal gods of Greece as it was to the demigod in arms, Solomon Guthrie, esq. as he had styled himself, who sat up in his piazza, with one or the other of his eyes open, to a late hour; and then peaceably falling asleep on a sofa, dreamed, in spite of musquitos, till daylight.

CHAPTER 22B.

Content thyself awhile. By the mass, 'tis morning!
OTHELLO.

THE morning had no sooner dawned, than our man of war (though he was a most peaceable creature, and had assumed his weeds of peace, having adonized himself in his own fashion—that is, with an umbrella hat, a light grey coat, or coatee—if we may use such a term,—and a pair of large white trowsers, which overwhelmed his boots) mounted his wall-eyed nag, and rode to Belmont, to satisfy his curiosity respecting the return of Mr Oliver Fairfax to the demesnes of his ancestors, the first of whom was of the family of that Fairfax who had cut such a figure in the commonwealth of England, and had been a contemporary friend of Hugh Guthrie, from whom our individual was descended. The young man Fairfax had spent a great portion of his early life in Jamaica, and had been the frequent inmate of Mr Guthrie's house, where he had had opportunities of forming his earliest attachment; and though he was eight years older than Mr Guthrie's daughter, that circumstance did not prevent the parents on both sides from flattering themselves with the prospect of a future and perfect union between their families. Individuals of each had intermarried in ages past; and some of them, dying without issue, had left their properties to be managed jointly by members of both families, with legacies and encumbrances to this cousin, and that aunt, the nephew or the grandchild; and, as too frequently occurs in Jamaica, (and all the other islands of the West Indies, unfortunately)—it happened that an estate was now and then ill managed; that there were bad seasons, bad times, oppressions to suit the policy of Great Britain with respect to her own private and peculiar interests, wholly independent of the colonies—(such as the navigation laws, war taxes on sugars, prohibitions of sending refined sugar to England or Europe, prohibitions of all intercourse with America, &c. &c.)—which occasionally prevented the estates from yielding any revenue, and even added to the incumbrances on the properties. In consequence, the legatees often got little or nothing, and being poor themselves, and sued by their creditors, were obliged to sue in return, and by such misfortunes disturb the harmony of all parties. The managing legatees were accused of incompetency; their successors managed worse; debts were accumulated, Negroes mortgaged, and difficulties of all kinds augmented (as they still continue to do) on the heads of that most unhappy class of landholders, that devoted party whose misfortune it has long been, whose crime it now is, to be the proprietors of other human beings with black skins. The late Mr Fairfax used to regret that he could not wash them white: for then the spiritual party in England, he said, would let them go to heaven or to the devil how they chose, and not pack off all their own rubbish, and the rubbish of England and Ireland, to help them there. A late celebrated author regretted the Irish were not black, as then they would have a claim to the merciful consideration of their white fellow-creatures, to which they have now no right whatever, as may be seen any day in the year.—But to return to Mr Fairfax: he had in his turn inherited the property of Belmont and other estates, with claims on them from half a score of Guthries and Fairfaxes in England and elsewhere; which claims the estates, thanks to the holy men of England (that is, the ultra pious, and others interested in the importation of East India sugar) could no more pay than the aforesaid pious pay for the property which they are most religiously pleased to confiscate in the West Indies, to save their own souls from the devil. The estates (some of them at least) were sold at a miserable depreciation; the half of the wretched price for which they were sold was as yet unpaid; and Mr Fairfax had found, after all his sacrifices, that he could not carry on this his reserved estate of Belmont without assistance from a merchant in England. Things were not then quite so bad as at present: an agent was found, money advanced, supplies sent, and crops returned, without any benefit to the proprietor. The debt increased; the saints demanded emancipation; the agent demanded, and obtained, a mortgage. Still the debt increased, as sugar and rum were worth nothing; the saints were clamorous for emancipation; the mortgagee threatened to foreclose. Lastly, sugar and rum being no better, the saints began to bully the government in England; the government in England began to worry the government here:—as

> 'The dog began to worry the cat,
> The cat began to kill the rat.'

The mortgagee got a judgment, and entered into possession.

Here his deputy had been for four years, without bringing the estate to sale, or rendering any account to the proprietor, the present Mr Oliver Fairfax; his father having died in the interim, and left him sole heir to all the remains of what his ancestors had enjoyed, with claims also to a certain extent on Mr Guthrie's estate, and to a gang of Negroes left to that gentleman under the ricketty will of an old lady whose heir-at-law young Fairfax had proved himself to be. The English mortgagee had disputed this will on behalf, as he gave it out, of Mr Fairfax; but literally to get the Negroes, between seventy and eighty in number, placed (for their *mutual* benefit, of course) on Belmont estate, to work out his debt; and the mortgagee seemed to have every prospect of succeeding.

It happened that the mortgagee, who had spent a part of his life in Jamaica, previous to his setting himself up as a merchant in England, and had amassed a considerable fortune there, had found it convenient to attach himself to the African Society about the same time that he commenced business; and some one or two of the members of this body had recommended the present deputy of the mortgagee, his attorney, the trustee in possession, to manage the estate for him.

Mr Fillbeer had been a saint! (*fuit Ilium!*) as well as a brewer of no credit, but much renown, who was fined so often for using villanous drugs in his composition that he was ruined, and came out to Jamaica to repair his fortune, or rather (as the old one was not mendable) to make a new one. His religious friends had put him at last into a good thing; and he lived much like other planters' attorneys—with all the consolations of this world, and nothing to pay for. His religion was still as good as new; for he was not likely to wear it out in his present birth. He wore it less often than his hat; but he had it, like the hat which hung half the day and all night on a peg, always at hand in case of emergency. At other times he was not particular about theology or divinity, and thought the Negroes worked as well, and as happily, and as profitably, as if they went to meeting on a Sunday, instead of selling their commodities at the Bay.

This heathen practice of keeping a Sunday market he affected to wink at, in compliance with the prejudices of his new neighbours. He allowed also his book-keepers to entertain themselves in adding to the happiness and gay costume of those sable or brown beauties whose charms they found irresistible; and he did not altogether escape the suspicion of a few such intrigues himself; although, as he had lately buried a termagant Presbyterian wife, who had long lived with him, such reports must have been all scandal and invention.

Such was the person in possession of Belmont; who knew, although it had only come of late to the knowledge of young Fairfax, that when the mortgage had originally been granted by the father, it had been so done only for his life. The young man had consented to the sale and to the mortgage of other properties; but his father had not permitted him to do so in this instance—at least he had not consulted him; and though the elder Mr Fairfax had appointed his English factor his executor, and made him trustee for the management of his properties, until they should be sufficiently relieved from debt, he had by a saving clause stipulated, that no act of the trustee should be valid without the approbation of his son.

After a partial education in England, Oliver Fairfax had returned to Jamaica at twenty-one years of age, and had remained there for three years; when he departed again for England very suddenly, to arrange some matters with his father's factor, difficulties having arisen out of the times, as before stated. During his residence there he had opportunities of renewing his acquaintance with Miss Guthrie, who had been sent *home,* as it is called, for her education. He had likewise contrived to meet her on the continent, and attended the party with whom she travelled through France and Italy. The intimacy which this tour allowed, had revived all the tender recollections of their youth. They were united by ties of kindred, friendship, community of interests and affections, of country, and even of locality. They were the last heirs of two honourable families, whose fortunes had within the last twenty years been wofully depreciated by the cruel and fatal policy of the mother country, and were now endangered, in addition to that depreciation, by the interference of the Emancipators.

The consciousness of this, which ought to form a bond of union among all West Indians, helped at least to draw closer the ties which united these young persons in heart and sentiment. They were aware that a marriage would be highly agreeable to their relations; and they knew that it would end all disputes and animosities on the score of property and inheritance. The lady returned first to Jamaica; the gentleman was speedily to follow; vows, promises, had been given reciprocally; and not the slightest apprehension on the subject had ever caused either party a moment's uneasiness until, upon her arrival in the island, Joanna had communicated the particulars of her connexion with Oliver to her mother, with whose feelings regarding it the reader is already acquainted. Roland had found it proper to his interests to put a bar to the union of the lovers, and had spread very extraordinary tales respecting Fairfax, who happened to have taken his departure from the island the morning after the fire at Mr Guthrie's, at the time when that gentleman was a prisoner in Guadaloupe. He had always entertained a great dislike to young Fairfax for his independent spirit, and for having taken the liberty of exposing from time to time the preacher's pretensions to sanctity. He had therefore denounced him as an atheist in his absence, and had laid the crime of robbery, at least of piracy, to his charge, for having embarked in a ship from which a part of the crew had been known to desert and join some adventurers in Cuba, who in taking a prize had exercised great cruelties on their prisoners in their endeavours to extort from them the surrender of their valuables, and had put some of them to death. Two of the party had been afterwards apprehended in the island, condemned, and executed; and Roland, who attended them spiritually before they suffered, had affected to bring from them a communication to Mr Guthrie, relative to the participation of Fairfax in the atrocities for which they were put to death. He had not scrupled to charge him with murder as well as piracy; and as he had already convinced Mrs Guthrie that Fairfax was guilty of a crime which had ruined her peace of mind, she was unable to refuse her belief to the otherwise almost incredible stories which the Missionary detailed respecting him. Mr Guthrie, being unacquainted with the aforesaid crime, was not so credulous as his wife, and doubted every one of the facts declared by the Missionary; but he was not aware of the machinery by which the will of his relation had been pulled to pieces; he gave Fairfax full credit for that; and although he had always felt the greatest regard for his young friend, he could not altogether forgive him for instituting, as he thought he had done, this process against him, and for threatening (as the trustee had done) to enforce his claims for certain legacies on the other properties of his old friend.

From these circumstances, Fairfax stood very low just now in the estimation of Mr Guthrie, and was absolutely execrated by his wife. Joanna wavered not; but he had no other friends that he was aware of, except that the old planter, in spite of his ill will, retained a sneaking kindness for him, and meant, now that his curiosity led him to Belmont, to lend him, if there should be occasion, any assistance that he might want to repossess himself of his estate.

CHAPTER 23.

Alas! it is the baseness of thy fear
That makes thee strangle thy propriety.
                                        TWELFTH NIGHT.

WITH this compound feeling of curiosity, animosity, and benevo-
lence, the old planter came jogging along on his white-faced
charger beneath the sunny rocks of the sea beach, with his valet on
a mule behind him; when he espied at a distance the evangelist
Roland rising from out the river, wherein he hoped he had washed
away all the abominations of the heathen orgies in which he had
been made to participate. There was no mistaking him: his solemn
walk—even in the river—his lank locks, and his demure cast of
countenance, betrayed him successively to each of Mr Guthrie's
eyes, and no less quickly to those of the horse, who by his starting
and snorting gave indications of feeling himself in the presence of
something very offensive or horrible to him.

The Missionary had hastened to the bank of the river as the old
gentleman quitted the sea shore, and had got on the chief of his
clothes by the time the charger could be brought to face him. His
coat was still daubed with dirt and blood, and his old brown castor
was squeezed up into all manner of figures, as if it were a piece of
rumpled brown paper instead of a hat. He placed it with an awkward affectation on his yet reeking cranium.

'Good morning, Mr Roland,' said the old gentleman. The
Missionary made a bow, at which the horse started, much to the
satisfaction of Roland, who wished that the old planter were
drowning, so his attention (though to his own death) should be
diverted from him and his disfigured garments. 'An early bath, Mr
Roland. Have you been far to windward?'

The horse made another horrible start; for, according to the
custom of the country of shaking hands at every meeting, the
Missionary put forth his arm to receive the salute of his acquaintance; and whether it yet retained the odour of the filth with which
it had been stained, or whether it was the mere caprice of the

beast, the latter seemed to be alarmed beyond measure by the
motion of the man of grace, wheeled round as often as the rider,
by rein, and whip, and spur, could bring his face to bear on that of
Roland, and snorted and reared, very much discomposing the seat
of the horseman. All this time the Missionary was hatching an answer or a story; but the old gentleman, still battling with his steed,
relieved him from his temporary embarrassment by observing,
that Roland must certainly have the devil at his elbow, which was
visible to the horse, although his own eyes could not penetrate to
the sight of the fiend.

'Your eyes are penetrating too,' said the other with a forced
smile. 'I hope your excellent lady is in good health; likewise Miss
Joanna.'

'No, indeed,' replied the planter; 'neither one nor the other. My
wife gets worse and worse. Here, boy, take my horse to the stable
at Belmont, and tell Mr Fillbeer, with my compliments, I shall
walk up and breakfast with him. Where have you been, Mr
Roland? Why, what's this? Blood on your clothes! Who has done
this? Are you wounded—hurt anywhere? What are these crosses?
My God—my God! *Dii quibus imperium*—Harlequin smelt
you—and your coat all bedizened as if you had been dragged
through a horse-pond—foh! I smell you myself. Where did you
get all this? In the storm? I ask pardon, Mr Roland: I hope I am
not impertinent.'

The Missionary was never taken more aback in his life. There
was a tolerable confusion in his face (as well as a few contusions)
before the planter had remarked it; but when Roland saw the two
eyes of his acquaintance running him over and over, and round
and round, like two galleys plying round a becalmed or distressed
frigate, one taking up a position to fire on its bows, while the other
blazes away on its stern,—he felt as much alarm and consternation individually, as that which the whole crew of the frigate would
experience collectively, and looked more woful, pitiable, and des-
titute, than the frigate would do by the time all her masts were
shot away, and she had seven feet water in her hold. The planter
could not help feeling for him, as the Missionary turned up the
whites of his eyes, and heaved a sigh.

'You have been beaten too: why, you have got a black eye!'

'It has pleased the Lord'—said Roland.

'What! to give you a black eye? By what natural means, may I ask—nothing miraculous?'

'It has pleased the Lord—'

'To drag you through a horse-pond?'

'A truce, sir, I pray,' said the Missionary, again turning up the white of one eye, and the black and blue of the other. 'It has pleased the Lord to chasten his servant. The Lord giveth and taketh away.'

'Well, well,' resumed the planter, 'that is some consolation at all events. Not a drunken frolic—you were chastened, eh? A cater-wauling? I beg pardon. And you lost your sweetheart—was it a black-fisted one? a Sappho? *Lesbia puella!*—And is this *your* blood, all over your clothes and your shirt? Did she give you a bloody nose as well as a black eye?—Unfeeling jade! *Infelix Dido.* What a Jezebel! She felt nothing. Why, what a figure she has made of you! You cannot shew yourself for a week.'

'Sir, sir!' exclaimed the preacher in confusion, 'you misappre-hend—you misunderstand. There was no Sappho, nor even a Dido, nor Jezebel, nor incontinent Rahab, nor any female con-cerned.'

'Then who has torn your clothes in this fashion? Have you been wrestling with the Lord?'

'Fie, Mr Guthrie! Knowing my persuasion, my belief on sub-jects of religion, my calling—as I may call it,—I should have hoped to hear from your lips nothing that could give me pain on that score.'

'Not a jot,' returned the planter. 'I ask pardon; I mean no of-fence to you or to religion; I wish only to avenge you on those who have maltreated you. *Antecedentem scelestum*, you know, with the club foot.'

'*Scelestum*, indeed,' muttered the Missionary, still over-whelmed with the conviction of his most pitiable situation. '"Vengeance is mine, saith the Lord: I will repay."'

'You would rather pay it yourself, Mr Roland, I suspect,' re-joined Mr Guthrie. 'But after all, what is it? Here has been a parcel of rascals at my house, to steal my daughter, and murder my wife and myself. If the storm had not smashed their canoe, we should have all been provided for by now.'

The face of the Missionary turned to a deadly paleness, as he listened to this communication. He dared not raise his head to encounter the keen glances of Mr Guthrie, who fixed on him his two eyes, each having a power like that of Tamerlane, or almost that of the caliph Vathek, on this occasion. Roland could have wished they were those of a basilisk, that he might have been struck dead on the spot, and so his conscience set for ever at rest.

But the old planter continued:—'We have reports of an insurrection to windward among the Negroes: where can you have been buried, not to hear of it? We wanted you yesterday too; the militia are on the alert; and I have further news for you; our neighbour Fairfax is expected here today; but this is a secret, I believe. But what is the matter with you, Mr Roland? Why are you so pale? or rather so black; for the whiteness of one part of your face makes the other look as black as if it were the devil's own. What ails you?—Let us go into the house: yonder is Mr Fillbeer looking for us; see, he is coming down the piazza steps to meet us. He will wonder, as well as myself, at your extraordinary appearance; and I am at a loss to understand why you make a mystery of it. Have the Negroes insulted you, or is it a white man? Or have you been wrestling with a duppie in your sleep—an incubus? Or have you been *Obeah'd*?'

'Ah, forbear!' said Roland with an expression of disgust. 'Make me not the subject of your mockery. I have met with an earthly affliction, which I must bear as a Christian.'

'But will you not tell us what it is, that we may do you justice?'

'Justice!' repeated Roland: 'justice!—I have been maltreated by Negroes; and, when occasion serves, I will call on you, my respected friend, to do me justice in the eyes of the righteous. Vengeance on my own part I disclaim altogether. Would that the whole island, the whole world, could forgive as well as I can!'

' Ah,' replied Mr Guthrie, 'we should have the golden age, the *Saturnia regna*, instead of Satan's reign:—but you must tell us of your discomfiture; our own safety requires it. The Negroes must not insult, much less strike, the Whites with impunity, and least of all a holy man of God, a delegate from the pious fraternity of Wesleyan methodists. Why, if we were not to inquire into your case, we should have a remonstrance from the house of commons in England to our house of assembly here, on the subject; we should be taxed with wilfully degrading you and your calling.— Mr Fillbeer, your most obedient.'

CHAPTER 24.

A little, round, fat, oily man of God,
Was one I chiefly marked among the fry.
He had a roguish twinkle in his eye,
And shone all glittering with ungodly dew,
If a tight damsel chanced to trippen by;
Which when observed, he shrunk into his mew,
And straight would recollect his piety anew.

THOMSON.

BY this time Mr Guthrie, with his disconsolate and bewildered companion, had reached the house where Mr Fillbeer, with an obsequious bow, was ready to welcome them to breakfast.

'Your humble servant, Mr Guthrie; pray walk in. Friend and brother Roland, I am charmed to see you.' (The word brother sounded hatefully in the Missionary's ear.) 'Hola! hola! man, what have you been fighting with?—Not with that terrible fellow they call Sebastian, who they tell me is coming here to take possession of the estate for a crew of pirates and revolted Negroes?'

'Hah!' said Mr Guthrie, 'is that the report?'

'Indeed is it,' replied Mr Fillbeer. 'Why, Roland, how did you pass the night of the storm? And why did not you put up here, or at the other estate above, when you spoke to the Negro girls? They told me yesterday of your having passed, as sweet as a nosegay; and that you inquired for M'Lachlan's estate, where the Negroes have run away. But how came you by this disfigurement?'

'Aye,' said Mr Guthrie, 'he's not so sweet now as he was before. He says that some Negroes have been thumping him; but where, when and how, he is loth to communicate.'

'The where is pretty evident,' observed Mr Fillbeer; 'and the how may be guessed at by the marks: these are not chops or stabs.'

'No,' rejoined Mr Guthrie, 'they are punches, fisticuffs. I thought at one time it had been a Medea, some jealous nymph, some enchantress, who had been dying his skin for him, without giving him an opportunity of any revenge—*Nil habet ista sui;*—but he denies it.'

'If it may please you to spare my feelings for a few minutes,' said the preacher, 'I will endeavour to relate some of the particulars by and bye; but in the meantime allow me to retire, and arrange my dress, before I sit down to breakfast.'

So saying, he stalked off into a chamber which was pointed out to him, where he pulled off his coat, and fell to washing out the blood-marks, though not before he had almost fainted at the sight of his black eye and his blue face, which he now saw reflected in the glass for the first time. 'What a catastrophe!' said he to himself: 'these blood-marks may lead to all sorts of suspicion. I cannot shew myself; I cannot give an account of myself: nay, my boy Cuffy may have already told of my encounter with the black idiot who would not be satisfied without cramming his thick head into a crown. Merciful heaven, what horrible nonsense! As if the tinker and the toy-man could consecrate the deputy elected by the Lord; as if—But where is Cuffy?—Come in, Cuffy, and shut the door.'

While the door is shut, let us give some account of Mr Fillbeer and his conversation.

The attorney was a round fat man, with a bald head, or partly bald, like the tonsure of an ultra priest. What hair he had was black, and—as Mr Guthrie was wont to say—'*Nimium lubricus aspici:*' it began just above the bump of philoprogenitiveness, extended round to the organs of acquisitiveness just in front of the ears, and reached down behind to his shoulders, as lank as so many rats'-tails. He had large grey eyes, a huge bottle nose, and behind, as much as beneath it, a mouth like that of Cerberus—a triple mouth, with a triple chin, and three teeth in all; two like the fangs of a wolf in the upper jaw, the third standing like a pyramid in the desert below, for men to wonder at. He had not *lost* the rest; as, according to his own account, they were all safe in his drawer, where he had deposited them *gradatim,* during an unpleasant salivation he had found it necessary to undergo a few years back. It was to the same cause that he attributed the loss of his hair, being, as he said, the only bald individual of his family; for not having yet reached his fiftieth year, he wished to consider himself, like

Falstaff, only in the vaward of his youth. He was almost as wide as he was high, and his circumference was fully equal to his stature; so that he had not looked upon his knees for a year or two, and all the buttons and button-holes of his waistcoat had parted company, or were bent on a separation, in spite of sundry efforts of the estate's nymphs to patch and attach them. He was not an ill-tempered man, where his interest was unconcerned—else he had not been so fat; and there was reason to suppose that if he had never affected the saint, he would not have thought it worth his while to take up the character just now. Yet he was bound to be consistent; and report said that he was in the habit of supplying the African Society and the Society for Suppressing Slavery with a few occasional tales, such as he had been taught would be most grateful to those liberal and enlightened gentleman. He was in fact, with all his fat paunch and his rubicundity of visage, what the world calls a deep fellow, subtle and clear-headed, and close-fisted; greedy and rapacious as the grave, and like that, retaining all that came within his grasp: he rendered nothing on which he had once laid his clutches. Hence one of the reasons why Mr Fairfax was still deprived of his estate, and why for four years he had had no accounts; the agent in London even complaining of the delay, and referring Mr Fairfax to his *locum tenens* on the spot.

Such was the fat, sleek, pursy gentleman who now very officiously poured out a cup of coffee for Mr Guthrie, and handed him some hot rolls, pointing to the other eatables with all the grace of which he was capable, and inviting his guest to attack them as he pleased—in detail, or at once in a pitched battle.—'Mr Roland,' said he, 'will be here anon; but what has happened to him? The Negro girls at the other estate said that he shook hands with them, and that he was all perfume and pomatum, and was certainly going to see some lady with whom he was in love;—but where? in the back settlements? I know of no habitations—'

'Have you here at present,' said Mr Guthrie, as if not adverting to the attorney's speech, 'a sailor in distress?'

'No,' replied the other; 'not that I know of; have you heard of such a person? I have heard only of a boat's crew who came to your house, and a brown man calling himself Sebastian, who I understand killed two of his comrades, and flung them into the sea, and talks of paying us a visit here. We shall be happy to see him.'

'Did you hear that there was a report of insurrection to windward?'

'No!' cried the fat man, as if surprised.

'Well, sir,' continued Mr Guthrie, 'I ought to tell you that a Negro who assisted the Sebastian of whom you have heard, says that not only is a revolt planned, but that a man named Combah is to be king.'

'I never heard the name,' said Fillbeer, perspiring at every pore.

'Nor I,' resumed the other: 'it may be true or false: and I think it right to apprise you as well, that the same Negro asserts, on the strength of this Sebastian's assurance, that Mr Fairfax is in the island, and will be here today, to take possession of his estate.'

'Here today!' cried the fat man, blowing out his cheeks.

'Here today,' repeated Mr Guthrie with a smile, helping himself at the same time to a slice of ham. 'Today—this very day.'

'This day!' re-echoed Fillbeer with a fiendlike snarl, such as one might expect from a goule or an ogre. 'Fairfax! Let him come at his peril; I have put the estate's people on their guard already; let him come if he dare.'

'He dare, be assured,' rejoined the planter; 'he is as brave as a lion; and if you know that he has a claim on the estate prior to that of the mortgagees, I am at a loss to see how you can refuse him possession.'

'Possession!' said this ton of man, half choked with fat and rage, as well as with a great gulp of hot coffee which had taken the road to his lungs instead of keeping to the alimentary canal: 'Possession!'—But he could not go on for coughing; and Mr Guthrie took the opportunity of repeating the word.

'You know, Mr Fillbeer, that this particular estate was entailed by his grandfather, and cannot be alienated from him without his consent: his right is indisputable. What other powers he has with respect to the other estates, I know not; however, the law will not only reinstate him here, but set aside altogether the mortgagee's claim for any advances since the death of old Mr Fairfax; and indeed the personal estate will only be liable for the previous advances.'

'He consented,' said Mr Fillbeer (recovering himself at last) 'with his father, that the properties should be placed in the hands of a trustee for the liquidation of debts; and let him attempt an entrance by force at his peril.'

'Why, what would you propose to do?' said the planter, squinting at him.

'I know how to resist him,' replied the other with a growl. 'He is a robber, if not a murderer; a pirate, and I know not what—'

'Until he is so proved, he is an innocent man,' rejoined Mr Guthrie. 'He is my neighbour, my kinsman; and if he should claim assistance from me, what will you consent to? Will you leave the business to arbitration?'

'No, I'll be—hang'd first, I mean—God forgive me. Here I am, Mr Guthrie, with a power of attorney from the mortgagee in possession:—I say no more.'

'Ah!' thought the planter, 'here stands a post—touch it, if you dare.'

'You are bound in some measure,' said the round man, 'by rights of hospitality: you would not sanction or encourage injustice.'

'Bound to yourself, you mean, Mr Fillbeer?' said the other. 'Aye; why, certainly, I have the highest respect for Mr Fillbeer; but I do not know how—when I am here, I always fancy myself the guest of my old or rather young friend, Mr Fairfax: these are his slaves, his buildings, his cattle grazing yonder, his provisions, raised by his Negroes on his own land, or sent out from England at his expense. He has been an unfortunate young man perhaps; but I cannot fancy him guilty of the crimes you lay to his charge— robbery, murder, and what not.'

'Mr Roland is my authority,' said the attorney.

'Mr Roland will be puzzled to prove any one thing with which he charges him;—but where is Mr Roland?'

'I will soon see for him,' said the host, and walked impatiently across the piazza to the chamber where the holy man was still wiping out the stains upon his clothes, and coaxing his neckcloth to hide the blood upon his shirt. The little man (little in stature) was so fat, so punchy, and so pursy, that his locomotion was anything but active or elegant; yet, as if sensible of the awkwardness of his whole figure, and of the *dumpiness* of his legs, he had endeavoured to adapt a sort of elasticity to his gait by rising on his toes before he lifted his feet from the ground; so that he seemed to walk with less ponderosity than might have been expected from his bulk; and while the floor creaked and bent beneath this hitch in his waddle, his lank rats'-tails waved up and down with a most laughable rise and decline on his round shoulders, rendered more ridiculous by the arrogant air with which he carried his big nose aloft, and puffed out his bloated and toothless jowls. Mr Guthrie could scarcely retain his gravity, as he saw him thus march off, looking something like a fat ox erect on the stumps of his hind quarters (on his houghs, for instance) to the chamber of the Missionary, with whom he spent some few minutes in private conference before they returned together to the breakfast table, where the planter with admirable *sang froid* kept up a very persevering attack on the coffee and cocoes during the time he was left to his own reflections.

CHAPTER 25.

I have been to-night exceedingly well cudgelled;
and I think the issue will be—I shall have so
much experience for my pains.   OTHELLO.

MR FILLBEER came back with the same jaunty spring in his
march, leading or rather dragging forward Roland, who came—
not like a lamb to the slaughter, nor yet like a sheep (though he
could not divest himself of a most sheepish look) but rather like a
bull dragged to the stake. His host, or his executioner in this case,
was scandalized at his appearance, and had made him don one of
his own shirts and neckcloths, while his friend's were washed and
mended. The former did not fit the Missionary over-tight; but as
the cassock hides all, we need not remark on that circumstance: it
was wide enough, if it was too short, and made up in breadth for
its want of length; so that literally it was as broad as it was long—
physically, and we may suppose also metaphysically; for the
preacher was too much hustled and confused to bestow a minute's
thought on such a circumstance as this.

Elated as the attorney felt at having a witness so ready at command, to ensure him a triumph over Mr Guthrie, he was notwithstanding very much astonished, and almost confounded, to find
Roland so unwilling to account for the black eye he had got, and
for the other marks of discomfiture and disgrace which he carried
about him: for still the Missionary was not a jot more forward in
his inventions, and feared, as we have seen in the case of
Drybones, to say anything by which he might commit himself, or
which might at present or at any future time be brought against
him, to prove the purpose for which he had gone to the scene of
his last night's adventures, and the business in which he had been
engaged. His bosom burned with spite and indignation against
both Hamel and Combah; yet how could he denounce them
without involving himself? He was a man of much superstition,
notwithstanding the general doctrine he preached; and though be
felt some compunction in breaking the hideous oath which had

nigh choked him, the demon of revenge had spirited him up already to a resolution of despising it; and he would not have halted
at any falsehoods with which his genius might inspire him for the
furtherance of his object, provided they could not be disproved by
circumstances: for he disdained the testimony of the Blacks, taking for granted that they would lie in their turns, and knowing that
if they spoke truth, their evidence would not affect him, a white
man: it could not be admitted against him in a court of justice.
Besides, he meant at all hazards to strike the first blow, though he
was puzzled how or where to plant it.

Never was assembled perhaps a more extraordinary triumvi-
rate, as to manners, morals, and appearance, than that formed by
the three persons who now sat round the breakfast-table at
Belmont. It would be a waste of the reader's time and patience to
recapitulate the particulars of their singularities: let him only recall to his mind's eye their figures and costume;—the planter's
club tail and crocodile squinting eyes; the face of fat Fillbeer, resembling at once those of Falstaff and Bardolph; the black eye of
the holy wight, his bruises and contusions. Then again, their
heads, and the expression of the passions which governed their
features; the attorney's rage and pride, mixed up with spleen and
subtlety; the confusion and dismay of Roland, which he attempted to gloss over with a varnish of cant; the solemn and yet
droll demeanor of Mr Guthrie, who could hardly keep his countenance at the sight of the other two, and who distressed the chop-
fallen Missionary, whenever the smile that was flitting about his
lips found its way to the diseased conscience of that gentleman.
Let him fancy them seated in a handsome apartment, and attended by two black footmen, almost bursting into laughter at the
sight of Roland, yet obliged to restrain their mirth. Let him paint
to himself the good appetite of Fillbeer, and the affected delicacy
of Roland (like that of Amine picking rice with a bodkin;) while
the old planter played away upon the ham as if he had been a lately
converted Israelite. And finally, let him calculate the particular
feelings which each individually entertained at this moment for
the other two, independent of extraneous circumstances; and
what portion of those feelings they betrayed in spite of their

efforts to disguise them:—he will present to himself a diverting picture.

The civilities of the table were exchanged for sometime before the ex-brewer felt it convenient to call the attention of Mr Roland to the stories he had erewhile told of Mr Fairfax. Roland seemed to shrink from the recollection: he had enough of other matters just now on his mind, and could well spare the oft-repeated explanation of this tale, which he had learnt (as he had given out) from men under sentence of death, and consequently believed himself.

'It will be no proof,' observed Mr Guthrie: 'those pirates may have lied. Why did they not unburden themselves to others? Why did not you, Roland, take their depositions before a witness?'

'The communication was confidential,' replied the Missionary.

The planter stared with surprise. 'Confidential! How if he should prove that he was never in company with the pirates?'

'Why,' said Roland, 'then he proves them liars.'

'Aye! so he will, I'll engage,' continued Mr Guthrie.

'He is in the country, Mr Roland,' said the attorney, 'according to Mr Guthrie's account.' The Missionary laid down his knife and fork, drew forth his pocket-handkerchief, and wiped the perspiration from his face.

'Yes, Mr Roland,' said the planter, 'I tell you as I was told, that he will be here today.'

'Today!' cried the preacher.

'Aye, today; at least so I learn from the Negro who assisted this hectoring fellow calling himself Sebastian, a brown man who has been a sort of something—I do not know what—to Mr Fairfax in France or in Italy. He is too fine a gentleman to have been his valet; I cannot think in what capacity he could serve him. The Negro says, Mr Roland, that Fairfax will be here this day; but he may speak false. He says also, speaking of the insurrection that is talked of, that a Negro named Combah was to be king of the island. Do you know such a person?'

'Who—I?' said the Missionary in great agitation. 'I?—not I. Combah? Who is he? What is he? A free man or a slave?'

'You don't know him?' continued the planter, remarking the confusion of Roland. 'I thought, among the many converts you have baptized, such a person might not have been unknown to you. You keep a list, I know, of all your flock: have you it about you!'

'I never heard the name,' said Mr Fillbeer, looking with some surprise at the Missionary.

'Where is your list?'

'I have it—not about me—let me see: no—I have left it in my portmanteau; or perhaps I lost it in the storm.'

'Ah! where were you in the storm, Roland?' said Mr Guthrie.

'My portmanteau and its contents,' continued the Missionary, 'were wetted in the river and in the rain; yet I will search for my memoranda.'

'Why the devil,' exclaimed the planter, 'cannot you tell us where you were in the storm, and where you got your black eye? My house was almost blown away, and this I should think was in danger. I am sure the roof of mine would have been taken off, but for the assistance I got from the pirates. It is an ill wind which blows nobody good.'

Roland was moving off to his portmanteau; but the old gentleman brought him to again.

'Roland! Where did you weather the storm? We shall begin to think you were intriguing some where or other.'

The culprit started at the observation, as if he had been stung by a rattle-snake. 'Intriguing, Mr Guthrie! Am I a person to intrigue with slaves and—'

'Brown girls, I meant, Roland. No offence, sir, I hope. I said nothing about intriguing with slaves; but the black girls above, yonder, say you were sweet upon them the evening of the storm— sweet in two senses, for you were perfumed with all sorts of scents. With your gallantry we have no right to meddle; and if your black eye is to be attributed to that, I have done, and shall only counsel you to hide yourself till these *damned spots* are *out.*'

'Swear not in my presence,' said the preacher; 'and do not injure the character of one who has always felt towards you as a friend, by oblique hints at transactions which my religion forbids.'

'I will leave it to Mr Fillbeer,' rejoined the planter, 'to say whether my hints are oblique or not. If there is no woman in the case there is only one thing besides to which I can attribute your absence, and your reserve on the present occasion.'

'Name it not,' cried the Missionary in a new alarm.

'Name it not!' re-echoed the planter. By —— I will. *Sit mihi fas audita—a—a—audita.*—Let me be heard. Perhaps brother Roland has been trying to convert the old watchman that lives by the cave yonder in the rocks—the old reprobate who is suspected of Obeah. You know, Mr Roland, what he said when our parson threatened him once with hell-fire for his practices—Stay, Mr Roland—Mr Roland, excuse me—'

'Excuse *me,* Mr Guthrie.'

Roland was not to be detained, except by force: he bolted into his chamber, on pretence of looking for his pocket-book, and bolted the door after him.

'Why, what is this?' said the planter, in some amazement, to the fat attorney. 'What, in the name of heaven, is this?—Roland is mad.'

'Very extraordinary,' replied Fillbeer, raising his eyebrows, and depressing the corners of his mouth, while he stuck his punchy thumbs into the two uppermost button holes of his coat, as if to support his *elephantine* arms.

'May I be shot,' resumed Mr Guthrie, 'if I don't think he knows more about the insurrection than he ought.'

'Than he ought, Mr Guthrie?'

'Aye, than he ought: for if he does know of it, he ought not to conceal his knowledge for a moment. Did you not mark his agitation when I mentioned the name of this Combah? And he actually took fright when I spoke of the old watchman and his character.'

'Why, what can the old watchman have to do with it?' said the attorney; 'you mean Hamel, do you not?'

'I know not his name,' replied the other; 'but there is always an Obeah man in every insurrection; there always has been; though I cannot say that the watchman is a dabbler in the art: I spoke at random to Mr Roland. He has been somewhere and in some company for which he is ashamed; that is evident.'

'Why, you know, Mr Guthrie,' resumed the attorney, 'Roland aspires to your beautiful daughter, and may dislike to own any piece of gallantry, successful or otherwise, to the young lady's father:—perhaps he will be more communicative to myself.'

'Try him, sir.'

'I will; but in the meantime I trust you, sir, will not sanction any illegal attempts on the part of Mr Fairfax to seize his property here; which must end in violence, if not in murder.'

'Hush—hush—Mr Fillbeer,' said the old planter. 'Murder! You, a disciple—no, no—an apostolic brother of Roland, a serious Christian—you talk of murder!'

'I am no brother of Roland's.'

'Indeed! I heard you call him so when you first accosted him.'

'No matter—I renounce him.'

'What! already, Mr attorney?'

'I tell you, Mr Guthrie, I will defend my rights here to the very last drop of my blood.'

'Body of me!' murmured the planter, 'here is a mighty soul in all this fat! Who could have thought it?—As for his blood, nothing shorter than a spit can reach it. Fairfax must treat him, if needs be, like a turtle, and lay him on his back.—Do nothing violent, Mr Fillbeer,' he added aloud; 'do justice, and love mercy, as you walk humbly with your God.'

'I am the best judge of my own actions and feelings,' replied the attorney. 'I have spoken my mind—I am not a man to change: let Mr Fairfax beware!'

'Adieu, sir,' said the planter. 'Here comes my horse, and yonder goes the apostle Roland. Why, this is worse and worse: there must he something wrong, radically wrong: see how he steals away— "how like a guilty thing!" This must be seen into.'

'It is indeed very extraordinary,' observed the fat man, waddling to the piazza door again, though his fat was set into a fermentation by his apprehensions respecting Fairfax, and the presentiment he could not help entertaining of a battle, for which he was firmly resolved.

Mr Guthrie saluted him, and rode after the Missionary; while Fillbeer, having watched him as long as the road admitted of his keeping him in view, and ruminated with a shrewd guess on the affairs of Roland, turned about at last, and sought the interior of his abode, like a wild beast retiring into the penetralia of his den; gnashing his three teeth with rage and vexation. He sent for his overseer and his three book-keepers, determining to hold with them a council of war; and summoned all the drivers, and the head men among the Negroes, to come directly up to the *great house* for the same purpose.

CHAPTER 26.

Poor worm, thou art infected:
This visitation shows it.   THE TEMPEST.

THE order of our story brings us now again to pretty Michal,
whom we left watching the slumbers of her dear and too sincere
Sebastian. If, by any fatality (as all things are predestined, even to
the note of a pigeon) he had set off into a vigorous snore, a person
of more sentiment, making the best of everything, might have ex-
tracted some consolation from the circumstance, some counter-
poise in the imagination to lighten the load of love which
oppressed her innocent and affectionate heart. But Michal could
have borne that, although he had outsnored the Seven Sleepers of
Ephesus, without letting fall a grain of the charity which possessed her mind, or deviating from the course of tenderness and
sympathy which her heart was but too ambitious to run. She
looked on him, and then on the lake, still watchful for the black
duppie—and then again at the object of her love, with a feeling almost akin to that with which a fond mother watches the slumber
of her first born—and then again on the little lake; and while she
gazed upon it, her thoughts wandering from scene to scene, her
mind became distressed by the mournful pictures it continually
presented to itself of disappointed hope; and her eyes were more
than once filled with tears. 'What consolation,' thought she, 'can I
derive from this, the punishment of my folly? If I could but serve
him—save him from danger, render him some signal benefit, to
ensure his lasting gratitude, I should still be happy. If he could
value the feeling that draws my heart to him, if he would think
hereafter of poor Michal as of one who would have laid down her
life to do him service—But no, no, no—he will think no more of
me; he makes a jest of me, of my presence, and of the motive that
brought me here. I had better, now he sleeps so sound, leave him
entirely to his repose, return home to my mistress and my mother.
He wants me not; he has this Negro almost at his orders; and his

177

master, or whatever he is—Mr Fairfax—is soon to be here:—I
had better go.'

She rose to depart; but the sight of the lagoon brought again the
duppie to her recollection. 'I must not leave him,' she said to herself: 'that duppie may do him some injury, if he should come up
again. I should like much to know what he can be, and where he is
hid. There must be some way under the rocks, where he has
dived; yet the shore is sand: but there is no water runs out of the
lake—I never thought of that before—and here are three little
streams running into it: where can the water go to?'

She sat down again, and thought of all the strange tales she had
heard in days of yore of ghosts and necromancy; but nothing
brought any satisfaction to her mind. 'Spirits,' she fancied, 'appear only in the dark; and this must be a man who walks about in
the day. He can be no good.' She walked quietly and softly round
the lagoon. The shore seemed to shelve gradually; but the centre
yet appeared too deep in proportion to the nature of the shore.
She threw a stone into the middle, and watched the bubbles rise
to the surface for at least half a minute—till she could almost
count a hundred. The next thought that occurred to her, was to
undress, and try to sound the bottom of the lagoon herself: for
the dames and damsels of Jamaica, not excepting many of the
white ladies, swim like coots. But modesty forbade this:
Sebastian might awake; or Hamel might return; or the duppie
might be somewhere about, and see her, though he pretended to
be blind; and he might take advantage of her situation to enter
the cave, and execute any intention he might have with respect
to Sebastian.

She returned to (her lover, he cannot be called) the being she
loved, who was still in a deep sleep on the spot where he had
awaked her with his kisses. These she had no thought of returning
just now; but she drew nearer to the bench, as if at least to gratify
her eyes with a good look at his features. 'He is not a Mulatto,' said
she to herself: 'his hair is softer than mine; and his face is as fair by
nature, though it is burned by the sun. What has he got here?' She
spied a black ribbon beneath his waistcoat, which went round his
neck under his neckcloth: it was tucked into the bosom of his shirt,

perhaps by accident. 'Let me see if there is anything fastened to it.' He breathed deep—the Quadroon stopped. 'If he should wake, and catch me here?' But no, his sleep was too sound, and Michal's touch was light and tender. She drew the ribbon out of his bosom. 'There is a picture—gracious heaven, it is Miss Joanna!'—A crowd of ideas and recollections rushed upon her mind, and she almost gasped for breath. 'Why, he *does* then love my mistress—at least he did not mean to mock me—he said he was engaged to marry her. Ah! she is handsomer than I am: what beautiful eyes, blue like the sea! And what pretty hair!—I know how pretty it is. But her cheeks are not so red as this: they are white, and she never smiles now as the picture does. That is old Roland's fault—an ugly disagreeable creature! Well, let us put it back again. What wonder shall we have next? There have been diamonds or some ornaments about it; for here are empty holes: they must have been pulled out, perhaps by robbers. Let me put it into the place I took it from. He is hardly fair enough, I should think, to marry my mistress: I wonder she did not know him. There must be some deceit or disguise: let us see if his skin is as dark as his face.'

The Quadroon peeped into the bosom of his shirt with a presentiment of what she was to see. 'Mother—mother of me!' she exclaimed, bursting into tears, 'he is a white man!'

'Hah! Michal!' cried Sebastian, starting from his slumber. 'What is the matter? Who? Where is that blind Negro? A white man, did you say? What is the matter, and why are you alarmed—and wherefore do you weep?'

The soubrette was upon her knees, hiding her face in her hands.

'My pretty Michal, speak: what has frightened you?—Ah! you are in possession of my secret:—get up—arise, dear Michal.'

He found the picture hanging loose from his neck, outside his waistcoat. She would not rise: she lifted her head, and presented her pretty face, suffused with tears and blushes, and crossed her arms on her bosom with an air of the most enchanting modesty, while she bowed before him.

'Forgive me, sir; forgive me.'

'Dear Michal, there is nothing to forgive.'

He raised her from the ground, and strained her to his bosom. 'Michal, we shall be friends for evermore: you know my secret, you deserve to know it: I am ashamed I did not confide it to you; I am happy you have found it out; indeed I wonder it escaped you hitherto. These are Hamel's drugs,' he added, pointing to his cheeks. 'I owe to them my safety, and my escape from Cuba. But I have worn them long enough.'

'Ah,' said Michal with a sigh, 'then you are Mr Fairfax! Oh, how happy will my young lady be!'

The pretty maid's tears began to flow afresh at the idea of her mistress's happiness being the cause of her own chagrin, and at the comparison which forced itself upon her mind between their relative situations. However, she had a generous mind, and taking the hand at the possession of which as she said she had too vainly aspired, she put it to her lips, and invoked a blessing—all happiness upon his true heart. 'But you must be on your guard,' she continued, recollecting herself anew: 'you are in great danger, and have a number of enemies against you. There is the attorney below at Belmont, and master Roland, who have abused your name, and say you are a wicked man: you remember what I told you at my mother's house. But the most extraordinary thing of all is, the dislike which Mrs Guthrie has taken to you. Master Roland has often told me that she cannot bear the mention of your name; and I have heard her myself speak of you as of the most unfeeling and merciless profligate on the earth. I know not why—I never heard her reasons; but I have often listened when she has talked with Miss Joanna about you, and I have always heard the same opinion expressed ever since I knew her.'

'How many years, is that, Michal? I wonder I do not recollect you; for it is little more than four years since I left the island. Rose and Eleanor I remember as children, not above eleven or twelve years old; but I have no remembrance of you or your mother.'

'No,' said Michal; 'we came from Spanish Town. We belonged to master Guthrie's aunt, who died about four years ago; and we came to him just after the fire, when you went away to England.'

'I must obtain an interview with Mrs Guthrie, if I can, and hear her objection to me. Old Guthrie too is my enemy. For Mr Fillbeer, the trustee, I care nothing. If I had not been robbed by the Cuba pirates, I had that which would have dispossessed him in an hour. As it is, I must make the best of the matter, and throw myself on old Guthrie's generosity for protection and assistance. But while his wife is so averse to me, I cannot hope for that.'

'Oh,' said the Quadroon, 'Mr Guthrie is a good man, and I am sure he will do anything for you.'

'Well, Michal, we must talk of that anon. Has Hamel been here again; or did the Negro rise from the water?'

'Neither,' replied the girl. 'I watched a long time after you were asleep: I saw him no more. But the lagoon is deep in the middle, and it must have a communication with some other place; for no water comes out of it. Let us climb the rocks, and look for the other little lake you told me of. Perhaps the water of this mixes with that beneath these rocks, and so the other lake should be close at hand; or what can have become of that strange duppie-looking man?'

'He certainly was flesh and blood,' replied Sebastian, 'and made as much splashing as an alligator would have done; and if he is not drowned, he must have come up somewhere long ago. But let us try to mount the rocks. Time was, l knew every path and every pinnacle about these wildernesses, and thought I knew every cave; but Hamel says I do not; and the trees grow so wondrous fast in this country, that even a house is upturned by them in a year or two, if it is deserted. No wonder I should be at a loss to know my own old haunts.'

While Sebastian (for so we must call him till he has parted with his brown face) was speaking, the Quadroon was engaged in looking round, about the mouth of the cave, at the rocks which rose above it to the height of eighty or ninety feet. She espied the semblance of a practicable ascent, the one before alluded to, consisting of some foot-holes chiselled out of the stone behind a mass of foliage which had found root in the chinks of the precipice, and hung over the face of the rock down to the very ground, where many of the parasitical plants taking fresh root, the whole were bound together as securely as if by ropes; and though not sufficiently strong to admit of a man's clambering up by means of them alone, they sufficed to steady his ascent by the foot-holes, while the umbrageous mass effectually screened him from observation.

'It was here,' said Sebastian, 'that the blind Negro disappeared the first time. Nothing can be easier—there is no danger; but let us have the gun, Michal, if you will follow me. We know not what we may have to encounter; for we are intruding into a comparatively undiscovered country, and Hamel says, as well as yourself, that it is all enchanted—all spells and demonology here. There must be something curious in my fate, I should infer; for these rocks were the lot of my ancestors at the capture of the island; and I never heard that any one of them even paid a visit here. The caverns have been the haunt of runaways, as they are said to have been the refuge of the Indians whom the Spaniards found here and hunted to death; and I dare say they could tell some strange tales, if they had the gift of communicating the scenes that have taken place among them. They are no doubt the haunt of runaways still, in spite of Hamel's denunciation; that is, if the runaways are not afraid of his credit as a conjuror. But let us mount.'

Sebastian began the ascent, with his gun slung behind him. The space between the rock, and the boughs which grew before it, was about a foot wide; and by the time they had clambered up about seven or eight yards, they reached a ledge or shelf which gave them a perfectly secure footing, and led them about fifty feet higher to an excavation, a natural arch in the precipice, through which they passed to a terrace whereon grew two beautiful orange trees loaded with fruit.

'So far, so good,' said Sebastian: 'this has the air of romance, and looks a little like enchantment.' The terrace was environed with high rocks, and sounded hollow beneath his tread. It was an area of about twenty yards diameter, covered with a fine soft herbage, across which a sort of track might be distinguished, leading to a few steps which might be natural or artificial, and by which they ascended to another opening in the rock—not, like the last, a perforation into daylight again, but a dark passage, low and narrow; where it would be necessary to travel on hands and knees.

'We will not venture here,' said Michal. 'This is too dark and dirty; and we cannot guard against surprise. Over the opening by which we entered is another ledge, where we may walk with ease, as it seems, to the summit of the crags.'

The Quadroon was right. They clambered a few feet to the aforesaid shelf, and holding on by the projections in the rock, wound along in a zigzag direction to the top of the precipice, whence they looked down on the whole estate of Belmont, with the ridges of the Blue Mountain beyond, and an immense extent of country besides, all glowing in the mid-day sun. The lagoon which they had left, lay just below their feet, illuminated like the rest of the landscape; and they could distinguish within it the same sort of overhanging rocks as those on which they stood, deepening in the centre, although the margin of the water was a shore of silver sand. It seemed, by its deep blue colour, to be a bason of immense profundity—a bottomless pit, as far as Sebastian and his companion could distinguish. On the other side they looked only into the little area adorned with the orange trees; but the second lagoon of which they were in search, must be beyond this, if it were indeed anywhere in this quarter. To satisfy themselves on that point, they clambered along the summits of these pointed and narrow rocks, with considerable danger and difficulty, scaring in their journey three or four little green lizards, which scampered before them, and stopped at every few yards to puff out their orange-coloured throats at them, as if they had been the *genii loci,* alarmed and angry at this violation of the silence and secrecy of their dwellings. The lizards did not offer to descend from the heights to which they confined themselves, until they had skirted one side of the area in which were the orange trees, and reached the rocks above the small cave which Sebastian and his companion had refused to enter. Here Sebastian, being first, looked over these crags, and beheld, as he had expected, the little lagoon which he had visited so many years before in company with Joanna. It was an area similar to that from which they had ascended, but of larger dimensions, surrounded by the same sort of

rocks, and of much greater profundity as they descended to the
level of the lagoon outside of the Obeah man's cave: indeed there
was reason to believe they descended still lower than that lagoon,
as the water rose in this with some little violence, gushing and
bubbling to the centre of the surface. They had gained the side of
this second area, opposite to that from which Sebastian and
Joanna had formerly descried the snake; and a palm-tree which
grew out of the rock beneath them, prevented Sebastian from
seeing the spot on which that reptile had been coiled. But although that was not visible, there was something on the farther
side of the lagoon no less interesting than the serpent, stretched
on the narrow shore, perfectly at ease, if not asleep; and this was a
Negro, the identical duppie who had disappeared in the outer
lake, and dived, as it seemed but too probable, under the orange
garden to this. His black shirt was hoisted to dry on a bamboo pole
which he had stuck in a chink of the rock; and he had at present
wrapped himself in a large piece of blue cloth. The only imple-
ment of any kind, offensive, defensive, useful, or amusing, which
he had with him, was a bonjaw, that is, a kind of rude guitar, which
lay beside him on the grass.

The Quadroon came forward in her turn to contemplate this
sleeping Proteus, whom she could have recognised by his features
(if there had been no evidence deducible from the circumstance
of the black shirt) to be the identical being who had jumped into
the lagoon before the cave; a conviction which satisfied the minds
of both spectators, as they had supposed the duppie was drowned.
Sebastian was as clearly convinced as herself, that it was the same
being whom he had seen before: and taking out the Obeah man's
glass, which he had still about him, he very diligently perused the
Negro's face by the help of it. His eyes were closed, but it seemed
he was not asleep; for as he lay on his back, he now and then kicked
up his legs alternately, then waved his arms, muttered and
laughed, as he articulated—'Cha! cha! the hangman tie him
strong—oh this white man! that looks so fair and smells so sweet.
Oh wicked, wicked man! Negroes are nothing.'

'What can this be?' said Michal, drawing back, as she whispered
to her companion.

'Who is he talking of,' asked Sebastian, 'that smells so sweet?'

'I know only of Roland,' replied the girl, 'that smells so sweet: he has always a mess of perfumes about his person, and smells of rose, and violets, and all sorts of English smells. But look, he is going to play on his bonjaw; listen to him.'

The duppie sat up, tuned his instrument, and making a sort of twangling noise which did not sound much amiss among the rocks which reverberated the music, began to sing—not the following words, but words to the following effect; for I regret much I must not give the story in its native simplicity, inasmuch as the lingo (I must not call it language) would be utterly unintelligible to all my uncreolized countrymen:—

'The night was clear, and the spots of fire were seen in the moon; but a brighter spot of fire was seen by the white man's house.

'What is so lovely as woman, and what is better than singing prayers to God?—Woman is better: the preacher knows it, for he preferred a woman.

'I heard her scream in the middle of the night: the moon and the stars heard it, and I heard it—I, I, I—

'His face was brown, but it was not true; and he was dressed like a brave man: his heart was blacker than my face.

'Oh he was sweet, like sea-side jessamine. I was a coward not to strangle him.

'This is the man the buckras send to teach poor Negroes,—eh? The white man's devil sent him here.'

'The white man's devil sent him here!' said Sebastian, echoing the last words of the song. 'What does he mean? He certainly alludes to Roland, and to the fire when old Guthrie was in Guadaloupe. But what was the scream and the woman?'

'Oh, that was the night,' said Michal, 'that Mrs Guthrie has never recovered. The fire was laid to you, Mr Fairfax; and my mistress always shudders at the mention of the circumstance.'

'I was on board of a ship in the harbour that very night,' said he in return. 'We saw the flames, and we came on shore to help to extinguish them.'

'This man,' continued Michal, 'could tell us who made the fire, and who caused the woman to scream, and who the woman

was;—but how can we get at him?—There is no way down the
rock, and it makes me giddy to look at him so far beneath; and if
we could descend, he would jump again into the water, and swim
away like an alligator under the rocks back to the other.'

'No,' said Sebastian; 'no violence will answer. What is so singular, even Hamel swears he knows not this strange man.'

'But Hamel is as strange a man,' replied Michal; 'and there he
stands—good heavens, look at him!'

Sebastian looked down, and beheld the Obeah man, attired as
we have described him when we first introduced him, with his
crimson bandeau and his scarlet poncho, leaning on his tattooed
wand of bamboo. The music had doubtless brought him to the
spot, though by what means, or by what passage, it was impossible
for the spectators to divine, as they could not see that portion of
the rock which formed the barrier of the lagoon beneath them;
and there was no visible aperture in front except a small cavity beside which the duppie was seated,—a passage where the Obeah
man could not have passed erect, nor in any way without stepping
over the amphibious gentleman; and that was a liberty he could
not have taken without alarming him.

The duppie had laid down his bonjaw, and folded his arms across
his breast, as if in the act of deep meditation; while the wizard stood
upright as a palm tree, extending his slim figure to its utmost dimensions, and not more than a dozen paces from him. He moved
not; and no breath of wind could find its way into these sequestered
courts to agitate his garments; but he kept his eyes fixed on the duppie, as if he had been a rattle-snake waiting to fascinate his prey by
glaring at him and overpowering his faculties with horror, the moment he should become sensible of his (the wizard's) presence.

Rattle-snakes, thank heaven, are not found in Jamaica; but at
this moment a large yellow snake issued very gently from beneath
the rock between Hamel and the duppie, whom it aroused from
his reverie by the rustling it caused among the dead leaves on the
grass. It had not displayed more than half its length to the spectators above (for Hamel kept his eyes on the man before him) when
it drew itself suddenly back again to its fastness, alarmed no doubt
at one or both of the beings it beheld.

The duppie looked round, and gave by his gestures too evident a sign of his having no defect of any consequence in his eyes. He unfolded his arms, placed them on the ground beside him, as one who meditates to spring from a sitting position, collected his legs under him, and cast a hurried glance towards the water.

'Who are you?' said Hamel, without moving; 'and where do you come from?'

'I am a man,' replied the duppie; 'and I come from the water.'

'And from the fire,' said the conjuror. 'I know you: what is your business here?'

'You should know that too, Hamel.'

'Aye, it is to evade the fire.'

'It is.'

An insulting laugh, no ways familiar to the Obeah man, seemed to treat this admission with scorn. 'Your efforts are in vain: you were a slave at Belmont; you dwelt with Roland?—Speak!'

'I did—I was—I did.'

'You must be my slave: your life is in my power.'

'No, no,' said the other; 'my life is yet my own.'

'It is forfeited,' replied the wizard; 'and you must obey me. You are an intruder here: will you swear to serve me?'

'No, never!'

'Swear then to serve your lawful master.'

'Whom?'

'Fairfax.'

'Alas, he is dead, or worse than dead—his good name is ruined.'

'But you can prove him innocent,' said Hamel, 'and clear his fame, although he were dead.'

'I can.'

'You will?'

'I dare not—I must die myself.'

'Not if he were to give you an assurance of his pardon?'

'Can he do that, if he be dead?'

'He lives—he lives, and could revenge himself at this moment, if he chose.'

'What! by your hands?' said the duppie. 'I am armed.'

'And I,' replied the Obeah man. 'Look up aloft.'

The duppie turned up his eyes to the summit of the cliff, and beheld the figure of Sebastian darkened against the bright sky, with his gun in his hand, ready to fire upon him, had he offered the least violence to Hamel.

'Swear then to him—before him,' said the conjuror, 'to appear at the summons of Mr Fairfax; to prove his innocence, though you betray your own guilt; to save his fame, though you die for it!'

'But Roland?'—said the duppie.

'Not a word of him. How has he repaid you? With tales of penitence, and threats of everlasting fire, if you betray him.'

'Well—I promise.'

'You will swear?'

'Yes, by the memory of my mother, I will speak the truth: save me from Roland.'

'Roland shall not harm you.—Will it please you to descend, sir?—I shall meet you at the cave. You,' said he to the Negro, 'must again to your element: give me your shirt, and dive into the lake: you know no other exit or entrance; and I shall teach you none. Down with you to the deep; away, man—away!'

The duppie obeyed his directions, delivered him his black shirt from the staff on which it hung, and throwing aside his garment of blue cloth, appeared naked, with the exception of a pair of cotton drawers. He sprang into the lake; and while Sebastian was still gazing at his diminishing form sinking into the abyss, the wizard had disappeared from the shore without being detected or observed. The agitation of the water subsided into the gurgling and bubbling sound which was natural to it; and the only vestige that remained of the scene which had passed, or the actors who had figured in it, was the duppie's blue garment lying beside his bonjaw on the margin of the lagoon, and his bamboo pole leaning against the rock.

CHAPTER 27.

No might nor greatness in mortality
Can censure 'scape; back-wounding calumny
The whitest virtue strikes. What king so strong
Can tie the gall up in a slanderous tongue?
                                    MEASURE FOR MEASURE.

By the time that Sebastian and the pretty soubrette had reached the base of the rocks, and descended from the orange-garden, the duppie was at the mouth of the cave, habited in his black shirt, waiting to receive them. His eyes were free from any blemish; and he owned, on being interrogated by Michal, that he had once seen the water in the lagoon sink so low, that he had descended by the rocks, and walked through to the inner lake, which had become quite dry; for there was a passage for the water, deep down on the other side of it, into a chasm called the Devil's Gully, where it fell into the Rio Grande. This occurred just after an earthquake. He said that it was always dry under the orange-garden; for the water passed along the floor of a cave there; and there was but a rock not three yards wide to dive under, to pass from that into the inner lagoon.

'You belong to Mr Fairfax,' said Sebastian: 'I remember you; and you came to see your children?'

'I was made free, master,' said the Negro: 'Roland bought me.'

'How so?'

'He taught me to counterfeit blindness, and bought me for nothing; but it was not to make me free: he would have sold me, and sent me away from the island. My master only sold me on condition that Roland made me free.'

'He did so, then?'

'He was obliged, and he has long thought me dead. I shall tell you more, before Mr Guthrie, of Roland's motives, and why he sent me away; my life is not safe, while he is in the island; and I can tell a tale of him—but in good time for that. I have two children here at Belmont, who are slaves: it is four years since I have seen

them, though I have been here more than once for the purpose.
I have often seen this watchman; I knew that he frequented the
caves; he is more acquainted with them than myself; but I did
not suspect, nor do I know, how he came into that court of the lagoon. *You* know perhaps that he was thought to be a dealer in
Obeah; but while I confined myself to the shores of this water,
nothing, I thought, could catch me; and no one could find out my
secret.'

'Tell me,' said Sebastian, 'in what respect the character of
Fairfax is affected by your own or Roland's machinations.'

'For my own, I can say nothing. Master Roland was too fond of
Mrs Guthrie: he did the deed of a villain. Mr Fairfax sailed for
England; Roland accused him of the wickedness which *he* had
himself committed. I was sent to leeward and to sea; for Roland
threatened to have me hanged, if I remained in the island. He said
his word was better than a Negro's, and that I set fire to the trash-
house at Mr Guthrie's.'

'And did you so?'

'I used no fire: I put something wrapped in a cloth, which he
gave me, among the cane trash; and when I saw the flames mounting above the shingles, I ran, not knowing what I did, into the
great house, and hid myself behind a bed. There was a lady in the
piazza: I heard her scream; and a white man brought her into the
room where I was hid. He spoke to her in whispers; but she heard
him not, for she had fainted. She was then beautiful, as she is now,
they say. I came from my concealment, thinking to rescue her
from the white man's violence. It was Roland: he knew me not at
first. I was a fool; he chased me from the house, and fled himself,
as if a wild boar had been at his heels.'

During this conversation the Obeah man, in his usual watchman's garb, was sauntering round the lagoon; and Michal, forget-
ful of her assumed sex, was sobbing ready to break her heart at the
tale she heard of her poor mistress. But what were the feelings
which agitated the bosom of Sebastian? Rage, indignation, compassion, sympathy. This however, he thought, was not a time for
giving way to feeling: they must act. 'Michal,' said he, 'let me conjure you to go home. Tell your master that Fairfax—(I wish I had

materials for writing: I have a pencil, but this wilderness will not produce a sheet nor a scrap of paper)—tell your master that Fairfax begs to see him directly at the sunken bridge between Belmont and his own estate—the bridge where Kenrick the robber was shot;—tell him what you please to ensure his coming, but spare the mention of his wife; and tell Joanna—'

'Stay, stay,' said Michal, interrupting him, and drying her tears; 'write in my hat or on my handkerchief with your pencil, on your own handkerchief—for it is here; and let me first wash it in the lake:—the sun will not be long drying it.'

So saying, she stepped to the lagoon: and having soaked and wrung the water out of the pocket-handkerchief, laid it on the sand to dry, while Hamel remarked to her that women's wits were seldom at a loss.

'Indeed,' replied she, 'I am at a loss to comprehend you; and know not but you may yet deceive us all.'

'Fear me not,' said he. 'I have great wrongs; but the owner of the estate yonder behaved to me with the kindness of a father and a friend; for his sake I could forego my deep revenge; for his sake at least it shall sleep till justice is done to his heirs. I am proscribed in many men's thoughts; and Roland has it in his power to raise the demons of the white man's law against me. I cannot come down to the bay, nor to Mr Guthrie's: my presence would defeat the object of your lover.'

'Alas! he is not my lover,' said the Quadroon, blushing.

'Your friend then, the lover of your mistress. The watchman Hamel, or the Obeah man:—in the first character I should be despised, in the second detested. But though I shall remain here, I shall be as useful as you could wish, and of more service than you expect.'

The handkerchief was but a few minutes drying; and the letter to Joanna being written out, was folded up and consigned to the bosom of the pretty maid, for it was hardly safe in the shallow pockets of her jacket. She took an affectionate leave of her late companion, whom she left with the Obeah man and the duppie, though not without some anxieties on his account; and assuming a quicker pace than corresponded with her heavy heart, she was soon lost among the woody forest that skirted what might be called the domain of the Obeah man.

She could not have less than six or seven miles to walk; and it was now about two o'clock in the afternoon. A couple of hours would bring her to her master's; but as it is not our intention to accompany her through every foot of her journey, we shall suppose that an hour at least is passed, and that she has reached the sunken bridge where Sebastian was to meet her master. She sat for a moment on a stone beside the river, a small stream which flowed over it, and had already tucked up her trowsers, to keep them from being wetted as she waded through, when she was startled at the sound of a horse's hoof clattering along the road; and looking forward through the trees which terminated the view before her, she caught a glimpse of mister Roland coming towards her at a good round pace, with a green shade tied over his eyes. He was alone, and had hardly taken any notice of her, but for her retreating back out of the water as he came through; for the consciousness of his black eye prevented him from gazing too much around, at least at any human being: so that he had actually passed her before he bestowed more than a very hasty glance on her. She turned about to see if he was gone, congratulating herself on escaping his notice; but she reckoned without her host: he had not proceeded many yards before he pulled up his horse, as if arrested by some sudden recollection; and turning round to reconnoitre, he observed that she was attired like a sailor. 'A sailor boy,' thought he: 'who said that Mr Fairfax was disguised like a sailor?' He called out—'Young man, may I ask your name?'

The Quadroon proceeded on through the water: the Missionary followed.

'Young man, what ho! stop; I wish to speak with you.'

Michal still hurried on, while Roland called to her; and finding that he was bent on stopping her, she darted into the wood to avoid him; but the Missionary, taking courage from her shyness, still pursued, and scrambling off his horse, rushed after her into the thicket. He was soon up with her, and seizing her rather rudely by the arm, demanded imperiously who she was.

'Begone, you hateful man!' she exclaimed. 'Let me go.'

'I will know,' he cried, 'if you are a sailor, and what ship you belong to. Let me see your face: this is no Fairfax:—let me see your
face.' (He pulled off her hat.) 'A Quadroon boy!—Why were you
afraid? And why this disguise?—The pretty Michal!'

'Leave me, sir; pursue your course, Mr Roland, and do not interfere with me: my mistress is ill, and wants me.'

'She is indeed,' said the Missionary, as if seized with a sudden
qualm. 'Young woman, I fear her hour is at hand.'

'What do you mean?' cried Michal, out of breath.

'I mean,' replied the Missionary, 'that the thread of her existence is unravelled, unspun; that she totters on the verge of eter-
nity: peace be with her! I have done all that religion could inspire;
I have endeavoured to give her all the consolations of faith; but
she has that upon her mind which turns hope to bitterness, honey
to gall: she will not be comforted.'

'Not by you, master Roland: you are her— '

'What, Michal?' exclaimed he, in some confusion.

'Look at me, Roland,' said the undaunted girl. 'You are her
murderer!'

Rage and astonishment contended for empire in the
Missionary's features; but he governed his passion. 'Michal, you
are mad: I heard that you were come to Belmont; but I dreamed
not of this disguise. You have been to see this furious Sebastian—
Ha, ha!'

'Do you beware of him, monster—murderer, as you are.'

'For shame, my beauty; but this passion becomes you. Your
sparkling black eyes speak a different language to him; and
you do not blush with anger in his presence; and he has toyed with
every chesnut curl that wantons on your pretty brows. What have
you written in your bosom there? Stanzas to love or remembrance, with a lock of his hair? Does he write on linen?'

He had espied the handkerchief, which her struggles to escape
him had perhaps caused to obtrude; and he resolved to see what
could be written on it, by foul means, if not by fair;—not that an
idea of Joanna had occurred to him on the subject; but he had
rightly divined that Sebastian was the author of the writing, as well
as the reasons for thus using a piece of linen.

'Let me see it, Michal,' he exclaimed, thrusting his hand over her shoulder towards her bosom: 'give me the handkerchief.'

'Hold off, villain!' cried the intrepid maid. 'I will die before you shall see it.'

'You shall not die,' said he; 'and I will see it—by my virtue, I will. Come what will, I will have it. There! there! gently now—I have got it.'

He had seized it, and it became unfolded in the struggle; but before he could assure himself of the possession, an unexpected ally approached on the side of the Quadroon in the person of the wizard Hamel, who told him, as courteously as usual, that the young girl was tired, and could not fight with a buckra; and begged him to restore the handkerchief.

'Touch me, at your peril,' said the preacher, holding the handkerchief.

'Oh, master Roland,' replied the Obeah man; 'brother Roland!—brother Roland—ha! ha! ha! Your horse is gone through the water, brother. Hah! you have pistols in your pocket. Hold still your hands, or you are a dead man: stir, and you die.'

Hamel observed him feeling for arms, as he guessed by his action and the quivering of his under lip; and being pretty familiar with the preacher's character, he knew too well there was everything to be apprehended from his violence: he sprung on Roland like a cat on its prey, and held a dagger at his throat, before the other could disengage his hands from his pockets.

'Oh, kill him not!' cried the soubrette, snatching back her handkerchief. 'Detain him only till I escape: hurt him not, monster as he is.'

'Fly, Michal,' said the wizard: 'you are safe;—and for you, brother, I will not hurt you, but I will fasten you to this tree for the present, with your arms still in your pocket: and I will then get your horse, and tie him beside you; and the next passenger shall do you a greater service than you intended to the pretty girl. Come—I shall not be rough with you.'

While he was thus talking, and Michal was hastening home, he took from under his frock two or three fathoms of mahoe rope, which he told Roland he always carried to hang those who violated their sacred oaths. He bound the Missionary by his hands, knees, and also by his throat, to a trumpet-tree which grew beside them. The Missionary did not take correction as a cat laps milk; but the Obeah man had the dagger ever in his hand, and Roland was effectually cowed. Hamel was however as good as his word; and having secured the rider, went after the horse, which he brought back through the water, and fastened to another tree in a more conspicuous place; telling the owner that it would soon attract attention, for Mr Guthrie was expected there in less than an hour, to meet a person whom Roland would be most happy to see—no other than Mr Oliver Fairfax, the proprietor of Belmont, and the affianced husband of Miss Joanna Guthrie. Having thus spoken, and waved a courteous adieu to 'brother Roland,' the Obeah man disappeared among the boughs of the forest.

CHAPTER 28.

Out, you rogues, you knaves! work for your livings.
There's no more charity among men
Than among so many mastiff dogs.
LIFE AND DEATH OF LORD CROMWELL.

IT is high time that we should give some account of our quickly deposed Brutchie Combah, and the troop of sable gentlemen and
ladies who had been scared from their festivities and imaginary
emancipation by the sound of a single word 'Maroons,' uttered by
the terrible Sebastian. As for the generality of these good folks,
they took to their heels, some to the estates around Port Antonio,
some to the eastward, others to the west. A few fled to the rocks
around the scene of their extravagancies; and half a dozen, among
whom was the Brutchie, towards the fastnesses of the Blue
Mountains in the interior. Happy to find themselves free from
pursuit, they attributed their escape very naturally to their own
talents and ingenuity, and wandered far from the spot where the
dreadful word was uttered, to await in patience a second and a
better opportunity of uniting again to put in force the occult,
mysterious, yet too well comprehended, recommendations of the
devout Missionary.

As most of the party had consisted of what the French call
canaille, we shall interest ourselves or our readers no farther with
their virtues or vices. But the Brutchie, inasmuch as he aspired to
a white beauty and a crown, is entitled to some additional notice
on the score of the first article of his ambition, even if he ought to
be despised on account of his desire for the second—the work of
the tinman and the toyman, as Roland remarked in his soliloquy.
The Brutchie had carried off the crown with him in his flight,
though it had become inconvenient to be worn, from the batter-
ings and squeezings it had received in the conflict with which the
new king had entertained his subjects at his coronation; an adventure without a precedent, proving that if Solomon were not right
in asserting that there was nothing new under the sun, the mistake

was excusable, inasmuch as Solomon had not discovered the continent or the islands of the West, where the cabbages are a hundred
feet high, the fish fly, and oysters grow upon trees. Such a scuffle
between a new crowned monarch of England and his archbishop
of Canterbury, hand to hand and foot to foot, would certainly strike
all Europe with amazement, and excite no little ridicule on the part
of our neighbours: and God deliver us from the chance of furnishing such materials for mirth! But in Jamaica, among ungenteel
Negroes of no condition and quality, and without any precedents
to the contrary, such an affair did not seem at all out of character or
place. It excited some admiration; and perhaps many of the spectators thought it a thing of course, a part of the ceremony; and as
such, who knows but the next king, which we are sure to have (I
mean of course in Jamaica) may repeat the scene, and that such a
scuffle may henceforth become as much a matter of importance,
propriety, and necessity, in coronations there, as the challenge of
our hereditary champion at a coronation in England.

However, to be more serious: his majesty (not his 'sacred
majesty'—as the oil, though duly consecrated, was not administered to the woolly pate of the monarch)—fled with as much
precipitation as any of his antidiluvian or postdiluvian predecessors, vying in speed with the unfortunate Darius, or the crazy
Charles of Sweden in his retreat from Pultowa, or Napoleon from
Waterloo, or any other discomfited king. He never stopped till he
had proceeded half a dozen miles at least, lasting thickets, sacred
to snakes, musquitos, pigeons, and toads, which last entertain
themselves by taking the air on the tops of the trees, as well as the
pigeons, though how they get there, none of them have told us.
He scrambled over rocks, amid waterfalls and ravines; now clambering like the youth who went in search of the waters of oblivion,
now diving, not into the water like our duppie, but into dingles
and bosky dells—

> Where the thrush and lark sing never,
> But the crickets scream for ever;—

now amidst groves of cedar and mahogany, o'er-topped by the
mountain-palms and the Santa Maria, or the huge juniper—

Where the huge axe with heaved stroke
Was never heard the nymphs to daunt.

In short, he never stopped till he reached the top of a naked rock
about six miles in a straight line behind Port Antonio, where he
found a brace of runaway friends quietly breakfasting under a
piece of an old sail, gypsy-fashion.

The Brutchie came up to them, reeking with perspiration, and
puffing with the race he had run; and dashing down his ginger-
bread crown on the rock, he exclaimed in a tone of mingled
ridicule and rage—'C—e and d—n all crowns and all kings, and
all preachers and Anabaptists! May the devil have them all, and all
that belong to them! I'll be a downright robber, not make laws to
rob. Let Hamel plot, and Roland preach and plot: I will be alone.
Fools, rascals, villains, and cowards!'

When knaves fall out, as the proverb says, honest folks come by
their own. This is not always true; but knaves themselves more
frequently come by their own in the shape of halters and whip-
pings, and by a certain portion of their own in the mutual surrender and acknowledgment of a few hard names, such as those
above recited. This was the case in the present instance; and his
majesty, king Combah, spoke with the accuracy of an oracle, as he
helped himself to the plantains and pickled herrings, and soothed
himself for the bumps which Roland had left on his head, and the
punches he had given him in his bread-basket or epigastric region.
But as Brutchie began to cool, and his limbs to get a little stiff, he
felt more of the subject than of the sovereign; and having acted his
part as well as he could before company, right royally, he thought
himself at liberty now to curse and swear as much as he pleased,
by way of easing his passion, as well as to revenge himself on his
enemies. This was a Chinese mode of vengeance in great vogue in
the time of the jesuit Le Comte, who relates that if a house were
robbed, the owner and his family would take it in rotation to sit on
the roof and curse the robber, keeping up an incessant tirade of
execrations, until (which usually happened) the thief was so
horrified as to make restitution of the stolen goods. A feeling
somewhat analogous prevails among the Africans, who will bear

blows more patiently than curses, and any violence rather than hear their mothers cursed; but it does not extend their hopes or their ideas to the recovery or to the restitution of stolen goods, although they attach more weight to curses which they utter than we are wont to do in Europe. There are other more ancient authorities for the importance and consequence of these awful denunciations, which we need not point out to the reader, who will be satisfied to hear that the Brutchie continued the fire of this artillery long after he had lighted his pipe, and until he had smoked himself into a stupor of repose.

He awoke, after a few hours' dreaming, with recruited hopes, energies, and intentions, resolving at any rate to make an effort for the young lady whom he had selected to be his bride, and if he could not reign as a king—an honour of which he did not altogether despair—to make war upon the Whites, and set the Negroes by the ears. He now felt the necessity of having advice respecting what was going on, and the importance of being on good terms with Hamel, who was, and always had been, his oracle. Beside which, the blows he had received from Roland had completely disgusted him with that vain and vacillating personage, and stimulated him to wreak his spite upon him by turning his preaching into ridicule, and exposing his schemes; and if opportunity should again serve, of securing his person, and taking vengeance on him for his duplicity, his vanity, selfishness, superstitious folly, and splenetic insolence.

His breakfast companions, as well as the few of his comrades who had followed him from the ruined settlement, were to him little more than so many mules or oxen, over whom he had as complete an ascendancy as a hog-hunter has over his dog. He was vastly their superior in strength of mind and body; and although he had been hurried away by the panic which had infected all his followers, he was by no means deficient in courage or resolution. He had slept amidst this crew, confident and unconcerned. He knew that they considered him next to invulnerable, except as to fists, on account of some charm he had obtained from the Obeah man, of whom they were all in great dread: swords and bayonets were not to hurt him, nor molten lead. They were but few who knew that he had ever been baptized; and even these suspected he had been so served only to flatter the vanity of the Missionary, without attaching any importance to the ceremony.

Combah got up from his slumbers, like the tiger from his lair; and without saying a word to Quashie, Quao, Diego, Tom, Jack, Fiddlestring, or Julius Cæsar, marched off with his machet in the direction of the Obeah man's abode, to learn some news of this so famous Sebastian, and to hatch some scheme against the miserable and yet mischievous Roland.

CHAPTER 29.

We had as good sit still, as rise to fall.

RABELAIS.

BEING perfectly familiar with all the passages through the jungles of Portland and St George's, the Brutchie travelled with no less expedition than secrecy towards the enchanted abode of his late host and ally, the magician Hamel; his mind burning, as his heat increased, with the recollection of his disgraceful overthrow before his subjects, and his no less disgraceful flight from the Maroons. Indeed, he began to suspect that there might have been some roguery played off in the concoction of that last adventure: however, time and the conjuror, he knew, would explain all; and he doubted not but that Hamel would assist him in his revenge on the Missionary, and in any scheme of retaliation on the hard-hearted and tyrannical Whites. He fell in with one or two persons in his route, from whom he heard nothing connected with the history of his own affairs; the sole thing he learnt of any interest being the report set on foot by Drybones, though sadly perverted in its circulation—that the robber captain, Sebastian, was coming to take possession of Belmont. 'The robber captain!' thought the Brutchie. 'A Mulatto too! He is a bold man: I should like to see him face to face.'

His course lay through the estate of Belmont; and being provided with a forged pass, he determined to investigate this report more narrowly himself, meaning at the same time not to run his head into any unnecessary mischief. The Mulatto captain, he concluded, must turn out either a rival or an ally to himself—in the first case an enemy; and he had naturally an inclination to know the worst that could befall him. Under this impression, he crept silently through the woods at the back of the house, keeping clear of the Negro huts, and got into a tree just behind the works, where he could overlook all the premises with great facility; and, as the sea breeze began to decline, could distinguish, amongst the gabble of the Negroes, a great deal of what at least interested them and the Quinbus Flestrin, as he was nicknamed, the attorney.

Mr Fillbeer was on his steed, haranguing some of his people as they kept dropping in, and telling them that a robber captain had threatened to come and rob the house, pretending that he was Mr Fairfax; that if he *were* Mr Fairfax, he would have no business here; and that he should treat him as a robber, and shoot him, if he offered to stay in violation of the law.

'No, no,' said one of the book-keepers: 'do not threaten that; you must not shoot him.'

'No, master Fillbeer,' cried a Negro, repeating the words, 'you must not shoot him. Let the poor Negroes see their old master's son once more before they are dead.'

'Who are you, sir?' exclaimed the attorney, turning round upon him. 'Hold your tongue, sirrah: do you wish to make a mutiny among the Negroes?'

'I tell you, master attorney,' replied the Negro, 'that if old master's son comes here, and has the law in his pocket, the Negroes won't shoot him, nor let you shoot him: they'll pull you down, and put him up in your place. I speak the truth; you may go talk to others who will flatter you and speak with a sweet mouth; but I tell you what you must expect. We know what is right, as well as white men; we know who we belong to, who gives us clothes, and grounds, and houses. For one, I long to see my dear master come home again, poor creature—God bless him! Sent to wander about the world, and kept out of his own house and plantations, and cheated of his Negroes.'

'Sirrah, sirrah,' cried Fillbeer, shaking the stick of his umbrella at him, 'you are a mutinous dog; you will be a great man in a rebellion; you want to be free, sirrah—you do!'

'Cha!' said the Negro.

'Do you answer me in that way, sir? I'll have you flogged for your insolence.'

'I say *cha,* master attorney, when you say I want to be free: what's the use of *free* to me? Who will give me a house and grounds, and take care of my children? I want nothing but to see my own poor master again, and for him to enjoy his own. I do not like you, master Fillbeer; that is the truth; I like my own master better; I love him, poor thing; all the slaves love him, and pray

Garamighty to send him safe home. And now, master attorney, you may flog me when you please.'

'Hold your tongue, sir.'

This speech affected the oily man of grace (to compare small things with great, or rather great things with small) much as his majesty king James the Second was affected at the shouts of his soldiery on the acquittal of the bishops. He thought for the first time of abdicating his authority.—Four years' accounts in arrear even to the mortgagee; dilapidations, appropriations, a few spoliations, all the confusion of such an establishment badly conducted,—all rushed into his head. 'But not yet,' said the man-mountain; 'I'll die with harness on my back: time enough to surrender when the enemy is in the citadel. You talking fellow!' (The talking fellow was gone to the field again.) 'Mr Saunderson'—(this was the book-keeper)—'pray keep these fellows' mouths shut: they are become so saucy, since there is this palaver of their freedom, that one dare hardly speak to them of their moral feelings; and there is no such thing as flogging them into silence and respect.'

'No;' said Mr Saunderson; 'there is not indeed; you may thank your sect for that: you came here with a psalm in your mouth—I heard you myself. You were not so fat then, it is true,' he added laughing; 'but you have set the slaves an example of liberty, as well as preached it to them.'

'How so, sir?' said Fillbeer with a grin.

'By living here like a lord, without rendering any accounts.'

'And how do you know that?'

'It is no secret, sir; all the parish, all the island, knows it.'

A second thought of abdication here intervened; but it was smothered in rage, which subsided gradually into chagrin. He turned his horse about, and rode away from the works in a mood which master Matthew would call melancholy and gentlemanlike; leaning his fat head tenderly on his bosom, while his big belly, projecting before him, prevented him from seeing more than the tips of his horse's ears. If the reader has ever seen Mr Lambert, of fat memory (his picture will suffice) his imagination may set that mass of mortality on horseback. No horse could have borne him;

therefore we encounter only what is supposititious in the picture of the mind;—but such as the reader may fancy the effigies of Mr Lambert in the saddle,—with the reduction of one-third perhaps as to quantity,—was the figure of this fat Fillbeer. Then let the reader stretch his imagination a little farther, and paint a few tears trickling round and down the glossy cheeks of this man of sentiment; fancy the sighs that stretched his leathern coat almost to bursting—sighs of contrition too; he appealed to heaven and to the spirit of Wesley. 'He,' said the penitent, 'was reproved for his negligence at Birmingham by a shower of hail: would it could hail here! I have been a sinner by omission, if not by commission: I was virtuous, religious, and all that, to a certain extent; everything prospered with me; but in my prosperity I forgot the hand that had raised me up; and now my cup shall be turned into bitterness, and I shall be sent forth upon the wide world again, bereft of every blessing—uh!—uh! The Devil take Fairf—Oh dear, there, what am I saying?—Oh Fillbeer, Fillbeer,—thou art an ungodly ass; and the name of Satan is as often in thy mouth as that of thy maker—uh! uh! uh!'

Thus he sat, and sighed, and whined, and repented; using a great many more expressions whose holy character prevents us from recording them to the prejudice of good men's feelings. Even Brutchie, who from his perch had heard the conversation, was affected by the sighs of the attorney—but it was with laughter. He saw him wipe his eyes with his handkerchief, and descried the convulsion which his huge shoulders repeated; like a telegraph, from the head-quarters of his diaphragm; not that his head quartered there—that was gently couched on his fat bosom, as before stated.

The Brutchie watched him turn his horse toward the cane pieces; and slipping down from the tree, took again to his heels, satisfied with the information he had acquired, as it did not point at himself in any respect,—Sebastian and Fairfax being the only names which excited any interest at present on this estate. He left the man-mountain in the *interval* (a most 'vile phrase,' used to signify an avenue or glade between the cane pieces) weeping like a glacier in the dog-days—tears and perspiration; and keeping the covert of the woods, he skirted the cultivated grounds as far they extended; then hastened on more fearlessly toward the cave of Hamel.

VOLUME TWO

CHAPTER 1.

—This affliction has a taste as sweet
As any cordial comfort.

WINTER'S TALE.

THE day was fast drawing to a close; the sea breeze had died by
that agreeable death for which philosophers so often sigh and sigh
in vain—old age and exhaustion; the faculty, the excellence, of it
enduring to the last; more temperate in its decline; and as the less
passionate, so much the more regretted when it was gone. What
would Jamaica be without it? As badly provided as the world is
without philosophers;—not that by philosopher is meant a
weigher of gases, or a writer of polemics, of books of political
economy, or theological controversy, cheap tracts, such as 'Tom
White' and 'Margaret Blue,' or books of any kind;—but by
philosopher is intended one who sees and knows, and by bearing
teaches or rather encourages others to bear, the multiplied incon-
veniences, vexations, and tribulations, of this weary life, (with
which Heaven knows it is most crammed,) making, in spite of
Candide, the best of everything.

Mr Guthrie rode towards the rendezvous, chewing the cud of
sweet and bitter fancy, having left his wife, as the Missionary had
stated in his conversation with Michal, on a sick bed, and—as he
apprehended—in a fatal condition. Yet his presence and services
were of no avail with her, and seemed in fact to add only fuel to the
fire which consumed her. He had received the tale communicated
by the soubrette with some astonishment, wondering how he
could have failed to detect the disguise of Fairfax, and—why in
spite of the Quadroon's explanation on the subject, Fairfax should
not have discovered himself. 'The return he owed to the rascals
who brought him from Cuba!—Yes, he was bound to let them get

away; there was some delicacy in his not shocking my wife and daughter, after all this law business, and considering the antipathy she has taken to him—and that I had. Alas, alas! Self-interest! But no matter for that—I must do my duty by the poor boy; I must give him my advice as a man, my assistance as a magistrate; I must seat him in the hall of his ancestors. And for Joanna—I suppose she will be twice as much in love with him as ever, since her mother has exacted her solemn promise not to marry him—and this romance in his character at present—his painted face, and his Spanish name, and his tossing robbers into the sea,—the girl will be downright crazy about him;—and a letter written on a cambric pocket handkerchief, and that silly Michal whimpering all the while she read it;—well, well, he is a brave lad.' The old man's heart yearned towards him, the nearer he drew towards the spot where he expected to find the son of his friend; his mind now reverting to past days, now looking to the future; sometimes recalling the comfort and independence in which both families had been wont to live, then contemplating the broken society in which, with impaired fortunes and blighted hopes, they were now struggling; and then imagining the horrors which, as *he* thought, must inevitably, soon or late, dissolve for ever the influence and authority of white men among a set (as he expected them to become) of fanatical and infuriated Blacks.

The sun was setting—(he sinks, in the Tropics, as if Phaeton always attempted to guide the steeds of Apollo)—and his long rays, shot from the ridges of the western mountains, gleamed on the giant shafts of the cotton-trees—(wands which would have been almost stout enough for Milton's hero)—and on their long streamers, hanging motionless in the becalmed atmosphere. The distant sea was fast subsiding into repose—scarce a wave murmured; the crickets thought it time to go to bed, and the bat and the owl thought it was time to get up; a few beetles and cockroaches were in the same mood; but the lizards still scampered about the road, as Mr Guthrie came cantering on, now flashing their grey jackets in the sunbeams, now whisking their long tails into the shaded bushes, and into the chinks of the rocks. Fairfax was already at the sunken bridge, which is a sort of dam made in rather a muddy

river-course, with bavins and gravel to afford a safe passage
through the water for mules and oxen, and the wains they draw; an
arched bridge not suiting the taste of many of these Jamaica
streams, which are apt to bury up such conveniences under a
mountain of rubbish, before they choose another course to the
ocean, perhaps half a mile distant from the old one. There had
been a few bamboo poles suspended across for foot passengers;
but the rain of the hurricane, swelling the river, had carried them
away; so that now it had become necessary for Fairfax to walk
through the water, or to remain on the eastern side. He chose the
latter alternative, being as yet uncertain whether Mr Guthrie
would attend to his request, and give him the meeting at this the
appointed place. Had he waded through the stream, he had
hardly failed to encounter Roland, whose horse was not tied
above a hundred yards from the bridge, and at about the distance
of twenty yards from himself.

Mr Guthrie had been made acquainted with the violence which
Roland had offered to Michal, though he was not aware of the result of Hamel's interference, as the Quadroon had not waited to
see the Missionary grafted, or rather inarched (to use a horticul-
tural phrase) on the trumpet-tree—a fit species of vegetable for
the occasion. Some sable Ovid, in future ages, may tell of the
metamorphosis of such a preacher into such a tree, and feign that
its name was thus derived because Roland was a trumpeter, and
the tree became as hollow as a trumpet, in consequence of this
oracle, this spouter, being so incorporated.

Fairfax at length heard the clattering of the whey-faced horse;
and looking anxiously down the glade, recognised the wall-eyes of
the beast, and the squinting eyes and pinioned locks of the kind
old planter. He in his turn espied the Mulatto Sebastian, who
doffed his sombrero in token of recognition, waving it beside the
streamlet where he stood. So anxious did the old man seem to
come up with him, that he mended his pace as soon as he caught a
glimpse of him, and without looking to the right or left, galloped
straight forward down the glade, dashed through the water, and
leaping with youthful activity from his horse, took the young man
in his arms, strained him as affectionately to his heart as if he had

been the issue of his own body—his own, his sole, his long-lost, darling son. 'My child, my child, may every blessing be yours! Welcome to the land of your fathers, to your own lands, to your inheritance, to my heart, to every heart that loves you!' (His lip quivered, and a tear or two forced their way from his eyes, in spite of his efforts to prevent them.) 'What is it, Fairfax? What can I do for you? I have left my poor wife dying, to come and meet you; but where is your copper-coloured face? You are as fair as ever, and look as handsome as if the grasp of sorrow had never wrung your heart.'

It may be supposed the young man was not unaffected by this ebullition of old Guthrie's affectionate nature. He returned his embrace, and kissed his old sunburnt hand with the submissive idolatry of a fond and doting child; but his heart was too full to speak. 'God's blessing!' cried the old man again, 'that I may heal all your wounds, and soothe all your cares! *Duras immittere curas,* of which my poor boy has had his share. Oh, Fairfax! But they are all lies; and we shall defeat the liars. I have told Fillbeer I shall take your part, and we must turn him out; but not to-night—it is too late—the sun is down; and we must do all in open day.'

'It is too late, sir,' replied Fairfax, wringing the old man's hand, which he still grasped in his own. 'Nothing but your kindness could enable me to bear up against the calumnies that have been heaped upon me, and the oppressions that have almost overwhelmed me,—misfortunes indeed of all kinds; but the worst is, that I have lost, by the pirates who took me into Cuba, my clothes and property.'

'Tush—fiddlestick!' said the old man. 'I will equip you from my own wardrobe. Besides, your own costume, for the present, cannot well be bettered.'

'And I have lost,' added Fairfax, 'a most important document—a power of attorney from Mr M'Grabbit in London, to supersede Mr Fillbeer here in the management of all his affairs.'

'You astonish me,' said Mr Guthrie, opening his eyes to the widest. 'A power of attorney from M'Grabbit! What! did the hypocrite relent at last?'

'He relented from persisting in the wrong,' replied Fairfax: 'he found I was informed of everything relating to my rights and interests; and Fillbeer is such an ass that he did not send the accounts, nor half the crops, to him. He was very glad of an opportunity to be revenged on Fillbeer: he gave me a power of attorney to be in fact my own trustee for all the estates that are mortgaged, leaving it to my honour, as he said, to arrange all matters relating to Belmont as my father's son would wish himself to do.'

'Very fine, indeed, M'Grabbit; no virtue like the virtue of necessity;—and this power of attorney you have lost?'

'Indeed I have. It was taken with my baggage and all my moveables, by a crew of pirates, who plundered our ship and burnt it.'

'I wonder,' said Mr Guthrie, 'you escaped with your life.'

'It was a wonder. That Negro Drybones—or, as we called him, Nimrod—belonged to my father; he knew me; it was he who managed to get our lives spared, on condition of a ransom from Jamaica; it was he who secreted me in Cuba, found me the plant which stained my hands and face—a secret I had from Hamel, one of my father's Negroes, a rebellious Coromantin whom he had bought at my intercession, when a boy, from another Coromantin his master.'

'I know the man,' said Mr Guthrie: 'he is reckoned a professor of Obeah.'

'This Drybones,' continued Fairfax, 'equipped me as you see, and got me a birth in the canoe which was destined to carry away your daughter Joanna, to be the wife of a black man who was to set up for the crown of Jamaica, to be king of the island.'

'There is no end to the extravagance of their notions now,' said Mr Guthrie with a sigh. 'We want to get hold of this king—this Combah, as he is called.'

'It was perhaps a fortunate circumstance,' continued Fairfax, 'that I was taken into Cuba, and got a birth in the boat which was freighted with a set of cut-throats who were to attack your house. The storm disabled the boat; but they would have made a second attempt, if I had not run the canoe on the rocks, and fairly bundled the crew on shore or into the water.'

'Alack, alack!' said the planter, musing over the circumstances he had heard: 'so you have lost the power of attorney: that is the most serious loss of all.'

'They left me nothing, sir,' rejoined Fairfax, 'but my shirt and trowsers, not even a hat:—yes, yes, they left me one thing—here it is—the picture of Joanna:' (taking it from his bosom:) 'it was set round with pearls, which they took out: the rest they did not value, Drybones procured it for me.'

The old man looked at the picture and then at Fairfax, and heaved a deep sigh. 'Ah, my poor boy,' said he—'but we'll talk of this tomorrow: we must go back to my house for to-night; Joanna will be too happy to—Ah, there again, all wrong! God only knows what fancy has possessed my wife: but I believe she would encounter Beelzebub rather then see you: the mention of your name is to her what water is to a man raving with hydrophobia.'

'Alas,' said Fairfax, 'she has but too much cause.'

'How!' cried the old man, with a start. 'What is the cause? Do you know it!'

'I know it but too well,' replied the other: 'I never knew it till today.'

'What the devil is it, then?' said Mr Guthrie. 'Tell me quickly, I pray and beseech you: her aversion is beyond reason, it seems to know no bounds whatever.'

'It cannot: it would not, supposing she were not imposed on. But I can never tell you, sir: it is impossible. I could tell her she is deceived; but to no one else could I explain myself, and least of all to you:—and indeed I would, if I might take so great a liberty, advise you never to inquire about the cause of her aversion to me; only—'

'I tell you, my dear boy,' rejoined Mr Guthrie, 'I hate all mystery, and care not a curse for the worst that I can hear; but I must know this bugaboo tale, be it what it may, except it involves your own character.'

'Oh, sir, not the least,' said Fairfax. 'Mrs Guthrie is deceived by the Missionary, Mr Roland.'

'Gad's my life, I thought as much,' replied the planter. 'That rank old vermin attacked my Quadroon, Michal, here today in this very spot, and tried to rob her of your handkerchief, and would have succeeded but for the interference of a Negro who chanced to pass by, and threatened to cut his throat if he did not desist. He

is always in some disgraceful scrape: I met him in the morning all
over bruises and bumps, with a black eye. Ha! there is a horse
neighing—who is coming?'

'I see no one,' replied the young man.

The horse neighed again.

'This is not a place to turn out horses; let us cross the water; get
up behind me,' said Mr Guthrie: 'Harlequin is not riotous; he will
carry us through the river goodnaturedly.'

The old gentleman mounted before; the young gentleman
seated himself behind on the croup, hardly containing himself
from laughter at his friend's funny tail, which stuck out so as to
tickle his face in the passage or the streamlet. He slipped off as
soon as they were on dry land; and walking forward a few paces,
they beheld the sulky Spanish beast of the devout Roland.

CHAPTER 2.

'Shew him up, sir? With all my heart, sir, up
or down, all's one to me—'

GOOD-NATURED MAN.

'INSTAR *montis equum*,' said the old gentleman; 'here's Roland's
Bucephalus; and see—by my stars, the *divina Pallas*—tied to the
trumpet-tree yonder! Did any one ever see the like of this? The
horse is safe; let us go to the rider. Is he alive or dead?'

The sun had been set some minutes; but there was a rosy sort of
effulgence still glowing in the atmosphere, which illuminated
every object with a mellow and yet perfect light; and as Roland
fronted the western sky, it gleamed with all its radiance upon his
solemn and sullen features, rendered ridiculous by the impressions of the royal fists of Combah, as before related. His green
shade had been wriggled from its position on his forehead, and
hung from beneath his chin. His hands were tied behind the tree
so securely, that all his efforts to loosen them had effected nothing
beyond giving him considerable farther annoyance. In fact, he
was almost as secure as if he had really become incorporated with
the tree, and had begun to take root.

Mr Guthrie, casting at him a look of commiseration and reproach, drew a knife from his pocket, and cut the bonds which
held his throat, before a word was exchanged between the parties; the young man assisting at the same time to liberate his
knees from the jessies that confined them. His hands were not
liberated with so much facility, the mahoe rope being twisted
three or four times round his wrists, and tied each time in a double knot; and it was necessary to untie these, for fear of cutting
the preacher's fingers, or any part of his hands. While the old
gentleman was thus engaged, he saw the butt end of a pistol
protruding from the Missionary's pocket, and ventured to make
an enquiry respecting it; but Roland was too sulky to utter a
word in reply. Mr Guthrie repeated his question; still the prisoner was dumb;—a second and a third time, and yet no answer.

His eyes were fixed on those of Fairfax with the sullen malignant sort of scowl that lurks beneath the overhanging brows of a viper.

'Give *me* the pistol, sir,' said Fairfax to Mr Guthrie: 'give it me.'

Roland shuddered. 'You will not take the law into your own hands,' said he: 'you will not murder me?'

'Murder you!' repeated Mr Guthrie. 'Why should we?'

'Give me a trial, at least.'

'He is mad,' said Fairfax. 'Let us discharge the pistol: it has two barrels—what can he want with it?'

'Why, Mr Roland,' said the elder gentleman, 'a man of your consideration and profession has no need of arms: what were you going to do with your pistol?'

'You see the bruises I have already received,' replied the Missionary: 'I did not choose to expose myself to a repetition of them.'

'Then why not keep out of the way of them? You said you could forgive; you disclaimed vengeance altogether.'

'But I might be insulted again, Mr Guthrie.'

'Not if you had told us who insulted you. We should have felt it our duty to avenge you, if only on account of the peace of the island. Who ever heard of an apostle of the Christian church travelling with loaded pistols in his pocket?'

'And here,' said Fairfax, drawing the charges, 'are a brace of bullets in each barrel.'

'Well, gentlemen,' said Roland, '*your* pleasure.'

The old planter smiled as he set him free. 'You told us, Mr Roland, that on the last occasion,—that is, the occasion of your getting that black eye,—there was no damsel in the case, neither Lesbian nor Carthaginian. This is a judgment on you of the right sort; for my Quadroon slave was the syren for whom you ran on this rock; but you must not complain of her.'

'No, sir,' said the Missionary; 'Miss Michal was not herself to blame; I have no reproach to make to her; I dare say she would not have broken her heart at any liberties which another person in my situation might have taken: my own profession of course prevented me from trifling with her—my avocation, my calling.'

'Ah, ha!' said Mr Guthrie, with a shrewd glance at Fairfax,— 'you took *her* handkerchief; you did not throw the handkerchief to her?'

'Perhaps, sir, there would have been—there was—no occasion: Miss Michal was dressed in man's clothes; and she may not set so much store on her virtue as she ought to do, were she—were she'—(he added, stammering)—'any where but where she is. You see, sir—you know, that in this country all ranks and colours admit of greater licence in matters of gallantry than would be endured in England.'

'The devil they do!' said the old gentleman. 'Then all I read of must be false. I have never been there, it is true; but I have always heard that no set of human beings on the face of God's earth can compare with the English in moral depravity, and the misery that attends it; that the metropolis swarms with prostitutes— swarms; that a young man cannot possibly (nor an old man, nor any man) walk along the principal streets after dark, without being literally besieged by women of this class, who feign, fawn, lie, flatter, try to cajole—nay, almost to drag him by force into the most filthy, horrible, and dangerous dens of vice. But I suppose it is all invention.'

'Altogether, sir, upon my honour;' replied Roland. 'The women are too religious to indulge in criminal passions: the Society for the Suppression of Vice has reformed them completely.'

'Reformed them!' said the planter. 'Then they wanted a reform. But, Mr Roland, how came that Negro to meddle with you, if Michal did not think your behaviour somewhat disagreeable?'

'That, sir, you must inquire of herself; the taste of women is unaccountable: Michal and her bully, sir, retired together into the bushes yonder.'

'What!' said Fairfax, 'you do not mean that the Quadroon and that old Negro went away together into the wood?'

'They went away together—that is, one after the other; but they went the same course.'

'*Dido! dux et Trojanus!*' said Mr Guthrie. 'What next? Do you know that the pocket-handkerchief was this gentleman's?'

'Oh! very likely,' said the Missionary.

'It contained a letter to a person under my roof, written on it for want of better materials; and this gentleman is Mr Fairfax.'

'I thought as much; I knew it, I believe,' said Roland. 'He is welcome to the island.—Gentlemen, I thank you for liberating me from my thraldom. Do you know the man who has thus insulted me?'

'I do,' said Fairfax; 'he belongs to me.'

'He is a dabbler in Obeah,' replied the Missionary: 'I denounce him to you, Mr Guthrie; I will prove upon oath that he deals in philtres and charms; that he practises; that he is looked on as a wizard; that he practises the most—that he dwells in a cave full of abominations.'

'A cave!' said Fairfax, interrupting him. 'Have you seen the cave?'

'I have.'

'Ah,' cried Mr Guthrie, 'it was there then that you got the black eye—What the deuce could take you into that cave? Curiosity? I guessed aright when I asked if you had not been trying to convert the old fellow who lives by the cave. Well, you have succeeded in a strange fashion: you gave him the precept—he furnished or found in you an example. The Quadroon says that you were very rude to her; that you held her by force, and seized the handkerchief from her against her will.'

'Ah, sir, you do not know her.'

'Do I not?' said Mr Guthrie. 'I think she is as good a girl as ever smiled—as kind-hearted and sincere.'

'Aye, aye,' replied Roland; 'the scoundrel Negro held a weapon to my throat, and vowed to stab me, if I did not suffer him to—to—tie me to the tree.'

'Well; yet he hurt you not, and you had arms.'

'He knew it not: I had not time to draw them.'

'What!' said Mr Guthrie, 'you would have shot him if you could; you would have done murder. *His* case is clear: he hurt not a hair of your head: he has not robbed you, not even searched you: the girl called to him for help. Master Roland, you are instigated by spleen to charge this man with Obeah practices.'

The Missionary scowled on the planter, and burst out into an exclamation—'Well, sir, it is as I thought; my word is doubted, and the tale of a Mulatto believed against me.'

'A Mulatto girl! No,' said Mr Guthrie, quietly interrupting him, 'she is a Quadroon.'

'The offspring of a Mulatto, the grand-child of a Negress,' continued Roland. 'A fine pass this, when Negro evidence is preferred to a white man's! But this is not the law yet, thank God! Sir, I give you notice I shall make this behaviour of your's a matter of especial information to the Society for emancipating the slaves.'

'Why,' said Mr Guthrie, 'it is what they wish, that Negro evidence should be good against Whites: you do not suppose there is to be an exception in favour of their own agents. *Humanum est errare.* You may sin, as well as others: Michal is a pretty girl.'

'Sir, sir,' cried Roland, 'she has no charms in my eyes. I will state this conversation by letter to——Your object is to bring me into contempt, to bring my religion into contempt; and that before this gentleman, who, I have not forgotten, entertains similar ideas on many points with yourself. But the English people, sir, shall know it: they shall avenge me.'

'What!' said the old man, 'vengeance again? Roland! *who* is it has brought you into contempt? How came you thus disfigured—with your face bruised, your eyes blacked, your linen torn, and your garments besmeared with blood and dirt, as I saw them this morning?'

'No matter, sir: I am a servant of the Lord, and must take all patiently.'

'Aye; and you must state all patiently. There are suspicions already afloat respecting you: we hear that you have been *night-preaching* at a ruined settlement in the woods to a gang of runaways, with all the *riffraff* of the Negroes, and this Combah, at whose name you were so staggered to-day.'

'Staggered!' repeated the preacher—(the twilight faded so fast, that Roland derived a sort of courage from the invisibility of the passion which his nerves only betrayed to himself)—'staggered! Mr Guthrie, you do not use me as you were wont. It is but a short time, a few hours, since I administered the last consolations of religion to your dying wife; and now am I in return persecuted and insulted by yourself, and your friends here.'

'No Mr Roland,' said Fairfax; 'I have said nothing; my turn is reserved for a future occasion; but were I in your place, I would desist from intruding again into Mr Guthrie's house.'

'Ah, sir,' replied Roland, 'you have your reasons for wishing so, I doubt not; and I have mine for despising them, and your advice. This gentleman may shut his doors on me; but otherwise I shall make my appearance as usual.'

'You had better not: your secret may be safe in your own bosom; but there is a point at which charity becomes a crime.'

'Sir, I heed you not; I scorn your advice; I shall come.'

'Then take the consequence.'

'What?'

'You will meet one there you little expect—one that will confound you.'

'Mr Guthrie, I wish you a very good night, sir: I shall pray for your amendment, that you may see the error of your ways.—A curse upon them both!' muttered the preacher in conclusion, as he rode away through the river, taking the road to Belmont; a little to the surprise of Mr Guthrie, who had thought, from comparing notes with Fillbeer, that he would not be very welcome there at present, with a cloud upon his character which shed an additional gloom on the mind of the attorney.

Here let us leave for the present this strange compound of villainy and hypocrisy, and attend Mr Guthrie, and his protégé Fairfax, to the abode of the former, situated but a couple of miles from the spot where this colloquy had taken place. The night was cool and agreeable; and the pedestrian without difficulty kept pace with the cavalier, whose head was full of crotchets which must be explained in the next chapter.

CHAPTER 3.

Oh villain, villain! Abhorred villain—unnatural,
detested, brutish, villain.

KING LEAR.

'*ANIMUM rege,*' said Mr Guthrie. 'It were an act of virtue to give
this knave a dry beating. Is it not a horror to be insulted with such
wretches? I should like to know how he received the black eye.'

'I can partly guess,' replied Fairfax, 'I saw him this morning, at
day-break, fighting with a Negro at M'Lachlan's deserted settlement in the mountains; and he had been preaching the Lord
knows what—something that finally displeased one of his audience, who had nearly throttled him, when I put the whole party to
the rout by almost a single word. I shouted out 'Maroons! The
Maroons are upon ye!'

'And they ran?' said Mr Guthrie.

'One and all—an universal rout. Roland had his horse there: I
tracked him for some miles from the scene of the exhibition.'

'What could take him there, and what did he preach, I wonder?'

'Treason, rebellion—so Hamel assured me; but in a mysterious
way.'

'The scoundrel!' said the old planter. 'If he were anything but
what he is, he would be laid by the heels in an hour—the very
Negroes would tell of him; but, with his affectation of sanctity, and
the support he may receive from the canters, I really am almost
afraid to meddle with him.'

'Sir,' said Fairfax, 'I would arrest him without delay.'

'Ah, my dear boy, you know not what it is to have to do with fanatics who have power. If you can *prove* anything against him, let
us go to work. Suspicion will not do: though the island were known
to be endangered by him, we must have proof before we move
against *him:* reasonable suspicion with others—but handling a
saint is as dangerous as handling a rattle-snake: the reptile has
fangs and poison; you must destroy him when you touch him, or
he will sting you to death.'

'I can bring proof, I think, of what I assert,' said Fairfax. 'But what should take this creature to my house? He is gone for consolation to Mr Fillbeer; to plot with him against my acquiring possession of my estate.'

'Let him plot,' said the planter: 'we will convene the *posse comitatus,* and have the *custos* to reinstate you. He has no right to remain an hour at Belmont against your will, even though, by your power of attorney being lost, he may retire to one of the other estates. But we must avoid wrangling or violence; for Fillbeer seems as obstinate as a tree, and will yield to nothing but main force, as he says.'

'We shall judge of that tomorrow.'

'Aye, tomorrow and tomorrow; but for tonight!' said Mr Guthrie. 'I am at a loss what to do: we shall find Mrs Guthrie in a sad state, I fear. A woful meeting for you this, if you do meet; but even there I am uncertain:—nay, so strong is the prejudice against you, I know not, I confess, even how to apprise her of your being in the house.'

'If she would see me,' replied Fairfax, 'I could convince her that her prejudice is (I will not say unjust) but wholly founded on a mistaken idea with which Roland has possessed her mind relative to myself.'

'What can this be, my boy?' said the planter. 'I am myself bewildered with your mystery: can you not make a confidant of me?'

'Not except Roland were to accuse me to yourself as he has done to Mrs Guthrie; and even then it were better that the charge were buried in oblivion altogether. I am wrong, sir, to intrude myself on her patience: you say she is almost past hope of recovery.'

'I fear it is the case, and more from grief of mind than from any bodily illness. Since I was taken into Guadaloupe, she has been a prey to melancholy. You remember, Fairfax, what she was—how amiable, how interesting, how cheerful and happy; and I the happiest of husbands and of fathers. You will see now what she is: still a young woman—thirty years nearly younger than myself—Ah! I should not have married her! When a man weds one so much his junior, he knows not what he undertakes. It is no little responsibility to guarantee the happiness of any woman; but it is an awful thing to be accountable for that of a young thing who is of course still a child in her mind, and who has fancies and caprices natural to her age, and wants all the attentions that one of a similar age would find time to pay her. But still, Fairfax, her conduct was unexceptionable: simpleton as I was to marry one so young, I never had cause to repent of my marriage for the first fifteen years. It was an age of happiness—a long, long age; and when I consider the mutability of human things, I ought rather to thank God for the happiness I *have* enjoyed, than to repine at the loss of it. I hoped my wife would have lived to close my eyes. It is a double calamity that her decline, if I may so call it, should come, too, in the midst of my other misfortunes; when our properties are become almost trash, and even those made subjects of litigation.'

'Say no more of that, sir,' cried Fairfax, interrupting him. 'You will not object—you will not forget that you have always honoured me with the title of your son: I shall soon put a stop to all litigations.'

'No,' said the old gentleman; 'you must have justice done you; you must not compromise your rights, though the result be fatal to me and mine. But what must I tell you, Fairfax? Joanna can never become your wife: we cannot end our differences in that way. Her mother has exacted from her a promise never to think of you again as a lover, nor even as a friend: she would have bound her down never to speak to you, never to listen to you, never to look on you; but this was too much, especially as the cause of her mother's dislike to you remains a secret.'

'It was—it is—too much,' replied Fairfax. 'But I hope she yet lives; I hope she will herself see me, hear me: I have no fear as to the opinion she will then form of me. But what is to be done with Roland? Are we to allow him yet to do such deeds? Good God! To preach up treason and rebellion; to plot against an honourable family, to ruin them; to spare none; your house to be attacked, your daughter carried off—your wife, yourself, murdered! This miscreant has—or had, I should say—a legion of runaways and rascal Negroes at his beck. If he had possessed talents to turn their strength to his own purposes, what might not already have been the result? The very ground trembles beneath our feet; we are walking on a volcano ready to burst into flames.—Ah! shall we suffer this incendiary to be at large? It was he set fire to your trash-house when you were in Guadaloupe:' (The old planter stopped his horse in amazement:) 'at least he gave some combustibles to a Negro whom he had bought of my father, to be thrust into the cane trash. I had the story from the Negro this day: he has sworn to come forward at my call, and prove the fact.'

'I am thunderstruck,' replied Guthrie, almost gasping for breath.

'And this too dreadful tale! Alas, he was witness even to that deed of which I am suspected! But his are crimes of horror, acts of cold-blooded desperation, and so contrived that nothing short of desperation on my part can bring them to light. However, let us see him again tomorrow. We must drive him from the haunt of men, from human society; and if he dares—but he will not dare—'

'No violence, Fairfax,' said the old man.

'No, sir,' replied the other; 'I will unmask him.'

By this time they had arrived at the chateau of Mr Guthrie, who rode on a few yards in advance of his companion, to prevent any surprise at his arrival, and especially to keep the circumstance from coming to the ears of his wife, lest it might affect her too sensibly; which there was every reason to apprehend it would do in her present unhappy state of mind.—He had not entered the house many minutes, before Michal came out in the moonlight to meet Fairfax, who had just reached the end of the piazza, and to give him some confidence and assurance, of which he stood not a little in need.

'Keep a good heart, my kind master,' said the generous soubrette in a whisper. 'There is one here who will be no less happy to see you than I am. You have nothing to fear: the antipathy of Mrs Guthrie is overcome; I have found means to tell her all.'

'Is it possible?' said Fairfax, while his heart beat high with surprise and gratitude.

'Yes, Mr Fairfax, I was resolved my mistress should not entertain an opinion unworthy of you for an hour, much less that she should carry such an opinion of you to the grave. I had a dreadful task, and was obliged to speak things indirectly, for her own mind to unriddle. She never answered me; she took no notice: but I watched her eyes.'

'How is she?' said Fairfax, interrupting her.

'Oh!' replied the damsel, 'she is very, very ill; but she is not worse since I told her. I watched her eyes, and saw them brighten and sparkle while I spoke; and she turned them upwards to thank God—I am sure of it: I know by the smile upon her face.'

'And did she give you no other token?' said Fairfax.

'Yes, the tears ran down her face; and but a little time ago, as I sat by her bedside, she took my hand, and pressed it to her bosom; and when she speaks to me, she calls me dear Michal. But come into the house softly; Miss Joanna is waiting to receive you.'

' Does she know anything of what you have told her mother?'

'Not a syllable: take no notice of it; I promised my mistress that the mystery was only known to you and me, and the Negro who told us of it.'

Mr Guthrie came to the door of the house, and taking the hand of Fairfax with an affectionate though at first a hesitating grasp, led him into an apartment removed as far as possible from that of his wife, who he said was asleep. The jealousies of the room, which reached from the cieling to the floor, were thrown open into the piazza beyond, where he saw a lady in white, seated beside the balustrade, leaning her face on her hand. The sound of footsteps recalled her from the abstraction in which she seemed wrapped; and as the old man said with a tremulous voice—'There, Fairfax— there is my only child!' the young lady rose from her seat, and received his salute, trembling under the effect of the mingled feelings and recollections which oppressed her.

CHAPTER 4.

—God be wi' you!—Now I am alone.
Oh, what a rogue and peasant slave am I!

HAMLET.

THE king of Jamaica, whom we left on his march to consult the chief of his majesty's Magi, or his Delphic or Dodonian oracle, arrived without any impediment at the lagoon before the cave of Hamel; where he saw, as might be expected, the water spirit—the diving duppie—seated on the sand, and affecting as usual to be blind.

'Where is the watchman?' said the king.

'I wait for him,' replied the other: 'he is gone down to the sunken bridge, where Kenrick the robber was shot.'

'Kenrick the robber!' muttered Combah.—'Ah, I remember Hamel warned him of the spot. What does he there?'

'He is gone to attend the meeting of a white man with the Mulatto Sebastian.'

'To attend the meeting! Why, Sebastian is a robber, is he not?—a captain of pirates?'

'I know not,' replied the duppie. 'The road is before you, if you are curious: you that have eyes can go and see the meeting; but you must make haste: the day is almost gone, and the watchman is already there.'

The Brutchie looked towards the mountains and his shadow; and hastening towards the little cave, mounted by the steps in the rock to the opening by which Fairfax and Michal had penetrated to the orange-garden. There was a descent from this, known to the duppie, by which he had himself travelled down to the farther side of the external lagoon, when the approach of Sebastian had induced him to take to the water; and in the path or ledge of rock which constituted this descent, was a hole large enough to admit a conch shell which was fixed into it. Combah, taking for granted that the duppie was blind, climbed without hesitation; and, approaching the aforesaid hole, kneeled down, and applied his lips

223

to the conch shell. He blew a faint note—a second, and a third; and finding that the Obeah man did not appear, he descended, as the duppie had done, among the foliage, repassed the lagoon, and hurried away towards the sunken bridge, to have a sight of this Sebastian. It was an hour's walk, even for a king; and the twilight was pretty well past by the time that his majesty reached the appointed spot, which was all silent and abandoned; the white man, or two of the white men, having departed for Mr Guthrie's, and the Missionary having trotted off to his friend at Belmont. Let us see how he was received there, while we leave the king to his own reflections beside the rivulet.

Mr Roland rode up to the house with some assurance, in spite of all his degradations, although a little annoyed at the whisperings of the Negroes who were lounging about the road looking out for their young master. The moment the sound of his horse's hoofs was audible, the murmur that ran among the crowd reached the mansion, which, as he approached, he was surprised and mortified to see barricaded; at least all the jealousies were shut, and the door, which was whilom open as the gates of death, he found locked.

He knocked with his umbrella. 'Mr Fillbeer—brother Fillbeer—allow me to enter, Mr Fillbeer.' He put his lips to the jealousies, to speak; and then his ear, to receive an answer: but he remained in the last position for a very short time, being almost scared by a sort of savage growl from the tenant within, resembling in tone and temper that of an hyena. 'What do you want? Fool!—(The last word was in a smothered voice.) 'Your machinations, your lies, have undone me.' (Still the same subdued grumble, though the preacher heard every word.) 'I will not trust him,' continued the attorney: 'he may be a spy, for anything I know, after all—false to everybody.'

'Mr Fillbeer,' cried the man of grace again, in a more supplicating tone, 'I pray of you to admit me to an audience.'

'Speak, sirrah,' replied the fat man: 'I can hear you.'

'Sirrah—sirrah!' echoed and re-echoed the Missionary. 'He is mad or drunk. You know not whom you address, Mr Fillbeer: it is I—do you not know my voice?'

'I know it, I hate it,' cried the attorney, waxing wroth at Roland's perseverance. 'Go along—get away, I tell you: I will let no Methodist in here. I know not but Fairfax may be a saint. You have been preaching up a rebellion to the Negroes.'

'It is a mistake, sir,' rejoined the holy man. 'Am I a dog, that you should use me thus?'

'I tell you—begone!' cried the fat man in a rage. 'You must put a crown, must you, on the head of a runaway Negro? Perfidious ass! Begone! I will not parley with so base a knave—a cogging, pettifogging knave. Take care of yourself; the officers of justice will be speedily on your heels. Though Mr Guthrie is so tame of heart with you, there are others who have no fears. Go, sir, to the gallows!'

Roland was as much astounded as mortified and enraged. 'Gallows!' muttered he to himself.

'Aye, gallows,' cried the attorney, overhearing him,—'Gallows. You are charged with murder.'

'Hush, hush, for mercy's sake!' cried the Missionary in an alarm. 'Mr Fillbeer, I take my leave; I came but to tell you I have seen and spoken with Fairfax.'

'It is a lie,' replied the attorney: 'you are all lies.'

'It is no lie, sir,' cried Roland in return. 'I parted but now from Mr Fairfax and Mr Guthrie; and let me tell you, sir, that the pirate Sebastian, whom you fear, is the identical Mr Fairfax, the owner of this estate.'

'Hah!' snarled the attorney—with a wolfish grin. 'A pirate again?—Do you know the watchman Hamel?—You are accused of murder, I tell you, you sanctified sinner—of murdering a child. I will neither harbour you, nor speak to you more:—begone!'

The Missionary took him at his word, remounted his steed, which he had held by the bridle during this dialogue, and rode away in a dejection of mind such as to this hour he had never before experienced. The violence of Combah, the satire of Hamel, and the indignities he had endured from him, much as they had outraged his feelings, had still brought with them a kind of encouragement to bear patiently—a sense that he had deserved them;—but this from his friend Fillbeer!—to be denounced as a murderer, to be shut out like a dog from his house, to learn from a fellow disciple in the spirit, that the officers of justice were after him, and yet to find no sympathy in that fellow disciple,—to be known as a murderer! A deep sigh escaped from the bosom of Roland, when he turned away his horse from the house; and as he passed his clammy hand down his features, it seemed to him there was a ghastly chill in his fingers; as if his blood, forsaking his extremities, had concentrated itself round his palpitating heart, throbbing with apprehensions to which it had been as yet a stranger.

'My God—my God!' said the preacher, with a second convulsive sigh,—'what will become of me?—Oh heavens, what horror! an ignominious death—murdered—hanged:—dreadful! Is there no mercy in heaven?—Is it then come to this ? I that aspired to an heiress—a beautiful woman, and to be the head of the church in Jamaica! I—to lose my life on a scaffold—to be hung by some black villain, blackguard, ruffian—oh, terrible! What must I do? Is there no escape? Who taxes me with murder? Hamel suspected I had shed blood: he said it was the skull of that unhappy child, a white man's child. No matter; I meant it not; what had the mother to do with a Negro lover? And what had the Negro lover to do with me? If she liked me, why did he dare to raise his hand against me?—Oh that I had struck at him, as he at me, with a less fatal weapon!—The child had not then run upon my dagger. I am a lost man:—I'll go to England; they will believe me there; I shall have a party for me. But how to get away? If I had kept friends with Combah or his delegates, even with those wretches of the Obeah cup, a boat had been at my orders, to take me if only to Cuba or St Domingo; and then I could return to England, and revenge myself on Fillbeer, and make out old Guthrie and Fairfax to be what I pleased—aye, and revenge myself on the whole island, Blacks as well as Whites. But the beautiful and accomplished Joanna— death and tortures! is Fairfax to possess her, after all? What an angel of loveliness—what eyes!—But whither am I wandering? I that am to be proscribed, I must fly for my life.'

In the midst of these and similar reflections, one while shuddering at the recollection of the past, then at the prospect of the

future, and sometimes breathing fire and slaughter,—the bewildered Missionary had reached the sunken bridge, on his return
home; the spot beside which the disappointed Combah still lingered, he knew not wherefore; as if his fortune, his stars, had kept
him there for this encounter with Roland, the person against
whom he felt most incensed on account of his late discomfiture.

'This very night,' thought the king, 'an attempt should have
been made,—a second attempt,—at Mr Guthrie's. If that
Mulatto-man Sebastian had not broken up the meeting, or if
Roland had done his duty at once, and crowned me, as he swore to
do, we should not have lost our time; our plans would have been
properly concerted; and by this hour perhaps the white woman
had been in my possession, and the white men had been (many of
them) in the other world. But here comes master Roland.'

The moon had just risen from the ocean: its yellow rays illuminated the cloudless atmosphere, and the cloudy face of the
Missionary, as he approached the sunken bridge, and presented
himself before the black majesty of king Combah, who stood by
the water side, contemplating the rider as he drew near, and med-
itating, without being able to decide exactly, how he should treat
or accost his former ally.

'Master Roland,' said he at length, 'how d'ye?'

'How do you, Combah?—You see I cannot travel about by daylight: you have so disfigured me by your brutal and unmanly conduct, that I am obliged to hide myself with the bats and fire flies by
day, and flit about like them when the moon shines.'

'Stop, master Roland,' said the king, who saw that the
Missionary was disposed at once to ride through the water: 'stop,
and hear me speak.'

'Make haste then,' replied he; 'for my time is short: what have
you to say?'

'Stop—stop,' said the Brutchie again, (for Roland did not much
fancy the rencontre, and was for passing the river at once.) 'Stop,
I say, master Roland: you have something to expect at my hands.
You beat and bruised me before all the people last night; and you
broke your oath: you did not crown me, as you swore to do; nor
pour the holy coco-nut oil on my head.'

'It was blood,' replied Roland. 'If you will deal with jugglers, you must expect to be played tricks. The phial which Hamel gave me contained blood:—would you have been anointed with blood? Who ever heard of such a fashion ? And for the rest you can but blame yourself: it was you that seized, that struck me; I struggled in my own defence; yet all might have been well but for that Sebastian, who said that the Maroons were upon us. It was not true: they would have followed us, if they had been there, and taken some of us. And let me tell you, Combah, *that* Mulatto-man is no other than the owner of this estate here at hand: he is Fairfax. It was he who came from Cuba with the Negroes in your service; it was he who beat them and flung them into the sea; and he is gone to —— to claim and to receive the fair-haired beauty as his wife.'

'Indeed!' said the king in a rage: 'he is gone to Mr Guthrie's?'

'He is: I saw them, left them here together; his face was as fair—aye, fairer than mine: I am sure he is Sebastian. He had the same dress, a Spanish hat, and a cutlass; and he threatened me, if l dare come again to Mr Guthrie's—'

'With what?' said Combah.

'Nay, he told me I should see there some one whose presence would be hateful to me.'

'Pshaw!' cried the Brutchie—'is that all?—Let us go and fire the house and the premises.'

'Ah!' said the preacher, hugging himself at the proposition— 'there is too much risk; there is a watch set: and what are you— how many?'

'I am alone,' replied the king.

'Alone!' ejaculated Roland—'Alone! What can you do alone? You do not know then that the militia have been called out; that the whole island is already alarmed; that a reward is offered for your head.'

'For my head?' cried the monarch. 'Who has betrayed me? Is it not you, Roland?'

'Me!' replied the preacher in affected amazement. 'There were a hundred like yourself spectators and hearers of all that was done and said. Can you trust *them*? How can I betray you, without betraying myself?—I tell you, Combah, flight is *our* only safety at present. If you will do anything, make any attempt for *me,*—we must have a vessel of some kind in readiness, to escape from the island as soon as it is done.'

'Why, what should I gain by that?' said the monarch. 'You would have me steal the white girl for you, and then drive me off the country; but you could not keep her by force—and whither could you take her? Not to England.'

'You are right,' replied the Missionary. 'And yet,' thought he, 'it were to be in paradise to possess her; to call her mine but for an hour; to anticipate, to blast the expectations of Mr Fairfax; to wring from him the cup of bliss which fortune offers to his lips; to snatch the rose, to rifle all its sweetness, then throw it like a loath-some weed to him, or to this blockhead; but he has not the heart to appreciate what we idolize: any white woman, an abandoned prostitute, would be still a queen for him, so she were white; any-thing for his ambition, for his vanity.'

His majesty was in a brown study, as well as his vicar; not alto-gether relishing the idea of having a price set on his woolly head. Had the canoe been undamaged, he would have got together a few of his associates, and decamped, first trying to carry off the young lady. He next thought of transporting the same pretty personage to the Obeah man's cave; but that genius (Hamel) had more influence over the Brutchie than the Missionary would have believed, and kept even the monarch at a respectful distance, when the privacy, and we may add the property, of his cave was in-vaded: Combah dared not carry the young woman there without the knowledge and approbation of the wizard, whom he was not a little anxious to see for the purpose of concerting some plan for fu-ture operations. For himself, he thought not of flight except he could first commit some signal act of vengeance on the Whites; al-though he began to despair of effecting anything at present to-wards establishing himself on the throne. The island being once alarmed, all precautions would be taken, not only to prevent an in-surrection, but to insure the punishment of all whose conduct could be construed into rebellion or treason. Combah knew too well the danger he had incurred; but he could shift his quarters:

except the Maroons should give him up, he had but little to fear:—
if the fastnesses of the Blue Mountain should fail him, there were
other wildernesses in the west, in Clarendon or Trelawney; or he
could seize a boat and steer to Cuba, conceal himself on board an
American, or get taken up by some English homeward-bound
ship. There were many modes of escape known to him; and he was
more occupied with the thoughts of his revenge than of his running away.

Roland was equally anxious on both points; but security from
justice was perhaps the predominant consideration with him at
this moment, terrified as he had been by the denunciation of Mr
Fillbeer. Harassed by the forebodings which this denunciation
had caused, it was little to be expected that he should take this opportunity of holding forth to the Brutchie upon his apostacy and
tergiversation from the faith which he had once sworn to hold; yet
as the least expected circumstances frequently get the better of
probability, so Roland, in the midst of his own troubles, began to
read the king a lecture on the evident interposition of Providence
which had punished him for his backsliding by destroying his
hopes of empire. 'Had you stuck to the true faith,' said the
Missionary; 'you had—but no matter. Why did you cleave to the
idolater, the worshipper of Baal, who with all his tricks has left you
in the lurch?—You have debarred me from the power of assisting
you.'

'Why?'

'You are an infidel. Had you remained a Christian, one of the
pure sect to which I belong, I could have taken you by the hand,
led you through fire and water, cried you up to my countrymen as
an enlightened, a devout, and intelligent enthusiast; I could have
made half Europe idolize you—nine-tenths of England canonize
you.'

'What's that?' said the king. '*Canonize*—shoot me?'—

'Pah!' replied the Missionary, taking courage, as humbled
courtiers are wont when they are agreeably astonished at the ignorance of princes. '*Canonized* means sanctified—a kind of mental worshipping. All my countrymen would have felt for you,
petitioned for you, invited you to England, to their houses, filled

the newspapers with your story, and the shops with your picture, made subscriptions for you; you might have brought away a *harem* of white women.'—

'Nonsense!' replied the king. 'The English are not such fools. Roland, you have deceived me too often: I know the English women abhor the Negroes. But leave off this: I will go home with you to your house; I shall be close to master Guthrie's; I can see what is going on there; I shall know how to deal with Mr Fairfax, and how to carry off Miss Joanna for my friend.'

'To my house!' cried Roland in amazement. 'To my house.'

'Aye, master parson, to your house: come on!'

'Never!' exclaimed the Missionary. 'Impudent Negro! What! shall I harbour you?—I receive a Negro as my guest!'

'Aye, master Missionary; no more words; we know one another: I shall come.'

The Missionary felt for his pistol, but recollected the balls had been taken out; and Combah had a machet. 'Now,' thought he at last, 'I can deliver him up—a glorious idea! Revenge and—Oh! the child—the child! But for that I had now triumphed.'

CHAPTER 5.

Monster, I will kill this man: his daughter and I
will be king and queen, save our graces!

TEMPEST.

'I SHOULD have gained a reputation indeed,' said the Missionary
to himself, as he rode through the water. 'This delivering up a
rebel—a prince of rebels—a villanous apostate—would have
made me whole—round and sound. God! What a fortune is here
marred, and by such a circumstance—a deed I thought almost
forgotten—unknown to the Whites. Oh the black dolt! To thrust
his head into the lion's jaws! Yet he shall pay for it. If I grind him
not for his apostacy, may I be ground myself! The rack, the gallows, were too good for him; his violence to me I could forgive—
his blows, his efforts to destroy me; but the insults to my religion,
his knuckling down to Hamel in my presence, and the d———n of
the Obeah cup. Ah, ha! He shall be racked for this. Fool that I was
not to invite him to my abode, though perhaps 'tis better he should
thus intrude; the rights of hospitality are not his due.—I have him;
he is mine.'

The Brutchie walked by the side of the horseman with a hand
on one of the reins, thinking that the trickified Missionary might
give him the slip: for rogue as he was himself, he never dreamed
of being given up by his vicar as a rebel; in fact, he thought himself
of too much importance to the preacher to be put wilfully in the
way of danger, although he was well aware of the aversion that
Roland would have to receive him as a guest in his house, especially as he was so far condemned as to have a price set on his head.

The Missionary, in his turn, thought of securing the royal personage, and getting the reward, which was something considerable; but the charge which Fillbeer had revealed to him,
distressed him to a degree of wretchedness and anxiety that coun-
terbalanced all the satisfaction he felt from having Combah in his
power. The Obeah man knew the fact of the murder, if such it
were to be called. The cause—the spectator of it—was the Negro

we have called the duppie. There had been but one other person, a Mulatto woman—the mother of the child—who witnessed the deed; and she had not long survived her offspring; she was in fact lately dead; but she might have told of the deed,—though still living evidence would be wanting to convict him. And where was the Negro?—Roland little imagined him so near at hand; yet he knew he lived,—and he knew the prejudice existing against himself, chiefly—as he flattered himself—on account of his ultra religious principles. He felt a conviction of the triumph his enemies would experience in his downfall: the cause—the cause of emancipation would be delayed, and his own sect brought into disrepute; but even this were nothing to his fears of an ignominious death. If he could escape the penalty of the law on account of the murdered child,—his association with rebels; his crowning a black man— the consequence of these he could avoid by turning informer; and his attempts at the abduction of Miss Joanna might be hushed up in the same way. Then came the recollection of Joanna's mother. His brain was almost maddened as he rode along; and when he came to the parting of the roads, one of which led to Mr Guthrie's, and the other to his own abode, he more than once thought of riding away from the king, and burying himself at the other end of the island, till he could find means, among the pure in spirit, of getting away in safety to America, or to England. However, Combah held his bridle too securely to allow of this escape; and they reached the house together, followed by a Negro who had joined them at the parting of the roads, and who proved to be no other than the Obeah minister Hamel, who begged to speak a few words to master Missionary—tonight if he pleased; or, if more agreeable to him, the early morning would do as well, and he would wait.

As soon as Cuffy had taken his master's horse, the Missionary turned about to the Obeah man, and bid him begone from his presence; denouncing him as a villain and a robber, an incendiary, a delegate of the devil, and half a dozen other equally amiable characters. The Obeah man smiled and begged pardon for his intrusion, which was caused, as he said, 'solely by his concern for brother Roland's safety.'

'Brother me no brothers,' said the preacher, pulling out his pistol. 'Infamous rascal, begone! Thank me for your life,—you have attempted mine.'

'I have a dagger,' replied Hamel very calmly; 'but I have not shed blood with it. I drew it in defence of innocence. Put up your pistol. Think you that I am ignorant of its contents? I come to save you. What, brother Roland!'

'Avaunt, fiend!' cried the preacher, overcome with rage and horror; 'avaunt! Combah, give me your weapon; strike him to the earth!'

'Softly, master parson! You have blood enough to answer for already. The officers of justice will be here again with the day light. Hush! You speak too loud! You are discovered! One of the rabble you called brother last night, has been brought into the town by the Maroons; he has confessed the preaching and the plan of revolt; and, to save his life, has undertaken to prove you the assassin of a child. Aye, aye, the mother on her death-bed revealed the circumstance to him.'

'Well, and what then?' cried Roland. 'Such evidence is good for nothing—a second-hand story—and for such a purpose!'

'True or false,' replied the Obeah man, 'you best know; but he who is taken has promised to produce a witness—a blind man, Roland, one whom, as he says, you bought from Mr Fairfax.'

'He was a slave,' replied the Missionary; 'his testimony would be unavailable; and he is dead.'

'Do you then know him? But no matter: among friends there are no secrets, master Roland: he was a free man; you made him free yourself.'

'He is dead, he is dead,' said Roland.

'Now let me advise you to be gone; there is a boat for you on the beach, and an American schooner sails tomorrow for Baltimore. Get out to sea, you and your boy Cuffy; the night is fine; you will be taken up by the American; and here are ten doubloons for your expenses. You will find some of your friends, some of your family, in America. I know, you see, something of your affairs; will you take the money? You have more of your own; pack up that and your goods, and farewell. And you, Combah—will you go with him? You

must fly the country. If we had the strongest inducement to bring
about a rebellion, at this moment it would be impossible. The
whole island is by this time alarmed; we should act like madmen to
attempt anything for at least twelve months to come.'

'I cannot fly,' replied the king.

'Nor will *I* fly with this man,' said the Missionary; 'nor will I fly
at all; let me go; leave me, both of you; this is my own abode; you
will not violate it: at least you, Hamel, shall not enter it with my
good will.'

'Master parson,' replied the conjurer, 'I know you have denounced me, but you have more to fear for yourself. I have done
my duty, and I shall leave you: I have done more than my duty—I
have foregone my revenge; but it was for brother Roland.'

'Miscreant!' cried the Missionary,—(his rage over mastering
his other passions)—'may the Lord judge between you and me,
and reward us both accordingly! May the spirit—'

'Hah, hah!' said the Obeah man, interrupting him with a smile
and a bow,—'Farewell, master Roland, for to-night; you will want
me, and you may find me tomorrow with the dawn, brother; and
for you, Combah, the spirits and the stars are against you. Stir not
in rebellion; and let me see you at the cave. Give me your
promise—you will do nothing against the family of master
Guthrie, nor against master Fairfax? The time is not fit; you will
bring down ruin on the island, on yourself, and the cause of the
Coromantins.'

'I will make no promise,' replied the king. 'Joanna must belong
to me; I will have her.'

'To *you*?' said the Missionary. 'To you, a miserable Black! What!
after all, then, it was for yourself that you would have stolen her?
And this is your faith, Combah!'

'Faith!' replied the monarch; 'say nothing more of faith. You
knew, I dare say, that I designed her for myself. Did you flatter
yourself that I would take such measures for you? Or did you
dream of retaining her, or any white woman? Ha, ha! vain and con-
ceited fool! We knew your thoughts, your hopes, your passions;
we soon discovered your treachery; we made what use of you we
could; little enough, for master Roland was false to everybody.

Get to the boat that Hamel says is ready; take the money, and begone; or this machet shall end your worthless life! A miserable
Black, a Negro, gives you your life, and bids you fly. Would you
have done as much for me? No coward! wretched, wretched coward! You may thank my mercy that I did not, that I do not, destroy
you; but you shall not remain here to betray me, nor any of my
subjects, nor Hamel; nor shall you live here to possess by any fortune this white girl whom you meant to steal—to violate, as you
would call it, master Roland. Do you think we were blinded with
your religion, with your pretences, your psalms, and hymns, and
prayers? Do you think we could not see the wild boar dressed up
in all this trumpery—the cunning, plotting, cheating, merciless,
murderous priest—the sensual hypocrite? Yes, yes, I grant you,
you deceived many; but think not you deceived me.'

'Not you!' said Roland. 'The wise, the prudent, the virtuous
Combah! Were not you deceived? Why did you wish to stuff your
stupid head into a crown? But why do I talk with you? You call me
a coward: it is you who are a coward. You are armed, and I have no
weapon; my pistol is unloaded. Let me go into my house and get a
cutlass. I will fight you.'

'I will cut you, if you stir,' replied the king. 'You shall hear me
speak my free thoughts before I leave you.'

'Let me get a sword,' cried the preacher, retreating to the door
of his house. 'You are a coward, Combah, to insult me with this
bravado, while you are armed and I am defenceless. I have no one
here but my boy Cuffy.'

' 'Tis false,' rejoined the Black. 'I saw a brown girl this minute
looking at you from the window.'

'Let me go! stand off!' exclaimed Roland, seeing the Negro still
advancing on him. 'Hold your hand, you brutal assassin! Open the
door, Rachel! Quick! open the door!—Cut-throat!

'Cut-throat and miserable Negro!' said the monarch. 'Villain!
hypocrite! take that!'

He cut at him; but the door opening at the same moment, the
Missionary slunk back sufficiently to escape damage; and before
the king could recover his position for a second blow, Roland had
discharged both the barrels of his pistol in the face of the assassin,

flung the weapon at the monarch's head, and retreating into his castle, shut and barricadoed his door against the discomfited Brutchie and his unmoved, and seemingly uninterested, companion—the dealer in magic.

Combah was stunned by the blow which he received from the pistol used as a missile; and his face was terribly burnt and disfigured by the gunpowder and wadding discharged from it. He had staggered, and fallen to the ground, where he lay, not altogether insensible, but rolling as if in agony; so much so, that Hamel suspected the Missionary had contrived to slip another bullet into one of the barrels before he discharged it. He picked up his companion, who complained that his eyes were burned, and begged of Hamel to kill him on the spot, and not let him fall into the hands of his enemy, and to take care of himself; for Roland had most probably more firearms in the house, and would shoot at him, and would murder both of them if he could: at any rate, he would kill the Obeah man, and reserve him, the Brutchie, as an acceptable sacrifice to make his peace with the authorities of the island. 'You said that you had a dagger, Hamel,' continued the king. 'Kill me with it; but first set fire to the house of this hypocrite. Though I cannot see, I shall at least hear the flames, and hear his groans! Take my sword! Kill him if he attempts to escape. A cruel beast! He has blinded me for ever! Curse him—curse him, his mother, and all that belong to him!'

'Hush, hush!' said the wizard. 'I have no fire; let us leave him to the law; and get you on my back. There are lights coming! The watch at Mr Guthrie's has seen the flash of the pistol, or heard the report. I can see Negroes running about with torches, and lights moving at the other house to the right. Quick, quick! And Roland is opening the jealousies to fire. I will carry you to a place of safety. You are not hurt seriously, I am sure. Get on my back. I can cure your eyes; and you shall have your revenge on this preaching beggar.'

The Obeah man got the Brutchie on his back, and staggered off with him just in time, by slipping round the corner of the house, to escape the contents of a fowling piece discharged at him by the apostolic Roland, who accompanied the explosion with a fraternal benediction. 'Brother, take that! The Lord rewards you according to your merits!'

But they did not receive the reward so piously intended by the Missionary, profiting only by the intention; for the gun hung fire; and while the powder was blazing from the touchhole, Roland lost not only his aim, but forgot the direction of the muzzle of his piece, and turned it too near the wooden wall of his house, where some of the rotten boards took fire from the explosion, while the curtain of the window was enflamed from the touchhole. The musquito-net of the bed was speedily in a blaze; and while the Obeah man, like another Eneas carried off his more juvenile and blinded Anchises towards the seashore, he looked back with more surprise than gratification on the dwelling of the preacher, which soon blazed to the heavens in one vast sheet of fire, illuminating the scenery around, and lighting the wizard along the rugged path leading to the rocks, among which he tottered beneath the cumbersome carcass of the king.

'I am not wounded,' said the latter, at length, descending from his bearer: 'I am but blind. Lead me where you will—I can follow.'

The wizard took him at his word, glad to be relieved from his weight. He placed him on his legs, and conducted him, with little bungling, to the sea-shore.

CHAPTER 6.

——Whatsoe'er we perpetrate,
We do but row, we're steered by fate.

HUDIBRAS.

SOLOMON the wise has said, that 'there is a time for all things;' but some other Solomon has insisted on it that there is no time when all things are to be said; and we must content ourselves to abide by the opinion of the latter, merely because it answers our purpose. It would, no doubt, be a very pretty and a very pleasant business to relate all the conversation, as well as to describe the feelings which caused and were caused by the conversation that passed between Mr Fairfax and the young lady of his heart, the beautiful and interesting Joanna. But besides that in reality such dialogues are only fitted for the performers in them, a third person, far from taking any interest in these matters, generally turns away from them, sometimes with a jest—often with pity, and it may happen occasionally with contempt. If such be the case in actual life, why should we incur the risk of exciting any of these inharmonious feelings in relating what belongs to actual life?

A painter knows it to be his business—at least in the higher departments of his art—to select from nature what is grand, striking, beautiful, and interesting. The deformities of the creation are to be concealed; the vulgarities are to be omitted, with all which is inefficient, dull, flat, stale, or unprofitable; and if the subject demand any of this, it must be clothed or disguised in some undefined vestment, some magic tint, of air or distance, of light or shadow. Much must be left to the imagination of the spectator; not because it spares the pains of the painter, but because it is the business of the artist to set the spectator's imagination at work. It is to the feelings and fancies which he can thus excite, that he will be indebted for the more flattering part of the triumph he is to enjoy from this successful exertion of his talents.

But our readers may already wish the author transfixed with his own pen for thus detaining them from the more important

incidents in this true story: therefore we shall proceed, first referring every lady and gentleman to her or his own fancy for every
word that passed on the occasion of the meeting between Fairfax
and Joanna. They will easily represent to themselves the very
looks which accompanied every speech, active and passive—how
handsome they were, both of them—how amiable, interesting;
and all the rest of the scene, not omitting the occasional œillades
of old Guthrie. The adventures of the gentleman were related;—
but still a very small proportion of happiness was elicited, after all,
from the conviction and contemplation of their present situation—the young lady under the sacred promise recorded in a former chapter; and the person who had exacted it—the unhappy
mother—lying, as they had but too much reason to believe, on a
death-bed:—dying in fact, if not of a broken heart, of the melancholy entailed on her by the inhuman conduct of the fanatic
Roland.

The others of the party were still in conversation where we left
them, when the double report of Roland's pistol called their attention to the window. Old Guthrie, taking on himself the office of
commander-in-chief, bid Fairfax remain where he was, and not
on any account venture out of the house. One of the watch that
had been set, came up to alarm the house. Others, trusty Negroes,
went fearlessly, with pieces of blazing torchwood, towards
Roland's house; and one or two went silently and secretly in the
same direction. The report of the gun accelerated their motions;
and Mr Guthrie was hardly satisfied that the sound proceeded
from Roland's small dwelling, before he saw that gentleman's
abode burst into a flame which raged with the fury of a volcano.
Still he kept his garrison at home, knowing that the contrivance of
a fire has been frequently resorted to for the purpose of enticing
the white inhabitants from their houses by Negroes intent on rebellion, that they might offer a surer mark for the guns of the
rebels, or expose themselves with more certainty of detection and
destruction to any weapons which the insurgents might be provided with. The death of the Whites, of the masters, the leaders,
must be the first object on such occasions. The slaves, without a
captain and without a plan, can of course offer no useful resis-

tance. They would be expected to run away, from a double motive perhaps; at any rate, they would not know what to fight for, if their master and his family were killed.

Therefore Fairfax moved not from the house; but taking his station in the piazza, by the side of Mr Guthrie, contemplated in silence the fire which, blazing at the distance of half a mile or thereabouts, would have exhibited very distinctly the performers in such a scene, had there been any; and as there were none visible, this circumstance increased the suspicions of both the spectators, who concluded, with greater appearance of reason, that an attack was meditated on Mr Guthrie, and that the conspirators were in ambush somewhere between that gentleman's house and the fire, calculating on his hastening to render every assistance in his power. The old planter and his comrade were provided with a sufficiency of fire-arms, and they had Negroes enough on the alert in case of an assault; but though the fire burnt fiercely, no one was visible except the Missionary himself, who was seen to mount his Spanish steed, and gallop impatiently towards Mr Guthrie's.

'Wonder of wonders!' whispered the old gentleman to Fairfax. 'Here is Roland coming to us.'—He whispered, for he feared to alarm his wife, who was still in a lethargic stupor.

'There never was infatuation like his,' replied Fairfax in the same whisper. 'It is not enough to say he is mad. Such a compound of abominations was surely never before heaped together in one human being. We must not let him disturb Mrs Guthrie: it might be fatal to her. There are two or three persons now about the fire; your Negroes I think;—but they may spare their pains, for the building is already destroyed, and the flames begin to decrease; and here comes this extraordinary, this execrable villain! With what confidence! He may have some wicked intention; for he is capable of anything. Let us be on our guard. I should not wonder if he were actually leagued with rebel Negroes, and at the bottom of this contrivance of conflagration.'

The illumination of the fire lighted the Missionary to the door of the house, where Mr Guthrie met him with a gun in his hand; and putting his finger on his own mouth, intimated to him, by that sign, the propriety of holding his peace; but Roland burst forth with 'Treason and rebellion!'

'Hold your tongue, sir!' said the planter in a tone somewhat above a whisper, looking at the same time with as much fierceness at him as he could assume in his funny face—'Hold your tongue, sir!'

The Missionary dismounted from his horse, and adopting the same tone of voice, affected to fall into an extacy of rage and indignation at the treatment he had experienced, as he said, for his religion's sake.

'Persecutions,—persecutions! My house burned!—A Negro I know to belong to Mr Fairfax—I shot at him.'

'You have not killed him?' said the planter.

'I know not—I hope I have. Had you not taken the balls from my pistol, I had ended both the rebels.'

'Who was the other, then? There were but two?'

'An apostate—a fellow who called himself king of Jamaica.'

'There were no others, then?' said Fairfax.

'I know not,' replied the preacher, offering to walk in; but Fairfax put himself in his way.

'You must not enter here, sir! The officers of justice have been after you already; they will seek you again. I cautioned you against presuming to intrude into this house. If you hope for mercy, for safety, pray begone, and do not tempt your fate beneath this roof. You are accused of murder, and though you may have no compunctious visitings, for your heart seems harder than brass or marble, you must at least be sensible to your safety. Your disgrace will dishonour your cause, and shame the religion you profess. You will meet with no sympathy, and if the charge be proved, you will have to suffer a public and ignominious execution!'

'It is all false,' replied the preacher; 'I am not that monster. I have no sins to answer for. Let me enter.'

'You have no sins to answer for!' said Fairfax.

At this moment Joanna made her appearance in the piazza, and the preacher started at the sight. He looked at her, and at his own blazing tenement; then again at the pretty creature whose anxious look (rendered palpable by the fire) and timid step caused her to appear more interesting in the eyes of Roland; and although they revived the passionate remembrance of the ardour with which he had long sighed for the possession of her, they awakened again the now bitter recollection of that fatal night when, by the blaze of a similar conflagration, he had beheld her once beautiful mother trembling from similar apprehensions.

'I shall not reproach you,' said Fairfax, 'with the scandalous tales with which you have endeavoured to poison the mind of this young lady. A crime of a deeper, of the deepest, die you have endeavoured to fix on me; and such measures had you taken to prevent its coming to my knowledge—But go: you are every way beneath my notice—keep your secret still; but begone.'

Roland stood trembling for awhile at the door, looking anxiously at Mr Guthrie, and then at his daughter, whose white garments were waving in the night breeze which streamed down from the mountains, and then again at Fairfax; and seemed to be hatching some fresh falsehood, some plausibility or some scheme which might yet leave him a hope, however vague, however extravagant, of aspiring to the possession of Joanna, whom he could not behold without almost adoring in his imagination. He admired—he actually idolized her, monster as he had shewn himself; and what seemed almost anomalous in his character, he had taste sufficient to appreciate her good qualities, her accomplishments, her kindness of heart, her affectionate disposition. He had even thought that with such a companion he could have been the happiest of men. He had pictured to himself the interest she would take in the fate, the fortunes, the domestic happiness, of him she loved. The possession of her person, that is, the thought of such a triumph, was fuel to the fire which these ideas kindled. Unfortunately, he had taken no measures which could have rendered him acceptable to her under any circumstances, and he knew too well the opinion he merited in her estimation. He was aware that he had but little chance of obtaining her by fair means, and he was one of those who reckon it not improper to use any other means in the acquisition of a wife or a mistress—as it might happen,—calculating that success justifies the attempt, as in cases of treason and rebellion. But within the last day he had thought of

Joanna with feelings of remorse, not originating in repentance, but emanating from the conviction that no successful revolt could be maintained by the stupid crew to whom he had preached, and the *roguish* leaders with whom he had to cope. Nothing less than a revolt, and that a successful one, at least for a time, could put Miss Guthrie in his power; and, with such associates, he found he had no chance of securing her. Still he could not endure to see her the bride of another, though a white man; and as he looked at her under the circumstances we have described, he felt that he could have sacrificed her to his despair, and slain Fairfax with her, if he could have ensured his escape after such a deed; for with all his unaccountable conduct, he had a sufficient self-love, and missed no precaution for his own safety. He had already tried all to obtain her, that his head or heart dictated—courtesy of a spiritual kind, cant, hypocrisy, lies of all sorts, scandal, slanders on his rival, treason, rebellion. There remained nothing but violence, and the affectation of repentance. The first he would have tried, but the means were snatched from him. He determined to have recourse to the last; and no sooner had he formed the resolution, than he attempted to put it in force.

'Miss Guthrie,' he said, addressing himself to her, 'and Mr Fairfax, do not condemn me unheard, as you hope for justice hereafter and mercy. I am innocent of murder—I have shed no blood wilfully—thank heaven! So dire a deed weighs not on the soul of the unfortunate Roland. My duty, my profession, expose me to all kinds of calumny. How easy is it to misrepresent! With the prejudice which exists against my calling, a Negro may report falsehoods of my doctrine, or of my conduct, and crowds will listen to him. A watchman of yours, Mr Fairfax, even now set fire to my house. Such a man may have told you lies of me. He is a dealer in magic—an Obeah man, whose poisonous practices are only rendered abortive and contemptible by the antidote of mine—I may say of ours—the only true religion;—for we are fellow-christians, Mr Fairfax—do not forget that!—although we may differ as to the degree in which religion should influence all our actions. This Obeah man has an interest in supplanting me in the estimation of all the neighbouring Negroes—in your estimation above all, Mr Fairfax; and what have I done to yourself? Forgive me if I presume to fancy—to have fancied myself—your—your—your rival, Mr Fairfax. My religion is a religion of love. In offering myself, with my humble possessions and pretensions, to this young lady, I knew I had little more to offer than an honest heart, Mr Fairfax. I could not expect to vie with yourself in person or wealth; but in the grace of divine truth, in humility of mind, in faith and hope, and the profoundest conviction of the importance of walking in the steps of him who died for us, I will yield, Miss Guthrie,—to no man, Mr Fairfax.'

Mr Fairfax was struck dumb at his assurance.

'I have used none but what would be considered legitimate *ruses de guerre,* in speaking of you to this lady. You would not have fought my battles, my young friend, had I been in your situation; nor could I have blamed you, nor did I blame you, except for making a joke of my seriousness when my principles were called in question—the principles, the fundamental principles, of the only divine revelation. Excuse me, Mr Fairfax, if I put such conduct in an unfavourable light. This young lady's parents did not forbid my suit, and we were led to believe that you never meant to return to the island; but in every case the field was open to me. I had a right to propose myself to Miss Joanna. I wished indeed, most devoutly, to open her heart to receive a better impression of divine truth. A religious love first of all inspired me; although, knowing Miss Joanna, I could not fail of loving her for the beauties of her mind and person. This latter is a more selfish feeling, I own; and this I could renounce, but her salvation is as dear to me as my own; nor shall I think I have lived in vain, except—except—My God! What's this?—Who are you?—Oh, begone!—Touch me not! Why, what art thou?'

The Missionary's locks began actually to bristle up, as he saw by the glare from his still burning mansion the face of that Negro whom we have ycleped the duppie, staring intently at him as he stood still at the door, making this his long-winded defence.

The duppie was clad in his black shirt, and had assumed the strange appearance of blindness which it was sometimes his pleasure to counterfeit. Roland drew back a step or two; and Fairfax,

looking out, beheld the object which alarmed the Missionary; an
object, of course, familiar to him. The duppie held his hand, or
rather one of his fingers, in a threatening attitude at the preacher,
from whom he was separated by some palings which inclosed a
garden; but on seeing the Missionary offer to recede, and being
sensible that Fairfax had also discovered him, he disappeared,
though very deliberately, among the bushes in the garden.

The preacher, though in a cold perspiration, had begun to pluck
up courage again, when he heard the voices of several people
coming, evidently from the fire,—some on horseback, others, and
among them soldiers from the Bay, on foot. The alarm had been
communicated from its too evident cause; and prompt assistance,
in the supposition of a Negro attack, was at hand. Several individuals, finding that the house was deserted (for the brown girl and
Cuffy had run away from it) were on their route to Mr Guthrie's,
who, still anxious to spare the feelings of his dying wife, sallied out
to meet them, to learn the particulars concerning the fire, and the
attack, if such it were, and to join with those who had come to the
scene of action. Among these came young Cuffy, who ran up to Mr
Guthrie, and told him that master Roland himself had accidentally set the house on fire, with the other particulars of the affair,
not omitting that one of the Negroes had cut at his master and
tried to kill him. The old gentleman was intent on disposing of the
strangers who arrived, and making excuses on the score of his domestic calamity; but hearing how the life of Roland had been actually threatened and endangered by a lawless Negro, he felt
bound so far to recognise the dues of hospitality, even in his case,
as to offer him an asylum till the morning. But for the vision which
he had just seen, the Missionary would have hailed and accepted
this invitation as an auspicious omen. The duppie however had
virtually blasted him and his last hope; and until he could dispose
of him in some way or other, Mr Guthrie's house would be no
abode for him, nor did he feel inclined to encounter the various
persons who had sought this rendezvous; but taking advantage of
the diversion caused by their approach, he made a respectful bow
to Mr Fairfax, and silently withdrew himself, leading away his
horse, which he surrendered to Cuffy, without being aware of

what he was doing; so absorbed were his mental faculties in bewildering ruminations on his perverse fortune. He returned on foot to the ruins of his house, by this time levelled with the ground, being built solely of wood. He had not even attempted at first to quench the flames; but throwing his few moveables out of the door and windows, and his writing-desk, with his small stock in hand, after them, he had loaded his brown housekeeper with the last, and taken himself off to Mr Guthrie's, as we have described.

He now found the place deserted altogether; his few chairs and tables lying untouched on the grass, and the smoke streaming from the smouldering embers into which the rest of his property was converted. His loss, however, was not great—a hired house, and but little furniture; nevertheless, the conviction of his situation, combined with the picture of desolation before him to strike on his heart a sensation of the deepest melancholy.

'What now remains?' said he. 'The measure of my cri—my misfortunes, is nearly full!—The officers of justice are to be *here* tomorrow. *Here!* What will they find?—Dust and ashes! The vanity of nature! But these cut-throats may first return to murder me, and that crew who must needs go blundering up to Mr Guthrie's because my wretched little home was on fire. The country is alarmed. I must begone, or be the butt for every arrow of scandal, malice, and uncharitableness! But whither shall I go? There is a boat on the shore, so Hamel said. He is not disposed—he did not seem disposed—to injure me. He offered me money of his own. It was that dolt, that idiot Combah, who was so cruel and ferocious. But what can be expected from an apostate? And to owe my safety to a dealer in magic—to an infidel! one condemned to everlasting—to the pains of hell for ever! to the fire which is not quenched! It might be Satan who thus tempted me—for he can tempt, and does tempt. He is the prince of this world. But I fear him not! With the armour of righteousness, and the shield of faith, I shall pursue my course in spite of his machinations. Satan, I defy thee! Nevertheless, I will not neglect human means for my temporal safety. The boat—the boat may be of use.—Cuffy, you heartless villain, why did you not stir in defence of your master?

You that saw the nasty blackguard Negro with the raw forehead attempt to take my life, and never moved a finger to assist or save me! Yet you saw the finger of heaven was there, coward! You saw the interposition of Providence to save—to rescue the servant of God! But what occasion was there for you to run with all that nonsense to Mr Guthrie, and to tell him that I set fire to my house myself? It was not I, fool! It was the fire of my gun directed at assassins, who were thus guilty of the crime of arson—that is, burning, wilful burning—Cuffy! You had no need to speak to Mr Guthrie at all. You should see only with my eyes and speak with my tongue. But some of these creatures are again coming from Mr Guthrie's. Let us retire among the bushes and watch them. Or stay! There is nothing they can steal: leave the chairs and tables, and come with me down to the seashore.'

'No, master,' replied the boy; 'I will stay here and watch the tables and chairs, and take them for Miss Rachel, the brown housekeeper. I won't go to the seashore at this time of night. Those two Negroes went down there; one carried the other on his back, master; I won't go there after them. They may kill me, for they have got a sword and the pistol you threw at them.'

'I have another, a better pistol,' said the preacher; 'loaded with bullets. They have no ammunition. I shall be a match for them!'

'No, no, master,' replied the boy; 'please go alone. Miss Rachel is gone up to her mother's on Mr ——'s mountain;—please let me run after her.'

'I command you to follow me,' said the preacher, 'or you shall have the Mosaic allowance tomorrow—forty stripes save one—from the workhouse driver, you little execrable rascal! Follow me!'

He spoke and threatened in vain.

As the voices approached, Cuffy took fresh advantage of his master's confusion; and as the latter mounted his horse again, and turned his head towards the sea, the former darted into the bushes, and ran with his utmost expedition towards the mountain, where Rachel had found a refuge in the abode of her mother.

CHAPTER 7.

There is a tide in the affairs of men,
Which taken at the flood to fortune leads:
Omitted once, it never flows again,
Or 'tis a tide of woes a tempest feeds,
Whose ebb the shipwreck'd heart expects in vain.

ANON.

ROLAND proceeded but a few paces when he was again overtaken by the Obeah man, who accosted him as civilly as usual, and told him that the marshal's man, whom he knew by sight, was come up from the Bay to take him on a charge of murder.

The sound of Hamel's voice made the preacher instinctively feel for his pistol; but the Obeah man cautioned him against the use of his weapon, and intimated, that he must be mad to confound thus his friends with his foes. 'Master Roland,' he said, 'I shall respect my oath, and I will never harm you but in self-defence. I have had you in my power. I do not seek your life. I came, as you must know, to succour you—to help you to escape from the law. My services are still at your command. Think, if you please, what must be the consequence of continuing here. You will be tried for killing a child! Stay! You may think to escape.'

'It was accidental,' replied the Missionary, interrupting him: 'I am not guilty!'

'But you will be tried,' rejoined the wizard; 'and you will be found guilty. The guilty man escapes often; the innocent man sometimes is unjustly punished. The justices and the White jury here will find you guilty.'

'You pretend to be a prophet,' said the Missionary.

'I am so,' replied the Obeah man.

'Pshaw!' said Roland.

'Farewell then—you will regret me tomorrow!' rejoined the wizard.

'Stay!' cried the Missionary, feeling disconcerted at the prospect of losing his last chance, according to the Obeah man's account. 'What is become of Combah?'

'You have burnt his face, and perhaps blinded him for ever!' said the prophet.

'Perhaps!' said Roland, echoing the word. 'You, who are a prophet, should say positively what is to become of him.'

'I could say it. I can tell you he will never recover the use of his eyes.'

'Where is he ?' demanded the Missionary.

'He sits beside a spring of cool water, bathing his face.'

'Where then is your boat?' said Roland. 'Combah cannot make use of it.'

'He cannot,' rejoined the prophet; 'nor can you, I fear. Cuffy is gone, Combah is helpless and desperate, and I have business in hand. I cannot attend you beyond the shore. If you can manage the boat alone—I will conduct you to it: if not, I will yet place you in a safe abode till morning—till tomorrow night; when I will find you a party sufficient to carry you to Cuba, or to St Domingo.'

'What is your business that you cannot go with me?' demanded Roland. 'Come with me, if you would fain save me. I will not trust myself with runaway Negroes and rebels.'

'They shall be Christians,' replied the wizard; 'some of your own making.'

'Ah! nonsense!' rejoined the preacher. 'They are brute beasts—guided solely by their passions: would I had never known or seen them!'

'If you remain at large,' continued the Obeah man, as if not attending to the last remark, 'you will be taken up for murder. You are accused besides of preaching sedition—of conspiring to carry off Miss Guthrie. There are plenty ready to betray you, and Mr Fairfax can tell you a tale respecting Mrs Guthrie—of the fire on that night when he last quitted the island—of violence.'

'Hush! hush!' said Roland in an agony. 'Mrs Guthrie is dying.'

'But she will know all.'

'How?' cried he again.

'Michal—Michal can tell her.'

'Michal? Who, what? How came that man? Hamel, I saw a strange Negro—that man of whom you spoke to me—him whom I made free: what does he there at Mr Guthrie's?'

The Missionary spoke in a voice half choked with the thirst arising from his anxiety; and the Obeah man, too sensible of the agonies which reached the mind of his rival, could hardly conceal the triumph he felt at the conviction of his distress.

'You thought him dead! You have no chance of safety,' said he, in reply to Roland's question, 'but in flight. Mr Fairfax is my friend; him I will serve. There shall be no rebellion; master Roland, you have gone too far! I hate the white men—I abhor them! I wish——But that is no matter.'

'That man!' continued Roland, interrupting him: 'that black man with the blear eyes!'

'Beware of him!' said Hamel.

'It is long since I saw him, Hamel!'

'Aye, four years! You laugh at me and at my prophecies,' continued the wizard; 'I can tell you, however, that your existence hangs on a thread. You must be ruled by me, or you are lost.'

'Well,' said the Missionary with a sigh, 'what do you counsel? It seems my own efforts must soon fail.'

'Had you consented to make use of the boat when I offered it to you,' observed the conjurer, 'I had persuaded even Combah to attend you; and you had your boy. That chance of escape is lost for to-night. You must let me put you in a Negro hut till the morning, perhaps till tomorrow night; or you may come to my cave. I will conceal you. Combah has access there, but he is blind—it will be many days before he is able to see at all.'

'Well, be it so,' said the preacher;—'but hear me, Hamel: you have some secrets—some power—and may perhaps be able to bring about some strange things. Put me in possession of Joanna. What is she to you? You have outlived the age of love. You may have never known what it is to love. You cannot perhaps appreciate the divine sentiments I feel towards that beautiful white girl. But, Hamel, I really adore her; and the less my chance of obtaining her becomes, the more ungovernable is the passion I feel to be loved by her.'

The wizard laughed in his heart at the mad folly of the enamoured wretch: but he bid the preacher think of his idol no more.

'There are other women,' said he: 'surely you have enough in
your own country, and as many as you please in this. Think rather
of your safety. Think of your difficulties, dangers; of Fairfax and
Mrs Guthrie; of your participating in the Obeah cup, of your ser-
mons, of the innocent blood you have shed, of your league with
Combah. Think of a halter rather than of love. Think of your religion—of your character.'

'Alas, alas!' said the preacher, interrupting him again; 'I can
think of nothing but Joanna—of nothing but the happiness that
awaits Mr Fairfax. If she is to be his, I care not what becomes of
me.'

'Cha, cha!' rejoined the Negro. 'Life is uncertain, and fortune
may present you with opportunities of success when least expected. Remember the night of the fire. But here is a hut in which
you may pass the remainder of the night, and a black woman who
will take care of you. Master Roland, though she is young, as you
see, and I am old, she is my wife; and I will answer for her that you
need fear no treachery here.'

The Missionary had been led by a roundabout way from the
course he had first taken towards the sea-shore, and now found
himself at the house of a Negress, belonging to a small proprietor,
a neighbour of Mr Guthrie's. The woman was as black as pitch, as
Roland could distinguish by the light of a piece of candle-wood
which she kindled from the still glowing embers of a fire in the
middle of the floor; but she was young, and amongst Blacks was
considered very handsome; and she received the preacher with
great civility and good humour. The Obeah man took his horse,
which he turned out in a piece of guinea grass, and having seen his
guest provided with a trash mattrass, left him, with a promise to
return by daylight, and to secure him a passage, in some mode or
other, from the island by the following night.

The Missionary was no sooner left alone with the black dame,
than the latter asked him if he was hungry or thirsty, and offered
him all she had to offer in the shape of refreshments; but he was
not disposed to eat. He threw himself on the mattrass beside the

embers, whose smoke kept the musquitos in some sort of subjection, and fell into a disturbed and unhealthy slumber; muttering, between whiles, something of death and paradise—then of judgment—and lastly of Jael and Sisera.

The black woman had squatted herself on the opposite side of the fire for some time; but finding that Roland still slept, although in so unsettled a manner, she retired to her own dormitory, an inner apartment, where she likewise fell fast asleep.

In the meantime, as the night waned, the Obeah man had returned to his majesty king Combah, whom he found venting his rage and grief in curses and vows of vengeance, and occasionally consoling himself with reflections on the mutability of human affairs, and the disgrace consequent on unsuccessful ambition: then dabbling his face with water, and holding it in the little pools which the rill formed in its course; then again bursting into a passion of execration, and vowing vengeance on the whole island for this one act of the religious Roland, committed by him solely in defence of his life.

The Obeah man was not dissatisfied, in one point of view, with the fate which Combah had thus brought on himself, as it put out of the question any farther proceedings, at least with regard to the king, in the matter of rebellion. By this means he could fulfil his wishes, and his engagements to Mr Fairfax. However, he would have preferred to dispatch his majesty to Cuba, or St Domingo, or anywhere out of harm's way, for the present, and to have got rid altogether of the Missionary, except that by holding him up to the Negroes in a ridiculous light, he exposed the pretensions of the zealot, and prevented his own persuasion from falling altogether into contempt among the black population.

'Combah,' said he, 'you must be carried to my hut at Belmont, if not to my cave, where all my arts, physical and magical, shall be employed to heal your eyes, and allay the burning inflammation in your face; but as the way is long, it might be as well to press the Missionary's steed into the service for an hour or so. He can carry one, if not two Negroes, as well as any other white man's horse; and whether Roland sleep or not, I can catch his beast without being overheard.'

'But where is Roland?' said the king. 'You talk of his sleeping. Lead me to him, and let me kill him, or cut him as he has marked me. Let me be revenged on his false heart for his cruelty. Do, Hamel, I pray of you! I will make war for ever on the Christians! I will banish their religion from the country! I will burn them all!'

The Obeah man laughed. 'Your power is gone, Combah; or at least, it is suspended till you recover your eyes. Wait here; I will fetch the horse; and keep this cloth over your face, that the moon may not shine on you, for that would make it impossible to cure your wounds.'

The king took the cloth, a piece of Osnaburgh sheeting, or some such thing, which Hamel had brought from his young wife's abode; but he was obliged to keep his face in the water still, to obtain at least a temporary relief. He counted the moments with much anxiety till Hamel's return, for the latter had found the horse not so easy to catch as he expected; and having deposited the saddle and bridle in the hut, he was unable to secure the animal when once in his possession.

Liberty! glorious liberty! thought the horse.

The Negro thought the horse a vile, self-willed, obstinate brute, but that idea would not serve him at present.

'A bridle you shall have, master preacher,' as he called him; 'though I go into the hut for it. But softly! What do I hear?'

The Missionary had awaked, and was engaged in prayer loud and long, expressed with all the mouthing and ranting of the most passionate enthusiast: but as it would be impossible to detail the terms of his supplications, we shall only state that the occasion detained the Obeah man a good hour and a half before the Missionary—recollecting the black dame, who lay all the while as mute as a fish—had called to her to accompany him, and join her prayers with his.

'Black woman,' said he, 'mistress Hamel—or by what name shall I address you? Negress!—sister in the spirit!—Canst thou so sleep while I am agonized with passion? Come forth, mine hostess. The fire is not extinguished! Come forth, and let us endeavour to improve the occasion by pious exhortation.'

The woman lay all this while as snug and silent as if she had
been in her grave, and seemed still disposed to retain her taciturn-
ity; but the preacher did not so much like his own company, and
began groping his way towards the inner chamber, vociferating all
the while texts from scripture, illustrative of his holy zeal.

'Holy Dunstan,' said he at length, apostrophizing the spirit of
that saint—'holy man, thou wert tempted by a beautiful devil. I
cannot fear a black one. It was a white one tempted him and me
too. And thou, too, fortunate Alvarez,* for whose sake even
Beelzebub was smitten with an amorous passion, as I have read in
the days of my youth; thine was a white fair devil with flowing
amber locks, and this, if a devil, is a woolly-headed one, and as
black as Cocytus. Quashiba! mistress! are you dead?'

'I am not dead, and no more devil than yourself,' said the dame
in a whisper. 'What do you make such a noise for?'

'Pardon me,' replied the Missionary; 'I spoke figuratively. You
are no devil nor witch, but a good woman. Are you a Christian?'

'Yes, master.'

'Then come and pray. Join with me in supplication to the throne
of mercy.'

'What for?' said the Negress. 'Why must I beg *Garamighty* at
this time of night? I want nothing. Please go lie down, and go to
sleep.'

'Alas, I cannot sleep,' said the Missionary. 'My brain burns, and
I am oppressed with many sorrows! Oh conscience, conscience, I
thought I had learned to still thee! Tell me, mistress—mammy, I
should say—are you the only wife of Hamel?'

'No, he has one more.'

'Only one?'

Silence seemed to give consent.

'Are you faithful to him?'

'As faithful as he is to me.'

'How old are you?'

'The overseer's book will tell; I believe I am near sixteen.'

'Have you no white love—lover, I mean?'

* Alluding to Cazotte's *Diable Amoureux*.

'No, none; and I want none. Go and sleep.'

'And do you not think that Hamel is inconsiderate, to leave me here with you alone? Suppose I were to offer you any—'

'No, no, master: go and say your prayers again.'

'I tell you,' said the Missionary, 'I cannot pray alone. I would fain have your company beside the embers.'

Here the girl burst into a loud laugh, which disconcerted the preacher, who reproved her for her want of feeling and respect with an affectation of the most profound gravity; but the more he argued, the more she laughed. They made such a noise between them, that Hamel took the opportunity of opening the door, which was only latched, and creeping into the hut on all fours, got off, unobserved, with the saddle as well as the bridle, and went to work again to catch the Spanish horse, as if indifferent to the interview or the dialogue which he had witnessed, wherein the preacher, as he thought, betrayed something like an inclination to gallantry.

The young dame still continued to laugh, although Roland had approached the bed in which she lay, and begged to know, in a voice rendered more croaking by an assumed tone of tenderness, the reason why she thus made a jest of him.

'You are young,' continued he; 'too young to be wilfully wicked; and you are pretty. Give me your hand.'

The Missionary lifted up a musquito-net with which the bed was protected, and felt for the girl's hand, although there was a sufficient light from the moon which shone into the chamber, to guide him in his search. Still the girl laughed, and Roland had almost plucked up courage enough to smile too, when he discovered, by the aforesaid light, that there were two persons in the bed before him. Had Combah fired the pistol in his face, he could not have been more disagreeably surprised.

'Mercy on me!' he cried with a deep sigh, letting go the musquito-net which he had still held in his hand. 'Peace be with you!—If you will not join me in prayer, at least allow me to pray for you.'

The girls laughed now, both of them, while Roland returned to his mattrass, sadly put out of conceit at the issue of his adventure;

for his mind, being humbled afresh, gave way to the distressing anxieties and reminiscences which crowded on it, together with the fears which assailed him from all quarters. He no sooner closed his eyes, than his fancy presented to them a portrait or an effigy of himself suspended on a gibbet, while a rabble of Negroes hooted around him. It was not necessary that he should sleep to see this vision; it was a waking dream which haunted him. Sometimes he pictured to himself the eternal gulph—the modern Tartarus—where he beheld the souls of his enemies, as he considered them, heaving on the waves of the fiery abyss, while he looked on complacently. The assurances of his faith had power to calm his soul as to any apprehensions of a future state, believing himself, as he did, elected, and inspired, and emancipated from the power of the devil, who could only enthral his mortal flesh in this world, and give it over to the Jack Ketch of the island. His immortal part gave him no concern, for that he considered safe. Nevertheless, he turned with horror from the vision of his dear flesh hanging between heaven and earth, and prayed most fervently to be excused such an unpleasant exhibition, preferring, as he expressed himself, to die of old age and a gradual decay, amid the consolations of faithful, affectionate, and pious relatives, leaving his character as a bright example to them and to all the partners in his religious belief. He persuaded himself that such an exit from this world would be more useful to mankind, and would tend more to promulgate and to recommend the infallible tenets of his persuasion; besides being so much less disagreeable than a public execution, or any violent death, though it were an apoplexy even, which he candidly owned he should prefer to being hanged by the neck. As he had again resolved himself into prayer, from which he had hitherto seldom failed to derive consolation, he gradually acquired confidence enough to enlarge his ideas and requests, and prayed now for a long life, and for Miss Joanna, and for riches and fame, and a triumph over his enemies; and began to disdain his black hostess and her wizard of a husband; and had actually resolved to sally forth and go home directly, before he recollected that his home was a heap of ruins, or rather that it had melted into thin air. This recollection brought back the conviction of his miserable situation, and satisfied him that he was a forlorn outcast as to the people of Jamaica, and that his best chance of escaping the evils which he dreaded, was to be found in abiding by the instruction of the Pagan, the necromancer Hamel. Yet even this idea brought with it an additional gloom, and so distracted him, as it mingled with his other recollections, that he could neither sleep nor even rest on his mattrass. He called again for the company of his hostess, told her it was near morning, and begged of her to make a fire, and roast him some plantains; besides, he was overcome with thirst, and wanted a draught of water.

The appeal to her hospitality was instantly obeyed by the black dame, who came out of her bed with no superabundance of clothes on her person, goodnaturedly displaying her white teeth as she smiled over the fire which she rekindled. She gave the Missionary a jug of cool water, and promised to prepare him a pot of coffee as she put the plantains down to roast. He in the meantime walked to the door of the hut, to breathe the fresh air, and avoid the smoke of the fire, as well as to look for the dawn in the eastern sky, for which he was sadly impatient. There was no appearance yet of morning; but as the preacher gazed intently through the moonlight, he saw a figure of which we must give some account in the next chapter.

CHAPTER 8.

Fine apparition! My quaint Ariel,
Hark in thine ear.   TEMPEST.

THE Missionary rubbed his eyes half-a-dozen times before he
could make out the object which fixed his attention. It was, in fact,
the majesty of the ex-king, mounted on the preacher's horse, and
surmounted by the Osnaburgh cloth, or piece of sheet, which the
magician had put over the singed and royal features of Brutchie
Combah. The wizard walked on the farther side of the horse, so
that he was invisible to Roland, who distinguished only the steed
carrying its unaccountable burthen, which gleamed in the moon-
beams, and surprised the Missionary into a belief of its being
something supernatural. He never entertained a thought of its
being his own horse, or of the figure being the Brutchie, but kept
his eyes steady on the apparition until it vanished among the trees,
more than half convinced that it was a ghost, although he was
doubtful of ghosts riding the highway. With footpad ghosts all the
world is familiar, and ghostly cavaliers have been known to take
the air in some of the German romances; but in spite of their great
authority, the Missionary was confounded, and remained in mute
astonishment for at least ten minutes after the spectre had vanished, when he returned into the hut, and sat down on his mattrass
to ruminate afresh on his unhappy condition.

'I am undone,' thought he, 'at last, if I remain here among a disturbed and suspicious neighbourhood, where the mere burning
of my house will bring the white population to inquire into the
cause of such an event; where the officers of justice have been in
pursuit of me, where the vengeance of Fairfax awaits me, and Mr
Guthrie will soon discover his wrongs and persecute me.' It was in
vain that the black woman exerted herself to keep up the spirits of
her guest. Her cheerfulness, her desire to please and console him,
only wrung his heart the more, and caused him now to reflect on
his own moral worthlessness with a pang of more intolerable an-
guish. The day added little to his quiet, for as it began to dawn, he

descried with new mortification the absence of his horse
equipage, and next the absence of his horse, which evidently was
not in the pasture where it had been turned out in the night.

'Ah!' said he to himself, 'this is Hamel's work. He has me now
securely. He knows I cannot escape on foot under the burning sun
of Jamaica. He means to await the reward which will be offered
for my apprehension, and then he will deliver me up, and I shall
die—he would not put me to death himself—he dared not; but he
has an enmity to me for my religion. He will expose me—humble—annihilate me! Would to God I had never meddled with pol-
itics, revolutions, or any such trash! My connexion with Combah
has been my ruin. What can I do? Mr Fairfax disguised himself as
a Mulatto. Why should not I blacken my face, and try to make my
escape as a Negro? Yet whither can I go? I cannot leave the island
publicly, except as a pretended seaman. My name must be put up
first in the secretary's office: but had I been at sea in Hamel's boat,
I might have escaped in safety. Common humanity would induce
the master of any ship to take me up and carry me, I care not
where, from this island for ever. I was a fool to reject his offer, but
perhaps he meant to deceive me. Yet he seems to possess a sort of
sincerity. But why has he taken my horse, and my saddle too? He
must have taken that while I slept; and for what purpose?' He
thought again of the apparition, and the idea which had so
alarmed him recalled as speedily a portion of his confidence. He
divined aright that it was the Brutchie, either equipped to protect
his burnt face from the night air, or dressed up to alarm any of the
Negroes from interfering with him; and he made no doubt but he
was on his road to the Obeah man's cave, among whose windings
and mysterious retreats he might set at defiance the scrutiny of
the whole island; and knowing how well the wizard was provisioned, he was no less satisfied of his capability to endure any
siege. Besides, he had always an escape from the Devil's Gully,
where he doubted not the Obeah man could find his way,
notwithstanding his declarations respecting that horrible pass. 'If
Hamel,' thought he, 'were really sincere, no place would be so
fitting for him until the hue and cry were over.' Combah's blindness rendered him incapable of revenge of any kind; nay, he

would be at the preacher's mercy; and the Obeah man was no less
interested than himself in casting a veil over all the transactions
which had occurred of late, and of keeping, as he began to persuade himself, even him (Roland) from being given up to the
authorities.

Being convinced of all this, he set about consoling himself for
the wretched night he had passed, by making a tolerable meal on
the black dame's plantains and coffee; calculating meanwhile on
the return of Hamel, and devising or trying to devise some mode
of disguise, by which he might get incognito to the wizard's cave;
although he trembled in imagination at the thought of passing the
Devil's Gully, the only approach to it with which he was acquainted. He found he must needs wait for the Obeah man, the
only disguise which he could assume (that is, with which he could
be accommodated) being some of the gear of Mrs Hamel, and
that on a scale infinitely too small for his figure. Yet he tried on the
feminine apparel, and set the two girls grinning again at the
strange appearance which the clothes gave him; while, as the daylight increased, his apprehensions augmenting likewise, rendered
the whole effect of his masquerade more and more ludicrous. At
length the women left him to attend their own work, and locked
him in the hut, hiding the key in a place where, they assured him,
Hamel was accustomed to look for it.

While the Missionary had thus been awaiting the daylight here,
the king was pursuing his course to the sunken bridge, with the
Obeah man for his guide, and clad, as we have described him, in
the Osnaburgh sheet. He arrived at the bridge just at the first
dawn of day; for Hamel had lost much time, first in getting the
horse, and secondly in mounting his majesty on it. He rode
through the water, his lord chancellor walking by his side; but had
no sooner reached the other shore than he heard the trampling of
a party of horsemen coming down from the eastward at a brisk
pace. These were in fact some of the Surrey troop of cavalry, riding towards the scene of the fire, as the report of it had been
spread abroad with great expedition, by emissaries dispatched in
all directions from the town, at —— Bay, before it was discovered
that the fire was accidental. These cavaliers were coming along

the road which Combah must of necessity take, except he turned to the right by the only other one which would lead him to Belmont. There was no time for deliberation. The wizard jumping up behind his monarch, put his hands around him to secure the reins, and stuck his heels into the palfrey's flanks to urge him forwards; but the horse was more than satisfied with one Negro, and determined not to carry two. He kicked a little; and what was worse, he turned restive, and began backing into the water again, just at the moment that the helmets appeared flashing in the pale moon-beams, at an angle of the road which led directly down to the bridge, distant from the horsemen not more than a hundred yards. The Obeah man dismounted as quickly as he had got up behind the king; seized the bridle, and led the horse again into the Belmont road, bidding the Brutchie ride away out of sight; while he himself darted into the bushes, and soon escaped the chance of detection—from horsemen at least. The king, in a royal passion of rage and fear, pummelled the horse with his fists, and kicked him with his naked heels, till he flew with his utmost speed along the road to Belmont; Combah being for the present so utterly blind, that he dared not attempt to direct him. But he had not escaped the observation of the troopers, who would not perhaps have noticed him, had it not been for the white cloth, which was too conspicuous and too uncommon an object to fail of exciting their attention. The horsemen set up a shout, and galloped after the ghost with as much speed as the Spanish horse could boast of; and he, as much alarmed by the pursuit as his rider, scampered as if a devil bestrode him, and stopped not until he had carried the king directly up to Mr Fillbeer's piazza door, where he had been accustomed to halt.

Mr Fillbeer had passed as dismal a night as his religious brother Roland; although his anxieties proceeded chiefly from temporal considerations, as he had found that his garrison at Belmont were worse than mutinous, being resolved to welcome their master, and open their gates to him the moment he should appear.

The fat man would only lose his revenue, his home, his authority, his respectability: but his life was at no risk, nor was his conscience burthened with deep crimes. However, he could not sleep; and no sooner had the day dawned, than he was at his window, looking down the road which led to the town, expecting to see his enemy, Mr Fairfax, coming with the *posse comitatus* to summon him to surrender. It was at this very moment that king Combah on the Spanish horse met his view, racing away from a party of troopers, who came up with him in a few minutes after he had reached the piazza—in fact, before the attorney had been able to satisfy himself as to the identity of this extraordinary visitor, or could comprehend why he was mounted on Roland's beast, or why he was clad in this white sheet. Combah himself was in no little alarm, for he distinguished, by the clatter of the horses behind him, and the shouts of the riders, that they were fast gaining on him; and when the Spanish steed halted at the fat man's gate, his alarm was in nowise diminished by any knowledge of his situation, as he was so effectually blinded as to be unable to decide whether it was night or day. The first sound he heard that could inform him of the spot where the horse had thought fit to plant himself, was the voice of Mr Fillbeer, growling from the piazza—'Who the devil are you?'

The king remembered the voice, and recollected likewise how he had laughed in his heart at the distress of the fat man the day before. This he thought was a judgment on himself, for he had his share of superstition; but the idea did not help him to any answer: not a word could he utter. He sat as silent on his horse as if he had been a real ghost waiting for the voice of the exorcist.

'Who the devil are you?' cried Fillbeer again, in a voice of thunder;—'what do you come here for, dressed up like a Jonkanoo Tom Fool? Speak, idiot, or I'll blow your brains out.'

'Fire!' cried the Brutchie; 'fire!'

The Brutchie actually wished himself dead: for what could he do? He was like Sampson in the hands of the Philistines, and felt assured that death in some shape awaited him, and must surprise him, at latest, in a few days. He disliked hanging as cordially as his vicar Roland, and cried out stoutly to the attorney to put him to death. Fillbeer was still more astonished, and being outraged at his impudence, put a gun deliberately out of the window:—it snapped.

'Try again,' said Combah; 'fire—fire! you fat beast, fire!'

He heard the troopers coming nearer; and Fillbeer saw as well as heard them. He was bewildered: he cocked the gun again, and pulled the trigger. The gun hung fire for some time, but at last it went off. The horse wheeled round in a fright, and scampered away, leaving Combah on the ground, lying flat and motionless on his back.

The troopers, drawing their swords at this, rode up and surrounded the Brutchie, who fancied or feigned himself dead, although the fat man had taken care not to hit him, meaning solely to put his mettle to the test, and supposing him to be a delegate of Mr Fairfax, to scare him from the premises, and give his master a hint at the same time. But as the king lay apparently dead, and as the gun had hung fire, Fillbeer concluded he had missed his aim, and really dispatched the ghost.

'He is shot in the face,' cried one of the troopers: 'his eyes are blown out.'

'What did Mr Fillbeer shoot him for?' said another.

The Negroes came running up from their houses, and being unable to get a sight of the Brutchie, on account of the troopers who surrounded him, took for granted, as they heard this last question, that the attorney had shot their master, Mr Fairfax.

'Master Fairfax is shot! The overseer has killed him!'

A simultaneous shout was succeeded by as simultaneous a rush at the great house. Door, windows, piazza, bars, bolts, gave way as if it had been the last day. The mob were all over the house in a minute; seized the ex-brewer, whom they nearly suffocated in their struggles to get at him, and, in spite of his bellowing remonstrances, pulled him out of the house by main force; some taking a leg, others an arm, (it required a score to carry his fat carcass) and others supporting his head. They bundled him through the door, and were going to hang him to a tree in the mill yard, but they thought his weight would break it. They then took him to the tree in which Combah had perched the day before, and a rope was actually round his neck before the troopers knew what was really the matter. They shouted in vain to the mob, who began to think that Fillbeer had employed them on the occasion, and were about

to make a charge to rescue the attorney, when their attention and
the purposes of all parties were arrested by the arrival of Mr
Fairfax himself, and his friend Mr Guthrie.

'Massa da come! massa da come!'

A lusty hurrah from the rear of the assailants confirmed the
news; and that sound which fat Fillbeer had anticipated as the
most hateful summons which his ears were ever to let into his
brain (except that of the angel of death) proved, as occurs very frequently, the most welcome tidings he had ever listened to in his
life. 'Massa da come!' said the Negro who had tied the rope round
the attorney's neck.

'Massa da come! Yander him tan!' (Yonder he stands.)

He did not wait to expostulate with the attorney, whom he and
others had hoisted into the tree, but slipping down from it himself, left Mr Fillbeer with the rope round his neck, seated in a fork
of it, habited as he had been found, in a long dressing gown of
white cotton.

Meanwhile the Negroes had crowded round their young master, whom they were ready to devour with caresses and congratu-
lations, and carried him in triumph to the house, where they
seated him in the piazza, and greeted him as if he had really been
a king. He received the same courtesies from the light-horsemen,
with many of whom he was acquainted; while Mr Guthrie stated
to them all (including the Negroes) the nature of the rights by
which Mr Fairfax took possession of his patrimony; as well as that
he really had had a power of attorney from Mr M'Grabbit to enter
on all the other properties on which that gentleman had any
claims as to possession, and likewise to transact all his affairs for
him in the island.

As soon as this little explanation had taken place, an inquiry was
naturally made for Mr Fillbeer, and the troopers were not a little
curious to know the particulars of the Brutchie's adventure; for by
this time it was found, that the attorney had completely missed
him, and that the singing of his face was attributable to a former
misfortune.

Combah was sulky and silent; but Mr Fillbeer, still seated in the
tree, to a branch of which the rope which encircled his neck was

made fast, bawled out at intervals to be taken down; as he was
fearful of turning giddy and falling into a suspension by the neck,
unless some one came speedily to his assistance. It was in vain to
look at him and hope to avoid tormenting him with a smile. His
long lank locks stuck out (as if they were electrified with fear) like
the quills of an angry porcupine: his gown was flying loose in the
wind, and his under garment, which was a pair of drawers only, in
addition to his shirt, was burst in two or three places, either with
the hauling he had endured in being thus run away with and
hoisted into the tree, or from the increase of fat which he had acquired since the purchase of these articles, which were probably
sent out on commission, and not calculated for the fattest man in
the Antilles. He had on a pair of slippers when he was thus borne
aloft, but these had dropped off, and left his legs and feet bare.
They were so loaded with fat that he might have shewn them
against an elephant's. One gentleman remarked, that all
Barbadoes* could not vie with them, or produce such another
pair. The toes were scarcely visible, except at the very extremities;
and they resembled two macaucas magnified by a solar micro-
scope to the size which they presented. How was he to be got
down? How got he there? Jack Ketch was obliged to mount to his
assistance, and cut the rope, preparatory to his descent by a ladder, which he trod as some may imagine those elephants step who
are taught to poise themselves on the slack rope. Once he missed
his footing, and had certainly rolled over on his back but for the
Negro who clambered to his assistance; for, being conscious of his
own weight, he begged that no one else would encumber or strain
the ladder. The last spoke but one actually broke with his load of
mortality, and let him slip to the ground, striding, to save himself,
across the ladder, where his legs and arms, stretched out at the
four corners of his carcass, gave him the air of a turtle; or perhaps
he as much resembled a woolpack. He came to the ground with a
rush which upset him, and he fell backwards into the arms of the
Negroes, who carried him, by direction of Mr Fairfax, into the
house, and into the room which he had occupied, where they

---

* Barbadoes is famous for big legs.

seated him on his bed, puffing and blowing like a grampus on a
shoal.

This lesson had been sufficient for him. The man of war was but
too happy to make peace, and promised to vacate the premises in
the course of the day; thanking Mr Fairfax, though in rather a
dogged way, for the salvation which he owed to his name—the
name of master. Another minute, and he had breakfasted in
Paradise! He was too happy at his escape from the aforesaid place,
to think, with the depth of feeling which he afterwards under-
went, of the information which Mr Fairfax gave him respecting
the power of attorney he had received from Mr M'Grabbit. For
the present he was not superseded as to the other properties; and
having dressed, and eaten his breakfast, he packed up his clothes
and his papers, and mounting his horse, turned his eyes for an instant to *the tree,* heaved a sigh, waved an adieu to the party, and
rode off the estate.

CHAPTER 9.

Have you not set mine honour at the stake, and baited it?
TWELFTH NIGHT.

THE next scene which the course of our narrative unavoidably
leads us to, is the sick bed of Mrs Guthrie, attended by the patient
and affectionate Michal, whose good fortune it had been (in the
pursuit of a romantic love-affair, which had added little to her own
happiness) to make a discovery respecting the cause of the melancholy which was conducting her mistress to the grave. She might
still have kept her knowledge to herself; she might have suffered
her mistress to pay the debt of Nature in ignorance of the real author of her death; she might have kept Joanna under the interdict
of her mother, and Mr Fairfax had still been a bachelor for her,
more majorum;—but the Quadroon's passion for that gentleman
was too pure, and too disinterested, to admit of her entertaining
any selfish feeling for an instant. Indeed, no thought of such a feeling ever occurred to her, and she had used the very first moments
of her return—that is, as soon as she had resumed her maiden
weeds—to tell Mrs Guthrie every particular she had learned from
the diving Duppie.

Her mistress, as the Quadroon related to Mr Fairfax, had
heard all without making any remark. She remembered to have
seen the Negro fly with her brutal assailant from the house. She
remembered, likewise, the perfumed state of the person of this
latter, corresponding with the still existing fancies of the
Missionary on that point. Mr Fairfax she had never beheld since;
and Roland, to whom the Negro then belonged, had insinuated
to her the confession of the Negro to himself, as to the outrage
she had endured. The absence of Fairfax, who left the island very
abruptly, gave a colour to the representations of the Missionary;
and he acquired a perfect mastery, for some time, over the mind
of Mrs Guthrie by his apparent knowledge of this adventure;
which the lady, from considerations of the most distressing
nature, wished to keep a secret from all the world, and more

especially from her husband, whose peace of mind she thought it would destroy for ever. Roland still triumphed in his success, for no suspicion had ever attached to him, he being, as the Duppie had related, disguised at the time even as to the colour of his complexion, and having, with no common ingenuity, perverted every circumstance of the affair to his own advantage, as to the future opinion which the lady should thenceforth entertain of him. There was but one other creature in the secret—the Duppie; and him the Missionary, after having long plotted against his life or liberty, had imagined to be dead, and persuaded the lady to the same belief.

The designs of Roland had first of all been confined to Mrs Guthrie; concluding, or hoping, that the captivity of her husband at the time would end in his death, the pirates generally disposing of their prisoners effectually. In such case, he would have proposed himself as the widow's husband, trusting to his secret, in case of need, to enforce his pretensions; but when, in a few days, Mr Guthrie returned, the Missionary decided on transferring his affections to her only child, then absent in England. Joanna was heiress to the property of her parents. He knew her, admired her, and being called home for a time on his own affairs, renewed his acquaintance with her in England; tried to poison her mind there respecting Fairfax; and came back to Jamaica, resolved to put in practice *all* means to obtain her as soon as she should arrive. He had found her wholly averse to him, and had therefore, as well as on other accounts, concerted his scheme with Combah to bring about a rebellion, and seize the young lady by force. But when, during the absence of Mr Guthrie, he had cast his eyes on her whom he expected to be a widow, he had taken, as he thought, the most effectual way to ensure his pretensions to her. Had she then lost her husband, her days of mourning must have retarded his suit for many months—perhaps rendered it altogether abortive; others would have had time to interfere to supersede him. He chose a cruel and a fatal scheme, to render her happiness, at least her peace of mind, dependent on himself. Had Mr Guthrie been slain, who could successfully oppose him? How could the widow refuse him who was necessary to the establishment of her

character, and the restoration of her tranquillity? He had employed therefore, in the dead of night, his Negro to fire the trash
house, which was at the distance of near half a mile from the mansion, knowing that all the inmates would run to the fire, while he
could at once take advantage of their absence and the lady's alarm.
The result has been seen. The lady's happiness was ruined: her
health had declined with it; while the monster who was the cause
of all her misery, had even made a merit of his forbearance in
keeping her secret, to urge his pretensions to her daughter. He
had seen her wasting away from day to day, almost from hour to
hour; yet his hard heart had never known a pang of compunction
or commiseration; nay, he looked forward to her death as the
means of accelerating to Joanna the possession, in which he
hoped to participate, of all her inheritance. This was the man who
had pretended to give her the last consolations of the religion of
which he boasted himself a righteous, an elected believer; and she
had received that awful dispensation at his hands but a few hours
before she was made acquainted with his real character, and with
the obligation she owed to him for the years of misery which she
had endured, and the untimely death which now hurried her to
the grave. Yet it was still possible she might be deceived, and
when, towards morning, she had awakened from the lethargic stupor in which her faculties had apparently been suspended, she expressed to Michal a wish to see Mr Roland without loss of time;
determined to know, from the confession of his soul upon his face,
if not from his lips, whether he were the villain he had been represented. It was then that Michal detailed to her mistress how
Roland's house had been destroyed by fire the previous night,
with the particulars of the alarm it had caused, and that the
deputy-marshal had been after him with a warrant to apprehend
him on a charge of murder.

A deep sigh acknowledged the impression which this intelligence produced on the mind of Mrs Guthrie, accompanied by a
hectic flushing, which was quickly followed by a death-like paleness.

'Where is he, Michal?' said the lady, after a pause. 'Have they
taken him?'

'No, mistress,' replied the soubrette. 'He was here during the fire, and was terrified at the sight of the Negro who told of his behaviour—he who set fire to the trash-house. He came here to prove, if it should be required of him, all that he has declared.'

'I would see Roland,' said the lady again. 'Where is he concealed?—and Fairfax?'

'Mr Fairfax is gone to take possession of Belmont. He was here last night, and Mr Guthrie is with him.'

'Thank heaven!' said the sick person. 'But I would still see Mr Roland. Oh Joanna!—you may be happy! I wish to release her from her promise. But let us be assured by Roland's self. Keep my secret, Michal!' A look from the Quadroon, beaming with intelligence and sympathy, satisfied and consoled her mistress.

'I have had,' said she, 'a hard fate; one that I have scarce deserved, and at the hands of such a man as the Missionary—if he is guilty! Send for him, Michal.'

By this time intelligence arrived from Belmont, of Mr Fairfax being peaceably in possession of his estate; of the resignation of Mr Fillbeer, after his narrow escape; and of the capture of the rebel Negro Combah, who had set himself up for the king of the island, and for whom a large reward had been offered: but of the Missionary nothing had transpired.

Michal, surrendering her post to Miss Joanna, who was now permitted to attend her dying mother, had set off to the place where the Missionary's house was used to stand, hoping to find some clue that might lead to the concealed abode of Roland. She found the premises as we have described them—little more than a heap of ashes. The stable, which was enclosed only with rails, was still standing, and some of the Missionary's tables and chairs, which had been flung into it, were lying scattered about, with two or three open trunks, displaying a farrago of old coats and waistcoats fluttering in the wind, together with a parcel of tracts and placards, with prints of a Negro on his knees in chains, which strewed the country for some score of yards to leeward. What seemed extraordinary to Michal was, that the coats and other habiliments should remain untouched, notwitstanding their being at the mercy of the numerous Negroes who had been to visit the fire. But this surprise on the part of the Quadroon, gave way to the evidence she soon discovered, of Hamel, or some such person, having affixed his *taboo* on the stable, in the shape of a glass bottle hung up at one corner, a bunch of chickens' feathers at another, and a large toad impaled against a post at the third. None but Christians would dare to encounter the anathemas condensed in these materials; and the Christians had too much reverence for the Missionary to meddle with his goods, or derive any profit from his misfortune. It was far from being generally known that the deputy-marshal had a warrant against him; and as Mr Roland could not be found since daylight, it was imagined by many whom curiosity led to the scene, that he must have perished in the flames. Michal was however better informed on the subject, as she had seen the pious man at Mr Guthrie's door whilst his own house was in flames. She was well aware of Mr Roland's existence, and thought, with sufficient reason, that the Obeah man could give the best account of him, tacitly making up her mind to go to the cave in case she should hear nothing of him in the meantime; for she felt the very greatest interest in gratifying the wishes of Mrs Guthrie respecting the interview of which she was so desirous. Not that she entertained any hostility to Mr Roland, at least any wish to bring him to the scaffold, detestable and execrable as she thought him; but she was aware that her mistress was dying, and she hoped to soften the asperity of her grief; and she was equally earnest in endeavouring to clear the character of Mr Fairfax from every tinge of suspicion. But the Missionary was neither to be found nor heard of. His boy Cuffy, who had returned from the mountains with Miss Rachel, said that his master had resolved to go to sea, after his return from Mr Guthrie's, in an open boat, with Hamel for his companion; and that he had run away to avoid being taken with him. Miss Rachel was as much at a loss as Michal; not daring to make any enquiries for Roland, lest they should lead to his detection and seizure by the officers of justice. She sat down on one of the buttresses which had supported the Missionary's dwelling, and gave vent to her grief, for a time, in a flood of tears; while Michal, at her request, collected some of the placards which were flying about, the tracts, and the old clothes, and placed them in the trunks for which Rachel had found the keys.

She was still lingering about the premises, endeavouring to console Rachel, and watching every face which curiosity attracted to the scene, when the black damsel, or rather dame—the Obeah man's wife—came, at the instigation of Roland (as it afterwards appeared) to reconnoitre the field, and to obtain, if possible, some information respecting the deputy-marshal, as well as to find out Miss Rachel, if she were there, and get her to take possession of his clothes, and bring them to the Negro woman's hut, if occasion should offer; and in case Rachel were not there, she was to seek her at her mother's, according to the direction which Roland had given her. The Negro woman quickly found the object of her search, suspecting, by her tears, that she must have been particularly interested in the fire, and the fate of him whose house had been the prey of it. She quickly related to her that she was the mistress of Roland's secret, and could lead her to the abode where he had found refuge during the night, and where he was in fact concealed at this moment. The Mulatto woman arose immediately to attend her guide, but not before she had confessed to Michal the intelligence which she had received, and supplicated her not to take any measures which could involve the Missionary in farther trouble.

All this poor Michal promised, bargaining only that Mr Roland should attend to the last request of Mrs Guthrie; after which she would assist in any way to help him in his escape from the island. It was agreed that they should follow the Negress in company together.

Meanwhile, Mr Roland had no sooner dispatched one of the women to whose care he had been left, than he, with his natural inconstancy, prevailed on the other, a frisky lass, to disguise and lead him to the Obeah man's hut at Belmont, as his mind was bent on finding a security among the caverns which Hamel frequented. The Negro girl dressed him up in an Osnaburgh frock; put a hat made of grass on his head; tied up the lower part of his face in a silk handkerchief, as if he had a sore mouth; and with a piece of charcoal made his hands and the upper part of his physiognomy of one colour—all of the same complexion as his black eye.

Thus disguised, he sallied forth from the hut, conducted by the Negress, who absented herself from her work at her own risk. He was armed with his pistol, and brandished a good cudgel in his right hand. They had to cross the cane pieces in front of Mr Guthrie's house, in order to reach the road which led to the sunken bridge; there being no other place to cross the rivulet, except by going a mile below, where it disembogued into the sea. The black girl knew, of course, the hut of the Obeah man, as well as the little cave above it. The entrance to the subterranean abode was known but to very few persons, and those only dared to enter it in company with Hamel, after they had summoned him by blowing a note on the conch-shell we have before noticed. But in this instance they had not the good fortune to arrive at the conch. As they crossed the interval in the cane pieces beforementioned, the Negress espied the deputy-marshal, as she rightly suspected, sitting on his steed beneath a tamarind tree, directly in their way. She communicated her discovery to Roland; urging him to put a good face on the matter, and walk boldly past; but the Missionary's heart failed him. He could not help sidling away gradually; not towards the sea, which would lead him to the town, and the haunts of many men, but towards the house of Mr Guthrie, which stood on his right hand. The minister of the law had observed him and his attendant, but without the least suspicion of his identity from first to last; but observing that the pair of Negroes, as he took them to be, had changed their course on seeing him, he conjectured they avoided him for fear of being questioned respecting Roland, knowing how loth all Negroes are to give any account of a culprit which may be the cause of bringing him into mischief. So, seeing that they still kept hauling off—to use a sea phrase—he weighed his anchor, and set his topsails to come up with them, increasing his pace the nearer he approached, as he distinguished the more certainly that they were intent on keeping out of his way.

Roland concluded he was known. At that moment he would have given his reversion of paradise to have been again in the Negro hut, or in the cave of Hamel, or on the ocean in a storm, a prisoner in a privateer, a jack tar fighting the enemy. The fangs of the law had more horrors for him than the clutches of Satan himself. He trembled from head to foot; redoubled his pace, and drew near, with long and hurried strides, to the dwelling of Mr Guthrie; the abode whose sanctuary he had violated—whose mistress he had rendered miserable.

Yet what was to be done? The deputy-marshal was determined to come up with him; and by this time he had got so near the house, that he must either enter it, or turn away from it altogether, and become at once the prey of the catchpole! A drowning man catches at straws. Despair encouraged him. He hastened up the piazza steps as the marshal galloped towards him, and ran for protection into the very chamber of Mrs Guthrie—the scene of his crime—now, at least, the scene of something like his expiation. He bolted the door after him, before Joanna, who was seated by the bedside, had time to address him; threw down his hat, and pulled the handkerchief from his face, clasped his hands together, and fell flat upon the floor.

'Save me! save me! Forgive me!' cried he; 'Save me from an ignominious death! Oh God! Oh God! Miss Joanna, save me!'

'Gracious heaven,' said Joanna in amazement, 'it is Mr Roland's voice!'

Her mother looked from her bed on the hideous figure before her, more astonished than her daughter at the black face of Roland; while the Missionary, crawling towards her on his knees, implored her protection in the most abject terms.

'Save me, spare me, forgive me! I am guilty, but save my life!—I will atone for all!—I will be your slave! Imprison—beat me, brand me!—I will worship my deliverer!—Mr Fairfax is innocent!—Would you shed my blood?—Would you seek my death—the death of a sinner? Let me live to make atonement, to make my peace with heaven, to redeem my soul from the gates of hell, from the lake of brimstone—the level lake, the burning billows of sulphur and pitch!'

There was a noise as of one trying to enter the room. The Missionary's blackened features assumed the character of a more ghastly horror. He felt for his weapon to destroy himself, but the incumbrance of his frock prevented, or delayed, his getting at it.

Still he was on his knees, exclaiming—'Is there no mercy,'—while his victim, to whom he addressed himself, alarmed at his figure and speech, and already on the verge of the grave, cast on him a last look of pity, and motioned with her finger to Joanna to open the door.

The Missionary sank again on the ground, but quickly recovering himself, ran to prevent the young lady from complying with the direction of her mother. He was, however, too late. The door was opened, and Michal made her appearance in time to stop the Missionary's hand from discharging the pistol through his own head in the presence of the dying woman and her daughter. The noise of his harangue, as well as the presence of the Negress, had brought the house servants to the door. The deputy-marshal too, acquainted, during her agitation, by the guide of Roland, that it was himself, sent in to claim his prisoner. Mrs Guthrie had breathed her last before he attended to the suggestion of Michal, and Roland hurried out of the window into the piazza, whence he leaped to the garden below. The marshal was on the look out, having summoned the servants to assist him. He caught a glimpse of his prey, and spurred his horse after him; while Roland drew forth his pistol and bid him defiance; but the man of war had no fear— or overcame it. He rode at him, and coming in contact with the Missionary, tumbled him headlong down with a blow of his staff, and springing from his horse, disarmed, handcuffed, and led him off in triumph to the prison at —— Bay.

CHAPTER 10.

Oh! 'tis a cruel sentence, whether it
In heaven for me or in earth be writ.
FAITHFUL SHEPHERD.

THE news of Mrs Guthrie's death was speedily conveyed to
Belmont, where Mr Fairfax and his ancient friend were preparing
to celebrate his return to his paternal domains, in company with
those of his neighbours whom courtesy or curiosity had brought to
the scene of Mr Fillbeer's disgrace. Mr Guthrie of course returned with the messenger who brought the news, lamenting bitterly the hard fate which had deprived him, first of his wife's
affections, and lastly of herself, before he could reclaim them; and
commiserating, at the same time, the long sufferings she had endured, from what had appeared always to him, a preposterous, if
not a capricious melancholy.

His opinion on the subject was not much improved when
Michal put a letter into his hands, which her mistress, anticipating
her end, had given to her charge some days before, to be delivered
after her death, conjuring him never to inquire into the cause of
her chagrin, or the malady which would prove fatal to her, but to
assure himself that she was his fond and faithful wife, who had
never loved any one but himself, and now consigned her daughter
to his constant and affectionate care.

She had expressed, by word of mouth, the same wishes to
Joanna; and bid her tell Mr Fairfax to use a similar forbearance if
ever there should arise a question on the subject. The old gentleman was contented, at least for the present, to abide by her instructions; and he grieved not the less for her untimely fate, and
the loss he had sustained, when he heard of the defeat and im-
prisonment of the Missionary Mr Roland.

'*Una dies,*' said he, '*aliquando parens—aliquando noverca est.*
The attorney overthrown, and the hypocrite unmasked and secured; the son of my old friend reinstated in his mansion and
rights—But the wife of my bosom—the partner of all my past

happiness—is gone for ever! For ever! That dreadful conviction, for ever! strikes on one's heart as if it were the signal gun for one's own execution! She will never come again!—Never, never! The joy of heart! Ah! that has been long gone, poor thing! The smiles of innocence, of affection, of rapture!—Ah, my God! Can I forget when Joanna was born? How proud she was of her, how grateful, how affectionate, and how beautiful she looked! And now she is dead—a cold insensible corpse! Yet she is beautiful still! Dry your tears, Joanna—and you, Michal.—Would it had been my fate, rather than hers! But we shall meet again, all of us—aye in a better world—for there is little use in this as far as I can understand it—except—except—except we can make those happy who depend on us for happiness, and a great many more too. God's will be done! I confess my ignorance: I know nothing of this world, and but little of any other: I had almost said less of any other. But we are born to suffer; that is evident: and why may we not die to be happy? Who knows? The books say so—some of them—and I think it really possible. Thank heaven! I have still my daughter left. You, Joanna, shall console me for my loss! Weep not, my child. You are young, and shall find consolation, as I did. Bear with me;—and you, Michal! We all owe God a death. You have lost a kind mistress, but I will do my best to supply her place to you, and so will Joanna.'

Thus sighing, and then consoling the mourners, then mourning himself, the veteran betrayed, without designing it perhaps, the sense he entertained of his loss, together with some little sparks of his religious and philosophical fantasies; and the night found him still exhorting his daughter, from time to time, to restrain the tears which his conversation as often recalled when he spoke of the amiable qualities, and the personal charms, of her whom he had on the morrow to consign to the earth. Let us leave him for the present, and give some account of the wizard Hamel, who sprang into the bushes between the sunken bridge and Belmont house, at the moment that the light horsemen were in pursuit of the dethroned monarch, the Brutchie Combah.

Hamel belonged to the estate of Mr Fairfax; and the king was too blind at present to see or make any appeal to him, except he

should give him warning, by his voice, of his being present; consequently he had little or nothing to fear. He allowed the troopers to
pass, and then altering merely the position of his hat on his head,
returned to the road, and followed them as quickly as his legs would
carry him; but not in time to see the scene between Fillbeer and the
ghost. He was overtaken by Mr Fairfax and his companion, in
whose rear he arrived before the house at that critical moment
when the attorney was seated on a branch of the tree, with a few
fathoms of rope made fast to his throat. He was himself too much
out of breath with running to announce his master, and it would not
have caused him to shed many tears if, by any precipitation, the fat
man had been fairly launched into the air; for he abhorred him. The
attorney was no favourite with any one on the estate, but Hamel
held him in utter detestation on many accounts, chiefly for having
punished and insulted him at the same time for some remissness in
his duty as a watchman, when a sheep had been lost from his domain—stolen, as it was thought, but afterwards discovered to have
been struck by lightning. It is not confessing too much on the part
of the Obeah man, to acknowledge that he enjoyed the agony of
Fillbeer, and would have kept him for an hour—a day—a week—
in the situation in which he saw him; nay, he made his way to the
foot of the gallows, and taunted him with his affected pity.

'It is but dying, master attorney,' said he. 'You see how the
Negroes love you. I'm sorry for you, master Fillbeer; perhaps they
won't hang you yet. I am too old, or I would climb the tree and cut
you down.'

Fillbeer had been too terrified to pay any particular attention to
what he said, though he was not insensible to it at the moment; but
Hamel, to make more sure of his revenge, had anticipated the retreat of the man of fat, and waylaid him (although he was thus
obliged to desert his sovereign for the time) in a narrow pass
through which his road lay to the upper estate, where he doffed
his hat at the ex-brewer's approach, and wished him good bye,
with many thanks for all favours.

Humbled as the attorney felt by his disgrace and defeat, as well
as his expulsion from the estate which he had threatened to keep
by force, his fears had yet so far given way to his feeling of present

security, as to admit of his rage rekindling at this shew of insult. His pale face was again reddened with passion; his cheeks swelled like the gourd of Jonas; and he gnashed his three teeth together as an alligator clashes his flytrap.

'Accursed villain!' cried he; 'you are that dabbler in spells and Obeah, who caused the turkies to lay rotten eggs, and the chickens to have the pip. D—n you! I'll pheeze you, rascal! You shall grace a gibbet yet.'

'Thankye, master. Master's too kind—master likes hanging himself. He grease the gibbet well.'

'Scoundrel, do you mock me?' said Fillbeer, riding up as if to strike him with his whip. 'It is you, you black monster, who bewitch the cows, is it?—who cause abortions among the women—who make your fellow-creatures eat dirt?'

'Dirt!' said the Obeah man, emphatically—'dirt, master Fillbeer? It is such as you and preaching Roland who make my countrymen eat dirt. Who brought us from Africa? Who made slaves of us? Who treated—and treat us still—as the dirt they buy and sell? And while they affect to be for making us free, and for saving our *souls*, are cramming us with dirt, and trash, and filthy foolish lies?'

'Do you call my religion dirt?' said Fillbeer, affecting a solemnity of look and manner. 'May the devil confound your impudence; d—n you, sir; d—n you, Hamel; d—n your mother and your father, your grandmother, and your great grandmother; and all her ancestry up to Noah!'

'Very well, master. Please to take care master does not damn his own grandmother's ancestors. Have you all these curses in your religion?'

'Aye, sir; and you shall be cursed to the lowest pit of hell, dirt as you are, yourself.'

The Obeah man looked at his own small figure, compressing his frock to display its true dimensions, and then extended his arms in a sort of half circle, as if to illustrate that of Fillbeer, who foamed at the mouth like a baited bull, and continued punching, with his fat heels, the ribs of his horse, to get him nearer the rock on which the wizard stood.

'I know,' said the latter, 'we are all dust and dirt—but master is more dirt than I am; ten-times, twenty times more dirt. If master please to go to hell too, when I go—'

'I go to hell, sir!' said Fillbeer with a grin, which was suddenly exchanged for a look of inspiration, as he turned the whites of his eyes to heaven, and assumed a smile he could have fancied celestial. 'No, sir, I shall mount—'

'I tell you, Mr Fillbeer,' replied Hamel, 'you shall dismount, if you do not take care. You shall march tomorrow at this hour to the mountains, or down to the Bay; for master Fairfax shall turn you out of the estate you are going to, and take away from you all the power you have had. You shall flog no more Negroes; and you shall dismount now, if you do not take care—look at your saddle.'

Fillbeer's eyes were on the route of Mahomet, travelling through the sixth or seventh heaven; and while he was extasied in this fashion, he lost, or forgot, the equilibrium of his weight, which preponderating, though in a very trifling degree, dragged his saddle on one side of his horse's back. He of course, slipped with it, and both were past recovery at the moment he discovered his mistake. Finding himself going, he thrust out his left hand as a prop to bear him up against the rock on which Hamel stood. His right foot being consequently hoisted on to the back of the horse, who, long accustomed to carry four and twenty stone (up to any hounds in the island) remained; fortunately for the rider, as motionless as those of Lysippus at Venice are at present. But the fat man could not recover himself, and beginning to doubt the stability of his nag under this uneven pressure, he was fain to ask assistance of the man he had been cursing.

'Hamel, you blackguard, help me up.'

The Obeah man laughed.

'Help me up, you idiot. Have you no bowels, no Christian feeling? Help me, Hamel, I beseech you. Will you let me fall to the ground? I shall be killed! Help me! stop my horse!'

The fat man rolled upon the ground, like a tame duck, after an awkward flight, alighting upon the earth, not being able to stop its course till it has performed a somerset or two. He lay at last flat on his back, gasping for breath to repeat his curses on Hamel, who stood calmly surveying him from the rock, without offering him any assistance. 'It is a bad omen, master Fillbeer! Think of it: you have brought it on yourself. You teach the Negroes to sing psalms and preach; now learn something from a Negro in return. Learn to be master of your passion and your tongue. Are you fit to talk of righteousness, and election, and salvation from hell fire,—who are proud and vain, cruel, merciless, and passionate? Think you the Negroes will reverence or love such a heap of flesh and fat as that which lies kicking before me? Who eats the dirt now?'

'Help me up, Hamel—I beg of you. You see I cannot stir!'

'I will not help you. You white men think us dogs till you want us. Help yourself. A time will come when you will pray in vain for life. Farewell! You have taught me to despise you—that is all I have learned from master Fillbeer. But I have given you a lesson from which you may derive some profit, if there is any glimmering of sense left in your dumpling of a carcase—so farewell.'

The Obeah man descended from the rock, and hastened back to Belmont, where he found that Combah had been recognised by some of the Negroes, who had brought him, disfigured as he was, to the presence of Mr Guthrie and his friend Fairfax. He would, however, give no account of himself beyond this, that he was burnt with gunpowder, and that, as he could not see his accusers, he would speak no more. The surgeon of the estate was deputed to examine and dress his eyes, and a book-keeper, with a couple of Negroes, dispatched with him to the Bay, where he was immediately put in durance, while measures were taken to summon a sufficient number of magistrates and jurors to an especial sessions, for the purpose of trying him on the following day. He heard all this without altering a muscle of his face, and calmly seated himself on a bench in the prison, merely asking to be allowed a draught of cool water, and to have permission to send for two children he had by a free woman whose residence he described; saying that, as he knew the buckras would kill him, he wished to give these (the children) a true account of the acts for which he was to be put to death.

This request was complied with: the children were sent for. He remained alone for some hours, reviewing his late conduct, and bracing up his nerves to endure the fate which he calculated on suffering, with firmness and propriety. In the midst of these and similar reflections, his ears were saluted with an accumulation of noises proceding from an assemblage of various persons who were escorting or following the unfortunate Mr Roland to the same durance in which his former friend, his late antagonist, his present partner in affliction, was confined.

Nothing could be more discordant than the sounds which accompanied the approach of the Missionary. Some persons could not help laughing at his ridiculous figure and costume; others, especially his late hostess, Mrs Hamel, crying bitterly. Many black dames shed tears on his footsteps; for with these the preacher was a great favourite. He was always sweet, and neat, and wondrous civil and polite, and very generous to them, as far as his slender means went; and then he preached for the fair sex, and told them of their rights—in this world and the next. They liked his religion extremely, and were very grateful to him on account of the consequence he gave them in their own estimation; a quality by no means despicable, although adulterated perhaps with a little vanity.

The Missionary no sooner entered the court of the prison, than he beheld the victim of ill-fated ambition, the ex-monarch Combah, seated on a bench, taking the air, with a green coco-nut in his hand, and a brown porous jug of water by his side. Roland groaned at the sight, and asked the officers, in a voice composed of sighs and murmurs, whether he was to be confined with this man, what the charge was on which he was consigned to a gaol, and who had committed him.

'The custos of the parish was the magistrate who had signed the warrant, and the charge on which he was imprisoned was twofold: murder, and conspiracy to excite rebellion. You are here for security,' continued the turnkey. 'The custos will wait upon you to examine you, and confront you with those who have deposed against you here; or you shall be attended to the courthouse, or to his own house.'

'Here will do,' said the preacher. 'Keep me from the gaze of the rabble, and give me some water to cleanse my person, and provide me with a Negro to fetch my clothes. There was a woman followed me, weeping. She has the garments I took off, and she can also provide me with clean linen; for in this dress I am too much cast down—but it is no matter.'

'None whatever, sir,' said Combah, interposing. 'I take it we are in the same ship, master parson. We have the same wind and weather to encounter. We have no mercy to expect from men—white men!'

'None!' replied the Missionary, with a fresh sigh—'none!'

'We should have taken to the boat,' continued Combah. 'We behaved like women and fools. We are justly punished.'

The Missionary cast a look of contempt, as well as commiseration, on his partner, which signified little to the king, as his majesty's eyes were bound up; but quickly relapsing into the grief excited by his own distresses, he gave way to the agony which oppressed him, and wept bitterly.

The king listened to his sobs for a long while in silence, despising the Missionary from the bottom of his heart; but at length the royal patience was exhausted, and he gave vent to his feelings thus:

'Master parson! what would you think of me if I were to cry in that way? And yet I am a captive through your means. If you had not disabled me, I had never fallen into the hands of the white men: certainly not alive.'

'I fired,' replied Roland, 'in defence of my life—you know it; you strove to kill me. It is you who are to blame for all—your own disaster and mine. You made me set fire to my house.'

'For that matter,' rejoined the Brutchie, 'you are safe. You will be cleared of the conspiracy. They dare not kill you for that, and no one could prove it on you but Hamel and myself.'

'What—what said you?' cried the Missionary, looking up.

'I say, master parson,' answered the Brutchie, 'I will not tell upon you.'

'I will not trust you—but no matter.'

'Then you are still and always a fool. Have not you a right to preach? I tell you nothing can hurt you on that score,—get over the charge of murder.'

'I am innocent—it was accident—the informer knows it was.'

'Then what have you to fear—and why do you sit blubbering there? What though you had told a thousand lies of Mr Fairfax; they do not hang white men for that. The white men are afraid of you. I wish they were of me. Get yourself bailed out of prison by some of the other preachers, and go away to America. You may begin the world again with all the knowledge you have gained by bad luck. I should be glad to change with you so far.'

'How, so far?'

'So far, and no farther; I would not change anything else with you—neither my skin nor my condition—nor my resolution to die as I ought. Have you nothing to say to comfort me? You have preached often of death, when it was far away. Tell me now how I should face it; and how you will endure it, if the white men should contrive to make you guilty.'

'Pshaw! Do not trouble me—you are the cause of all my calamity. If you had not sought to take my life, I might now have been on the sea, as independent as the waves themselves; I might have turned my back for ever on this hateful island, and all whom it concerns.'

'There is no consolation here; you are making bad worse. But, if you have nothing more to say, at least wipe your eyes; stop your tears; do not disturb me with your womanish grief. We are here on a sort of equality, I own; for though I am a king, I am a prisoner like yourself; but that does not authorize you to torment me with sobbing and crying.'

The preacher was struck with the assurance of the Brutchie, notwithstanding the extravagance of his own grief; however, he took a hint from his majesty's behaviour, and endeavoured to suppress his emotion, while he washed the charcoal from his face and hands, and assumed a more appropriate dress, sent to him by one of his own fraternity—a brother Wesleyan—who, in common with all the inhabitants of the town, had been apprised of Roland's misfortune. Still he whined, and moaned, and whimpered, and sighed; while Combah, from time to time told him how he despised him, and would die with less reluctance to be relieved from the annoyance of his lamentations. His prayers no less vexed the king: everything he said or did seemed to Combah the result of a puerile and a contemptible cowardice; and at times he felt so enraged at the Missionary for thus wearying him, that he wished only for his eyes and the liberty of his hands, that he might seize him and dash out his brains against the prison wall. The Missionary however continued inconsolable.

CHAPTER 11.

It was nearly dark before the Obeah man, Hamel
proach the town of ——, to reconnoitre the priso,
nicate if possible with his incarcerated ally, the
attempt anything for his companion of the Obeah c
tracted and bewildered Roland. He entertained b
hopes for the first, on account of his blindness; but he was as anxious to save the preacher as one devil would be to assist another,
where their mutual services tended to bring about the same end,
the object which the wizard had long entertained—the subversion of the power and authority of the whites throughout the island. It is true this feeling of his had been somewhat neutralized
by his sense of obligation to Mr Fairfax, but still a time might
come. He would not willingly part with so efficient an agent as
Roland, who was exactly the character which Hamel would have
sought or desired, to create a confusion in the island, and revenge
him and his countrymen on their oppressors. He had a scheme
which, if he could have written, might have been easily communicated to the preacher: but though Hamel could formerly write a
little Arabic, he knew not a letter of Anglo-Saxon; nor did Roland
comprehend a word of any other language, except Latin, and perhaps a sentence or two of bad Spanish. Hamel, however, was not
long baffled on this account. He soon found a pious dame, whose
daughter (a girl of ten years of age) had learned at the Missionary's
school the art of inditing letters. The mother was delighted to
shew the talents of her child, and highly interested in saving the
precious life of the man of grace. The daughter was commissioned
to obey Hamel's direction, but not in the presence of her mother.
The wizard would have no witness. He took the child aside, and
having furnished her with a piece of paper, and a pen and ink, dictated the following letter:—

MASTER PREACHER,—With the dagger contained in
this paper the least wound will be fatal, for it is poisoned.

btain the key of the outer door, and you will find
n horse ready for you on the hill at the church gate,
ne beside it, to ensure your safety. Had you followed
e advice of him who writes this, and staid where he left
you, you had before now been in safety. If you take my advice, remember I shall be in waiting, three hours after sunset, at the prison gate; and when you hear the ship's bells in
the harbour strike the hour, your gaoler will come to see you
safe, and lock you up. Then is your time! Judge for yourself.'

The letter was sealed, and secured in the lining of the
Missionary's own coat, with which Rachel had by this time arrived
from the hut of Mrs Hamel.

The dagger was a very small instrument contained in a sheath,
and, being inclosed in the letter, escaped the knowledge of
Rachel, who took it to be a file intended to extricate her master
from bars and bolts. She knocked at the prison door, with the
Missionary's clothes tied up in a bundle, and asked, with tears in
her eyes, to be admitted to the speech of Roland, which, as he was
only committed for examination, of course was not denied—the
gaoler merely introducing her. She put the bundle into Roland's
own hand, taking care that the letter, inclosing the dagger, should
touch his fingers; although there was little risk on the subject, the
goaler having locked up the brown nymph with the two prisoners,
until she should knock to be let out.

'Roland!' she said in a whisper. 'Dear master! Take courage!
The other Missionaries will beg you off.' Then, seeing the gaoler
was gone,—'Cannot you change clothes with me, and get away?'

Roland had not spirit to move a muscle; but the Brutchie, overhearing what had been said, and beginning to jeer him for his insensibility, he rose from the bench, and made an attempt to take
off the borrowed coat he had on. The brown girl had also commenced disrobing, when another visitor was suddenly announced
to the two prisoners, and the gaoler, entering with him, observed
Rachel's manœuvre, and civilly cautioned her against any such attempt as that she was engaged in.

It was a brother missionary who was thus introduced, and
whom, at the moment, Roland wished in the third heaven, as his

presence had marred one chance of escape, however desperate. He was a good and righteous man, who came to condole with Roland, and assist him in preparing for all that *could* happen to him, if guilty, and to keep up his spirits, and give him assurance of clearing his character, supposing him innocent. The stranger hoped the best, not being informed of the particulars of Roland's crimes; and wishing to console him by quoting an example of the universality of sorrow in this world, told him that his late friend and patroness, Mrs Guthrie, was dead that day, and that all her family were in the greatest affliction on account of her decease.

The poisoned dagger could not have inflicted a more painful wound to the bosom of Roland, than the news of this catastrophe. He had, at one time of his life, entertained a superstitious fancy, originating in a dream, that his own fate depended on the life of Mrs Guthrie; and although in his hours of prosperity (if any such of his might so be called) he had thought lightly of this piece of su-perstition, yet the event, taking place at the moment of his own in-carceration, on the day of his own most perilous lapse into the jaws of justice, brought with it the recollection of his former conceit, embittered by the conviction of his guilt. 'She should have died hereafter.' If the cause of her death were known, how many hearts would it harden against him—and would it not be known? Michal knew it: Hamel knew it: Mr Fairfax knew it; and the Negro who had fired the buildings seemed to have risen from the grave to tell of it.

The Missionary was absorbed in melancholy thought for some time after his ears had drank the words of his brother; but the Brutchie, who had listened to the intelligence, had no mind to let it pass without a remark.

'Master Roland,' said he, 'you can have Miss Joanna now, since you have blinded me. If I had my eyes and my hands! But no —— I can assist you no more.'

'Who is this?' said the stranger. 'And how have you blinded him, Mr Roland?'

'In self-defence,' replied Combah. 'We were friends, and we quarrelled. I tried to chop him, and am justly served; but master Roland has no business here: he is innocent as a child. He is silent because he grieves for the lady who you say was so kind to him.'

'How were you friends?' demanded the stranger again.

'Oh! we were like the cotton-tree and the fig-tree,' answered the king: 'we were bound together. The Missionary was the fig-tree, and has hugged me to death. Take him away, master, if you please. He has no business to die yet: he is not fit to die.'

'What is he accused of?' said the stranger, as if regardless of this remark.

'Only murdering a child,' replied the king. 'He meant, so Hamel says, to kill a Negro man: you must forgive him for that. What is a Negro, master parson? No more than a hog, or a dog; not so much as a horse: and he is accused of setting up rebellion; but I can clear him of that.'

'How so? You are a prisoner yourself on that score.'

'Yes, but he did no good: we should have been better without him. Take him away, if you can.'

'Alas, I cannot take him but by a course of law. But tell me, Roland, does this man say true?'

'Demand of me nothing,' replied Roland. 'There are ears to hear us in all directions. When will Mrs Guthrie be buried?—Tomorrow, I suppose—and the rector of the parish will perform the ceremony. If you will come again, and pray with us, you may perhaps console us, for we are very miserable.'

'Why miserable?' said the Brutchie.

'If you are innocent,' observed the stranger, 'why do you grieve and weep? This is but a trifling casualty. Bonds are the inheritance of every true Christian. Cheer up, Mr Roland. Let not your soul be cast down. The righteous shall flourish, and virtue is rewarded even in this world.'

Rachel was seated during this dialogue by the side of her master; and while the tears ran down her brown cheeks, she had taken his hand, which she held affectionately in her own, and now pressed to her lips. It was dark, or at least the little glimmering of twilight did not suffice to betray this action to the stranger; but the tender pressure, and the tears which he felt bedew his hand, acted on Roland's feelings so powerfully, in conjunction with the moral remarks of his brother Missionary, that he again relapsed into a passion of grief, wringing his hands, and even tearing his hair, while he walked up and down the prison, more like a bedlamite than a Christian martyr; cursing his folly and his hard fate.

'Talk not to me of comfort,' said he to the stranger. 'I know the *ferocity* of my enemies; I know they will strain every point to bring me to the scaffold. The Negro evidence, thank God, is nought: that is, the evidence of slaves; but Fairfax saw me—heard me; and who knows but they will take the evidence of slaves, and admit it to confound one whom they call evangelical, and hate on that account? Oh, they will hang me if they can! I thank you, brother, for your good-will. Come again tomorrow. I have not yet been examined or confronted with any accusers; when I have faced them, I have yet to come before a jury. Leave me now.'

'No, Mr Roland,' replied the stranger, 'I will not leave you in this temper of mind. Let me rather stay and pray with you.'

'I am not really in the vein,' rejoined Roland. 'Leave me, I beseech you! This poor girl will be within hearing of the prison. Will you not, Rachel? She will bring to you my wishes. Let me not detain you now.'

The turnkey came to tell Rachel at this moment that she must retire; and the stranger walked away with her, still pressing upon Roland his reluctance to leave him, and conjuring him to resist the temptations of Satan: but the preacher was resolute. He wished to examine the contents of Rachel's bundle.

No sooner was he alone with the Brutchie, than he felt into the lining of his coat, and drew from it the wizard's letter. It was too dark to allow of his reading; but he could, without difficulty, discover that it was a dagger which the letter enclosed. He called to the turnkey, who at his request furnished him with a light in a small glass shade, and left him again for the present to the society of Combah; telling him, as he went away, that he should come again at nine o'clock, to furnish him with food if he desired it, and remove the Negro to a separate apartment for the night.

Roland read the letter, and examined the dagger with a suspicious eye, congratulating himself that he had not felt the point of it in the dark; a circumstance that might have been fatal to him. Still it was a satisfaction to have the means of death, to avoid a public execution; and yet again this very reflection seemed to sink his soul into the earth. He dared not die, he dared not kill himself, although the point of the dagger, the prick of a pin, would effect his death.

'Oh, the horror of yielding up one's breath, of feeling one's heart cease to beat—of falling into nought, or worse than nought!'

He drew the dagger again from the sheath; looked on its point darkened with a brown and gummy sort of varnish; replaced it in silence, and put it in his pocket—not that of the coat he had on, for he was literally afraid of having such a terrible weapon on his person—but into the pocket of his own coat, which he hung on a nail projecting from the wall, that he might re-peruse the letter at his ease.

The Brutchie heard the rumpling of the paper, and speedily conjectured what it was. 'A letter from your friend of the Obeah cup, master preacher? Tell it me. Hamel has not forgotten us. But he can do nought for me, blinded by my own folly. Yet if I were at liberty, I might again recover my sight. The doctor at Belmont is a good man. He has cured me of all pain, and he promised me, now I remember, that he would come and dress my eyes and my face again tonight. Yet it is of no use. The justices and the jury will kill me at once. I wish they had left me the means of putting an end to myself and my troubles. But what says Hamel?'

A new idea burst on the Missionary's mind at the second perusal of the letter, and at the remark of Combah respecting his wish to destroy himself; and he was loth to answer the king's interrogatory until he had considered the effect the letter would be likely to produce on him. This idea was—to get the Brutchie to use the weapon on the turnkey, as he (Roland) was unwilling himself to shed more blood, or to commit any crimes he could avoid; and he did not consider it so criminal, we may suppose, to compass the gaoler's death as to be his executioner—certainly not so very disagreeable. But how to do it? Combah could not read, even if he could see. He was desperate, reckless of life; and might be induced to take for granted whatever Roland should tell him as to the contents of the letter. But if he should doubt his reading, if he should hesitate, the dagger might be used to rid him of both. The death of the turnkey might be attributed to Combah, and *he* might appear to have committed suicide. His blood curdled at the thought: yet something must be done, if possible. His conscience told him what was murder; what risk he incurred by taking his trial; the infamy even of an examination, such as his might be;—a participator in the filthy ceremony of Obeah—leagued with a Pagan and an apostate; an incendiary himself—a traitor—a rebel—a——. Yet he could not again shed blood: he dared not, even to escape from the almost certain prospect of death. He would have had the gaoler intimidated into the surrender of the keys, and he sighed to think that Combah lacked the use of his eyes; for *he* would have had no scruples, and would have made sure work; and then they might have escaped together,—or himself might have escaped under cover of the Brutchie's desperation.

The king had become impatient for the letter.

'Brutchie;' said the Missionary in a low voice, 'here is a terrible letter from Hamel. He says you are condemned already to be dragged to the gallows.'

'No, no, parson—he does not say so. Do not lie. He knows better.'

'But he does say so, and has sent—hush! Combah!'

His voice sunk into a whisper, and from that into a sort of sepulchral croak.

'He has sent you a poisoned dagger.'

'What for?' said the Brutchie, calmly.

'To stab the gaoler.'

Had the Missionary seen his own features as he uttered these last words, he had gone wild with horror at the sight; or sunk into the earth with shame and apprehension, had the Brutchie seen them; but as the king was blind, he merely remarked that Hamel should have commissioned him (the Missionary) to do the deed; 'for,' said he, 'I cannot escape, and I cannot see to strike the blow.'

'A scratch will suffice,' replied the preacher; 'the dagger is poisoned.'

'Poisoned or not poisoned, you can see to do it: you are not manacled. Look at these chains. Free me from these, and I might hope. Give me the dagger, master Roland.'

'No,' replied the Missionary, 'except you will engage to do what is necessary. When the gaoler comes to lock you up for the night, Hamel will be ready, at nine o'clock. He will be waiting for us both, with horses.'

'Where are the horses?'

'By the church gate.'

'And where is he?'

'He will be just outside the door of the courtyard.'

'Had I my eyes,' said the king, 'I would smite the gaoler to the earth. Roland, you must do it.'

'No, Brutchie, it is your business: 'tis you that are condemned.'

'What!' said the king again; 'am I condemned without being heard? Is this the white man's law? Oh, Roland, you are cheating me—I know better.'

'Well but,' replied Roland, 'you are already judged in their minds; you have no chance of escape. They know the evidence they have against you. They have got witnesses without end, from the multitude that assembled yonder at Mr M'———n's plantation.'

'The same witnesses heard you preach, master Roland; they know what you meant. I tell you again, you are in the same danger as myself. But I know your scheme; you will not impose on me.'

'Your life is in my power, master Brutchie; make no noise—you talk too loud!'

'Take it,' said the king; 'I value it at nought. If I am condemned to die, *you* may as well kill me, if you like to do it. If you had not deprived me of my eyes, I might have served you now; but Hamel is your friend—do what he bids you.'

The Missionary sank down again on his bench in a state of incertitude and anxiety, not knowing what to do. To tamper farther with the Brutchie seemed altogether useless; yet he was afraid to strike the gaoler himself; or his passion required excitement, as a flint yields fire only on being struck, at other times cold and insensible: resistance or violence would drive him to do anything, no matter how desperate; otherwise it was his nature to use scheming and treachery, rather than force, to accomplish his ends.

At this time the doctor was admitted who had engaged to apply fresh remedies to Combah's eyes. It was already past eight o'clock;

and as the door opened, the Missionary looked anxiously and wistfully down the passage which led from it, to form his calculations
on the possibility of escape.

The doctor saluted him very respectfully, though without entering into conversation with him, and applied himself immediately to the business for which he had come.

'What do the people say of me, master doctor?' said the
Brutchie. 'And what do they think of Mr Roland?'

The doctor shook his head.

'I am but too exposed to calumny,' added the preacher. 'I have
no chance of justice.'

'You know best,' replied the doctor; 'but were I you, Mr Roland,
I would lose no chance of escape; the feeling is so violent against
you. An idea is got about that Mrs Guthrie owes her death to you;
that you have destroyed her by poison; and that you had hired a
gang of Negroes to carry off her daughter.'

Roland was overcome with horror; a death-like sickness
seemed to take possession of him, and the perspiration dropped
from his brows. 'I have,' said he, 'no chance of justice; nothing is
more clear.'

'Indeed,' replied the surgeon, 'the prejudice is strong against
you: you have such influence over the Negroes, and there is so
much apprehension of rebellion. We are afraid, that if any one of
your profession chose to give the word, he might raise a commotion in a few hours, and make himself, if he pleased, high-priest or
king of the island.'

During this conversation the eyes of the Brutchie were
dressed, and in spite of the misery he endured, he discovered that
he had not lost his vision. His face, it is true, was wofully blistered
and burnt, but his eyes were still safe, although he could make little or no use of them, as they were, of necessity, bound up again for
the present.

The doctor retired, and Roland remained again absorbed in
thought, endeavouring to work himself to such a pitch of courage
as might enable him to follow the wizard's advice, in case all other
means should fail. Yet, when he had wound himself up to the
point, his nature revolted again from the execution of the plan he

could devise with so much consistency. Sometimes he regretted
the absence of his spiritual brother, whose company would have
impeded such thoughts as those which his mind harboured, and
would have prevented the execution of them, had his mind given
way; and then he congratulated himself that the coast was clear, in
case an opportunity should occur to effect anything of importance.

The apartment in which he was confined was about twenty feet
square; built of stone, with iron gratings at the windows, which
were not glazed. It opened into a passage, which again opened
into a court, communicating with the public road, or street it
might be called, as it formed the main thoroughfare of the town.
He might have scaled the walls of the court perhaps, could he
have got out of the chamber in which he was confined, and have
had sufficient time to clamber: but nothing short of the violence
he had meditated could enable him to get clear of his bars. The
windows were eight or ten feet from the ground; however, he contrived to scale one of these, and seating himself in the ample recess of it, as well to breathe a cooler air, as to look out upon his
possibilities, he thought he could hear the voice of Hamel outside
the wall of the court, humming some African ditty as he paced up
and down the road. It was a bright moonlight, and he could distinguish that the person who was thus parading, and occasionally
singing, threw up something into the air from time to time: it
might be a coco-nut or a shaddock, which he perhaps was tossing
up and catching—but no, it had a string to it. It is, in fact, a rope—
an insult to his misfortunes? No! it is meant for his escape—the
rope is flung over the wall, and hangs down into the court. If he
could get into the court! But he is not active enough to mount by
means of the rope, even if he could rush by the gaoler when he
comes to lead him to the apartment in which he is to sleep, or
rather to pass the night. Another foot is heard—another and another. There are several persons arriving at the prison gate. They
knock and summon the gaoler, who unlocks the court yard gate to
hear their business. They are white men, two of them troopers;
and although they speak in an under tone of voice, Roland can distinguish that their conversation regards him.

'Directions from the governor to guard the Missionary strictly. He is accused of the most infernal crimes; and an example must be made of him. The white inhabitants of the island have long wanted such an opportunity to expose the machinations of these meddling hypocrites. He has no chance for his life; but he must be separated from the black man, blind or not—they may assist one another in any desperate attempt.' These, and such like *snatches* of the conversation, reached the ears of the too vigilant Roland, and confirmed him, as far as his vacillating nature could be confirmed, in a determination to make at least one effort for his deliverance. Combah could not, or would not, assist him. He would make no confidant of him; but furnishing himself with the fatal dagger, for which he had descended from his position, he now remounted to the window for any further information, and sat there until he heard the ships' bells in the harbour strike the hour, for which he had waited with some such feeling as that with which he would have expected the hour of his own execution.

The court-yard was all still; the troopers and their companions were gone; and while he was yet counting the number of bells, the gaoler opened the prison door and called to him. 'Mr Roland, I am come to shew you your bed-room—Where is he?' The gaoler looked rapidly round the chamber, and seeing only the king on his bench, concluded Roland had escaped by some means or other. Confused and amazed, yet without looking up to the window where the Missionary sat, he ran back down the passage, and called to some of his family for arms, crying out that the prisoner was off.

His family, with the exception of a drowsy Negro, were all in bed, according to the early habits of Jamaica; and while he was engaged in taking down a gun from the wall, the Missionary had descended from the window, and found his way to the door in the passage, which was bolted in the inside, where he fumbled for a few seconds; while the gaoler, hearing him from his own apartment, and recollecting he had left his keys in the door, ran back, as he thought, to secure Combah. The Missionary, meanwhile, had opened the passage door, hurried across the court, and seized the rope, by which he ascended the wall more expeditiously than he could have expected. It had been made fast on the outside, so that it held stoutly, and bore the weight of Roland, who had reached the top of the wall at the moment that the gaoler seized him by the legs, calling all the while to the Negro to come to his assistance. The Negro came forward with the gun; but his master, having hold of Roland, bid the slave hasten to the prison door, and secure the blind man first. He obeyed: he ran to the door of the apartment, in which Combah sat as if perfectly unconcerned—turned the key in the lock—bolted it on the outside—and scrambled again into the court yard, where he found his master alone, leaning against the wall, his neckcloth torn as if with struggling, his white waistcoat disfigured with blood, and his pale face rendered more ghastly by the moonlight which illumined it.

CHAPTER 12.

I do follow here in the chase, not like a hound that
hunts, but one that fills up the cry.

OTHELLO.

THE patient and compassionate Rachel sat (like Judah weeping
for her children) beneath a palm tree fronting the prison wall, ruminating on the bitter fate that awaited Roland, as she thought;
now turning her eyes, which were dimmed with tears, to the
bright moon, as if to implore her interference, then to the dazzling
ocean beneath it, and then to the gaol again; invoking the spirits of
heaven to save her good-for-nothing master. She heard the ships'
bells give the hour, which only caused her to think with regret that
so little of the mournful night was passed. She knew not the contents of the letter she had delivered—Hamel trusted no one with
his affairs; but she had seen a Negro walking up and down the
road, tossing up a ball of some kind as he sang. He had taken an
opportunity of throwing the rope over the wall, when her gaze was
diverted to the sea. She had listened, too, with redoubled grief to
the conversation between the gaoler and the troopers; and lastly,
after the bells had been struck, she heard the scuffle in the court
yard, and saw with joyful surprise the Missionary mount the
prison wall. He had not lingered on it; he dropped at once into the
road without accident, cast a hurried glance around, and with his
utmost speed followed the Negro, who, after tossing up the rope,
had listened with some anxiety, and had decamped at the first
sound of the scuffle.

The Missionary ran faster than Rachel could follow him; yet she
still kept him in view by the moonlight, although he seemed to
quicken his pace, if at any time she thought for a moment or two
that she gained upon him. He ran eastward from the town, and
turned up on the right hand towards the church, seated on an elevation about a hundred feet above it. She had lost sight of the
Negro; but as her master reached the wall of the churchyard,
which was whitened with lime, and attempted to climb over it, she

saw another form arise from within it, at whose presence Roland was so much dismayed as to shriek, and letting go his hold, she saw him fall backwards to the earth. She was quite out of breath, and her panting prevented her hearing distinctly the sounds, which yet did not altogether escape her. She stopped to listen, putting her left hand on her fluttering heart to pacify it, while the right was erected and expanded behind her ear, to catch with more accuracy the words for whose import she was so anxious.

'Come, murderer! come!' said an insulting voice; 'your victim is behind you! Coward, and traitor, and assassin! Mount! here is your horse. Quick! before vengeance shall overtake you! Mount, mount; and begone!'

Another person came galloping round the outside of the wall, leading a second saddled horse for Roland. 'Give me the reins,' said he, putting his foot in the stirrup; 'give me the reins.'

He mounted with difficulty; and before he was fairly seated, his guide was already at full speed, rushing down the hill from the church. The steed of the Missionary followed, in spite of the rider's efforts to moderate his pace; bounding down the narrow and rocky road, now snorting, then launching his heels into the air, and springing over the bushes that lined the sides of it. Roland was nearly unhorsed at every other moment; and fain to secure himself, seized the mane of his courser with one hand, while with the other he assured himself of his stirrups. His guide (black, brown, or white, he could not tell) still urged the same headlong pace, without looking back even to see if he was followed, and utterly inattentive to the Missionary's prayers to travel more gently. The road itself, hewn out of solid rock, was strewn here and there with fragments of stone, until it descended to the plain beneath, where a scanty pathway among shrubs, and stubs, and tangled trees, was still encumbered with the ruins of those which had fallen in the late storm. These would have arrested the speed of an English fox-hunter by daylight, but the Missionary's guide seemed to heed them not by night. As he rushed down the hill, there was something almost awful to Roland's ears in the rattle and clatter of his horse's hoofs, and to his eyes in the flashes of fire which seemed to burst from beneath the charger's heels. The rider sat unconscious

of danger or difficulty, apparently as much the master of the animal that bore him as if horse and man were really incorporated—
as if they had formed a Centaur, governed by one mind, and every
muscle moving in obedience to it. Not so the affrighted follower:
he expected every moment to be his last; shuddering at the loose
rocks which waylaid him in the descent of the hill, and shrinking
from the trees, and beneath the boughs, which, without seeming
to cause any obstruction to his guide, threatened to dash out his
own bewildered brains at every step. He sat with his face lower
than the horse's head, holding the neck with his arms, resigning
himself at times to his fate, as a dreaming man drops in imagination down a precipice; and then, when a little ascent retarded the
hurry of his guide in ever so trifling a degree, assuming a thought
of hope and courage, and raising his eyes to contemplate the fate
which seemed to await him in every stride of his charger. The road
was intricate as well as entangled, tortuous, and sometimes zigzag;
crossed by two or three small rills of water, over which both horses
appeared to fly as if the touch of that element would have been
fatal to them. The Missionary's brains began to falter. He fancied
that it was a demon that conducted him, and his memory revived
a train of long-forgotten lore—of necromancies, charms, and
spells, dissolved by running water. They were making for the
sunken bridge.

'There,' thought the miserable Roland, 'we must needs ford!
We shall see whether the demon, if he be one, can evade the
proof. But he leaves the sunken bridge!'

They turned up the savannah towards the ruins of his own
house; and being upon a more open road, the Missionary discovered with new dismay that, although he had a bridle rein in his
hand, there was no iron in his horse's mouth. He was at the mercy
of his beast, who plunged and snorted, as they rushed over the
blackened threshhold and the dilapidated fragments of his late
abode. There were his trunks and his furniture still lying about.
His guide rode towards the mansion of Mr Guthrie, and turned
down a green glade, where a blaze of light burst on them from
burning torches, by whose red glare he beheld a man dressed in
black, reading the funeral service over a coffin supported on

tressels by the side of a new-made grave. There was Mr Guthrie in
deep mourning at the head of it, and Fairfax supporting the trembling and weeping Joanna, while Michal sat on the ground by her
side, with a white handkerchief over her face, to conceal, if not to
excuse, the tears which she could not control. There were two
or three other gentlemen in attendance—the overseers, book-
keepers, and an immense crowd of slaves, forming a half circle behind them. The grave had been dug at the foot of a clump of
bamboos, whose leafy plumes waved in the night wind with a
graceful yet melancholy motion over the house of death beneath
them.—The pale faces of the Whites and the swarthy features of
the Negroes were illuminated by the ruddy flames of the torches
which blazed among the crowd, and rendered the scene, already
brilliant with the yellow effulgence of the moon, almost as palpable as if the daylight had not been wanting. The minister
stopped in the midst of the ceremony, and looked around and
down the glade towards the horsemen, whose approach was but
too audible. A similar curiosity affected the multitude. The
torches were raised aloft, and every eye turned towards the
spot from whence the sullen tramp of the horses was distinguishable—a sound deadened by the sod on which they travelled. The whirlwind, the blast of the hurricane, the shaft of the
lightning, had scarcely exceeded the rapidity with which the
Missionary and his guide were hurried past the gaze of the astonished multitude, who had barely time, many of them, to make a
way for these intruders, before they were again lost to sight and
hearing. Yet they had galloped over the very confines of the grave,
and the flame of the torches had displayed the wild and haggard
features of the Missionary to more than half of the assemblage.
He was bare-headed, and as he had ridden thundering past, many
an eye descried him, recognised him, and many a tongue murmured or muttered his name—'Roland!'—All was silence
again—astonishment, fear, or indignation! Some thought it was a
demon whom he followed; others took himself for his own wraith;
and a few concluded that he was even come thus to insult their
grief. A minute or two elapsed before the ceremony was recommenced. Meanwhile the Missionary and his conductor pursued

their course like the waters of a swollen torrent raving over every obstacle that opposes itself to their impetuosity.

'We shall not pass the sunken bridge,' said Roland to himself; 'the mountain road is before us, and the stream is dwindled to a thread!'

Yet it was buried deep down beneath the rocks of the ravine. The horses sprang over it, and the murmur of its rushing was heard only for a moment.

'Quicker, now quicker!' thought the preacher. 'Alas! whither am I hurried?'

The fields of Belmont were beneath them on the left; the Rio Grande on the right. Here is the second estate of Mr Fairfax, and Fillbeer sits in the piazza still, with candles burning beside him. He is writing letters to England to —— and —— and the Society for Suppressing Vice or Slavery—no matter which. But there is a clatter in the mill yard. He starts—he rises slowly, like an elephant from his lair, and bawls to the watchman—'By heavens, 'tis Roland! stop him!—And a fury leads him!' They are gone. Their passage was like that of a falling star—a gleam of light through the elements—but from whence, and whither does it hasten? Fillbeer distinguished too plainly the expression of the Missionary's features; but he was past. His steed began to gain on that of his conductor, as they wound round the hills which encircled the estate; but his guide still kept his face averted.

'He is black,' thought Roland, 'and dressed in black—that demon that blasted me at Mr Guthrie's door!'

The horses strive as if for the prize of swiftness, yet the road is again rocky. They fly past some Negro grounds, and the hut of the watchman Hamel. They are hurrying to the crags of his cave; and the lagoon before it sparkles in the moonlight. 'Stop—stop—stop my horse!' cried Roland in despair.

He cried in vain! His horse came up at the same moment abreast with that of his conductor, who turned upon the Missionary, and exhibited the features of him he dreaded.

They rushed into the lake—men and horses—and sank awhile beneath its waters, which gathered again over their heads. The Missionary parted company with his beast, and struggled for his life; but when he rose again to the surface, bewildered as he was, he could see, as he strove to reach the shore, that the steeds had regained the land, and were shaking the water from their flanks. Where was his guide? Another stroke of his arms had placed him in safety, but a hand from beneath seized his feet, and dragged him down in spite of all his energies! He lost his powers of resistance. He concluded that all was over—he resigned himself to his fate, and sank! His memory—his consciousness—were gone! He had suffered all that death could inflict, all the agony of apprehension, all the horror, the pain of parting with his life.

Yet, as the reader will readily enough imagine, Roland was not dead. His black guide had introduced him to his own extraordinary residence, in the extraordinary way by which he was accustomed to travel there himself. The Missionary came to his senses in half an hour after his plunge into the lagoon, and found himself in the grotto which we have before mentioned as being always dry—the cave beneath the orange-garden. He was lying on the edge of the water, not altogether in darkness, for there were two or three chinks or clefts in the rock above, which allowed some rays of the night light to stream through, and one fissure admitted a moonbeam.

'I am not dead,' thought he; 'or have I reached the mansions of the damned? All is silent. Is this Styx or Lethe—the *inamabilis unda*—the limbo lake—Hades? Oh, what a vanity is life! What fools are men! Children always: selfish, sensual; scrambling for toys, then throwing them away! Do I live or dream? Have I passed the gates of death? Is it the air of mortality which I breathe? This is water, and I am clothed, and my garments are drenched with water! I am alive. Alas, alas! Why did my envious fate snatch me from forgetfulness? Have I to die again, of darkness, sickness, hunger, or old age, or by—Merciful heaven! Has not this water washed the blood from my hands? There's madness in that thought!' A deep groan issued from the Missionary's bosom; and he sank down again on the bank where he sat, fainting, exhausted, and insensible.

CHAPTER 13.

Lay her i' the earth; and from her fair and
unpolluted flesh may violets spring!

HAMLET.

THE climate of Jamaica—at least the lowland part of it—being at
once hot and moist, renders it necessary to inter the dead as expeditiously as possible; sometimes within a few hours of their decease. This is to many a very painful circumstance. It increases,
nay doubles, but too frequently, the pangs which rend the hearts
of parents, friends, or lovers, to part thus quickly with a beloved
object, for fear of its becoming a source of disgust; to hurry to the
earth the being we have idolized; to close the tomb at once upon
our affections! May not this feeling have been one of the inducements, on account of which the Egyptians took so much pains to
embalm their dead? We are indeed told that their cares were
owing to an expectation they entertained of returning to life after
a lapse of three or four thousand years; but whether the circumstance be correctly reported or not, it is undoubted, that they frequently—nay constantly—kept their deceased relatives, thus
preserved from corruption, in their houses.

There is no idea of the sweetness of the grave in Jamaica.
Everything connected with dissolution is revolting, even to the
rich and rank earth in which the dead are often laid. No tombs
mossed with age; no cool sequestered aisles or cloisters; no idea of
the companionship with the great, the illustrious, the amiable, of
former days, to console the living mourners of the deceased. All is
comparatively new, rank, festering! At any distance from the
towns, a private burial ground is preferred to the churchyard, the
consecration of which has little or no value in the eyes of those
who have once or twice crossed the Atlantic; and the tombs of a
family may often be seen from the windows of the mansion house.
Yet here, as in some parts of England, may sometimes be found
roses and jessamine, cultivated to adorn these humble mau-
soleums; the scarlet ipomea exhibits its bright petals, and many

other plants contribute their fragrance to the air which breathes around. We have described the spot which had been selected for the interment of Mrs Guthrie. It had been long sacred, in some measure, to the ancestry of the family: and Mr Guthrie and his friends were on the point of consigning the mother of Joanna to the tomb, when the funeral ceremony was interrupted by the extraordinary appearance of Roland. We have already described the feelings which that appearance excited. However, the ceremony was soon completed; the last looks bestowed on the coffin; the earth had rattled on the boards, and the melancholy 'dust to dust' been uttered over the inanimate remains within them; the minister and the mourners were returning to the house, and the Negroes following with confused and melancholy murmurs respecting the mistress they had lost, when a new cause of surprise occurred, in the arrival of a Negro, mounted on a white mule, who came at a pace, though inferior to that which had marked the progress of the Missionary, yet not much short of the utmost speed of which it was capable, as mules seldom do their best except it be for their own pleasure. The doctor was wanted. In Jamaica, as in England, the disciples of Esculapius are accustomed, after the proverb, to carry home their work. The doctor was a man of eminence: he was called to attend the gaoler who had been stabbed by Mr Roland.

'Stabbed by Mr Roland!' The words were echoed by a hundred voices.

'It was a poisoned dagger,' said the Negro; 'and the gaoler is dying.'

'Dying, and stabbed by Roland!'

The doctor mounted his horse and rode back with the Negro, while the rest of the party proceeded forward on their return to Mr Guthrie's mansion.

Let us see what had followed the escape of Roland.

The gaoler had retained scarcely sufficient strength to tell his Negro that Roland had stabbed him. The wound was not deep, nor would it have been serious but for the poison with which the dagger had been drugged; for Roland had struck with a reluctant arm.

The Negro, who had come from securing the door on the ex-king of the island, was perfectly at a loss what to do on the occasion. His master was bleeding, fainting, almost inanimate, and—as he felt assured—dying. The lock-up houses in Jamaica, not often overflowing, as in this happy and moral country of Great Britain, are less encumbered with *canaille* to keep the prisoners in safety. Mungo was the only deputy of his master, whose family were all already in bed; and Mungo was no surgeon. He began to bawl strenuously for his master's wife, who, half asleep, put out her head from a small window which looked into the court, and hearing what was amiss, came running out in her undress, with her hair flying about her shoulders, wringing her hands, and dumb with consternation. The dying man said that the knife must have been poisoned. The Negro was dispatched by his mistress for a surgeon; and the lady, beside herself with the fright and horror occasioned by the scene, took the keys which Mungo had left, and without more ado led out Combah from his prison, and promised him life and liberty if he would save her husband—if he would but tell her how to cure a poisoned wound! His majesty had already made up his mind for death; but if life were in his choice, it might yet have some allurements— some consolations. The lady unloosed the bandage from his eyes, with one of which he found that he could at least see to run away, if he could remove the shackles from his legs.

'What can I do?' exclaimed the woman. 'My husband will be dead.' (He had fallen into a mortal paroxysm.)

'Take off these chains,' said the king. 'I know of many herbs that would cure him directly; but we have none here. Take off these chains: the key is there upon that bunch, I am sure. Cocoon—that is a certain antidote. But stay—the first three different leaves you can find—that leg is free—unloose the other—I will run for his life!'

'Ah!' said the woman in an agony, 'you are deceiving me.'

Her husband groaned, and she turned to raise and support him; while Combah, freed from his chains, walked away deliberately through the gate which Mungo had left open.

He thought no more of antidote cocoon, or any other counterpoison; but using the privilege of his existence to move about on

two legs, was soon out of sight of the gaol and of the town, marching with his utmost celerity towards the fastnesses of the Blue
Mountain, where he was accustomed to quarter.

He had not proceeded far, before he was joined, first by one
Negro, and successively by six or seven more of his ancient companions, whom the report of his incarceration had brought to the
Bay, if not to his assistance. These were his friends of the Obeah
cup, who told him they had again mustered strong in the mountains, and meant to have attacked the prison that very night, to set
him and Roland free.

'Aha!' said the king, 'it is Roland who has set me free: he has
killed the gaoler. I thought he had not had the heart; and he is
gone to meet Hamel in the churchyard; but I will never again
count on him, notwithstanding; for nothing but despair urged
him.'

'Is there no other white man you will trust?' said one of the
Negroes; 'or shall we kill them all? There are two men from St
Domingo, who have a large canoe concealed among the mangroves at the little Turtle Crawl Bay, to windward off Port
Antonio. They are of some consequence in their own country, and
will assist us with their advice here; and if we do not succeed, we
can get to the canoe and sail away. But first let us punish the magistrate who put you in prison.'

'It was Mr Guthrie,' replied the king. 'Let us take away his
daughter, and set fire to his works. We must kill him if we can, and
all the Whites. I tell you we have no chance but by extirpating
every buckra in the island.'

'Here are men,' said one of the Negroes, 'from Hanover and
Westmoreland. The Negroes to leeward are all ready to rise, and
some of those in Portland and St David's. Let us at least make one
attempt before we run away, for we can (all of us, and more) escape to a certainty.'

While this conversation occurred, the monarch and his satel-
lites had arrived at the junction of the roads opposite Mr Guthrie's
house, and could distinguish, by the torches which the Negroes
carried, the return of the party from the funeral. Mr Fairfax had
taken the road to his own abode; the doctor and his guide (the

gaoler's Negro) had already passed them in their way to the town;
but the Negroes belonging to the estate were too much about to
admit of any attempt being made on the individuals of the family
at present. Another night would offer a better opportunity.
Meantime it was necessary to apprize the rest of their companions
that Combah was free, as well as to secure the good-will and assistance of Hamel, without whom many of the conspirators were unwilling to stir. The circumstance of Roland having slain the gaoler
might perhaps do more harm than good to the cause with some of
the party, although there were others who would value any volun-
teer in the cause in proportion to the crimes which would render
it imperative on him to die rather than capitulate under any circumstances. These would reckon on Roland as a good ally. On
Roland—the wretched Missionary whom we left in the Duppie's
grotto, among the obeahed or enchanted crags of the wizard's
abode! They knew him not.

Meanwhile the king and his comrades continued their march
into the interior, meeting from time to time with some of their
companions on the lookout, and having once narrowly escaped
falling in with a party of troopers who were watching the em-
bouchure of one of the passes from the south side of the island.
They flung into the thicket at the sound of the horses' feet, and
heard the riders laughing, as they passed, at the story of the
Missionary's black eyes, and of Combah having had *his* blown out.
They had a prisoner with them, whom by the moonlight one of
Combah's friends suspected to be Nimrod, alias Drybones: his
voice confirmed the supposition. That Negro had returned from
Kingston with a portmanteau, of which one of the troopers had
taken possession. It contained, he said, property of Mr Fairfax,
which he had recovered for him from pirates who had taken it in
Cuba. He had a pass from Mr Guthrie, and another, as he assured
them, from the governor's secretary, to whom he had been sent.
More they could not learn.

The troopers had passed by; and the eloquence of Nimrod, who
was not unwilling to be in such custody, was wafted by the land
wind away from the too curious ears of his late comrade. It was
near midnight before Combah arrived at the rock furnished with

the tent of sail-cloth, from which he had sallied two days before, to wreak his vengeance on the man of grace—the treacherous and inconstant Roland. What a variety of adventures had his fate, his very passion rather, we may say, crowded into this little portion of his existence! And how completely had all his exertions for the gratification of that passion recoiled upon himself! Every way foiled in his own intentions, he was, at least indirectly, indebted to his unhappy victim for his own life, rescued from a violent and disgraceful death by the crimes (it is true) of the false Missionary, whom he had himself endeavoured to assassinate. But he had shewn the feeling which almost all savages possess in the hour of peril and despair: he had betrayed no fear of death; while, on the other hand, his religious adversary had been overwhelmed with horrid apprehensions, and to escape from his prison had at last committed a deed of open violence, at which his nature and his conscience alike revolted. The Brutchie had so far triumphed here, though to Hamel was due the merit of having driven the Christian to extremity. He was the demon to whom Roland owed his life; for which, even in his own thoughts, he began to fear that he had compounded with his salvation. The Brutchie was the gainer by the compact, and prepared to put in force the schemes which his present good fortune had encouraged him to entertain.

CHAPTER 14.

There's nothing serious in mortality:
All is but toys.   MACBETH.

THE morning had scarcely dawned, when Joanna, rising from her almost sleepless couch, walked down from the great house, attended by the pretty Michal, to visit the tomb of her mother. The black garments worn at the funeral had been exchanged for a robe of cooler texture, whose sable ornaments yet marked the customary mourning. She had no head-dress, except a black veil which flowed down to her feet, and would perhaps have better suited the shadows of a cloister in the temperate zone, than the raging heat and dazzling sky of the tropics. Her aspect was pale and melancholy, but her gait had yet the elasticity of youth; and although her eyes were dimmed with tears, the tenderness and the delicacy of her grief would scarce have detracted from her beauty in the estimation of any beholder. But beauty is a perishable flower, and youth turns to age, and roses wither, and 'vanitas vanitatum!' as the preacher says—'omnia vanitas'—all is vanity! Yet roses are beautiful till they fade, and seem to require the notice of every beholder. Who would pass without bestowing a look on them—without entertaining a thought of their colour and their fragrance? The pretty Michal—she was also a rose, and carried with her a basket of roses, to strew upon the grave. This was suspended on her left arm. With her right she held an umbrella over her head, in imitation of her mistress, although the sun had not yet risen

'—from under this terrestrial ball.'

But Michal was bareheaded. They seated themselves beside the grave, on which they began to stick the flowers, while the melancholy yet affectionate office revived afresh the sorrow of Joanna, and renewed the sources of her tears. Yet she did not delegate the task to her handmaid. The roses were planted, and various seeds sown in the fresh mould, and many a sigh breathed over them,

311

which at least consoled the living, if the dead beneath, or the spirit of the dead, could heed them not. There is a luxury in grief like this—a sacred luxury

'None but the deeply wounded ever know.'

But we must not turn moralists. In the midst of their grief and occupation they discovered a Negro man gazing at them, and at the grave, from behind the trunks of the bamboos whose feathery boughs waved over them.

'Who is this?' said Joanna to the maid.

The Negro bowed, and *made a foot*—as the dialect has it. 'I am a slave of Mr Fairfax.'

'Hamel!' said the Quadroon, a little surprised, 'What is the matter? And what do you want?''

'I came, like you,' replied the watchman, 'to look on the grave of this buckra woman;—and to see you shed tears over your dead mistress.'

'Hamel,' replied the soubrette, 'you had better have been at your work; at least, at your post, watching your master's property.'

'It will take no hurt,' rejoined the wizard. 'There is one there in my place, who keeps a good look out, though he seems to be blind. You know, Miss Michal, who it is I mean.'

'But last, or least of all,' continued the Quadroon, as if regardless of his answer, 'should you come here to interrupt my mistress in her sorrow.'

'I ask pardon, Miss Michal,' replied the Obeah man, 'and of Miss Guthrie: I did not mean to interrupt you. I could mourn too, for she was a good woman, and everybody loved her. Well, she is gone to a better country: is she not, Miss Michal?'

Michal gave no answer.

'When the African *slave* dies,' continued Hamel, accenting the word slave, 'he is told, and he thinks perhaps as he dies, that he goes back to his own country'

'And don't you believe it?' said Michal.

'No, mistress;—no more than you do. Where should I go to? To that country from which I was dragged into slavery—to be seized, and bound, and sold again? I had cows, and goats, and horses.'

'And slaves too?' said the Quadroon, interrupting him.

'Yes, I had slaves; it is true. God is just. I was not a cruel master; but I had sold slaves—I had even taken them—made war to take them: but it was the custom of my country. Ah!' seeing Michal about to speak—'You are right, mistress. I know what you mean. I seized black men—men and women too, of my own colour, and sold them! I deserved to be a slave myself—but it was an abominable injustice. The white men tempted me to commit the crime; the white men punished me for it;—and they will themselves be punished in their turn.'

'How so?' said Joanna, interposing.

'God is just,' replied the wizard. 'Are you not punished now? Are not the white men punished in their wives, and children, and grandchildren? Is it not a crime now-a-days to be the master of slaves? Who sends the Missionaries here to tell this to the Negroes? All the planters hate and fear the Missionaries. They are the ministers of vengeance, the agents of men blinded by vanity, who, without knowing anything about the matter, send them here to torment the Whites—aye, and the Blacks too. They will have vengeance in their turn.'

'Who? The Negroes?' said Joanna.

'Yes, mistress—the Negroes;—look at Hayti. And they will again be punished for what they do. Look still at Hayti.'

'There are few Negroes who think as you do,' said Joanna. 'Most of them are too fond of the Missionaries.'

'If they knew them, as I have seen them! Look on the grave before you. I tell you that some of them are worse than devils—but God is just. Ah, Michal who will shed tears or scatter flowers on my grave? I am old, and ready to die!'

'Why should you wish to die?' said Joanna.

'Why should I wish to live?' rejoined the Obeah man.—'A slave—a despised, denounced Negro! I shall see no more prosperity; and, when I die, what soul shall mourn for me?'

'That can signify but little,' said Joanna, 'when you are dead.'

'But it may signify to think upon it while I am living. If it signify nothing to the dead, as indeed it may not, why do you come here to lay flowers on the tomb of this buckra woman? You would like to think that some friends—some little one—or at least this pretty Michal, would take care of your grave, were you to die, and come sometimes to look at it; and you like to think that her heart would swell while she looked, and the tears come into her eyes as she would say—"Poor young mistress! God bless her!"—So you say now; and think so of this kind-hearted lady whom they have buried here. You say, God bless her; and you fancy that her spirit hears you and is pleased. I should be pleased to think that any one would do so much honour to my grave; but it will never be—I have no children to bless my memory.'

'Well but, Hamel, you are not going to die,' said Michal.

'Indeed I am,' replied the Obeah man.

The soubrette could scarce restrain a smile.—'Die, Hamel! When, and where, and for what reason? You had better go home to your cave, and leave my mistress and me to ourselves. The sun is already risen and will soon drive us home; and you should know better than to intrude yourself upon any persons.'

'It is always so,' replied Hamel. 'We are unwelcome, and intruders, even when we come to do the most important services.'

'Pray leave us,' said Joanna.

'Do you know,' replied the wizard, as if scarce heeding her, 'that Roland has escaped?'

'Yes, yes,' rejoined the soubrette. 'We saw him riding last night like the wind. He seemed to fly, and your companion of the cave was before him.'

'And Combah,' continued Hamel, 'he too is escaped.'

'He has lost his eyes,' said Michal.

'He can yet see,' rejoined the other. 'He has seen you this half hour, and only waits my departure, to seize your mistress, and carry her off.'

'Heavens!' cried Joanna, 'Who is this, Michal—this Negro whom you know so well?'

Michal in alarm was gazing round the landscape in search of the object of her terror, at least for a confirmation of the Obeah man's important though somewhat mysterious assertion. 'He is a watchman and a faithful slave to Mr Fairfax,' said she; 'and you may trust him.'

'You think your mistress may trust me,' replied the Negro. 'I thank you even for that: you may certainly trust me. Mr Fairfax should have been in sight before now.'

'Quick, Michal!' said Joanna, 'Let us return to the house; there may be danger.'

'There is danger,' continued the Obeah man. 'There was a plot laid last night against your family, and your father's Negroes are even now alarmed; and there must be soldiers—I heard their drum: but you must not stir. My presence, insignificant as I am, has kept yonder ruffians hitherto at bay. Had you been alone, had you returned, you had fallen into their hands. And see—they come!—There are three skulking towards us, and three or four more, with guns, half hid beneath the bushes.' The Obeah man made a step or two before the grave, and waved his hand to the Negroes to retire; but they heeded him not. He called in an authoritative voice, and held up his right hand again; but they ran only the faster towards him. Joanna and Michal had fled. Still they came towards him; and when he cursed them by the spirits of his own country, they only smiled at him in derision.

'Your children shall be the slaves of slaves,' said he, 'and yet they shall laugh at your own shame, and trample on your bodies before you are dead! Begone! The ants shall gnaw your bones, and the vultures struggle for your flesh! I curse you by the spirits of earth and of hell! Your joints shall be rottenness, and you shall eat dirt like the worms!—Tremble, and begone!'

His imprecations had the effect of startling the Negroes for a moment, though by this time they were within a few yards of him. They had come forward with a smile—perhaps an assumed smile—of self-confidence. Hamel knew them not: they were strangers, and told him now, with something like a sneer, that they were Christians, and defied his charms. The Obeah man defied them in his turn.

'See,' said he, 'if your christening shall prevent the fortune I have told you. Miserable fools!—Is it for such a purpose as this that you are turned Christians?—Seize me, take me, kill me!—I curse you again by the moon that is growing less and less—by the darkness that is gone—by the fire of the earth, and the thunder of the mountains!—You shall die like the wounded hogs of the woods; and your bones shall whiten and wither above ground! You have dared to interfere with me—you know me not—back to your silly master!'

The Obeah man had fairly talked them and their courage down. The Negroes looked at one another, and then at the wizard, beneath whose scowl they were actually abashed.

'You are then a friend of the Whites?' said one of them. 'Why should not the king of the island have this white girl for his wife? A black man is as much worth in the eyes of God as a white man; and God Almighty knows no difference of colour.'

'Peace! fools and brutes, and begone!' replied the wizard. 'I am a black man, an African slave, and a——I tell you you are the scum of the earth—worse than the trash of the sugar cane, and the dunder of the still.—Hark! that is the scream of Michal! Villains and murderers, your comrades have gained upon the women!'

He set up a loud shout as he drew from a cutacoo, which he carried on his left arm, a small arrow or dart, scarce a foot in length. The Negroes seemed aware of his purpose, for they turned about and took to their heels; but they ran not fast enough to escape the Obeah man's revenge. He placed the arrow in a hollow stick, which he had held in his right hand, and putting it to his lips, blew it with sufficient force to wound the hindermost of the Negroes in the back as he ran: a second, as hastily taken from the cutacoo, flew as swiftly after the next of the black Christians, and stuck in the right shoulder of that baptized gentleman. The third Negro escaped. The others ran a very few yards before they found it imperative on them to stop. The first drew his machet, and faced about, but fell as he wheeled; and the second, already on the ground, discharged a horse-pistol which he carried, with as little aim as discretion. The ball flew over the wizard's head, and the report of the weapon served only to call the attention of the soldiery, and of Mr Guthrie's Negroes, to the scene of this catastrophe.

CHAPTER 15.

A plague upon them! Wherefore should I curse them?

HENRY VI

'I WAS wrong,' said the Obeah man, 'to give Roland the means of escape, for it had been better that Combah had died on the scaffold, than that my friend—my friend?—yes, yes, he has been my friend—my friend Mr Fairfax should be injured in life, or property, or happiness, or hope. Combah was a minister of my revenge, but master Fairfax redeemed me from a tyrant. For his sake I had forgiven—I forgive—the white men, and will do for them all that can be done by Hamel before he dies. Where are the women? Are they safe?' continued he, addressing some of the troopers as they rode into the glade, which was soon filled with soldiers and Negroes, men, women and children, all in confusion, calling aloud for Miss Joanna.

'Who fired the gun?' cried one of the cavaliers, apparently more bent on learning the particulars of the conflict, if such it may be called, than of attending to the Obeah man's request respecting the women. 'Did you shoot these two men?'

'I have no gun,' replied the Obeah man. 'See to the women—see for Miss Guthrie! Is she safe?'

The confusion became greater as all parties were crowding—some round the wounded Negroes—others straining to get a sight of Hamel, among whom Mr Guthrie in his regimentals, and mounted on his wall-faced charger, exclaimed aloud for his daughter, and endeavoured to force his way towards the wizard.

'Master Guthrie,' cried this latter, clambering into the bamboos; 'master Guthrie, where is Miss Joanna? Have you found her?'

The man of war looked aghast. 'No! no!—I have not,' said he. 'Where is she? Whither is she gone?'

'Hear me,' rejoined the wizard, trying to make himself heard above the murmur of the crowd, and almost participating in the

317

despair of the old buckra;—'hear me!—Her maid screamed—
some Negroes have certainly carried her off.'

'Where and by whom was that shot fired? We heard the scream
and the shout; and the shot brought us to this place.'

'What a misfortune!' said Hamel. 'That shout has misled them,
and that fool's pistol—Seek for Miss Guthrie. She is gone, carried
away—these Negroes will tell you where.'

'They are insensible,' said one of the cavaliers; 'dying, if not
dead.'

'No, I can revive them,' cried the Obeah man. 'Dismiss the
crowd, hunt the woods, I can direct you. There are Maroons here,
who know the runaway huts by the great waterfall—let them
search in that quarter—look to the leeward road—these men
came from the west—the robbers cannot yet be far away—get rid
of this crowd.'

As this was an affair of gallantry in some sort, to liberate a
damsel, a prisoner among a crew of ruffians, the crowd began to
disperse very rapidly in pursuit of her; the Negroes to the woods
and mountains, the troopers to spread the alarm in all possible
directions. An estafette was sent off to the governor, to beg that
martial law might be proclaimed; and a reward of one hundred
doubloons was offered for the recovery of the young lady, whose
loss occasioned almost as much confusion as the rape of Helen in
times past.

Where was Mr Fairfax? Hamel had sent him notice before
cock-crow; himself had dogged the ruffians, little expecting to see
the object they were in search of thus expose herself unconsciously to their intentions.

The crowd was quickly got rid of; and Hamel, not over anxious
to exhibit his skill to the multitude, drew forth his antidotes,
from the same cutacoo which had furnished his poisoned weapons, and applied them internally as well as externally to his victims. But though he was reputed a conjuror, his remedies had
but little effect for the present; and all the intelligence that could
be obtained from the ruffians amounted to an intimation that
Combah would have taken the white girl into the mountains of St
Ann's. Threats, promises, the assurances of recovery, or of cer-

tain death, elicited nothing farther; for in fact they had nothing farther to disclose.

The Obeah man stood before them, leaning on the tube with which he had shot his arrows, and surveyed their features with that appearance of calm indifference which seems the property of the Carib, or the North American savage, under similar circumstances; but they did not bear their torments, or rather the apprehensions of death, with the firmness which is attributed to those unchristian vagabonds. The Negroes gazed occasionally on him whom they called a cruel and heartless tyrant, with a mingled expression of horror and thirst for vengeance, fear of dying, and disgust at their murderer.

'Did they feel no remorse at their conduct?' said the wizard. 'Were they to go to the heaven of the Christians, although they died in the commission of a crime which the Christians denounce?'

The Negroes begged to have a doctor and a parson; and although the hand of death seemed to be on them, their nature yet revolted at the taunts of the Obeah man, whom they without hesitation condemned to the bottomless pit, and to the everlasting fire. Hamel smiled at them; and would have turned away, but that Mr Guthrie, and the two or three persons who continued with him, were somewhat solicitous that he should give some account of himself.

'Take me,' replied he, surrendering his arms, that is, his tube and his cutacoo, into which the old gentleman peeped rather fearfully: 'take me, do with me what you please. I am ready to lay down my life; the sooner the better, for I am weary of this world. I can tell you, I was at the bottom of this plan of insurrection—yes—never start nor stare. I am determined to yield up myself—my life—everything. I would have revenged myself on the buckras for bringing me away from my own country, and selling me to a Negro. I would have made Combah king of the island, to revenge myself on the missionaries, and secured to him your daughter, and half-a-dozen more white women, to teach the buckras that black men have as much courage, and power, and knowledge, and strength, and right, as white ones. They will repay one day on all your heads. There is justice upon the earth, though it seems to sleep; and the black men shall, first or last, shed your blood, and toss your bodies into the sea!'

Notwithstanding his great affliction, which had almost over-powered the feelings of Mr Guthrie, his hair would have erected itself, if its ligature would have allowed it, at the prophetic denunciations of the Obeah man, but too accordant with his own long-entertained ideas and those of the rest of his companions. He heaved an involuntary sigh—a gasp it might be called—and asked the wizard what he was to do with him.

'What you please, master Guthrie. I am now on your side. Yes—you may believe me; or why have I brought these villains to the ground? I am for Mr Fairfax. He is my master; and though I am his slave—his slave!—still he has been my friend. I will lay down my life for him, for I am no more worthy to live. I have betrayed the cause of my companions; and if they do not deliver up your daughter, I will betray them all—every one of them: I gave them notice.'

There was a silence of some minutes, which ensued, while Mr Guthrie betrayed, by his vacant stare, that various thoughts were passing in his mind.

'I know not,' he said at last, 'that I am justified in leaving you at liberty. Yet why should I apprehend you? Can you pledge yourself to be true to me?'

'To Mr Fairfax I am pledged. Yes, I vow to serve him with my life. But it is not for the hope of life or liberty that I swear. Do with me what you will. If you shut me up, I am useless; if you leave me so—free—I will find your daughter or die in the attempt. Please yourself; I ask no favour.'

'Go, in God's name!' replied the old planter. 'I know the confidence which Mr Fairfax puts in you. Go—find my daughter.'

The Negro made a bow to the buckra, and turned about, having received his cutacoo and his tube, with the two arrows which he had withdrawn from the Negroes. He marched off, after having given the white men a look of much signification, and some satis-faction, and murmured as he walked along—'These Christian white men are not all bad. There are many—slaves in their heads and their hearts—fit only to work in their own sugar mills. It is a pity that all should be confounded together, and that when the Negroes *do* rise, the good and the just, shall—must—be punished all alike.'

He was soon lost to view; while Mr Guthrie, distracted with his various occasions for anxiety, and almost overpowered with grief, rode hastily back to his house, leaving the wounded Negroes to the care of his comrades, who, equally weary of continuing at this spot, and finding that their prisoners were fast sinking into a lethargic, if not a mortal stupor, retired one by one; each, in turn, consigning them to the rest, until the last bequeathed them—or the care of them—to two of Mr Guthrie's Negroes, who ultimately bequeathed them to the sky and the winds, stretched on the earth, a few paces distant from the grave of the white lady, adorned with its roses and other flowers, which had already began to wither beneath the rays of the sun.

CHAPTER 16.

Hear, all ye spirits, that in hell lament!
Hear a new sort of pain and punishment.
FAITHFUL SHEPHERD.

THE Obeah man, assuming the pace which his years had not yet o'ermastered, marched off incontinently to Belmont; learning by the way that Mr Fairfax was missing, and that his people were in pursuit of the robbers, who had carried off Miss Guthrie, assisted by no less a personage than fat Fillbeer, who had volunteered his services for the occasion, having fallen in with some of them, whom he encountered on his road to the Bay, whither he was bound for the purpose of detailing the circumstance of his having seen Roland led away, as he thought, by the devil or an evil spirit, into the interior. His idea was not weakened when he learned, in return, that Roland had stabbed his gaoler, and escaped. From hence the wizard betook himself to his cave, before which he saw, as he expected, the water Duppie, with his arms folded, saunter-ing slowly round the little lagoon.

'Then Roland is here,' thought he. 'My life has been a life of strange vicissitudes, but all unhappy; yet not so cursed as the life of this hypocritical villain. And now what are we to do with him? He sticks at nothing for his own ends, and is even now stained with the blood of his fellow Christian, the gaoler, to escape the penalty due to his crimes. If I were in love with life, if revenge had any charms left me, I might be proud enough of my success, my tri-umph here. This Christian, most Christian Missionary!—this man who denounced me, who cursed me in the presence of Combah, who would fain have been great high priest of the island,—this man, full of crimes and wretchedness, is in my power. He has drank pretty deep of the cup of affliction, yet he has never been a slave—the goods, the property of a Negro—like myself. But I have done with the world, with life, and all it has to offer, since I have been obliged to betray the cause in which I embarked. I shall renounce everything, and all hopes—and set this scorpion free!

322

I think his sting is taken out of him, and that he can do no more with Christians, or with those he calls Pagans and Idolaters. He shall have the boat that is hid in Turtle Crawl; and he and his brown wife may depart together.'

With these reflections, and this resolution, the Obeah man approached the lagoon, from which the Duppie, according to his custom, retired at his approach; a ceremony still kept up between these mysterious personages, although they had now a good understanding. Hamel followed him among the recesses of the rocks, and learned from him every thing he desired respecting the unhappy wretch whom he had imprisoned in the vault beneath the orange gardens. His grief, his repentance, his horror and distraction in the solitude and darkness, together with the oppression of his own thoughts, had begun to unsettle his wits.

This was a situation in which Hamel by no means desired to keep him, as to his mental aberration, nor physically, as a residence for his yet breathing body; but how to get him out of the cave, was a question not easily solved—a feat not easily executed, more especially in his present state of mind. The Duppie knew no means but by persuading him to dive beneath the rocks into the inner lagoon, and, in case of his refusal, to push him into the water, and drag him as before. But this, the Obeah man concluded, would effectually destroy his reason. He chose a different plan.

The recesses of these rocks, their hollows and their winding passages, all communicating in some way with one another, were but too well known to the wizard. They formed (they yet form, as any man may see who will explore them) a labyrinth of vaults, of which, since the destruction of the Aborigines, perhaps no one has even thoroughly made himself master, except this African magician Hamel; not quite so desperate a personage as he who has been immortalized by Scheherazade, yet no mean subject, notwithstanding.

He retired into his penetralia, and lighted a lamp, while the Duppie was commissioned to watch from the terrace above; then threading the intricacies of his dungeons, he exhibited at length the rays of his light to the eyes of Roland, through a narrow passage in the rock, about fifteen or sixteen feet above the floor of the

cave, where he was seated by the water's brink, ruminating somewhat in Malvolio's mood, not of Pythagoras or wild fowl, but of
darkness and the fiery abode! He looked up timidly and wistfully
at the light, and descried (which he had never done but by means
of it) the chasm by which the rays streamed into the vault. The in-
equality of the surface, or wall, it may be called, of his dungeon,
enabled him without much inconvenience to clamber sufficiently
high to look into the passages. The light was gradually withdrawn
as he mounted, and by the time he had entered the opening on his
hands and knees, it was removed to such a distance as to be
scarcely visible. Still he followed, murmuring invocations all the
way as he travelled, to be shielded from the power of Satan, to be
spared from the temptations of the flesh, and to be supported
against the weaknesses of this frail nature of ours. The light was
carefully withdrawn as he approached it, and without once getting
a sight, or even conceiving suspicion, of the Obeah man, he was
peaceably conducted to the inner lagoon, where he beheld once
more the light of heaven, and found some food already placed for
him by his diligent host. Yet wearied and oppressed as he felt,
Roland was not sufficiently reconciled to mortality to know the
claims of hunger. There was a fire in his veins which he in vain essayed to allay with water, and even at this his stomach revolted. He
sat awhile beneath the palm tree, out of the sun's rays, gazing at
the inaccessible rocks around and above him, until his exhausted
nature could hold up no longer. He then stretched himself at full
length on the grass, and fell into a heavy and undisturbed slumber.

Meanwhile Hamel, leaving his prisoner to his dreams, bestowed a few minutes on himself to break his fast, and make some
provision against the fatigue he had to undergo in the pursuit
which he intended of those who had stolen Miss Guthrie and the
Quadroon. He was somewhat surprised to have heard nothing of
Mr Fairfax, and was almost tempted, at times, to suspect that he
had been made away with by some of the gang who had attached
themselves to the fortunes of Combah: if not, he must certainly be
in pursuit of her himself. Having taken his hasty meal, he
equipped himself with a gun, in addition to his poisoned weapons,
and having delegated his office of watchman to the Duppie, de-

scended to the works. A rumour had now got abroad that Mr
Fairfax was dead—murdered; and reports had arrived from the
westward, intimating that St Mary's parish was nearly all in rebellion, as well as many other districts to leeward; that the Maroons
had resolved to be neuter in the business, or were in fact rather
disposed to take part with the rebels than to come to points with
them. Some of the Maroons, it was supposed, had got a warp from
the apostles of the true religion, and having long contemplated
the struggle which all had anticipated, had perhaps thought it
most prudent to let the Negroes begin the fray, waiting, before
themselves should move, to see what advantage they would be
likely to reap from joining either party—or whether it would not
be the better plan to let the Negroes master the Whites, and then
themselves to make war on the Negroes.

These reports had alarmed the White inhabitants of Belmont,
as well as the Negroes, who were variously affected as each opinion seemed to prevail—there being, as on most estates, men of all
dispositions; many faithful, sincerely attached to their masters;
many timid, irresolute, and fearful of any violent change, yet
rather hoping, like the virtuous of Great Britain, for better
times—for liberty and property, women and wine, and all the
etceteras of luxury, not perhaps excepting slaves—free slaves of
course—to work for them, dress them, adorn them, and think for
them, if such a thing could be effected! Most of the people of
Belmont, however, were engaged in pursuit of Mr Guthrie's
daughter, or in search of their master. The rest, that is, the very
young and the old, the infirm and the sickly, had assembled at the
door of the hospital, round that huge mountain of flesh, the
Quinbus Flestrin, Mr Fillbeer, who, seated on his horse, was haranguing his audience on the vanity of human life, and condoling
with them on the loss they had sustained in their young master
thus suddenly snatched from them. The Obeah man made him a
bow as he passed, at which the fat man swelled himself out to his
greatest dimensions, and said with a sneer, 'What! you too are
going in pursuit of your master! Is there none here,' looking
round, 'that will revenge me of that traitorous villain? He is confederate with the damned spirits in the burning lake—a dealer in

charms and magic; and by his spells, or his more wicked intrigues, has spirited away your young master.'

The Obeah man halted a moment, and cast a look of contempt at the orator. 'Master Fillbeer,' cried he, 'do you learn wisdom so slowly, and at such expense? Have you forgotten that, but a short time since, you had a rope round your neck? Mark me! If my master is not found speedily, you will be suspected of having spirited him away, in revenge for his having treated you as you deserve. Look at that tree!' pointing at the one to which the fat man had been attached. Fillbeer hung his head. 'Take the advice,' continued Hamel, 'of one whom you call a companion of devils and the damned. Begone from here! Begone from the other estate! You have no longer a home there. Mr Fairfax is in the possession of it.'

'Ah, sirrah!' replied Fillbeer, gnashing his teeth, 'what is it you tell me? You are a prophet, are you? Mr Fairfax in possession of Red Castle! Stay, let me speak to you. Then he is alive still?'

Hamel had delivered his oracle, and attended no farther to the summons of the fat man, who, in spite of his rage and pride, was astounded and disconcerted at the discourse of the Negro, and disengaged himself from the circle that had been listening to him, to follow awhile, for farther information, the object of his abomination; but Hamel was already in the thicket, attended by another Negro, who had met and joined him at the works; and in his company the Obeah man marched along briskly and contentedly.

Mr Fillbeer was alarmed at the threat of the Obeah man; for as such it seemed to affect him. 'His power of attorney!' thought he. 'There is no packet arrived, nor any ship, in this quarter; but a duplicate may have arrived at Kingston. I am a fool to delay longer here. My course must be to the old world, and fortunate I shall be to reach it; for here are coming troubles and turmoil, battle and murder, and sudden death.' He put his hand unconsciously to his neck, as he uttered this last remark, and heaved a deep sigh. 'Yet what is to become of me in the old world? I have been improvident, not dishonest. What have I to look to, what to live on?— Preach! My mass of flesh will hardly go down with the righteous overmuch; and that trade is already overdone: besides, I have not the *reading* which it requires now-a-days. The youthful aspirants at evangelism would cut me out. They are mathematicians, classical scholars, adepts in chemistry, and music, and drawing. They have fifty ways of insinuating themselves into the graces of the fair sex, the rich, the powerful, the persuasive; besides youth, and simplicity of looks at least. For their hearts, it signifies little. Theirs is the road to preferment—D——n. Hah! I forget myself.

Balnea, vina, Venus, corrumpunt corpora nostra.

Living in Jamaica is altogether bad for the morals. There is Roland has flung himself headlong to the devil!—*Balnea! Vina! Venus!*—Poor Roland! How shall I live? These are not times of the buccaneers; and even for that trade I am too unwieldy. Too old to make love—a second wife! mercy on my body!—Heigho!'

With these and similar reflections the mind of the ex-brewer was in a state of fermentation, as he rode up the valley to his abode, where he learned, according to the declaration of the wizard, that Mr Fairfax had been to demand possession in virtue of a power of attorney from Mr M'Grabbit, which he had received from Kingston by the hands of a Negro named Nimrod. The power of attorney qualified him to act in all matters relative to that gentleman's affairs, as Mr Fillbeer saw by a copy which had been left him; so that he was wholly superseded, and required to settle his accounts, and pay to Mr Fairfax all balances due to his employer in England. With the copy of the power, Mr Fillbeer found a very polite and obliging letter from his successor, desiring to make everything as easy and agreeable to him as possible.

'As agreeable as possible!' muttered the man of fat. 'He turns me out of house and home, takes my revenue, the means by which I live, and calls me to account for years of management in the way the easiest and most agreeable possible! 'Sbl—d! I wish, G—d forgive me, that the rebel Negroes may make M'Grabbit's heart ache for this; and Mr Fairfax's too. I had half hoped,' (he whispered this to his conscience) 'that he had really——that the report of his death, of his being missing, had been true.'

The book-keepers and the overseer had seen the power of attorney, and Mr Fairfax was gone to Kingston to have it recorded. The white men were all in arms, and Mr Fillbeer was invited to equip himself, according to the laws of the country, in his military array.

'Never again, by heaven!' cried he. 'I have nothing at stake: what is the country to me? If it were at the bottom of the sea, I should be as well pleased, so I were out of it.'

While he was yet speaking, a musket was fired at no great distance, the ball of which whistled over the house. He popped down his head before he was aware of it; but though another and another succeeded, his courage seemed rather to revive than to be humbled at the sound. He was walking along the piazza, and as the firing continued, he demanded his horse, notwithstanding the resolution he had but lately made, and determined to ride to the scene of action.

'Let me put myself,' thought he, 'in the way of fortune. If I am to be killed, amen! if not—Give me a musket' (This was aloud.) 'There's firing all along the woods. I may be deceived by the echoes, but I think some of the shots are half way up the Blue Mountain. My horse and a musket!'

A light horseman arrived in a full gallop at the house, with an order to prepare accommodations and provisions for a company of soldiers now on their march.

'With all my heart,' said Fillbeer, reading the note. 'I am but a passenger. Burn the house, if you will. What can your soldiers do in these woods?'

'They can do little,' said the trooper in reply; 'but they are a protection to the neighbourhood. There will be another party at M'Lachlan's ruined settlement. You know the road; will you lead them to it?' Fillbeer thought a moment. 'This may be a path that leads to fortune. I'll shew the way; where are your troops?'

'They will be here anon.'

'I will lead them, and send provisions for them beforehand. It is a dangerous place, environed with woods, which are infested with runaways, and was but a few days since the scene of a grand meeting.'

'Aye,' replied the trooper, 'your friend Roland preached there.'

'My friend!' rejoined the man of fat in amazement.

'Nay, no offence. Roland, who has murdered the gaoler at the Bay, is said to have taken refuge there.'

'Indeed!' replied Fillbeer. 'He galloped in that direction, but I rather think it was the fiend of hell who led him, for he flew past this house.'

'No fiend,' answered the trooper, 'but a black rascal who took two of our best horses from a stable in the town. His name is Hamel—a rebellious idle vagabond, and a dabbler in Obeah. But I must begone again. See to the men, and let your Negroes carry provisions to M'Lachlan's. There is no roof to the house; but there is a cellar, and some of your workmen may patch up a covering of fan-palms, or any kind of thatch.'

'I will do all this,' replied Fillbeer, 'and render all the service in my power. The sooner your men arrive the better, for there is skirmishing in the woods already;—and look! see! here are two Negroes bringing a third a prisoner.'

'What are they?' said the trooper, riding towards them.

'Maroons,' replied Fillbeer; 'and the first fruits of our war—a wounded runaway. This is most likely one of Combah's men, the villain who has stolen Mr Guthrie's daughter. Welcome, my friends, (addressing the Maroons.) And you, sirrah! (to the prisoner) where is the buckra young lady? Where is your master? Where is this Combah who had his eyes shot out, and yet finds his way from a prison, and contrives to carry off the prettiest girl in the country? Tell me, or the truth shall be wrung from you.'

'Master Fillbeer,' said one of the Maroons with whom he was well acquainted, 'there is a reward of one hundred doubloons for bringing in the young lady. We mean to find her. This man is a stranger; he met us in the woods, and fired at me; but he is a bad shot. We hit him, as you see, and we must leave him with you.'

'I did not mean to hit you,' said the Negro; 'I fired at another man, one that carries poisoned arrows, and has stolen the young lady for himself.'

Fillbeer paid little attention to the Negro's remark, his head being filled with the thoughts of the doubloons promised to him who should bring in Miss Guthrie.

'One hundred doubloons!' said he to himself. (533*l*. 6*s*. 8*d*.) 'I would I were in the secrets of Roland; for here is a little fortune to one in my unfortunate circumstances.—What said you—' cried he aloud to the Negro, 'one that carries poisoned arrows?'

'Yes,' replied the other,—'an Obeah man.'

'Ah that Hamel—his life is too precious for such a hand as thine! The villain!'

He gave the trooper his congé, and called again to the Maroons. 'Hear me!' (The wounded man was carried into the hospital.) 'Take me with you. Where is the young lady? Do you think the white men will give you the reward of five hundred pounds? No such thing. They will not trust so much money among you in these times. Bring the young lady to me. I will claim the reward as my own, as if I had found her; and you shall share the money with one another, and with myself. Mark you—I am going to M'Lachlan's in the mountains, with a company of soldiers,—to the ruined and deserted settlement. Will you bring her?'

'We must first of all find her,' replied one of the Maroons, laughing; 'and Master Guthrie will keep his word. But do you hear the firing yonder in the woods? The white men will bite the dust—and here come your soldiers. Good bye, Master Fillbeer.'

'Will you bring the white girl to me?'

They ran away laughing.

'D—n it,' said the ex-brewer: 'if I had but Roland's persuasion! Why, they would go to the bottomless pit to please him; and they make a joke of me. Rogues! I should not wonder if there be treachery in all they say and do.'

The soldiers took possession of the house; and having refreshed themselves, the company which was destined for a farther march, followed Mr Fillbeer along the mountainous and narrow path towards the ruined settlement.

CHAPTER 17.

Every man is fixed to a spindle by threads fine as
those of a spider's web.

LUCIAN.

IF we have compared the fair Joanna to the Proserpine of
Schedoni, at her first introduction to the reader, the situation in
which we last left her must be allowed to have enhanced the
resemblance in a double point of view, inasmuch as she had here
the garland at least in her hands, if not the chaplet on her head;
and she was carried off by a Negro who might well have sat for the
figure of the Pluto, though perhaps he resembled the infernal
monarch in no particular but colour. It was not Combah himself.
The majesty of Jamaica was yet too much afflicted with burnt eyes
to undertake this manœuvre. A sturdy deputy snatched up the
young lady, and a couple of his fellows made little account of the
pretty soubrette.

The whole party was quickly in the heart or the forest, where
Combah had prepared a mule to hasten the flight of Miss Guthrie.
No plan having been concerted for the seizure of Michal, there was
no second animal to convey her; nor indeed did she require it, being
perfectly capable of traversing the woods on foot; and although the
Negroes once or twice mounted her behind her mistress, she persisted in walking, and gave her solemn promise that she would not
attempt any escape while Miss Joanna was a prisoner.

Nothing could exceed the horror and agony of the young lady at
finding herself in the power of a set of ruffian Negroes, who affected to console her, as soon as her mental distress admitted of
her listening to reason, by an assurance that Combah would not
offer her any violence, but would marry her according to the laws
of the Christians, as soon as they should arrive at his abode in the
mountains. Nay, the robbers assured her, in the hearing of
Combah, that they would themselves kill him, if he did not, in
every respect, conform to the customs, moral and religious, in
which she had been brought up.

331

As for himself, the monarch walked behind her mule, at this remark, with some such dignity as that with which Alnaschar threatened to treat the vizier's daughter at the moment that he kicked down his fortune. His face was yet tied up, except a space only sufficient to allow him to see his path; so that, fortunately for his feelings, the expression on his features was invisible; for he was wofully ashamed of himself, notwithstanding his previous threats. Nay, he felt more disconcerted in the possession of the object (which his vanity had required for its gratification) thus unlawfully and brutally obtained, than he had done in the anticipation of a public and ignominious execution. First, he saw that the young lady abhorred him, and was overwhelmed with distress and confusion. His black majesty was not altogether devoid of human feelings: he could resist violence with force, parry treachery with cunning, assail the strong, and shed blood where there was a desperate or a dangerous resistance: but the tears of Joanna,—the beautiful, the helpless, the innocent,—in his clutches, or in the fangs of those whom he knew to be more brutal and inhuman than himself, affected him with a real sympathy.

In the second place, the king—this sable monarch—lost all his majesty in the presence of his captive, all his monarchical self-assurance. Among Negroes he fancied he felt a superiority; but in the train even of a beautiful and elegant white maiden, an accomplished European, and a Christian (for there was something in the conviction of that idea which confused him) he sank even in his own estimation into nothing, or worse than nothing—into the character of a blackguard freebooter, who thus disgraced his title to supremacy, and set an example to his subjects, which he ought to punish as an offence to be expiated only by death. He despised himself for what he had done.

And, in the third place, he knew not what to do with this beautiful and delicate creature, whom he had seized in the execution of a pious duty to her dead parent,—where to bestow her, or how to entertain her, until the fortune of rebellion should put him in possession of a better sort of palace than the hut which formed his present abode.

Altogether, he felt with regard to his hapless prisoner, as a sportsman sometimes feels at sight of a woodcock which he has merely pinioned and caught alive. The ardour of the chase being cooled by the possession of the game, he contemplates the shape and strokes down the plumage of his prey, while he gazes on its large and expressive eyes, so bright, so mild, and so harmless, until his heart revolts at his being the cold-blooded executioner of a creature which actually excites his commiseration—a feeling enhanced by the consciousness of its helplessness: he must kill it, to spare it farther sufferance.

But Combah had not arrived at this extremity. It is true, he wished the damsel to escape, while he apprehended the impossibility of her so doing, except by means of his assistance; and to offer that openly would have staggered his followers, who would have immediately entertained a notion that he was about to betray them, and thus to make his peace with the white people. Yet he was determined that the young lady should suffer no indignity which he could avert—a strange resolution to have formed so suddenly, and upon the very heel of his offence. But what is man, even in his soberest moments? A changing, whimsical, and capricious being; vacillating between duty and passion of some sort or other, till all his passions forsake him. And what is he when the restraint of duty is suddenly and wholly removed, when he feels himself master of the law? A compound of still stranger contradictions— according to his phrenological bumps, of course—an agent for great vices and some virtues. In short, Pluto changed his mind, for want of some one to quarrel with about his Proserpine. Had Roland been there to interfere with him, and dispute his title, the young lady had perhaps fared very ill on the occasion.

But although the royal Combah entained these charitable thoughts towards the fair maiden, his delegates were not affected in the same degree, nor indeed, in a similar manner. They had not just escaped a halter; they had not sprung back from the precipice of death, after having trembled on its brink. They were successful,—they had carried off the prize for their Brutchie; an overt act which committed the whole party, and the Negro cause, to that issue which fortune or providence might please to give it. Their minds were inflamed with various passions, all turbulent; and they were ready for anything—fire and slaughter. Yet as they themselves meditated no farther violence to the lady than to make her queen of Jamaica, they hardly thought her an object of pity, notwithstanding the dreadful anxiety and despair in which she was involved, which they from time to time endeavoured to mitigate by assurances that she should be lawfully married as soon as a parson or a missionary could be found to perform the service.

The pretty Michal walked beside her mistress, and supported her at intervals on the back of her mule; for she made a virtue of necessity to avoid the contamination, the touch of the Negroes, who would have carried her in their arms, and sat in her saddle with all the fortitude and resolution of which she was capable, not knowing what to say or what to do; whether to make an appeal to the good feelings of the Negroes, to throw herself on their mercy, or to excite their cupidity by offers of reward. Threats she had too much apprehension to use; and indeed, so young, so inexperienced, and so alarmed as she felt, it was not without difficulty that she retained the command of her reason and her speech, and was able to conduct herself without a more humiliating display of her horror and disgust.

Yet if she was so incapable of hope or consolation in her terrible calamity, as indeed the reader may well imagine she must have been, what could her faithful Quadroon do for her, being subjected herself to the same circumstances, without the protection which her mistress derived from her rank? She was exposed to all the indignity that might be heaped on her; an object of desire to the rebels, no less than her mistress; and there was no question of marriage respecting her. Yet her feelings were as delicate and as refined as those of her mistress, as to the endurance of any personal insult; although the recollection of that impression which she had received from her acquaintance with Mr Fairfax as a Mulatto, came over her mind now and then with rather a melancholy foreboding that this calamity was a sort of judgment on her. Yet she could escape, she made no doubt, but that she would not leave her mistress. When the firing commenced in the woods, and the mule and its escort were turned into another path, amid the

confusion that ensued from the shouts of the Maroons, and some
of the rebels endeavouring to mislead them by their fire, an opportunity offered, more than once, of darting into the bushes, or
gliding down some of the precipices—for she was active and
courageous; but to leave her mistress was impossible.

They travelled for three hours, without halting, by some of the
mountain paths which were barely accessible to mules; occasionally striking into the thicket, and crossing from one of these roads
to another, to avoid pursuit; for they were soon sensible that there
were followers after them; and the firing of the Negroes, as signals
to one another, served as a warning to them which way to steer.
But they sought not the mountains of St Ann's: it was to the huts
by the great waterfall, as mentioned by Hamel, that their course
was directed; and this spot was far into the interior, towards the
foot of the Blue Mountain. The waterfall itself was seen by
Joanna, for some time before they reached it, issuing apparently
from the base of the great eastern cone; but in order to reach it,
they had to cross numberless streams and rills, and traverse a jungle that ages of peace could hardly bring into cultivation. Their
path for some miles lay through an extent of plain, overgrown
solely with grass, but this so high and thick that it formed a perfect
wall on either side, and shut out the view of everything but the
mountains, which towered beyond. The heat was here suffocat-
ing, and almost overpowered their captive; but the firing which
they heard below, and which they apprehended to proceed from
the Maroons—perhaps sent after them, or otherwise engaged
with their fellow runaways—deterred them from halting to relieve her. Every step which they proceeded appeared to Joanna to
add another link to the chain which she fancied would prevent her
return to civilized life, and increased the weight which hung upon
her heart. They came up, at length, with a party of their comrades,
who were squatted beside a sort of tent on the flat surface of a
rock, which rose above the rest of the plain sufficiently high to afford a view over this wilderness of grass, and of any party or person who might attempt to make towards it. The Brutchie was
saluted as their monarch; and they accosted the young lady with
an affectation of great politeness, which was extended, though

with less ceremony, to the soubrette. The party consisted of about
a dozen individuals, including two women, who laughed immod-
erately at the approach of Joanna, yet still as if they designed no direct offence in giving way to their mirth; for on being called to
account for it by some of the males, they begged pardon, and retired. These gentry were all very scantily clad; and their costume,
of rather a ridiculous order, would have excited the mirth of a beholder on any other occasion. Their garments were mostly stolen
perhaps, and in many cases seemed designed by the wearers
rather for ornament than use. One man, for instance, had
crammed his head into the laced cap of a child; another wore an
old regimental coat, without anything under it but his black skin,
and a blue apron or petticoat round his waist: a third had an old
cocked-hat, with no other vestment than a pair of drawers; and a
fourth wanted soles to a pair of military boots, with which he was
equipped, being, with the exception of a dragoon helmet which
almost overshadowed his eyes, as naked as any of the heroes of
baron David, and indeed not much unlike his Romulus, or Leonidas, as to costume; those warriors being clad in some such fashion,
that is to say, with only helmets and sandals, whereas this sable
warrior had a helmet and boots. There was not a shirt among the
party. One or two had ragged frocks, and some made but a very
slender sacrifice to decency. Miss Guthrie and her maid were
more than once horrified at their appearance, so whimsical and
savage did it seem. Yet the individuals were not uncourteous—
nor even less than polite. They were drinking coffee and eating
cocoes on their arrival, and after rising to receive the new comers,
they ushered the females into the tent, and brought to each of
them a small calabash of the former, and a plate full of smoking
plantains, with a little pot of salt butter, and a couple of pine apples; and having commended them to the care of their own
women, closed the tent, and left them to their own thoughts.

CHAPTER 18.

Ta. How now, good fellow? Wouldst thou speak with us?
Cl. Yes, forsooth, and your mistership be imperial.
TITUS ANDRONICUS.

JOANNA and her maid had not been long relieved from the presence of the runaways before they began to plan an escape, and endeavoured to prevail on their black sentinels to oblige them with their connivance, if not with their assistance; but Mrs Wowski and her friend Patch were made of sturdier stuff than to be twisted so suddenly to such a purpose. Joanna promised them money—they did not want it: their freedom—that they had taken: houses, lands—those they meant to take: finery, dresses, and ornaments: these staggered them, but they were also to be won. They seemed to enjoy the thoughts of seeing the white women brought down to their level, and resisted all offers of bribes, and entreaties. But it is more than probable they were intimidated, or had it not in their power to be of use.

Meanwhile, the conversation of the black men was at times audible in the tent, and Michal distinguished, with some new feeling of horror, that their debate turned on herself. The gentleman in the laced cap, whose voice she recognised, expressed his determination to marry her; while another of the worthies intimated an idea of his right to have her without marrying or any such trumpery. But these were not the only aspirants for the honour of possessing her: Michal was very beautiful, though not wholly of European descent; and as the beauties of the fair sex were some of the charms which led these Negroes into rebellion, the desire of obtaining her affected all the group. They thought not of winning her with suit or service, or courtesies of any kind; the only question with them was as to the right of preference or precedence, a kind of claim which many referred to the Brutchie, though one or two were so refractory as to talk of fighting for her.

Combah bid them be peaceable, and let the women alone, until they had at least assured themselves of the possession of the country, of the destruction or expulsion of the white male inhabitants, and of the annihilation of the buckra soldiers. 'You seem,' said he, 'to pay no regard to the firing, which may yet be distinguished below us and around us. You think we are safe from the red-coat soldiers; but we are at the mercy of the Maroons, if they will not join us; and you know the white men have great offers to tempt them with; and no doubt a great reward is already offered for this young lady.'

'I believe it,' cried he of the cocked hat. 'Brutchie, we are not safe upon this rock. The white tent can be seen from many estates below us. We shall have the militia after us before night, if not the Maroons. The houses will be secured along the sea-side, and defended; and though the Negroes rise to leeward this very day, or at least this night, we shall be attacked, and perhaps cooped up here, if we do not move off. The firing is from some of the militia: they are shooting at our men in the bushes below, who are gone to steal master Fillbeer's cattle.'

'Master Fillbeer,' said another, 'is a missionary: we must not thieve his cows and his goats.'

'A missionary!' exclaimed Cocked Hat. 'He that was nearly hanged the other day by the Negroes at Belmont! He is no missionary. He is a preaching attorney, and no worth; a cheat, and a cruel beast. But the cattle are not his; they belong to a Scotchman in England, and we have a right to them. Why does not the Scotchman come and live here himself, and defend his own? Has not Roland told us we have a right to them?'

'Yes; yes,' replied the type of Leonidas; 'and the English people over the water say so too: all the books, and the newspapers, and the petitions, say we have a right to everything in the island, if we can win it; and I shall win the Quadroon girl, and have her myself. I will fight any man that says I shan't have her.'

'You are a fool, sir,' said another of the party; 'I can kill you in a minute.'

'You are a fool yourself,' was the reply; 'I will have the girl.'

'You are both fools,' exclaimed the Brutchie; 'and if either of you draw a cutlass or a pistol, I will toss him down the rock.

Here—see—are two of your comrades coming with a prisoner—
a Maroon. Is this a time to be wrangling about a girl?'

The two Negroes arrived, bringing a prisoner. They were the
men whom Fillbeer had thought to cajole out of the reward, and
whom he only knew as Maroons, while they were in fact runaway
slaves, and had left to the care of his surgeon one of their own
comrades wounded by the Maroon they had in their clutches.
The first news they communicated to the assembled gentry was
the offer of the reward for the restoration of the young lady—
one hundred doubloons: but the idea of restoration was quickly
abandoned, as the company made no doubt of acquiring thousands. They were more disturbed at the account of the soldiers
being quartered at the different estates, as these would serve for
rallying points, and keep the slaves in subjection. They would
serve to encourage those who were attached to their masters,
and intimidate those who were disposed to revolt. A Negro or
two may run away, and take to the woods; but women and children are not so easily exported to the mountains; and Quashie
does not like to abandon house and furniture, his pigs, his
turkies, and his cocks and hens, to those who may make a merit
of staying with their masters.

'But what makes the Maroons fight against the free Negroes?'
said the chief with the cocked hat to the prisoner. 'How many
Negroes have you taken in at different times to the white men?'

The Maroon was a tall handsome black, of a bold and dignified
mien, and not in any way daunted by the circumstances of his
present situation.

'I have done my duty,' said he. 'We have rules to govern us, as
you ought to have. We are bound to obey the laws made and
agreed to by the white men when the last war was over with them.'

'But, sir,' replied the Negro, with an ironical politeness, 'why do
you meddle with us? How did your fathers and grandfathers get
their liberty? Have we not a right to do as you did? You rebelled
and succeeded, and you killed plenty of white men, and you have
been free ever since.'

'With your freedom,' replied the Maroon, 'we have nothing to
do: but a reward is offered for the daughter of a planter you have

taken away; and all the Maroons of this part of the island are after her.'

'And if they are,' said the Negro in return, 'they shall not have her. Why is not a black man good enough for her? It is not for you to say or think otherwise. The people in England, and Ireland, and Scotland, say we are all of one colour—all Christians. Don't they steal women there, and take them, and marry them, from one country to another? Don't the white men here, planters, book-keepers, doctors, soldiers, sailors, parsons, and all, take black wives, and brown girls; and why are not black husbands fit for the white women, hi? A pretty thing truly! Suppose you had taken one of us, what would you have done with him? You would no doubt have delivered him up to the white men to be hanged—would not you? Speak, if you please, sir.'

The Maroon was still silent.

'Sir,' continued the Negro, 'I shall put you to death, if you do not answer me to my satisfaction.'

'What!' exclaimed the Maroon, 'without trial, and in cold blood? Is this the way in which you mean to conduct your new government? The Maroons will all fight against you, if this is your plan: and be assured my death will be revenged by the death of at least a hundred of you.'

'Sir,' continued the Negro, 'we don't want advice from the Maroons, and we are not afraid of them.'

'But we wish to be in friendship with them,' said Combah, in-terfering. 'For shame, shipmate, that you talk so like a fool.'

'Me a fool' retorted the other; 'you fool yourself.'

The Brutchie pulled the handkerchief from his face, and gave his comrade as fierce a look as he could manage with his scarred features and sore eyes.

'If I were free from wounds,' said he, 'you dared not have replied to me in this way. But I will make you obey me while I live and am your king. Here—all the rest of you—listen to me—come round me!'

They all rose from the ground, and half a score, in addition to their former numbers, came from the adjoining bushes, and min-gled with the herd. They were in all about five and twenty persons, besides the Maroon; as extraordinary a looking group, perhaps, as the eyes of an European ever beheld. Most of them had muskets or fowling pieces, in addition to their cutlasses and pouches, slung over their shoulders, or girded round their waists, to carry their ammunition. Some had likewise bayonets; and of those who had no firelocks, two were armed with pistols, and a third was equipped with a couple of billhooks, and a few fathoms of rope.

'Hear me all!' said the Brutchie. 'Am I not your king?' They answered *yes*—with the exception of the culprit in the cocked hat.

'Here is a man,' continued the monarch—pointing to him—'who calls me fool, and disputes my authority—what does he deserve?'

'Brutchie,' replied the semblant of Leonidas, 'he is sorry for it; he did not mean it.'

'No, no,' said the Cocked Hat, 'I am not sorry. Combah called me fool first; and I am not a fool, nor a coward, but as brave a man as he is, and as wise. I have heard the Missionaries, and am a Christian; and I think I know more about God Al——ty than he does—and about salvation and faith. He is in darkness and the shadow of death. He is blind to the true light!'

'Silence!' cried the king, thinking, from the sneer on the face of Cocked Hat, that a double allusion was intended to the physical as well as moral obstruction in his vision. 'Your religion is your own: no one has reproached you with that. I ask again, what does he deserve who insults the king you have chosen? You have sworn to obey—for remember, you have taken an oath!'

'Brutchie, Brutchie,' said one or two of them, 'he is a silly man, and knows no better.'

'Not more silly than you,' cried the culprit.

'What does he deserve?' continued Combah. 'Does he not deserve to be shot?'

There was a dead silence.

'What is a king without authority?' said his majesty. 'We must have some rules to be guided by. This man wants to provoke all the Maroons against us—the Maroons, who are used to arms, and hunting hogs, and know all the secure places among the mountains, and can follow us anywhere and everywhere. They are capital shots, and will have great rewards offered them for taking us. And shall we begin by killing one of them in cold blood, because he has tried to win the hundred doubloons offered for this white girl? We ought rather to make them friends; and if it is a question of importance with them, let them have the white girl, and restore her to Mr Guthrie, and get the money. You think I want her for myself, but I can give her up for the general good, so that the Maroons will join us, or even swear to let us alone, and give us ten men in exchange for ten of ours, as securities that they will not make war upon us, nor assist the Whites or the Mulattos, if they offer any resistance.'

The silence that followed this speech was interrupted by a laugh on the part of one of the Negroes, who caught a glimpse of Michal peeping from out the tent; and he of the cocked hat answered with a sneer, that Brutchie did not mean to return the girl; or if he did, that it was to make friends with the Whites, and could not be to serve the cause of the Negroes.

'But it is to serve their cause,' rejoined the king, 'if I surrender her. Let the white men get out of the island.'

'Ah, cha, cha!' cried two or three voices at once. 'If the white men get out of the island, they will come back again with ships and soldiers, as they did at St Domingo, and burn our provision grounds, and catch and hang many of us. No, no! Kill the Whites—all but the doctors!'

'Not the parsons,' exclaimed Cocked Hat, 'nor the bishop.'

'Pooh!—hang the bishop too,' said the counsellor in the laced cap. 'What do we want with a white bishop?'

'You are a beast,' cried Cocked Hat, addressing this last. 'You want to shed the blood of the saints, and you demur about shooting this heathen Maroon, who has fired at one of us.'

'He fired at me first,' said the Maroon, 'and two others with him; but will you give up the girl? You, sir, who call yourself king of Jamaica?'

'*I* call myself king!' retorted his majesty, rather in a huff—'I *am* king—these men call me king.'

'You are welcome to be called so,' replied the other; 'but you do not expect the Maroons to call you their king. Do you not hear the

firing all around? What will you do with this girl? Give her to me;
I will take her to her father, and give you the reward, or you may
come with me.'

'Hold your tongue, sir!' said the man of the cocked hat, again in-
terfering. 'If the Brutchie, because he is wounded and half
blinded, and was near hanged, is afraid to keep the girl, I will have
her.'

'I have a better right than you,' cried the Laced Cap.

'I will fight anybody for her,' said Leonidas, stepping towards
the tent, which he would have torn open.

The Maroon stopped him; but he bid him get out of the way,
and called him villain, threatening him at the same time with his
bayonet, and proceeding still as at first.

The Maroon detained him a second time, and even used some
degree of force to prevent his entering the tent; on which the
Negro, swinging himself from his grasp with a look of sovereign
contempt, struck him a blow on the breast with his fist.

'Take that,' said he, 'for your impudence;' and drew his cutlass.

The king demanded silence and attention, and bid them fall
back and respect the white girl, who was their queen; but while he
was endeavouring to make himself obeyed, the Maroon had returned to the gentleman the blow which he had received, and
levelled him with the earth, where he lay sprawling in a state of
insensibility.

'Keep your cutlasses quiet,' said Combah, 'and your muskets.
The Maroon has done well to punish the insolence of this man
who lies before you. He did but strike him with his fist, and you see
how he has stunned him.'

The Maroon had seized the musket of the fallen man; but he
was in evident confusion, for what could he do against a host? The
Negroes were some of them levelling their guns, but Combah
threw himself before the object of their wrath, and bid them
desist in a voice of thunder.

'He is our prisoner,' said he; 'a Maroon and a brave man. You
shall not kill him, but through my body, and the first man that
moves a hand, dies!' The Brutchie had his firelock in his hand, and
directed his imperfect gaze to the half circle before him. 'Villains!

traitors!' exclaimed he—seeing two or three disposed to violence. 'Down with your musket, sir—drop your arms!'

The rest of the party had torn the weapons from those of their comrades who offered to resist; but Cocked Hat was too outrageous to be controlled. Whether his particular spleen was excited against the Brutchie for calling him fool, or against the Maroon for having caused the conversation which had drawn upon him that odious designation, he struggled to get from the grasp of his companions, and, in spite of their efforts to prevent him, got round upon the flank of his antagonist, still levelling his firelock, which was at length wrested out of his hand, at the moment it was discharged. His aim had been destroyed; and the ball passed through the top of the tent.

The Brutchie looked around him for a moment; while the rest of the Negroes withdrew from their exasperated companion. He stood alone and in some disorder, finding himself in fact disarmed; but he had not much time for deliberation. The monarch profited by the opportunity, and pointed his own piece at the refractory Negro. It was the impulse of the moment, and a moment served for the execution of that impulse. Leonidas rose from the ground; but at that instant the Brutchie's musket was discharged, and the chief with the cocked hat reeled to the verge of the rock, where he clung, a minute or two, to the bushes that fringed its sides; but his grasp was soon too feeble to sustain him; his knees sunk—his head fell on his breast; and before any one of his ambitious comrades had reached a hand to support him, he had dropped from the rock into the long rank grass which waved on the plain beneath it.

CHAPTER 19.

Come on sir; here's the place: stand still. How fearful
And dizzy 'tis to cast one's eyes so low.

KING LEAR.

'He deserved his death,' said the Brutchie, seeing that his subjects were in some alarm. 'So perish all the enemies of Combah—all your enemies! Let us make friends with the Maroons. We have a common cause, and this man is indebted to us, to me, for his life. Go,' continued he, addressing himself to the prisoner, 'go to your friends, and tell them what you have seen—what we have done to deserve their friendship.'

The Maroon looked on the chief with a scrutinizing glance, as if the scene which had just transpired had surprised him not a little.

'I go,' said he; 'but, trust me, the friendship of the Maroons is not to be bought at this rate. They will give you a king. They will not take an African for their master; and nothing that you have done will induce them to desist from the pursuit of this girl. Let me offer my advice. Send her home, and her maid with her.'

'What is the use of that?' cried he who had proposed to marry Michal. 'If the Maroons want to give us a king, why should Brutchie do anything more to please them? Cha! We are strong enough without the Maroons, I think; and we had better make it their interest to beg our friendship, than submit to them in any way whatever. We shall be a great many thousand hundred, and they are but few. Though they are used to arms and to the mountains, so are we. I think the runaway Negroes are quite as good as Maroons; and as to giving up the women, that they may get a hundred doubloons for them, I hope Brutchie won't be so mean as to do that; besides, we won them—we have a right to them. There will be many more taken before tomorrow morning; and if these are returned, we shall only be laughed at.'

The scene that had taken place, the conversation which ensued, had all been overheard by Joanna and the Quadroon; the

345

latter indeed, from time to time, peeped through the opening of the tent, and continued to give her mistress some detail of the proceedings which we have related; but when she saw the Negro struggling to get loose his musket, that he might kill the Maroon, and when the shot had been discharged through the tent, both mistress and maid, overcome with new horror, and beginning to fear for their lives in the scuffle, would have certainly made an attempt to escape, but for the intervention of Patch and Wowski, to whom these bursts of passion, these heroic squabbles, were a little more familiar.

'Never fear, mistress!' said one of them, half laughing; 'the Brutchie must be king and master, or the Negroes will all be killed.'

'Oh, heaven!' replied Joanna, 'save me from these horrid men!' Then turning to the females—'You have women's hearts; you have been young, and have known fear: have mercy upon us, as you will one day have to appear before the God of all men, and give an account of your actions! Think what it will be to have on your consciences the crime of having overwhelmed in misery and ruin two of your own sex, whom you might have saved! Think of this! Think of your children, if you have any. Think what my father must feel for me, his only child—my father, whom all the Negroes love!'

The heart of Wowski was touched; and Patch could not look at the blue eyes of the suppliant, streaming with tears, without being sensible of pity. She hid her face in her hands, and walked to the opening of the tent, as if to go away; but Joanna, seizing her scanty petticoat to detain her, again implored her, by the compassionate feelings which God had rooted in her heart, to take pity on their desperate condition. She was on her knees before the Negress, and strove to force away one of her hands with which she had concealed her face, in order to oblige Mrs Patch to be a witness of her grief and distraction.

There were tears in the eyes of the sable dame; and when, in the natural and rather affecting struggle, the black and the white hands came in contact, that of the Negress not only pressed the fair hand of her suppliant in a way which was intended to inspire confidence, but the black lady, unobserved even by Michal, and her own companion, pressed it to her thick lips and kissed it.

If she had said aloud—'Fear nothing; I will save you—I have power to save you;' those words, consolatory as they would have been, had failed to inspire the confidence or gratitude which Joanna derived from this genuine triumph of human nature—of the black woman's best feelings over all other considerations.

Mrs Patch looked at Wowski, and Wowski looked at Patch.

'What do you cry for?' said the latter; 'you silly somebody—wipe your eyes:' and she wiped her own.

The conversation without had ceased, and Combah burst into the tent. 'What are you at? Fear nothing,' cried he to the Blacks. 'Tears!—and for what? You are in no danger. But we must be stirring. Miss Guthrie, you can ride no farther; but we will take care of you. To the waterfall, Wowski! We cannot leave you here. Keep up your spirits. And you too, Mrs Michal! There are soldiers in sight, and a crowd of armed Negroes, and a host of Maroons: but we shall be a match for them. We know the fastnesses as well as they; and in this wilderness those who pursue are sure to fall into the ambush we shall lay for them. Quick! quick!—The firing increases, and there will be danger here.'

There was a grin upon the faces of some of these worthies, in spite of the horrid scene of death which they had just witnessed, as the women came out of the tent. Joanna was refreshed by the hope she had conceived, rather than by the food she had taken or the short repose which had been allowed her, and expressed her readiness to walk; but a sort of litter had been fitted up by some of the Negroes for her use, consisting of a couple of poles with boughs laid on them, in which the polite monarch intreated her (his intended spouse) to deposit herself; and Michal seconding the royal request, the poor young lady at last ventured to trust herself to the care of two sturdy revolutionists who took this, her palanquin, on their shoulders. Michal walked by her side.

They had already attained such an elevation that the climate no longer oppressed them with heat; and as they ascended at almost every step, they speedily gained a region devoid of all inconvenience on that score. They were now in a dense jungle of

various trees, through which it would have been difficult to penetrate but for a narrow path lately cut, which conducted them towards the waterfall. They formed a considerable procession, the
Maroon being in the van, guarded by two or three Negroes—as it
was thought he might be useful as an hostage or an ambassador:
the motley multitude followed, in the midst of whom were Joanna
and her maid, attended by the two Negresses, and Combah, who
preceded half a dozen of his new subjects, employed to fill up the
path, as they passed, with prickly bushes, as well as to cut here and
there other openings into the thicket, which might mislead their
pursuers, and throw them into a confusion, of which his majesty
and his friends meant to take an occasional advantage from many
spots in their course which commanded portions of the route by
which they journeyed. They had not quitted the rock half an hour,
before a shout announced the arrival of the enemy at that station;
and as they wound along the path which Combah's party had
taken, his people, already posted in every favourable situation,
kept up a mischievous fire on their pursuers below. The army of
the monarch mustered stronger as they proceeded, and could not
amount at present to less than a hundred Negroes; but their numbers were invisible to their pursuers, who in vain returned the fire
of the rebels in their march; it was only by watching every projecting rock, or overhanging tree, in these circuitous gullies, that
the avenging party got a shot at their enemies; and then so cautious were the rebels in exposing their persons, that scarce a shot
did any execution. The path at length terminated in a wider road,
which led along a track of level ground for at least a mile, through
the same undying, undecaying forest, where the traces of men
were visible in many directions, and small glades, from time to
time opening into the roadway, betrayed the avenues by which the
wild hogs had been often pursued into their sanctuaries. Within
these coverts the rebels had stationed many of their men, with directions to lie down till the approach of the enemy, and having allowed him to pass, to give him one volley in his rear, before they
shifted their position. No one would dare to enter the thicket; nor
could any danger be apprehended from such a pursuit, except the
enemy had dogs; and in that case flight was safety. There was an

impregnable station by the waterfall, which was to be the rallying point for all the subjects of king Combah.

It was past noon when the rebels had gained this their favourite position; and the sky, which had been for some hours threatening a change of weather, was by this time entirely shaded with grey clouds, which dissolved into a small rain, unlike that poured down on the lower realms by the Aquarius or the Jupiter of the tropics. The climate was altogether temperate, and even cold to some of the Negroes, whose fiery constitutions exult only in the raging beams of the sun. The murmur of the waterfall had already informed the females of their approach towards this citadel of the Blacks; yet it was too faint to have inspired them with a sufficient idea of the awful and tremendous scene which they were soon to behold, or of the quantity of water which there precipitates itself to such a depth, that it is nearly dissipated in spray before it reaches the bottom of the gulph into which it falls. The murmur it produces arises rather from its chafing the rocks through which it rushes to the perpendicular cliff down which it is lost, and from the reverberation of the wind that rages upwards, than from any farther obstruction which the river encounters, although, for the first few yards of its descent, the clashing of the different streams, as they emerge from its bed, causes perhaps some additional roar. If the fall were half the height only, the noise would be multiplied tenfold.

A tortuous and narrowing path brought the train to the edge of the cliff opposite this scene, where the water, gushing over the rocks, seemed almost whirled by the wind into the mid air between them and the spectators, before it descended into the chasm beneath; a depth so involved in mist and spray, overhung with trees, and entangled with withes, that the bottom of the gulph might have been as low as that through which Milton has described the *chute* of Satan, for any thing that could be seen to the contrary. Here and there a rock, covered with the moss of centuries, protruded its green head from the mist which encircled it, like waves rolling round an emerald island; yet every line which these formed in the picture before the spectator, was intersected by the long shafts of the giant palm-trees which grew out of the crevices and in the hollows of the rocks beneath, and spread their plumes into the mid air. These feathery tufts might be distinguished as far as the eye could penetrate through the gloom; but the trunks which supported them yet eluded the observer's penetration, and the bases of their shafts were altogether lost in the denser atmosphere below; so that a poetical fancy might have compared them to spirits called up from Hades or from the smoke of Tartarus; and as they waved backwards and forwards in the wind, a more serious beholder would have thought, with Roland, of ill-starred, unelected Christians:

> —— 'imprisoned in the viewless winds,
> Or tost with restless violence round about,
> This pendent world.' ——

The tortuous path above mentioned brought the rebels to the edge of the precipice, opposite that down which the river precipitates itself. The fathomless abyss lay between them; a ravine widening to the northward, until it forms an opening of immense proportions; on the south, that is, towards the line of the mountain, the gully contracts gradually until it is not more than forty feet across, and farther towards the interior probably ceases altogether: but in that quarter the ground is so broken, and precipitous, and loose withal, that it would be impossible to pass along it without grappling-irons and ropes, anchored in the firm land on the top, as a security to hold by. The weight of a man on the verge or the side of this (as it is there called) Runaway Land, would loosen a sufficiency of earth and rubbish to overwhelm a little army; and although along the plain there are some remains of rotten and decaying crags, yet there is not wood enough to shelter an invader from the fire of those who might be stationed on the opposite side, where the rock is of the firmest texture, and covered with a wilderness of bushes, which would effectually screen the attacked from all danger of suffering from the fire-arms of their adversaries. The rock down which the water falls juts out into the widening ravine like a modern bastion; and from the edge of the stream southward, along the cliff, to the spot where the chasm becomes narrowest, were seen a range of low huts, scarcely rising above the bushes. Here a couple of trees, laid and bound together, side by side, formed what in England is called an alpine bridge, without battlement or parapet, nor even a rope to assist the dizzy passenger, who must be somewhat adventurous to attempt it, if not urged by any necessity.

Many of the Negroes, long familiar with the passage, strode over the bridge with as much confidence as if they depended on wings wherewith to save themselves in case of a false step, or being alarmed, or losing their balance. Others sat down and trembled; some crawled on all fours; some were dragged along by their companions, clinging to the trees with their arms and legs; and some were altogether afraid to encounter the passage. One man, disdaining the apprehensions which assailed him, assumed a courage that scarce belonged to him, and stepped awhile fearlessly along the shaking trees, until he had gained the middle of the ravine; his spirit failed him here, at this critical moment—he staggered, and fell! But although, according to the Negroes' remark, his head was gone, he had not loosed his hold with the loss of his balance: his body swung beneath the trees; but he held still, like a monkey, with legs and arms, and even with his teeth.

A comrade sallied to his assistance—one with whom the reader is already acquainted—the hero in the laced cap. He kneeled on the bridge, and seized his friend by the arm; for he had no clothes except his drawers, which were out of reach for the other to lay hold of; and a Negro has no hair that can be grasped. They struggled together for some time on the trees, the one to save, the other to be saved; until the first, bewildered with the terrors arising from his situation, let go his hold of the bridge with his hands, to grapple the arms of his friend stretched out to assist him. The weight overcame the muscular strength of the other, who in vain bid his friend recover his grasp of the bridge: he could not induce him to let go the present hold on which he depended. There were others, seeing their danger, who hastened to relieve them, but their efforts were too late: the man of the cap, and he whom he would have saved, went down into the abyss together, while the air rang with the exclamations of the spectators, whose shout was heard even above the roaring of the wind and the raging of the water. They sank into the abyss, as Curtius is said to have sunk into the fiery gulph, and no trace remained of them.

They might, as far as human eyes could penetrate, have been said to have fallen into chaos. The vapour of the mountain, the spray, the winds, the elements, received them. Their sooty limbs, descending through the haze, shewed fainter and fainter, until the hue which it imparted to them mingled with the grey mist of the waterfall, and they vanished from human eyes for ever, engulphed perhaps in the boiling whirlpools below, buried beneath the moss of the rocks, or stretched on some bare crag, to feed the hawks and vultures which, startled at the sight of them as they rushed through the air, flew upwards in alarm, from haunts which nature has made sacred to them, and to them alone.

CHAPTER 20.

Mislike me not for my complexion,
The shadow'd livery of the burnished sun,
To whom I am a neighbour and near bred.
                              MERCHANT OF VENICE.

IT would require the hand of a Raphael to paint the passions expressed on the features of the rebellious rabble who witnessed the catastrophe just detailed. The fair form of Joanna was not unworthy such an artist; nor would he have disdained the pretty face of the Quadroon, or the kind and unsophisticated feeling which it betrayed. She clasped her hands in an agony of surprise and consternation, while her mistress, already pale with grief for the death of her mother, and for her own misfortunes, swooned at a sight which staggered not a few of the men of war who had yet to cross this frightful bridge.

'They are gone—they are lost!' said Michal to the black Wowski. 'Oh, heaven! what a terrible place! We never can pass the gully!—Oh, for God's sake!' turning round to Combah, 'do not drag my mistress over this fearful pass!'

'What is the lady to you?' said the king, somewhat confused at the accident, and at the loss of so valuable a comrade as him who had been wont to adonize his grim features with a laced cap. 'What is Miss Guthrie to you? You are a slave; you are liable to be flogged if she pleases, or set in the stocks, or sold, if you offend her; and you have to bear all her ill humours, and to dress her, and curl her hair, and to wait on her. Why had not you better be free, and have women to wait on you, and curl your hair, and lie down at your feet? Patch and Wowski, see to the young lady.'

The black king looked round in all directions, and wished inwardly that he could send the women, or at least the white one, away in peace.

'Michal,' continued he, 'if I were to send home your mistress, I would not part with you. If she dislikes me because I am not altogether a Christian, perhaps there is no law which would prevent

my keeping you as my wife—as one of my wives, at any rate. I like
you.' He whispered in her ear as he took her apart—'I love you!
my heart longs for you! Peace! Silence!' He saw she was about to
speak. 'Will you listen to me—will you live with me?'

'Oh no, no!' replied the damsel. 'For God's sake, do not talk to
me in that way! If you are to be a king, do something worthy of a
king; and if you are not, and will not be a Christian, at least shew
that you have some religion which is better than the Christians',
and do that which will shame the Christians, and make them envy
you the fame you will acquire.'

The king looked a little blank. 'What a time,' thought Michal, 'to
be making love; and to me! This Combah is a perfect fool.'

The bridge had yet to be passed by a great proportion of the
party; and after the catastrophe that had occurred, there were several so much alarmed, that they absolutely declined making the attempt, and preferred to climb the cone of the mountain among the
trees that far overtopped the runaway land already described,
rather than risk the dangers that hung upon this frightful passage.
This circuitous mode of getting at the fortress on the other side was
a very unwelcome business to the king and his bolder followers, as
it caused a serious division in his forces for the time, and some
hours must be expended before they could reunite at the huts opposite. Meanwhile the firing continued below; a desultory warfare,
calculated to teaze and irritate, as well as being fatal in some instances. And as the sound of the shots approached nearer and
nearer, some of Combah's outposts, from time to time driven in,
came always with a dismal tale of the number of the pursuers, and
of the accuracy with which they fired, exhibiting their wounds as
evidences of this fact. They had not a surgeon among them; a circumstance that, now first thought of, filled the heart of many a hero
with something like fear, and encouraged them to assist in stretching what they called a *tie-tie* of tent ropes, hempen cordage, mahoe
bark, and bush ropes, all spliced together, to form a little security,
a guide for those who could be induced to cross the bridge.

While this was in hand, the monarch, again taking Michal aside,
while he commissioned Patch and Wowski to attend her mistress,
bid her give him a direct answer to his proposal. 'You think me

mad,' said he, 'to talk to you at this moment about my loving you; but, mind me! you must hold your peace; for if you betray me, in one moment I can toss you down the gully.'

'Toss me down the gully!' repeated the girl, internally. 'He is moon-struck.'

'Look you, pretty Mrs Michal,' (he himself looked cautiously around), 'there is no one can hear me but yourself, amidst this roaring of the waters;—I really love you, and you shall be my wife. If you say *yes,*' he continued, gazing on her black eyes, 'here is an opportunity to let the white woman go free. The Maroons and the buckras will be here in a few minutes: we have only to send the Negroes all over the bridge before us. I will lead you; and the white woman, with her fits and fancies, shall be left behind. We will be the last. I will cut the cord they are stretching, as we pass; and the bridge shall be tumbled down the gully the moment we have gained the other side. The Maroons or the buckras will seize the white woman: they will get the reward; they will take her back to her father. Will you save your mistress? If you say no, come with me quickly—both of you—over the bridge. The rope is stretched. You have but a moment to decide!'

'I am in your power,' replied Michal, trembling. 'Leave us both, Brutchie. What would be the use of my telling you lies? I cannot bear you; I hate you; I am afraid of you!'

He seized her hand, and led her rather roughly to the bridge.

'Help me to carry over this white woman. And you, Brutus— quick! here! The buckras are coming: I saw a red coat cross the glade. Drive these foolish beasts—these Negro cowards—over the bridge. Awake, Miss Guthrie! Arise! Is this a time to be faint-ing and whimpering, while the bullets are flying around us, dan-ger before us, and death behind? By my father's bones, they will kill her! Fire, all of you! Give them ten for one! Michal, go over the bridge.'

He put her behind her mistress, whom he would even have guarded with his own body, and looked as tenderly as his burnt face would allow of.

'Michal, is it yes or no? Will you save the life of your mistress— or will you sacrifice her? Shall she be'—

'Hold, hold, for God sake, Brutchie! Let me stay with her till the white men come up, and then I will follow you. I cannot desert her here!'

'Save yourself,' said Joanna. 'Never mind me. Better let me be killed by the guns of the soldiers, than remain in the hands of these men!'

Her words wrung the heart of the Brutchie.

'Take her over the bridge. This Maroon will help her,' cried he, addressing him. 'But why—how—by heaven! what is this? The Maroon a buckra—a white man!'

The Maroon was indeed a white man; and the small but incessant rain, mingled with the spray of the waterfall, had begun to bleach his painted face. The Brutchie drew his cutlass as he let go his hold of Joanna, whom he was raising from the ground, and flew at his antagonist with the fury of a game cock. Their swords met and sparkled in the contact; while Joanna, divining but too accurately the identity of the Maroon, and the intention of his disguise, sprang from the ground, and endeavoured to throw herself between the combatants. Their swords had well nigh pierced her bosom, but for the presence of mind with which Michal restrained her. The conflict was but momentary. Combah, the monarch of the island, was disarmed, as if he had been an infant, hurled to the ground, and the sword of Fairfax was at his throat.

'Spare his life!' cried Joanna, 'spare his life! We are in the hands of his people, who are worse than he is. Spare his life.'

'Oh yes, let him live!' said Michal.

Fairfax looked round him. The noise of the wind and the waterfall, the confusion in passing the ravine, the danger, and the pursuit, the firing and the whizzing of the balls which flew about them, had prevented the rest of the party from paying any decided attention to the scene while it was taking place, and rendered it impossible for those who did look on, to hear the conversation which passed, or to guess at the meaning of the scuffle: and when the spectators from the other side of the ravine had become aware that something was amiss, the Brutchie was on his legs, commanding those about him to take care of the Maroon, or the buckra—for such he was universally found to be—and to spare his life.

The approach of the adverse party put farther parley or deliberation out of the question. Joanna was hurried over the bridge
with the assistance of Fairfax; the black dames went next; and the
Brutchie followed close behind the beautiful Quadroon, amidst a
shower of bullets, one of which knocked his hat from his head,
while a second grazed his ribs and drew blood from the inside of
his left arm. He staggered, but recovered himself, and passed the
bridge in safety, with his three captives, who were no sooner
landed on the rocks beyond, than they were buried behind them,
ensconced in the jungle, and effectually screened by their projections from the fire of the Maroons and soldiers, whose approach
prevented the followers of Combah from destroying the bridge.

Many lives were lost at this crisis. Two or three Negroes who
followed the monarch were shot on the bridge; and a fourth, tumbling over the dead body of his comrade, which hung across it,
plunged with him into the gulph, notwithstanding he grasped the
rope which had been supplied for their assistance. At the same
moment the rope was cut by those who were even hacking with
their bills at the bridge itself. Still he grasped it as he fell, and did
not loose his hold till the jerk with which he reached the end of his
suspension, disabled him from farther efforts. He was dashed
against the precipice be had quitted, in sight only of his own party,
who revenged his death by a volley across the ravine, which
mowed down three or four of the soldiers, and wounded half a
dozen more. But the fire was returned; and the soldiers, taking a
hint from the Maroons, sought each a barricade—a breastwork of
some rock or tree—to secure themselves from the fatal aim of the
rebels, who were ultimately obliged to abandon the destruction of
the bridge.

Some of the Negroes were taken prisoners on the western side
of the ravine, having been afraid to cross the pass; some escaped
into the woods around and above it, where they gradually fell a
prey to the guns of the Maroons, who picked off all in sight, who
had attempted to make a circuit round the runaway land.

But this victory, if such it may be called, was attended with no
trifling loss on the part of the conquerors; for many of the runaway Negroes continued their fire till they were shot themselves;

knowing that they had no mercy to expect, and finding all retreat cut off, they determined to sell their lives as dearly as possible, and avenge their fate before they submitted to it; a sort of gallantry not uncommon on such occasions, where the enslaved fight for liberty, among any of the races of man.

CHAPTER 21.

——Dar'st thou die?
The sense of death is most in apprehension.
MEASURE FOR MEASURE.

HOWEVER successful the soldiers and Maroons had been in following up the rebels to their stronghold, the main purpose of the
pursuit had yet to be achieved. The white damsel was still in the
hands of the rebels; and what was almost as serious a calamity,
though unknown to the pursuers, Mr Fairfax was her fellow prisoner, taken in disguise, and as a spy. He reckoned rightly that he
had but little mercy to expect from the multitude, however the
Brutchie might be disposed to grant him his life; and was preparing his mind to meet his fate with decency, when the Brutchie,
who had before commanded his subjects to spare the white man's
life, came behind him, and whispered to him to take heart. They
were perfectly secure from the fire of the Maroons, who dared not
attempt to cross the bridge, so well defended by the rebels that no
soul could pass it alive; and the women were soon seated beneath
a canopy of fern and palm branches, which protected them from
the rain. The figure of Fairfax was sadly grotesque, resembling in
colour one of Jacob's lambs, though his eyes might have betrayed
to an intelligent spectator something of the emotion and the resolution which animated his bosom. If they killed him, what would
be the fate of Joanna? If they spared his life, how could he still rescue her from her ravishers, before she could have been sacrificed
to the brutal appetite of one of them at least? And the pretty and
affectionate Michal, who sat by the side of her mistress, and strove
to comfort her, while her own heart seemed ready to break, what
must become of her? What would she think of the violence to
which she must submit? Would *she* rather die than yield to it? For
Joanna, he felt assured, dreadful and desperate as the alternative,
would rather be precipitated down the ravine, or fall beneath the
musquets of either party, than become the victim of a Negro's passion: and if need were—if there were no other alternative—no

chance of escape—down that precipice would he leap with her. They were not so closely guarded but that they might run to the brink of the rocks before anyone could stop them. And there seemed no chance of escape: notwithstanding the assurance of the Brutchie, the rest of the Negro council, if they may be so called, began to clamour for the execution of the white man. The circumstance of his disguise had excited a feeling of indignation in their bosoms, in addition to the revenge which they already meditated against the white population; and the fury of the battle in which they had just engaged, left them not one jot of mercy to extend to such an enemy in their power.

There were various modes of execution proposed—decapitation—crucifixion: one would have hewn him in pieces with a billhook, or hanged him with a rope, which constituted one of his offensive weapons, being formed into a lasso after the fashion of those in Peru, whither he had been transported, some years before, for threatening the life of his master in Jamaica. Another proposed to hurl him down the gully; and a third would have had him shot. All seemed impatient for his death, except Combah, who insisted that he should not be killed without a trial; a preliminary which very few were willing to grant. Indeed the Brutchie, fearing he might be torn in pieces, gave him a cutlass, which he snatched from a comrade, and bid him defend his life, if there were need to do so, while he himself exclaimed aloud to his subjects, that the white man might have killed him, and did not.

'I owe him a life,' continued he. 'You shall not put him to death. Hear him speak, at least. Speak, Mr Fairfax:—and if any one of you dare touch his skin, or shed a drop of his blood, till he has been heard and tried, I will fire this musket through the heart of him that does so, and Hamel shall curse him and all his family!'

The Brutchie had his hands full of business. The noise of the elements, the gabbling of the Negroes, the firing of the enemy and of his own party, caused such an union of uproar, that he was obliged to speak at the top of his voice, and could not depend on his hearing to guard against any portion of the mischief he dreaded. His eyes were occupied with a scene affecting even to him: Joanna, on her knees, implored the compassion of Fairfax. She had taken his blackened hand in her own, and while she kissed it with a passion bordering on madness, she entreated him to save her from the violence of these merciless men.

'There is no hope, Fairfax! Death has no terrors: think not of it. Kill me. By the memory of your own dear mother—by all, by every recollection—faithful friend, husband—lover—brother! Oh! we shall be happy in another world! Strike!' She kissed his hand again. 'It will be heaven's mercy'—

The Brutchie was near enough to hear this; and Michal, at his feet, was offering to devote herself for him she adored—(such is the perverseness of destiny)—and vowed that, to save Fairfax, she would be whatever the black king desired!

It was at the command of his sable majesty, that Fairfax, holding the hand of Joanna, who still knelt beside him, addressed the black rascals who seemed to pant for his last breath.

'Hear me! This young lady is my wife: we have been promised to one another since we were children. You stole her away; I disguised myself to get her back again, because she is mine. She loves me, and I love her. I never wronged any one of you, nor did she. And which of you, who calls himself a man, would not have done as I have done?'

This pithy speech affected those who heard it; but the noise and confusion prevented it from reaching the ears of those who, farther removed from the stage on which these actors were performing, trusted only to their eyes for an assurance of the scene;—and who can believe his eyes? They clamoured for the execution of the youth; and one or two muskets would have been discharged at him, but that the incessant rain had rendered most of the firelocks useless. Nevertheless, the clouds had begun to break, and the thunder, which gave proof of it, added its clamour to the confusion that already reigned. The lightning seemed to cleave the very air breathed by the performers (we may so call them,) followed instantly by such a clang, that a stranger, unused to these tropical explosions, would have fancied the world at its crisis as the mingled din overwhelmed his hearing. It is in this fashion that the storms of Jamaica subside.

The monarch, always master of himself, had fired his musket on one of his rebellious subjects, and was denouncing the rest of the refractory as a gang of brute beasts, mules, steers, and asses, while he endeavoured to detain Fairfax, who, leading Joanna with his left hand to the brink of the precipice, defended her, with the cutlass in the right, from the grasp of several who would have laid hold of her. Michal still clung to the Brutchie, around whom the rabble were closing fast; and they had already gained the verge of the rocks, almost in view of the enemy, when a flash of lightning seemed to sever him from her hold. He reeled—he might be said to have whirled round on the top of the crag; yet he recovered himself, though but for an instant, and put his right hand on his heart, while with his left he appeared to wave a farewell to Fairfax.

The thunder which followed convulsed every individual of the rebels, as well as the unhappy lovers. They were many of them struck to the earth, but Combah was precipitated into the abyss.

'He was shot,' cried one of the Negroes, as the king vanished amidst the spray. 'He was killed by a bullet: I saw the blood stream through his fingers from his heart. It was not the thunder.'

'Stand off, villains!' exclaimed the party-coloured prisoner, still fighting his way to the edge of the precipice.—'A moment and we are free!' (These last words were addressed to Joanna.) 'It *was* the thunder—Heaven's vengeance that will overtake ye all!—Oh, Joanna! God of mercy, what an alternative! Leap with me! Leap!'

The young lady had fainted at his feet; he held her hand, or rather his own was yet convulsively grasped in hers. Michal had caught her garments as she fell, and would have dragged her back from the precipice.

'I cannot shed her blood,' said he. 'Michal, let go your hold! Would you save her? For what, for what?'

The Quadroon replied only by a look that would have wrung the heart of Fairfax upon a happier occasion: it was not a reproach; it expressed neither fear nor horror. The thought which had passed through the mind of the poor girl, was to this effect—that she wished the sacrifice of herself could save Joanna for the man she loved; but, as that seemed impossible, she was determined to die with them: and some such notion was conveyed in that look of hers to the mind of Fairfax.

The firing had ceased from the opposite side, whence the Maroons and soldiers had beheld the women as they approached the precipice, and would fain have crossed the bridge to their relief, but that it was yet too well guarded. Old Mr Guthrie descried his daughter, and a black man (as he thought) dragging her to the brink of the chasm. He saw likewise king Combah, whom he knew by his sore eyes; and though, like the rest, somewhat confused by the shock of the lightning, he distinguished plainly enough the descent of his majesty into the watery gulph, and cried out instinctively, 'The king is dead! the king is dead!' These words were repeated by a hundred voices: and Hamel, at the same moment, with a musket in his hand, and his red turban on his head, made his appearance among the rebels, and commanded, by gestures as much as by his voice, that the firing should cease.

A ray of hope beamed on the heart of the widowed and well nigh childless father. 'She lives, she lives yet!' he exclaimed, his agony of passion dissolving into tears. 'The Obeah man has saved her honour and her life! See, see how the rebellious cut-throats cringe before him! *Instar Jovis!* He treats them like the dirt they are. And ah! he kneels to Fairfax, and lays his master's hand on his own head!'

The clouds were dissipating apace; the thunder was expended; and the sun in its splendour burst out upon the mountain, the rocks, and the waterfall augmented by the rain. It lightened up the figures of this grand landscape, and displayed to either party but too palpably the dreadful situation from which the females were relieved.

Joanna was assisted to the bridge by Fairfax and the black women, while Hamel conducted the pretty Quadroon, her features yet retaining some expression of the passions which had agitated her artless bosom. He called from the rebel quarters, that there should be a truce, and that no Maroon or soldier should attempt to pass the bridge, or fire a shot, or interfere in any way, while the ropes were repairing to enable Miss Guthrie to return back to her father. A shout of assent from the besiegers encouraged their late opponents to proceed to work. The ropes were refitted; and the Obeah man, preceding the party which conveyed the young lady and her maid across the ravine, delivered her to the arms of her parent. There was a wildness in his manner little corresponding with his usual habits. His eyes were bloodshot, and the muscles of his mouth were somewhat inflamed with passion.

'I told you, mistress,' said the Quadroon in a low voice, 'that you might trust this man. He has been faithful.'

'He has indeed!' said Joanna in reply.

The Obeah man heard the dialogue, though not intended for him. He put his hand to his heart, and heaved a deep sigh; but he spoke not. His eyes were fixed for a moment on the pale yet conscious features of Miss Guthrie. He then looked round the circle of Maroons and soldiers who stood admiring him—for they saw he was no ordinary man in the estimation of his fellow Negroes—waved a submissive sort of adieu to his master and Mr Guthrie; and turning quietly round, strode over the perilous bridge with the confidence of one indifferent to fear, and with an assurance scarcely belonging to his advanced years.

The rebels immediately cut away the ropes and the trees which constituted the bridge, and it sank, like the wretched beings who had preceded it, in silence to the abyss below.

CHAPTER 22.

Now for our mountain sport: up to yon hill:
Your legs are young; I'll tread these flats.

CYMBELINE.

THE Obeah man, perfectly familiar with all the passes of the Blue
Mountain, and indeed with all the wildernesses of that part of
Jamaica, had arrived at the retreat of the rebels by an obscure
route, known to few besides himself, at the most fortunate moment to save his master, and the young lady whom his master
loved. The influence he had acquired over his fellow Negroes by
means of his superior talents, his spells, and his magic, had rendered him a person of more consequence in the island than the
sovereign monarch whom the rebels had chosen to accept, partly
at his hands, partly at the recommendation of the preacher
Roland. The orders of the king had been disputed without hesitation; but his high priest, in addition to his human powers, and his
mortal weapons, carried with him the vengeance of heaven, and,
according to the fears of the Negroes, that of hell likewise. As absolute as Cromwell with the members of the Long Parliament, his
conduct served as one instance more to shew that a religious, or
rather a superstitious influence, is the most powerful weapon
which can be put into the hands of any man, whether to govern an
enlightened or an unenlightened mob.

No sooner had the bridge been destroyed, than the rebels, feeling themselves in comparative safety, began a consultation as to
their future procedure. The wisest (in their own estimation) presented themselves for this purpose, whilst the youngsters were ordered to bury the dead, and, with the women, to attend to the
wounded. The Obeah man was requested to give his advice, and
to take upon himself the direction of their movements; but he had
seen too clearly the inefficacy of any attempt to command
subordination, except by means of his religious tricks—if they
deserved that epithet; and his respect on that score, as he well
knew, depended much, if not altogether, on the caprice of the

multitude. A Christian preacher, or an hour's success, might divest him of the now unlimited influence which these misfortunes had conferred on him. He declined, on the score of his age, his cares, and his being obliged to set his master free when he was in their hands; a deed, he said, which heaven demanded of him, although it was a fatal blow to the conspiracy. Moreover, he told them, he had a forewarning that their enterprize would fail; and, to the surprise and consternation of many of his audience, he recommended to them, either to return to their masters; to separate, and secrete themselves in the woods; or to get off the island altogether as well as they could.

'For himself,' he said, 'his life was in their hands, for he had violated his engagement in delivering up Mr Fairfax; but he had stopped the effusion of blood; and he felt assured, that by that act he could (if they chose he should do so) stipulate successfully for a pardon to every one of them who would come and surrender himself by a given period. Nay, more; he thought he could stipulate for their being transmitted off the island to Sierra Leone, or to some of the British plantations on the continent of America, where they would belong to king George, and serve him as soldiers or sailors. As to these points, he was ready to serve them with his talents and advice. If they meant to stand out in arms against the government of the country, he had done with them, and with all things else; and if they pleased, they might take his life, or let him go home to his cave, and die there.'

This speech met with much approbation, especially from the wounded and from the women, who found sufficient excuse for his late conduct, and begged him, with tears and groans, to go and intercede with the buckras for the lives and the pardon of all the survivors.

He would have obeyed them on the spot; but the bridge being destroyed, he had no means of coming again to the speech of Mr Guthrie, or of his master Mr Fairfax, but by the roundabout way which he had chosen for his approach to this wild spot, unless he could bargain for a parley with the enemy on the other side, and obtain permission and assistance to construct a new bridge. But this he thought again would hardly be practicable, as in all probability those gentlemen, the only persons with whom he could hope to treat, had already begun their march homewards.

The Obeah man resolved to take the road by which he had arrived, followed by those Negroes who chose to attend him, and accompanied by the two women, Patch and Wowski, whose influence, they thought, would avail almost as much as his own, in consequence of the consideration which they had shewn for the fate of Joanna.

Let us now see what had been done by Mr Fillbeer, and the party of soldiers who had stationed themselves at the deserted mansion in the wilderness.

After rummaging among the ruins, and examining the cellar and the rest of the premises, the man-mountain—conscious of the evil report which attached to the place—recommended to the officer commanding the little party, to scour the woods around the amphitheatre, and mounting upon the craggy pinnacles that enclosed it, to take what reconnoissance these might afford, as far at least as the eyes of his men could penetrate through the jungle. But the captain was of opinion that the soldiers, whose faces were heated to the colour of their jackets, had already exhausted themselves sufficiently with their march, to endanger their lives from an attack of the island fever; and proposed instead, that the Negroes should perform this service, with the fat man at their head, while he and his own men should spread the canvass they had brought over the unroofed and disconsolate-looking dwelling, and proceed to cook themselves some hot dinner.

Fillbeer smiled at the proposition. 'I mount the pinnacle!' said he. 'Not if Satan would take me there. Look at my bulk. I should be food for the carrion crows before I had clambered half way up; and so out of breath, that they might pick out my eyes before I were dead, for any resistance I could make. But please yourself, my noble captain. Your meal may perhaps be a little broken in upon; or the gentry who have evidently been here of late, as you may see by their footmarks and their fires, and the stink of gunpowder, and rum, and tobacco, which is so rife among the ruins, may give you such a desert as you will not perhaps think you merit. Here seem to have been rare pranks performed upon this plain, where, according to report, Mr Roland came to convert all the runaway Negroes at once. Dancing, I see, must have engaged them in some measure; for only behold how the sand is trampled, and these feathers and rags still scattered about! They have had a heathen priest among them, I suspect. Perhaps that execrable Hamel, with his charms, and drugs, and trumpery. Well, sir!' still addressing himself to the captain, 'I see you are bent upon eating and drinking, and so am I; and as to sending these Negroes to rummage among the bushes by themselves'—

'You fear to trust them,' said the captain, interrupting him.

'Trust them!' replied Filbeer, 'trust them! Why certainly, they might take a fancy to join any runaways with whom they should happen to fall in; or they might set off and run back to their houses, for they do not like being shot at, and they are not devoted to the buckra soldiers, as you may have understood. But the main fact is, that they are altogether afraid of danger, and will not incur it except for those they love; and even then, sir you must give them arms. Now, I presume, you will not disarm your veterans to put weapons into the hands of these barbarians.'

'Why do you call them barbarians?' said the captain, fanning himself with his hat.

'Why!' replied Fillbeer, applying the sudarium to his smooth features. 'Some of the same sort as these mounted me to a gibbet but two days ago—at least to a tree—where they would have hanged me but for the interposition of Providence.'

The captain could not refrain from smiling. 'Let us,' said he, 're-fresh the men and ourselves a little, and we will then examine the bushes, and post a sentry or two on the highest peaks; although I see but little use in doing so; for what eyes can penetrate a hundred yards or a hundred feet into this forest? A red-coat on one of these rocks will only be a mark for the rebels.'

'Oh!' replied Fillbeer, affecting to be satirical, 'ever while you live send red-coats to bush-fight in the woods of the tropics; and cocked hats for the officers, and glazed caps for the men; never mind how much the sun roasts their faces, or how cumbrous the caps are in such an enterprise. Button up the men, and let them be hot. But come, "let us eat and drink," as St Paul recommended in such cases, "for to-morrow we die."'

'Like enough,' replied the captain: 'there are more blows to be expected here than dollars—more danger than glory, and no great prospect of booty or prize-money.'

'No, captain,' replied the Quinbus Flestrin, as he seated himself among the ruins. 'Here you may have your prayer, your toast—"A bloody war, and a sickly season." A most unchristian invocation, to be sure.'

'We must not stand for Christianity,' replied the soldier; 'interest, my fat friend, promotion, rank;—we must do the states' duty. It is the road to all that Christians desire, whether fighters or preachers.'

'Humph,' ejaculated Fillbeer, 'I believe it is; and yet I doubt the lawfulness of bringing up men to kill one another—mercenaries that hack and hew for pay. A Christian nation, an evangelical nation, ever meddling with the consciences of all its members in some way or other, yet trains up a proportion of its youth in the art of *massacring;* that is, the science of killing most at the least expense, and with the greatest certainty! And this trade is respected above all others; nay, kings and princes patronize it, and grace it with all their influence; to say nothing of lavishing upon its members all the finery of the earth—stars, ribbons, knighthood, orders, companionships, and what not. Even monarchs who have never seen a shot fired, except at hares and pheasants, must wear the costume of their mercenaries upon state occasions, and bedizen themselves with tags and tassels, despising the garb of peace, and the more sober, and quite as appropriate, garments of a gentleman and a philosopher—of a man of peace.'

'Hah! my boy!' said the captain, patting him on the shoulder, 'you're right, and kings are right. You would make a preacher methinks—a bishop, by all that's fat and heroic! Come, don't be offended; the capons begin to smell savoury, and the porter invites: if Quashie will let us eat in peace, we'll drink to his health and prosperity.'

During this dialogue, which was interrupted occasionally by various orders which the officer communicated to his deputies, the men had piled their arms, taken off their knapsacks and their jackets, and began to make provision for their dinner and for their temporary abode. A good fire had been kindled, and a score of pullets and capons, which had been brought up by the Negroes, impaled on wooden spits, now smoked around it. The plantains were piled about the embers, and the camp-kettles seethed with junks of beef and pork. The only want was that of an appetite to devour all these good things; many of the men, not inured to the climate, having experienced such great fatigue in the march, that they sighed in vain for the calls of hunger, and strove to excite their fainting stomachs with hot coffee, which lent its fragrance to the perfumes of the dinner. A tent or two had been pitched on the bar-becue, and pieces of canvass, as before observed, had been spread over some of the ruins; but as these could only guard the soldiers from the sun, and would yield a passage to the first shower of rain with which the elements might favour them, it was necessary to adopt a different covering, to some part of the building at least; and the two fan-palms, noticed in a previous part of this history, were devoted, by general consent, to the purpose of thatching a portion of the house. Spars and joists lay among the rubbish, which some of the Negroes quickly accommodated to the walls; while others, to save the trouble of felling the palms, clambered easily up their taper shafts, with bill-hooks to trim off the branches, or rather leaves, from the tufts which formed their summits.

Meanwhile, the captain and his two subalterns seated them-selves alongside of fat Fillbeer, and fell to eating with as much good humour as the scene would admit of, and drank to one an-other's healths with all the conviviality usual on such occasions, while their men followed their noble example, and detached themselves in little messes, in various parts of the amphitheatre; and the Negroes brought them their refreshments, as they re-quired them, from the house where the headquarters had been established. Some of the soldiers were imprudently bathing in the rivulet which flowed beneath the rocks; and there were not in all more than three sentries under arms, and even these were seated on the grass in the shade at their different posts, little apprehen-sive of any attack, or of any enemy being near. The fat man, who had loosened his waistcoat and removed his neckcloth, for the benefit of breathing as he eat and being at more liberty than usual, turned up his little twinkling eyes to the summits of the palms, which the Negroes were trimming with great perseverance. These trees grew close beside the house, on the east side of it; and as the breeze blew fresh, the ex-brewer was apprehensive that some of the branches might in their fall invade his homestead; and, as he looked up from time to time at the havoc committed aloft, a fresh idea sprung up in his mind.

'Can you see over the rocks?' cried he to the Negroes.

'Yes, master, towards Blue Mountain.'

'And what can you see there?'

'Nothing, master.'

'Can you see the mountain?'

'No, master. All is clouds and mist between us and the mountain, but it is clearing away.'

'What *can* you see?' rejoined Fillbeer: 'Can you see anything nearer?'

'Nothing but bush, and trees, and a pigeon flying about.'

'A pigeon!'

'Yes, two or three more—twenty pigeons—flying about.'

'Something disturbs them,' said the ex-brewer. 'Watch the spot. There must be some one in the forest there.'

'The pigeons,' continued the Negro, 'keep flying more and more this way.'

The soldiers had begun to prick up their ears, and the captain had rather hurried down the two last bumpers of Madeira. Filllbeer felt for his neckcloth.

'They must be far away yet,' said he.

'Oh yes,' replied the Negro, attending to the remark, 'one, two, three miles.'

He continued chopping, and the brewer took another glass of Maderia, which did not render him altogether as pot-valiant as he expected. He took another. 'Master,' exclaimed two of the Negroes at the same time, 'I see a man.'

'How many men?' said the captain.

'One man,' replied the Negroes, 'and a woman.'

'A woman!' cried the brewer in a flurry (a new light breaking in upon him.) 'A woman!'

'One, two women,' replied he on the tree; 'and three men.'

'Can you see them plain?'

'Yes—no—they are hid again in the bushes. One of them was dressed in a black cloak.'

The face of Fillbeer became ten times more rosy than the reddest rose. 'A black cloak!' said he internally, not daring to question the Negro further; 'a black cloak! Five hundred and thirty-three pounds, six and eight-pence. This is the queen of Sheba bringing presents to Solomon! This is the daughter of Solomon Guthrie!—Joanna, and her ravisher, and her maid!'

The captain soliloquized aloud—'A black cloak! A prize, by G—d! The old planter's daughter in her mourning weeds. Can you see them yet?'

'I saw them again for a moment,' replied the Negro; 'they are out of sight again—and now they cross the top of the hill, and are going to the gully where the water runs down to Red Castle Mill.'

'Hearkye, blackee!' shouted the captain. 'Are you sure it is a black cloak? Is it not a black woman?'

'It might be a black woman: I suppose it was,' replied the Negro, 'or a Quadroon.—('A Quadroon!' sighed Quinbus to himself.)—'I could not tell; but I am sure she had a black something on, for I saw it wave in the wind. I see it now again; and she has got an umbrella.'

'An umbrella!' exclaimed Fillbeer.

'An umbrella!' echoed the captain. 'What shall we do?'

'They are gone now out of sight,' continued the Negro. 'I shall see them no more. They are in the gully.'

'Stay, stay!' cried the captain to the Negroes, seeing them seized with a sudden fancy to come down. 'Stay a moment!'

'No, master, no—no use,' replied one of them; the other two, who had been his companions, seeming in too great a hurry to answer. 'No use, no use.'

'What the devil,' said Fillbeer, rising in a rage, 'brings them down so fast? Are they bent on catching the girl? Stop, you fools, and get up the tree again.'

'No, no!' replied the Negro he had seized, who spoke without seeming to heed him. 'Let me go! let me go!'

The two others had decamped already with all the speed of which they were capable, and were racing down the path from the arena.

'Let me go!' continued the Negro; 'I shall be killed.'

He got behind fat Fillbeer.

'Let me go, please God, master. There are other Negroes in the bushes, on the rocks. They pointed guns at us. Let me go—let me go!'

He ran from them after his comrades; and the captain shouted, 'To your arms, soldiers!' At the same moment a volley was fired from the heights around, and a score of ragged and half-naked Negroes rushed into the arena, and made for the arms piled up, as described before, some of which they had the good fortune to secure. The captain was shot in the face, and Fillbeer in the *derrière*. Fortunately neither shots were dangerous, and the latter scarcely drew blood. The soldiers, who had their side-arms, made uglier work with the Blacks, many of both parties biting the dust, for the rebels were provided with knives: but as they were all mixed up in the scuffle, those of the assailants who remained on the heights discontinued their fire for fear of killing their companions; while the captain and those around him entrenched themselves behind the walls of the house, whither the whole party of the military rallied themselves at last, saving those who had fallen in the fray, and kept a continued fire where the bushes could harbour an enemy, until they had silenced half of the rebels, or until the rebels had thought fit to desist. It seemed an afterthought, that the Blacks had had no immediate intention of attacking, and would have deferred their attempt till the evening, the twilight, or the night, but that they were discovered by the palm-cutters in the trees, whom they might have shot, had they been so disposed. The possession of the arms had been their chief object.

The captain of the company, in some confusion from his wound, and the surprise which he had suffered, for want perhaps of attending to Fillbeer's advice, now looked around for that gentleman, whom at last he descried riding away at his horse's speed, without his hat, which he had lost, and followed by the rest of the Negroes who had attended him to the ruined settlement. How he had escaped appeared incomprehensible to those who remained; or how he had prevailed on the Negroes to hoist him upon his beast; for without their help he had never disengaged himself from *terra firma,* as it was but too evident. The officers shouted after him, and taxed him with cowardice; but he had no ears for aught which they could say. Fear was behind, and hope before him—(the hope of obtaining the prize.) He did but point to his wound, as he galloped off, congratulating himself in secret that he had left the soldiery with their hands too full of work to interfere with him. 'Let them perish by the sword,' said he to himself; 'they who live by the sword! Faith, they will have enough of it! I have enough already. Thank God, it is no worse! Would we were down at the Bay; for we have a dismal route as yet to traverse.'

So saying, and encouraging the Negroes to keep up with him, he kicked and flogged his jaded nag until it staggered about in going down the narrow pass, so that the rider was every other minute in danger of falling off into the river, or knocking out his uncovered brains against the rocks which overhung it. He had felt but little pain from his wound at first, which was not more than a contusion, the ball having struck a wall, from which it recoiled against his rear: but with the bumping on his saddle, and the heat into which he was jolted, he began now to experience some inconvenience and annoyance, and was a little alarmed lest, becoming unable to continue his career, he might lose the chance of the century of doubloons which glittered before his imagination.

The Negroes continued in his company, notwithstanding the expedition he employed—nay, sometimes (by cutting off the angles of the ravines) were in advance of him; while he, like an old huntsman, cheered them along in a sort of demi-voice, for he feared to alarm the echoes of the woods or rocks among which he was fain to scamper, lest the ruffian Combah and his female companions should be made aware of his near approach. But although Combah was far beyond his hearing, and those whom he sought had not yet a suspicion of him, the clatter of his horse's heels had betrayed him to three or four runaways who were posted on the bank of the Rio Grande, to which he was hastening, where the rivulets which turned the mill of the Red Castle estate disembogued from the ravine in which the Negro from the palm-tree had seen the black cloak disappear.

These Negroes were skulking about as spies or scouts, and knew as yet nothing of the death of their king; but as they saw Fillbeer, a white man, bare-headed, racing away from the deserted settlement to which he had attended the soldiers in the morning, they concluded that he was either flying for his life from a defeat, or to get a fresh supply of troops. With this impression, they made bold to post themselves in his way, and signed to him with their hands to stop, one of them affecting to present a musket at him.

'Hold, there! Get out of the way, you villain!' cried the alarmed attorney, endeavouring to pull up his tired horse. 'What do you want with me, an unarmed man? Spare my life! I am undone—ruined—exiled—one of you—almost an outlaw. Stop my horse!' He pulled with all his might; but his beast had got so much headway, that it was in vain to tug at him, the sole effect he produced being to pull himself and the saddle over his horse's ears, where the Negro received him, more courteously than he could have expected, in his arms.

'Where do you come from?' said the Black. 'Speak! Where are you going, and what's your business? Speak—make haste!'

'Give me time to get my breath,' replied Fillbeer, panting and gasping; 'I am wounded.'

'Wounded! where?'

'Here, on this—this thigh.'

The Negro still held him; and his companions, espying those who attended Fillbeer coming up, proposed to kill him, and throw him down the dingle: and although be begged hard for his life, it would have gone harder with him, but that in the auspicious moment the wizard Hamel leaped down from the rocks above, and bid them desist on pain of death!

'Touch him at your peril!' said the Obeah man. 'Begone, and provide for your safety. All is lost! Begone, I say!'

The Negroes slunk into the bushes, as if it had been a deity who commanded them, and vanished from the eyes of Fillbeer.

'Soh!' said he, recovering his wind: 'There is some virtue in this
fiend. I thank you for my life. Set me down on the ground, and let
me get my breath. Hamel, you have a power, but it is the power of
the Evil One. All is lost, as you say. The soldiers are, by this time,
all murdered at M'Lachlan's. A gang of your countrymen, of rebellious cut-throats, burst in upon them from the rocks and woods
around. They shot the captain in the face; I saw his blood! They
shot me here, in the—the behind part of my thigh. See what a rent
they have made in my clothes! All is over. Let me escape with the
remains of life, and leave this accursed island to its more accursed
inhabitants—Pagans or Christians! Would they had been Pagans
still! They have the worst qualities of both—of all—of the whole
human race; the tricks of savages, the courage and the cruelty of
the most refined, civilized—I may say—religious nations. Oh,
heaven! deliver me out of the hands of these mine enemies!
Where is Miss Guthrie?'

The fat man looked around, as if suddenly recollecting the
prize for which he had been riding, and caught a glimpse of
Patch and Wowski, who were peeping down from the rocks
above.

'The black cloak! the black cloak!' cried he. The women had
vanished the instant they observed that Fillbeer beheld them.
'The black cloak is Miss Guthrie's!'

'It is,' replied the wizard, calmly.

'Good heaven, Hamel!' rejoined the other; 'give her up to me.
Let me restore her to her parents—aye, even to her lover, though
he has undone me.'

He raised himself, as he spoke, from off the earth on which he
had been seated, though, by the time he was on his fat legs, he
found they were hardly sufficient to support him, and placed his
hand instinctively on his wound, while he reconnoitered the rocks
on which he had caught a glimpse of the petticoats. Hamel had
sent one of his Negroes to bid the women descend.

'Give her to me,' continued Fillbeer. 'Let the last act of my
commission here be to make my peace with Mr Fairfax, and to
oblige Mr Guthrie; for I shall decamp. Nay, you may grin, Mr
Conjuror; but I shall march.'

'You will march, master Attorney—yes, you will march. Well, you shall have all you desire. Here is Miss Guthrie's cloak, or veil rather. You did not think I had the young lady to give away, did you?'

The brewer stared as if he had seen a ghost, looking at the black legs of Wowski as she approached, and then at Patch, and then again at the wizard; and after that, examining the two women more critically. At last he muttered between his teeth, 'Incarnate fiend! Not even Belzebub is more d—d. The villain! he has murdered her, or sold her! Gracious heaven!' (turning up his eyes) 'is this thy providence? And hast thou left the innocent, the virtuous, the helpless, in the fangs of these demons?'

He heaved a deep sigh, and wiped his clammy features, while he continued apostrophizing the spirit of the universe, and now and then adverting mentally to the discomfiture of his hopes, and to his despair respecting the hundred doubloons. 'Is my own life safe?' added he, in a sort of under voice. 'This ruffian has long owed me a grudge.' He cast a timid glance at Hamel, who was engaged in replacing the saddle on the horse, having meanwhile given his musket to one of the women; for the Negroes who had attended him hither had taken their departure. 'No; he cannot mean me harm, or he might have left me to those rascals who stopped me. Yet what has he done with Miss Guthrie?'

The Obeah man overheard part of this soliloquy, but declined paying any particular attention to it. He had replaced the saddle on the fat man's steed, and assisted him, whether he would or would not, to mount. In short, he hoisted him on his beast, and very courteously invited him to lead the way to the rocks that overlooked Belmont, to his own watchman's abode—his cave.

'*I* lead the way,' said Fillbeer, in alarm, 'to your cave! What have I to do there?' (The Obeah man examined the lock of his gun.) 'You will not murder me?' continued the brewer. 'It is true, I am in your power; but you that have saved—given me my life, cannot intend to take it away again.'

'Your life is not safe except you follow me, be assured,' said Hamel. 'I have business for you at my cave. I want you, and you must come. Even the Negroes who attended you have fled. You

are alone, and all resistance would be vain: but in my company you
have nothing to fear. Or, if you prefer it, give me your promise to
go with these women to the cave, and I will not trouble you with
my presence.'

'Not so black as he is painted,' muttered Fillbeer. 'A pestilence
on his Paganism—a demon may have one redeeming quality. I
shall go, Mr Hamel,' he added aloud; 'I give you my word.'

'Be it so,' replied the wizard. 'You shall have no cause for fear or
regret; but in case of danger from any strange interlopers who
may be on the look-out, this woman shall carry the gun for your
use.'

'Nay, nay, give it me,' cried the fat man. 'I can carry it easily
across my saddle-bow. My honour is pledged.'

'Take it then,' rejoined the Obeah man; 'and remember, if you
see danger or want assistance, whistle aloud: my comrades are
within hearing in the woods.'

'The devil they are!' said the fat man, as if alarmed at the circumstance. 'But I cannot whistle; I have no breath to spare. I
could no more whistle in such a case than I could fly.'

The Obeah man, as if heedless of this observation, had darted
again into the bushes, leaving Quinbus with his Amazonian escort,
screwing up his lips into the least dimensions of which they were
capable, and vainly puffing out by starts the little wind which he
could spare from his fat corpse, to effect the sound which was to
assure him of succour in case of need.

CHAPTER 23.

Aye, but to die, and go we know not where!
To lie in cold obstruction and to rot!
This sensible warm motion to become
A kneaded clod; and the delighted spirit
To bathe in fiery floods, or to reside
In thrilling regions of thick-ribbed ice!
To be imprisoned in the viewless winds,
And blown with restless violence round about
This pendent world,—or to be worse than worst
Of those whom lawless and uncertain thoughts
Imagine howling.—'Tis too horrible!

MEASURE FOR MEASURE.

WE left the ill-fated Roland sleeping within the precincts of the Obeah man's abode, beside the little lagoon environed with inaccessible crags. His slumber was neither sound nor refreshing. A raging fever had taken possession of him, the consequence of the fatigues of mind and body which he had suffered, the excesses and vicissitudes of which he had lately been the sport.

The sun was shining bright when he awoke from this sort of stupor rather than from sleep; and he surveyed, with the calmness of despair, the rocks that imprisoned him; for he felt a conviction that the hand of death was on him, and that although he had escaped the murderous passion of the monarch whom he had anointed, and the more horrifying apparatus of the gallows, yet his time was come! He had to surrender up his breath to the Being from whom he had received it; and, according to the vulgar creed, to give an account of his conduct while he had enjoyed it. Not that he had formerly considered himself accountable for all the works done in the flesh. Like many of his predecessors in his peculiar persuasion, he was averse to judge his actions by the standard of reason alone. He had made a merit of obeying impulses which he flattered himself were divine; he had felt affections which he considered as inspirations, and had assured himself of his election and illumination. Considering himself the servant, the soldier, of the most high God, he had never questioned the motives which induced him to effect this or that purpose, or halted to consider what might be their consequences. His confidence in the Almighty had never faltered; his faith in a crucified Redeemer had been imperturbable. He had always been satisfied that he was right; and, without referring to his mortal career, anticipated a crown of glory in the world to come.

We may suppose that during these assurances he was in a sound mind, for now that a mortal sickness had attacked him, every one of these impressions vanished. His brain was in a state of excitement bordering on delirium; and while his body, becoming more and more feeble, had parted with every passion that had been wont to interfere with it, this, the sensorium, the soul, lay at the mercy of the spirit which had summoned it from this life. In short, his conscience began to be troubled, and he hesitated to assure himself of the infallibility of his former hopes. Yet whom could he consult, or where could he look for assistance in this melancholy hour, estranged—exiled—from the haunts of civilized men; cooped up in a sort of prison; wasting with exhaustion; dying of disease? In vain did his troubled memory conjure up the recollection of past assurances, the triumphs of his faith and of his fortune, when something like prosperity on earth had smiled upon him; when he was believed, and believed himself, to be the deputy of his God, beyond the reach of temptation, beyond the chance of falling into nought. His past humility was arrayed now, before his imagination, in the garb of pride, of insolence to all other Christians—of intolerance. He had fancied himself a more useful servant, more zealous, faithful, more religious, more important, than a host of the merely virtuous and moral followers of Christ. He thought that, in affecting to engross the merits and the honour of *true worship,* he had been merely soothing and sacrificing to his own vanity. He felt that he had been a despot in religion; arbitrary, unjust, tyrannical, vain, selfish, even when most sincere. Then crowded on his mind the guilty deeds of the flesh; and as every circumstance of his excesses appeared in review before him, each seemed a demon striving to goad him for his cruelty, his

sensuality, his merciless pertinacity in worldly schemes. The
chain was counted, link by link—the chain of all his misdeeds—
the chain that had bound him to the earth, and that now seemed
to bind him to the bottomless pit,—*the level lake of brimstone!*
The fetters were rivetted on his soul, and wound around him by
the Arch Enemy of mankind—the apostate spirit—the *gran'
Diavol del Inferno* in his own proper person. The heart of
Roland, which had been used of late to throb, now beat as if his
bosom were too narrow to confine it; and his brain, almost riven
with the conviction, began to wander as in a wilderness. He raved
on Mrs Guthrie, on the name of Fairfax, and Joanna; at one while
invoking the mercy of Heaven, at the next moment uttering sighs
and murmurs of despair. The rocks that imprisoned him reverberated these sounds of woe; and whenever their silence was restored, the solitude of the scene inspired him with fresh
inducements to lamentation. The fever in his veins awaked the
recollection of the fire he had kindled, and the frightful figure of
his delegate again stood before him—the Negro whom we have
called the Duppie.

'Samuel! Samuel!' said he, (his apostrophe partaking of invocation as well as soliloquy,) 'thou shouldst have disobeyed me, or
thou shouldst have died, or I should have died, before my soul was
blackened like this throbbing, hateful heart! Must thou too rise in
judgment against me? Oh God! How dreadful is this world! How
terrible is that which is to come! Samuel! Samuel!'

In the midst of the apostrophe, the diving Duppie, known to
Roland by the name of Samuel, arose from the little lagoon on
which the eyes of the despairing man were fixed, and stood on the
shore before him. The bubbling of the troubled waters had first
arrested the attention of Roland; and as he saw the Negro form
emerging from the pool, his fancy, again wandering with alarm,
presented to itself the idea of a demon ascending from the condemned pit, and he thought again, for a moment or two, that he
had already passed the gates of death.

The Negro and the preacher exchanged a look of recognition.
The languor and the sadness of death were on the features of the
last, and those of the former betrayed no sign of triumph. There

was a pause of many minutes before the silence was broken, the
Duppie standing in a fixed yet rather respectful position, while
the gaze of Roland was bent upon him, watching the drops of
water which fell from his head or from the skirts of his black shirt,
and trickled down his ebony looking legs.

'Samuel,' said the preacher, at length breaking silence, 'what
wouldst thou?'

'You called me, Roland,' replied the Duppie. 'I heard you
plainly ask for Samuel.'

'You have betrayed me,' replied the preacher with a languid
sigh; 'but I forgive you: I am dying—dying, as I have deserved,
without one friend to soothe my conscience in my last moments,
to comfort this expiring body, or to close my eyes when I am dead!
Oh, Samuel! Say at least that you will bury me, if only here beneath this sod. Leave me not a prey to the hawks and vultures, or
to that ghastly snake that but now was wreathing its horrid folds
beside me!'

'Master parson,' rejoined the Duppie, 'you are not going to die.'

'Parson! Parson!' re-echoed Roland, interrupting him. 'Call not
me parson, nor preacher, nor missionary, nor even man. I am a
monster! Where did you come from? From the abyss of H——?
How can you live under the water? I remember—it was you that
dragged me beneath the waves into that dungeon. Had I but
served my God with half the zeal I served *myself!*—I a parson!
Would to heaven that I had been a real, reasonable, conscientious,
minister of the truth; ordained by some religious bishop, educated with men of honourable feelings and of generous hearts, instead of having herded with wretches, miscreants, sensual
fanatics, and interested hypocrites, ever seeking whom they may
devour! Samuel! tell me truly—'

'What, master?' said the Duppie, answering with an expedition
which startled the sectarian.

'Samuel! do you not abhor me? Tell me sincerely; do you not
look on me as a monster—as a fiend? You, alas! who know me—
am not I a horror and a shame? A firebrand plucked out of the
burning, to be left as a beacon on the top of these mountains, to be
a warning and a teaching to every man?'

Samuel looked down with some contempt on the wretched sufferer, and answered in a tone as little offensive as possible—'Master Roland, you *are* a bad man—a d——d rascal—to be sure; but God is good and merciful, and if you are really sorry, he will forgive you.'

'Never,' said the Missionary—'never!'

'I tell you he will,' rejoined Samuel. 'All the parsons say so; and I am sure of it myself Why, *I* forgive you, though you made me do a great wickedness; and God Almighty is more merciful than a poor Negro.'

The Missionary raised his head and looked the Duppie in the face, and, after heaving a deep sigh, sank down again upon the grass, apparently *in articulo mortis*. Yet, after the lapse of a few minutes, he resumed his cogitations aloud, muttering in a sepulchral tone, that Samuel had the knowledge of all the law and the prophets. 'An ignorant heathen,' continued he, 'preaching consolation to an expositor of the Evangelists, to a minister who has been courted and followed by the multitude—the mob whom he had led astray! And, in his last hour, one whose credulity he had abused—poor Negro Samuel—tells him, for his comfort, that there is mercy in heaven for sinners! Give me a cup of water to quench this burning thirst. I am dying, Samuel, but my soul is not relieved! I tremble to think where I am going, and almost wish I had, like thee, been born a heathen; for unto whom much is given, of him shall much be required.'

Some food had been left by the side of Roland; and Samuel, at his request, took a calabash which had been set on the grass, filled it with water from the lagoon, and presented it to the Missionary, who drank every drop of its contents, and returned it to him for more.

'Mine,' said he, 'is the thirst of death! But hark! What noise was that? Oh, heaven and h——l! are these the ministers of justice come again to seize me for murder? The murder of whom—of what—of how many? Of that angel mother of the unfortunate Joanna! Horror! It is Fillbeer's voice. Is not Mr Guthrie with him?'

The Duppie, looking up to the fissure in the rock by which Roland had been introduced to the area of this lagoon, and

beholding the fat paunch of the late attorney of Belmont squeez-
ing through the narrow chink, handed with the utmost expedition
the second calabash of water to his former master, and plunged
headlong into the lake.

'I thank thee with my heart and with my soul,' said the
Missionary, grasping the calabash.

The Duppie was gone. The eyes of Roland followed him till he
had disappeared beneath the bubbling fountain; and those of
Fillbeer, having witnessed this finale, were rivetted with astonishment upon the undulating circles, which, breaking upon the shore
in some confusion and commotion, assured him that what he saw
was real.

'What's this? Who is this?' ejaculated the fat man in the pauses
of his puffing and panting. 'To whom do you give your heart and
soul? Can I believe my eyes? Is this the Tempter, who thus has
darted into the pool and vanished in its depths? Roland, forbear:
it is your death and your d—n—n!'

He would have snatched the calabash from the dying man, if he
had possessed sufficient agility to reach it in time; but his bulk
prevented him. The Missionary had emptied it of its contents, and
lain down again in a state of exhaustion from the exertion, by the
time that the fat man had waddled up to him. 'Touch me not,' said
he to Fillbeer: 'let me depart in peace; detain not my soul. What I
have done, I have done, and I am beyond the reach of the law!'

'How so?' cried the astonished and again confounded attorney.
'What have you done? Have you sold yourself to hell? Have you
bartered for a cup of water your right to immortality? Have you
surrendered your soul?'

'Touch me not,' repeated Roland; 'I am dying! It would be
needless to hurry me from hence. I cannot live to satisfy the ends
of justice. Let them not treat my wretched corpse with ignominy!'

By this time the Obeah man and his two attendants, Patch and
Wowski, had followed Mr Fillbeer into the little area, and ranged
themselves in front and around the dying man. The women knelt
down at once to assist him, being moved by the compassion natural to their sex; and the wizard, leaning on his musket, was
satisfied to contemplate his fallen foe in melancholy silence; his

black features rendered more sombre by the expression of his gloomy and mournful imagination.

The Missionary at length exchanged a look with him, having for some time closed his eyes, as if he feared the sight of the wizard would blast his scarcely surviving hope.

'It is even so,' said he. 'Hamel! you have conquered, and you are avenged: but you may tremble in your turn.'

'Never,' replied the wizard.

'God grant it may be so!' continued Roland. 'Let us exchange forgiveness.'

The black man gave him his hand, which Roland squeezed, and even put to his lips; and Hamel would have repaid this compliment, but the Missionary, quickly loosing his grasp, whispered with a convulsive shudder—'No, no—there's blood upon it!'

'His head is gone,' said Wowski, scarcely refraining from tears, as she wiped the perspiration from his clammy face with the end of the handkerchief which she wore on her neck—'his memory is wandering.'

'Not so,' replied the Missionary. 'I am still sensible, and I thank you. Alas, poor Rachel! She too was kind, faithful, and affectionate.'

He raised himself again, as if inspired by the recollection of this devoted adherent; and addressed himself with a peculiar energy to the fat man-mountain, whose portentous figure was occasionally convulsed with a mingled sympathy of pity, horror, and alarm. 'Mr Fillbeer,' said he, 'we are in an error. No life can be pleasing to God, except it be an example useful to men; and all is vanity except the services we can render to our fellow-creatures. I believe in God; and, worthless ideot as I am, I yet dare hope for mercy through the merits of his Son!'

With these words he sank back in a mortal paroxysm, at the same moment that the waters of the lagoon, beginning to be troubled again, rolled in rapid circles from the centre to the shore, and distracted the gaze of Fillbeer from the dying man.

'It is his fiend again,' said the brewer, trembling with alarm, 'incensed at the mention of the name of him whom we adore.'

'Whom you adore!' observed the Obeah man with a calm and inoffensive smile. 'But he is no fiend who rises from the water:

regard him well. Are you so silly—such a simpleton—as to believe a fiend, a devil, could appear on this or that occasion? Master Fillbeer, the Missionary is dead. You have seen him die—are you satisfied? Will you take his corpse, or will you bury it here? This fiend, as you fancied him, tells me I must begone from this abode.'

Fillbeer was in a dreadful perspiration, arising from fear and fat, and knew not what to engage to do.

'I must leave you,' said the Obeah man, preparing to go. 'Resolve quickly: if you will commit your friend to the earth, this Negro shall assist you; if not, begone from hence for ever!'

'No, no!' said Fillbeer, in a fresh alarm; 'Roland is dead, it is but too evident. You may leave us awhile, if you wish it, and we will inter him.'

While he thus addressed the Obeah man, he fixed his gaze upon the Duppie; and although he could not account, in his own mind, for the mysterious visiting of this Negro, he was satisfied that his appearance and disappearance were not altogether supernatural.

Hamel retired. The Duppie brought a spade from the interior of the rocks, and began to dig a grave; while the women seated themselves, one at the head, and the other at the feet of Roland, and without meddling with his apparel, laid him out with becoming decency, and fanned the flies from his corpse while the work was proceeding. They offered the attorney some of the provision prepared for Roland, which he did not refuse; and by the time that the sun had set, the body of the Missionary was committed to the earth; Fillbeer reciting over it, from memory, the service for the burial of the dead.

CHAPTER 24.

What! have you let the false enchanter 'scape?
Oh, ye mistook, ye should have snatcht his wand
And bound him fast.

COMUS.

THE morning had dawned, and the sun shone brightly over the Atlantic waves and the green island which they surround—the scene of our narrative—when the Obeah man, refreshed with some hours' sleep, made his appearance at the house of Mr Guthrie. He was attended by the two women, Patch and Wowski, as his intercessors, and half-a-dozen of his runaway friends, who had demanded his presence the previous afternoon, when he was summoned from the inner lagoon; and the cavalcade (or rather procession, as all the rest of the party were pedestrians) was closed by the portentous figure of the ex-attorney, who accompanied the wizard, thus far at least, as an hostage. He was of course mounted on his steed, all other means of locomotion among the rocks and mountains he had traversed being utterly denied him; and like a knight true to the cause for which he had taken up arms, he carried over his shoulder the black veil of Miss Joanna—the prize which she had left in her hurry at the waterfall.

Mr Fairfax was already there before them, with a crowd of guests and soldiery, besides a multitude of other persons, curious to behold this wizard, his influence having sufficed to regain possession, for her father and her lover, of the young lady whose destiny might otherwise have led her to a throne; a royalty not altogether contemptible in itself, if we consider the honourable notice which some of the European governments have bestowed on the emperor and the president of Haiti.

The Obeah man requested, and was admitted to, a private audience, wherein he bargained for his comrades that all who should surrender by a certain time should be secure in life and limb. He would have stipulated that some few more should have the privilege of quitting the island, at least of being furnished with passports;

but the right of other individuals here interfered, and without permission of the governor no such indulgence could be granted.

Hamel still requested to see Miss Joanna, who came forth at his solicitation, and thanked him for the services he had rendered her.

She likewise received the black women, not refraining from tears at the recognition. One was a free woman; the other had lived the life of a free woman, (the creoles will understand this;) and both came, not to supplicate for themselves, but to intercede for many who, they said, had been induced by Roland and others to take up arms in support of the rights which Mr Wilberforce had obtained for them.

'They told us so, mistress; they told the Negroes so, who were slaves. They preached to us that the king of England had given liberty to all, had paid for their freedom; and they read out of big books, and little books, and Scotch books, that we should put the knives to the throats of the buckras, who then would own it was true. But Roland is dead.'

Joanna shuddered; and Michal, who stood beside her, trying to conceal the tears which obtruded in her eyes as she listened to the tale of the black women, asked very innocently where he had died, and what was become of him.

'Oh! mistress,' replied Wowski, 'he died beside a little pool of water among the rocks yonder, and we gave him a handsome funeral. These men were there, and Hamel and master Fillbeer preached over him; and we buried him on the spot where he died—where he breathed his last breath.'

While this dialogue was passing, the Obeah man was in deep consultation with Fairfax, who gave him a written paper, and after another word or two, waved to his companions to depart with him. At the same time he placed in his hands a weighty bag of gold; and having assured him that an escort of four troopers should attend him by way of safeguard, he bid him for the present farewell.

'Will you be a friend to these women?' said the wizard. 'They are innocent: they would have saved this buckra lady, if they had had the power. She knows what they deserve. Farewell; and may fortune smile on you both for ever!'

The eyes of all the witnesses to this scene had for some time
been fixed on the Obeah man, who was about to retire from the
presence of his master, and the multitude assembled at Mr
Guthrie's, with a respectful yet rather dignified obeisance; while
those of Fillbeer ogled only the bag which he was to carry off, the
bag wherein, as he guessed, were deposited the century of doubloons for which he had himself but vainly sighed. The wizard, as
he looked around the circle, encountered and detected the prying
glance of the fat man, and halted to make him a particular reverence. He seized the opportunity likewise of addressing a few
words, by way of adieu, to all the rest of the party—Mr Guthrie
and the militia, as well as the military officers.

'Gentlemen,' said he, 'the rebellion is all over. The runaways
who fought with the soldiers at the abandoned settlement yesterday, are many of them killed: the rest ran away. Some are gone to
the governor; some will be here to surrender to day; and some are
gone back to St Domingo, where they were invited to come from,
by —— and ——. Your Missionaries have persuaded the Negroes
that they are free; and they believe the king's proclamation, telling
them they are still slaves, to be a forgery! It will not be long, therefore, before they rise again; and they will take the country from
you, except the king of England, and the governor here, keep
these preaching men in better order. What do you want with
them? You have a bishop and regular parsons; good men, who tell
the Negroes their duty as slaves, and try to keep the poor ignorant
things quiet and happy. If you let any other people turn their
heads, believe me, they will twist off yours. I declare to my God, I
never saw such trumpery. Your king, your governor, and all yourselves (forgive me, gentlemen) are afraid of these white Obeah
men. What a fuss is made with them, and what strange nonsense
they preach! You all knew Roland—you think so at least; but I can
tell you that he was the basest of mankind, and ten times more
wicked than any of you think. Your missionaries are not satisfied
with telling the Negroes their duty; they must preach about freedom, or the Negroes will not come to hear them. Then there are
as many sects as preachers, and they hate one another like dog and
cat. They will not eat or drink with one another, or speak to one

another. The Negroes follow their example; and you have
Methodists, Muggletonians, Anabaptists, Moravians, all pulling
at one another. Is this the wisdom of white men? Pshaw! you must
be cowards to allow it. Had Combah been king here, he should
have taught the white men how to treat such turbulent ragga-
muffins, I promise you. You remember master C—— who sold
his master's books for gin—ha! ha! One sheep is much like another.
Take my advice: I am an old man; decide on what you are to do. If
you or your king wish to make the Negroes free, do it at once; say
they are free. Your white man's country has room for you all, and
land and *nyam-nyam* enough. They are rich, and can pay the
planters for their slaves, and houses, and estates, and works; but if
they are not to be free by the law—forbid anybody to deceive
them, on pain of death. I would hang or shoot the cunning, sneaking, fawning, fanatical, murderous villain, who tampered with the
passions of my slaves, or dared to hint at such a circumstance as
that of master Quashie holding a knife to his master's throat. But
you are no worth—(forgive me, gentlemen—I spoke without caution)—I mean you are afraid of the white Obeah men.'

So saying, while his swoln eyeballs seemed to flash with indignation, he repeated his salaam, and hurried away.

Of course Mr Hamel used the dialect of his country, the creole
tongue; sufficiently understood by all the assembled party, who
occupied the piazza and the apartments adjoining in Mr Guthrie's
house, to allow this his farewell to make a considerable impression. Fat Fillbeer yet sat on his horse, amongst the crowd without;
and as the Obeah man concluded his speech, he so far forgot himself as to call out—'Bravo!' The expression excited some attention, and a titter was communicated round the circle, which
somewhat disconcerted him, as his own conscience was awake to
the recollection of some pieces of information with which he had
favoured the white Obeah men in England, of whom the wizard
had spoken. He had often adverted to the resolutions of the Wesleyans in September 1824; and remembered that the ministers
who subscribed to them were censured and recalled by the rest of
the society—the *gang* (as he termed them to himself) in England.
He knew what sort of news would be acceptable, and had often

made it to suit the occasion. A little pained with these recollections, his eyes encountered suddenly the pretty features of the Quadroon, who saluted him from a distance, and waved to him to come near the window, at which her mistress stood. 'A pretty girl,' thought Quinbus. 'What is your will with me?'

'The veil, the veil,' replied the damsel. 'You are a brave man, and deserve to have saved my mistress. These women, Patch and Wowski, have told us of your intentions towards us, and how you took the field to fight the runaways.'

'And of my wound too,' thought Fillbeer, who by this time dismounted from his steed, marched very solemnly up the piazza steps, and delivered the veil into the hands of Joanna, whose kind words and kinder looks consoled him, though in a small degree, for the loss of the doubloons.

Mr Fairfax, who offered him his hand, hoped that all animosity might be laid aside between them, and assured him that he would endeavour to further his interest in the island, if he chose to remain, or render him any services in his power in England, supposing he thought fit to return home.

The fat man accepted his salutation, and thanked him for his offers of assistance, while his eyes unconsciously wandered towards Miss Guthrie, and his soubrette, the charms of whose person seemed to engage his fixed attention.

'The rose!' said he to himself, and then surveyed his bulk. 'This too should have been a queen, and a brave one she had made for the black monarch, or for a white monarch—aye, or for me, were I ten, fifteen, twenty, twenty-five years, younger.' He heaved a sigh as he turned away; a sigh that was echoed by the pretty damsel, whose thoughts were wandering to other scenes and sights than those before her. She was in a cave, and half asleep, and a Mulatto man was on his knee by her side, kissing her hand. She blushed at the recollection, and then she beheld the fair face and the blue eyes of her mistress, cast a glance at Fairfax, and sighed again.

'Ah!' thought she, 'I am a poor silly somebody, but I shall see him happy, contented, with his white and beautiful wife.'

She did not observe how many eyes were fixed on her own pretty figure, which had thus been brought into notice by her

address to Fillbeer; how many of the soldier buckras were pe-
rusing her, as well as the militia officers crowding towards her, as
Fillbeer thought, like wasps round the honey-pot. Indeed, no
one of the male sex could regard her with indifference, and few
of the female sex could ever have surpassed her in personal
attractions.

But as her history may perhaps serve a future opportunity and
another pen, it would be premature to say much more of her in
these pages.

Her first love, it seems, was to be renounced; and though this
necessary abdication pained her affectionate heart, yet she bore
her mortification with firmness and resolution, arising from a due
conviction of propriety as to her demeanour and ideas, and a sincere attachment to her mistress. Still we would not have our readers imagine that she had less sensibility than the fair beauties of
Great Britain, or even than the darker damsels of Italy or Spain; or
that she was unaffected by any of the little circumstances which
constitute the pains and pleasures of lovers—a look—a word—
the accidental touch of a beloved person. No: poor Michal was
sensible of all this without adverting to it, and to much more
which, in the course of time, oppressed her heart and spirits, and
caused her to think how often—

> 'A sincere and tender passion
> Some cursed planet overrules.'

Such a person, in such a situation, cannot want admirers, such
as they are; and lawless as their views may be, the whole race of
Mulatto women, Quadroons, and Mestees, are all equally exposed
to them, and generally entertain the same ideas respecting them.
The passion of Michal, however, had put her above these; and the
red-coated gentlemen ogled, and nodded, and looked languish-
ing, enchanted, and enraptured, in vain. She even felt more consideration for fat Fillbeer, of whose valour Patch and Wowski had
told rather more than the truth. It is true, that a few of the soldiery
had shewn her some little marks of gallantry on the descent from
the waterfall; but they were so taken up with the wounded and the
dying, that they had but little opportunity of attending to her or

her mistress, who returned as she went, first in a litter, and latterly on a mule, as soon as the road became practicable.

Mr Guthrie was exalted to a pitch of something like happiness, notwithstanding all his afflictions, at the recovery of his daughter and the escape of Fairfax; nor could he cease to wonder at that power which he had seen the Obeah man possess and exercise over the minds of his fellow Negroes: a power, as he felt assured, existing as much or more in the ignorance of these, than in the talents of the conjuror, who still was a clever fellow, however, as he allowed, more especially since he had heard his parting speech.

But it is time that we should return to our tale, and relate what little remains to be said of this dabbler in magic, who posted off to his abode with the bag of doubloons, followed shortly afterwards by Mr Fairfax and Mr Guthrie on horseback.

There was a brown woman seated within the little cave which looked on the lagoon, (the same in which Fairfax had found Michal sleeping,) who advanced at their approach, and presented the features of poor Rachel bathed in tears. She accosted Hamel, and told him that the gaoler, whom Roland had stabbed, was yet living and likely to recover; and she begged to be allowed to visit the tomb of her former master. The Obeah man complied with her request, and led her by sundry tortuous ways to the inner lagoon, where he left her to her meditations, while he exhibited the rest of his dwelling to the two gentlemen who had followed him.

A more extraordinary labyrinth cannot be conceived. In some of the passages were chasms scarce three feet wide, down any of which an unguarded stranger must have fallen, as it were into a bottomless pit, for the Obeah man assured them he had never been able to fathom their depth. Some had water, others breathed only a cool air, which rendered the climate of these recesses even agreeable. In one court was a gulph like the crater of a volcano, where, at the depth of a hundred feet or so, a subterranean river might be heard and seen rushing impetuously into some deeper cavity. We have formerly described some of the apartments in this strange abode, around which the Obeah man had always laboured to weave a net of mystery, by tales of enchantment and prophetic warnings, to keep all intruders from prying into his secrets; and we

need say little more of the rest of them. Provisions of all sorts
abounded—weapons, gunpowder, spears, a score of muskets,
which had been used of late, and even two small brass cannons,
which Hamel confessed he had, many years before, got from a
Spanish bark which was wrecked on the coast.

'It is all yours,' said he to Mr Fairfax. 'Use it, and defend your
property, and your wife that shall be. No Negro, no man but myself, knows the intricacies of this cave at all—nor the very entrances—for there are several; and you see how easily any one
may be lost among these windings. I blindfolded the attorney
Fillbeer, when I brought him here to bury Roland, who was drawn
in through the water in front of the rocks.'

The wizard, in short, laid open to his guests all the natural and
artificial contrivances of his dwelling, and, before they quitted it,
led them to the gallery by which Roland had first clambered from
the banks of the Rio Grande below. Hence they beheld far off at sea
a large canoe filled with Negroes, standing away to the eastward.

'My comrades,' said Hamel, 'the subjects of king Combah going
back to the land of freedom—Haiti—with some of the wretches
whom it vomited forth for your destruction, at the recommendation of the Obeah Christians in England. They will make up a
pretty tale, no doubt—but they might have conquered.'

The young gentleman and his Negro exchanged a look of mutual understanding. It meant, on the part of Hamel—'I have
sacrificed everything to serve and prove my gratitude to your
father's son. I want, I deserve, no thanks. I hope I have done my
duty.'

On the part of the white man, it signified an acknowledgment
that he felt and appreciated all this, and wished to repay him in
any and every way.

'No, no,' said the Negro, returning with them towards the
minor lagoon. 'Here is Rachel sobbing for the loss of her worthless
master. Let us give her some of the doubloons. It is a slave of
yours, Mr Fairfax. Make her free, or let her live unmolested, and
await a better fortune than that which she has had torn from her.'

They led her as before, blindfolded, to the outer air, where
Samuel, the Duppie, tarried, to accompany the Obeah man upon

his last expedition, in Jamaica; namely, to the Turtle Crawl, where had been left concealed a smaller canoe, in case of need, for him or his friends to make sure of their escape from the island.

Mr Fairfax accompanied them, as did Mr Guthrie, led on by curiosity to see the last of this extraordinary man; having dismissed the afflicted Rachel to her own abode with half the gold, which Hamel insisted on her taking.

'He did not,' he said, 'sell his companions; he did not even betray them. He had tried all fair means to stop the mischief which he knew must be fatal to Mr Fairfax, if not to the whole island; and when all other means failed, the king—Combah——but no matter, he is dead,' continued the wizard, 'and the hour of Hamel will shortly arrive!'

'The king was shot,' said Mr Guthrie to himself, turning over in his mind what he recollected of the scene: 'his majesty was not struck by the lightning—an ounce bullet gave him his *hic jacet*.'

The Obeah man meanwhile, with the assistance of the Duppie, had launched the canoe from among the mangroves and anchovy trees, and deposited within it his musket, with his ammunition and a basket of provisions, a keg of rum, and a few other articles, about all of which he seemed very indifferent, and but for the officiousness of Samuel would have left behind. He then took leave of his ally, and commended him to Mr Guthrie as an innocent man, who had been forced or seduced by Roland to do all of which he could be called guilty. He was likewise a free man, at least had been sold to be *emancipated;* and as his children were living in this part of the world, he was allowed to remain at Belmont, and received the remainder of the gold, which Hamel bid him keep.

Mr Fairfax took this opportunity of again soliciting Hamel to remain there also, and pass the evening of his days in peace.

'You have,' said he, 'saved my life—saved the daughter of this gentleman! We can never repay you sufficiently.'

'I would not have you repay me,' said the Obeah man. 'I have employed your gold as a satisfaction to yourself; but I would have the conviction of having devoted myself, at least, with my companions. I could dwell here no more. I have ruined myself in the

estimation of those to whom I had *sworn* fidelity; but I have saved
you and her whom you love. Farewell, master!'

'But whither are you bound?' said Mr Guthrie, observing that
Hamel had hoisted his sail.

'To the land of my birth—my mother's country.'

The wind was blowing fresh at north-east; and the wizard, having paddled out of the lee occasioned by the rocks and trees, set
his sail, and stretched away to the eastward.

'There were tears in his eyes,' said Mr Guthrie: 'What a strange
fellow! He is going to deliver himself up to the rebels, whose triumph he has spoiled.'

'Strange, indeed, sir,' replied Fairfax;—'but they dare not touch
him.'

They rode to the top of the rocks which overhung the sea,
whence they could, by the help of a spy-glass, for a long time distinguish the Obeah man sitting in his canoe, in a pensive posture,
gazing on the deep blue waves that heaved around him. The wind
freshened, and the sky became overcast, yet still they could descry
him in the same attitude. They watched him without regarding
the time they so misapplied, until his little boat had diminished to
a speck. The sun declined; the twilight sank into darkness; and although the moon arose in splendour, they saw no more of Hamel
or his bark. The Duppie gazed till he was almost blind in reality,
and Mr Guthrie gazed in two or three directions at once with no
better success; indeed none of them could assign any reason for
gazing at all. Hamel was never heard of more!

THE END

NOTES ON THE TEXT

These are intended to identify allusions to historical events and persons, mythological allusions, and also quotations and literary references—though a few of these have escaped me, in spite of considerable efforts with both traditional concordances and more modern research tools such as the LION (Literature Online) database. In addition, I have provided glosses for words and phrases in languages other than English, for items of Jamaican or Caribbean English vocabulary which may be unfamiliar to some readers, and for some of the more obscure or obsolete British English words.

JOHN GILMORE.

The following abbreviated references are used:

Bailey	Nathan Bailey, *An Universal Etymological English Dictionary* ... , sixth edition (London, 1733)
DJE	F. G. Cassidy and R. B. Le Page, eds., *Dictionary of Jamaican English*, Second Edition (Cambridge: Cambridge University Press, 1980)
Long	Edward Long, *History of Jamaica* (3 vols., London, 1774; reprint by Ian Randle Publishers, Kingston, Jamaica, 2002)
	All references to Shakespeare are to *The Riverside Shakespeare*, ed. by G. Blakemore Evans et al. (Boston, MA: Houghton Mifflin Company, 1974)
Title page	Quotation is from William Shakespeare, *The Tragedy of Othello, the Moor of Venice*, I, ii, 77–9, where they form part of Brabantio's complaint that Othello has only obtained the affections of his daughter Desdemona by witchcraft—the 'arts' which are 'inhibited and out of warrant' (that is, prohibited and illegal). The source begins 'I therefore apprehend ...'
p. 1	Quotation not from Shakespeare, but from the adaptation of his *Richard III* by Colley Cibber (1671–1757), first performed in 1700 (I, 165–6).
p. 2	**spatterdashes** Gaiters.
	Osnaburgh A kind of coarse linen or woollen cloth, often used for slaves' clothing. (Originally so called from Osnabrück in Germany.)

Cuffy A name commonly given to slaves; originally a West African day-name for a male born on a Friday.

castor A European-style top-hat made of beaver-fur (*castor* is Latin for beaver).

p. 5 Quotation is from 'Jamaica, A Descriptive and Didactic Poem', by Bryan Edwards (1743–1800), first printed in *Poems, written chiefly in the West-Indies* (Kingston, Jamaica, 1792; a collection including poems by Edwards and others) and later made more widely available by its inclusion as an appendix in the fifth edition (five vols., London, 1819) of Edwards' well known *History, Civil and Commercial, of the British West Indies,* at V, 215–33. The original has 'transfix'd' rather than 'them fix'd'. It is part of a passage in which a Jamaican Amerindian is imagined calling down divine vengeance on the Spanish who have destroyed his people.

p. 7 **Bucephalus** Here ironically applied, this was the name of the horse of Alexander the Great, King of Macedon 336–323 BCE.

p. 10 Quotation from Shakespeare, *The Life and Death of King John,* V, ii, 45.

p. 11 **contoo** 'A heavy woollen cloak' (*DJE,* citing this passage).

bonjaw A kind of stringed instrument of the guitar family, a banjo. In Jamaica, most commonly *banja,* though *DJE* cites other references for the spelling *bonjaw.*

vomitories Entrances, exits (from the Latin word *vomitoria,* referring to the entrances and exits of amphitheatres in ancient Rome, from which large numbers of people would pour out at the end of a show).

p. 13 **gombah** Also *gombay* or *goombah;* one of several types of drum, 'but all seem to be played with fingers rather than with sticks' (*DJE,* under *gombay*).

p. 14 Quotation from *The Puritan, or, The Widow of Watling Street* (I, ii), a play first published in 1607 and sometimes attributed to Shakespeare, though it is now generally credited to Thomas Middleton. The names of the characters speaking are given in abbreviated form by the author of *Hamel;* they are George Pyeboard and Peter Skirmish. See the online edition of Middleton by Chris Cleary at http://www.tech.org/~cleary/middhome.html.

the great house (as the principal dwelling is called)
One of a number of passages where the author makes a point
of explaining something for the benefit of readers outside
Jamaica or the English-speaking Caribbean.

piazza Often used in Jamaica to refer to a verandah.

p. 19   **such a stir making in England** After the abolition of the
British slave trade (1807), it was widely assumed that
the condition of slaves in the colonies would improve
significantly as (so it was argued) their owners would have to
look after them better since they could no longer replace
them easily with new ones. The passage of time showed that
this was not happening, and in the 1820s in Britain a new
popular campaign against slavery in the colonies began. At
first this aimed merely at improving the condition of the
slaves by increased government regulation, but it soon became a call for the ending of slavery altogether. This was
achieved by a law passed in 1833, which provided for the
abolition of slavery throughout the British dominions with
effect from 1 August 1834; while anti-slavery agitation in
Britain itself certainly contributed to this, increasing rebel-
liousness and resistance among the slaves themselves was
also of major importance. There were major slave revolts in
Barbados (1816), Demerara (1823) and Jamaica (1831).

p. 23   Quotation from Shakespeare, *The Comedy of Errors*, III, ii,
12–15.

p. 27   **machet** A cutlass; the spelling represents a common
Jamaican pronunciation of *machete* (with the stress on the
second syllable; see *DJE*).

p. 28   Quotation from Shakespeare, *The Tragedy of King Lear*, IV,
vi, 11–12.

    the Devil looking over Lincoln Possibly a reference to
the small medieval stone carving in Lincoln Cathedral in
eastern England, which is generally referred to as the
Lincoln Imp. Legend says this was originally a devil blown
into the cathedral by a storm, and turned into stone by the
resident angels when he began to misbehave.

p. 30   **dingles** A dingle is defined by Bailey as 'a narrow Valley
between two steep Hills'.

p. 31   **viceroy over him, as Trinculo happily observes**
Apparently adapted from Shakespeare, *The Tempest*, III, ii,

108, and *The First Part of Henry VI*, V, iv, 131, which uses the phrase 'viceroy under him'. The suggestion that Roland, while nominally subordinate to Combah, will be able to control him, owes nothing to Shakespeare's text, which is presumably being misquoted from memory.

p. 33   Quotation from Shakespeare, *Cymbeline*, II, ii, 14–16.

p. 34   **beaufet**   Buffet, sideboard.

        soubrette   Maid-servant (French).

p. 36   **Proserpine**   (Or Persephone) was in classical mythology carried off to the underworld realm of the dead (**Tartarus, Erebus** or Hades) by its ruler **Pluto**.

        Schiavoni   Unidentified; possibly Luigi Schiavonetti (1765–1810), an Italian engraver who worked in England from the 1790s (but see also p. 331 below, and note on that passage).

        Sambo   A common slave name, which was often used by whites as a derogatory term for any black man. However, it may here have the more precise meaning of a person of mixed racial ancestry, specifically the offspring of a black and a mulatto, or anyone of light black complexion. See Long, II, 261.

        Hercules   Hero of classical mythology, famous for his physical strength.

p. 40   Quotation from Shakespeare, *The Tragedy of King Lear*, III, iv, 24–5.

p. 43   **your doubloons, and your dollars**   Spanish colonial coins provided the normal circulating medium in Jamaica. The term doubloon was used in English for a range of Spanish gold coins, particularly those of two and four escudos. The escudo was equivalent to two dollars, but in Jamaica the gold coins were deliberately valued above their equivalents in silver, in an effort to keep them in the island. The dollar was a large silver coin equal to eight *reales*; in the late eighteenth and early nineteenth centuries it was generally valued at four shillings and eight pence sterling money of Great Britain, or six shillings and sixpence Jamaican currency. Long, I, 578–89, offers a survey of the extremely complicated question of money in Jamaica and the values of the many different types of coin which circulated in the island.

p. 44   **John-crows**   'The red-headed turkey-buzzard *Cathartes aura*' (*DJE*). A carrion bird well known in Jamaica, but *DJE* notes that the first recorded appearance of the name John-Crow is in 1826 (only a year before the publication of *Hamel*). It was earlier called simply the carrion crow.

p. 47   **such a serpent as that which stopped the march of the Roman army**   Apparently a (not very relevant) reference to a story told by Livy (Titus Livius, 59 BCE–17 CE) in his history of Rome (book VII, chapter xvii), in which the Romans are at first terrified by the snakes brought into battle by the priests of their enemies, the Falisci and Tarquinienses, but recover their nerve after being rebuked by their leaders, and go on to win.

p. 49   Quotation from Shakespeare, *The Tragedy of King Richard the Second*, I, i, 177–9. The original edition of *Hamel* misprints 'loom' for 'loam'.

p. 51   **perhaps by Mr W——?**   Probably a reference to the famous British Member of Parliament and anti-slavery activist William Wilberforce (1759–1833).

p. 55   Quotation from Shakespeare, *The Tragedy of Richard the Third*, I, ii, 252–4.

   a huge white sombrero beaver   A kind of hat; although referred to as a castor a few lines later (see note on p. 2 above), the use of 'sombrero' is probably intended to suggest it had a low crown and broad brim.

p. 61   Quotation unidentified—though 'Are these the confines of some fairy world?/ A land of Genii?' appears in *The Art of Preserving Health: A Poem* (II, 371–2) by John Armstrong, which was first published in 1744 and remained popular for many years.

p. 63   **Brutchie**   Explained below (p. 64): 'the Brutchie, by which they understand a king or prince'. Possibly an Ibo word; *DJE* (under 'brechie') cites two earlier examples from the 1820s, both referring to the marking of the forehead, as mentioned later with reference to Combah.

p. 68   Quotation from Shakespeare, *The Tragedy of Julius Caesar*, III, ii, 210–11, 221–4 (with slight variations).

p. 71   **Did not those of St Domingo make themselves free?**   A slave revolt broke out in 1791 in the French colony of St.-Domingue (the western part of the island of Hispaniola, often referred to by English-speaking writers as St Domingo, though strictly speaking Santo Domingo was the Spanish colony in the eastern part of the same island). After many years of bloody conflict, the slaves secured their freedom and the independence of their country, proclaimed in 1804 under one of the old Amerindian names for the island, Haiti. The success of the Haitian Revolution was an inspiration to slaves elsewhere, and a nightmare for slave-owners and their supporters.

p. 72   **Empedocles**   Greek philosopher (*c.* 450 BCE), said to have killed himself by jumping into the volcanic crater of Mount Etna in Sicily.

Lycurgus   A perhaps legendary figure in ancient Greece, who was said to have laid down the rules which gave the Spartans the austere way of life and strict military discipline for which they were famous.

p. 74   Quotation from Shakespeare, *The Tragedy of Titus Andronicus*, V, ii, 98–103 (omitting 'the wicked streets of Rome' after 'Look round about').

Eleusinian mysteries   In classical antiquity, religious celebrations held at Eleusis in Greece, in honour of the goddess Demeter. They were open only to initiates, who faced the severest penalties if they revealed any details of the rites to outsiders.

eboe drum   A kind of large drum favoured by the Eboes (or Ibos, a people from what is now Nigeria). See *DJE*.

p. 76   **Coromantins**   A name given (with numerous variations in spelling) to slaves brought to the Caribbean from a particular port on the Gold Coast of Africa (modern Ghana). They had a reputation for bravery and ferocity.

p. 77   **Mocos**   Moco is described by *DJE* as 'An African tribal name of doubtful identity'. The alleged cannibalism of the Mocos was referred to by Bryan Edwards.

p. 82   Quotation from Shakespeare, *The Tragedy of Titus Andronicus*, V, iii, 11–13.

p. 85   **Orpheus**   Figure in classical mythology, who descended into the underworld ('the abodes of Pluto and his bride') in an ultimately unsuccessful attempt to regain his dead wife Eurydice. The music which Orpheus played on his lyre was supposed to be able to charm all living things. Referring to the underworld as 'Pandemonium' suggests an allusion to the famous epic poem *Paradise Lost* (1667, 1674) by John Milton (1608–1674), where Book I, lines 756–7, refer to 'Pandemonium, the high capital/ Of Satan and his peers'.

p. 86   **pennistons**   Defined by Bailey (who spells it 'penistons') as 'a sort of coarse woollen cloth'.

sumpter mules   Intended to carry luggage or other goods on a journey (rather than for riding).

kittereen   One of the definitions given by the *Oxford English Dictionary* is 'In West Indies, A kind of one-horse chaise or buggy', though the definitions supporting this are later than *Hamel*.

p. 87   **almost Lethean sleep**   Deathlike (from the river in classical mythology which the recently dead had to cross in order to enter the underworld).

p. 90   **Carrion-crow Hills**   Possibly what are now called the John Crow Mountains, in the east of Jamaica. Portland Ridge is in a completely different part of the country, in the peninsula which forms the southernmost tip of the island, though there is a Portland Gap in the Blue Mountains (which are a little to the west of the John Crow Mountains). The parishes of Hanover and Westmoreland are at the western tip of the island. The different names mentioned in this passage may be intended to suggest that Combah was planning a slave uprising on an island-wide scale, or they may perhaps indicate limitations in the geographical knowledge of the author. Fires on Portland Ridge, for example, would scarcely be visible on the north coast of the island, or anywhere in Hanover or Westmoreland.

p. 92   **Ah! master W——, S——, B——, and the whole tribe of you**
Probably intended to refer to British anti-slavery campaigners. The most likely candidates for the initials are William Wilberforce (see note above on p. 51), James Stephen (1758–1832) and Thomas Fowell Buxton (1786–1845).

p. 93   Quotation from the end of Book I of Edwards's 'Jamaica' (see note on p. 5 above). The island's Amerindian population, on the verge of extinction, seeks consolation in the thought of a hurricane inflicting divine vengeance on the Spanish colonists ('the pale coward slaves'). Here, the author of *Hamel* applies it to slave rebellion.

p. 94   **puntees**   Some sort of charm, the exact nature of which is obscure, as is the origin of the word (see *DJE*).

make love to all the women yourselves   This does not have its usual modern meaning, and merely suggests flirtation.

p. 96   **him of Hayti**   Henri Christophe, ruler of the northern part of Haiti from 1807 to 1820, made himself king in 1811 and surrounded himself with a European-style court and nobility.

barbicue   Paved area for spreading out coffee beans to dry (normally 'barbecue').

p. 97   **that of Lombardy**   The Iron Crown of Lombardy was an ancient symbol of royal power in Italy. It consists of a small circlet of iron, enclosed in gold plates. The iron was believed to have come from one of the nails used for the crucifixion of Christ. It had been used for coronations since medieval times, and Napoleon crowned himself with it as King of Italy in Milan in 1805.

Bacchus   Classical god of wine, son of Jupiter and Semele, usually portrayed as a good-looking young man. He was said to have conquered India, and is sometimes shown riding in triumph on an elephant in commemoration of this. He was brought up by his tutor **Silenus,** often portrayed as a drunken old man riding a donkey.

Titian   Famous Italian painter (Tiziano Vecellio, or Vecelli, *c.* 1477–1576).

Poussin   Famous French painter (Nicolas Poussin, 1594–1665).

Rubens   Famous Flemish painter (Peter Paul Rubens, 1577–1640).

p. 98   *chorea sancti viti*   Latin term for St. Vitus's Dance, a nervous disorder characterised by involuntary jerking movements.

sotto voce   In an undertone, quietly (Italian).

Hottentots   Derogatory name given by Europeans to the Khoi Khoi people of Southern Africa.

fum-fum   *DJE* cites Long as the earliest reference for this, with the same meaning of flogging.

p. 99   **Pindarics**   Verses of irregular stanzaic form, supposedly imitated from those of the Greek poet Pindar (*c.* 522–443 BCE).

p. 100   **he could not render the *tiara recta***   In other words, he could not make the crown sit straight on his head. The word *tiara* was originally applied by ancient Greek and Roman writers to a kind of mitre or turban worn as a head-dress by men in Eastern countries; the *tiara recta*, or upright tiara (with a point to it) was supposed to be particularly the emblem of royalty, while ordinary men wore the tiara low and flat.

p. 101   **cudjoes**   Cudjoe was a West African day-name for a male born on a Monday. As it was a common name, it may here be used for slaves generally; *DJE* interprets this passage as indicating that it could be used to mean a driver in particular, but gives no other examples to support this.

p. 104   **Bonduca**   A reference to *The Tragedie of Bonduca* (1610–14) by the English dramatist John Fletcher, which was printed in a number of editions, both separately and as part of the collected works of Fletcher and his collaborator Francis Beaumont. Several adaptations of the play, by different writers, were produced between the late seventeenth and early nineteenth centuries. The title character is based on the British historical figure better known as Boadicea or Boudicca, famous for her resistance to the Romans.

Maroons   Descendants of escaped slaves, their personal freedom and autonomy as a community were guaranteed by eighteenth-century treaties with the colonial authorities. In return, however, they were expected to help the authorities with the recapture of slave runaways and the suppression of rebellions, a role they performed as late as the Morant Bay Rebellion in 1865.

breadbasket   Stomach.

p. 106   ***coup-de-théâtre***   (French, correctly *coup de théâtre*); sudden and spectacular stage-effect (or, more generally, any sensational and surprising action).

p. 117   Quotation from Shakespeare, *A Midsummer Night's Dream*, II, i, 214–19.

          videlicet   Namely, to wit (Latin, more commonly encountered in the abbreviation *viz.*).

p. 119   **Houris**   Beautiful women (as imagined in Western views of the Islamic concept of the afterlife).

          Praxiteles   Famous Greek sculptor of the fourth century BCE.

p. 120   **Archer's Catechism**   Unidentified.

          Romeo's two blushing pilgrims   Romeo thus refers to his own lips in Shakespeare, *The Tragedy of Romeo and Juliet*, I, v, 95.

          so redolent of youth   Quotation unidentified. Possibly a reminiscence of the phrase 'redolent of joy and youth' in the 'Ode on a Distant Prospect of Eton College' by Thomas Gray (1716–1771).

p. 126   Quotation from Shakespeare, *The Tempest*, IV, i, 51–4.

          tête-à-tête   (French, literally 'head to head'); private meeting or conversation, usually (as here) between two people only.

p. 128   **Love, light as air**   Quotation from Alexander Pope, 'Eloisa to Abelard', 11, 75–6 (first published 1717).

          Here love his golden shafts employs   Quotation from Milton, *Paradise Lost*, IV, 763–5.

p. 133   Quotation from *The London Prodigal*, a play first printed in 1605 and sometimes attributed to Shakespeare, though this attribution is rejected by most modern scholars.

p. 135   **duppie**   Commonly used in Caribbean English to refer to the spirit of a dead person, a ghost (also *duppy*).

p. 139   Quotation from Shakespeare, *The Tempest*, 1, ii, 418–20 (Miranda speaking of Ferdinand).

p. 143   Quotation from Shakespeare, *The Tragedy of Othello, the Moor of Venice*, V, ii, 303.

          I have no pass   Slaves were not supposed to leave their own plantation without a 'pass', or written permission from the owner or manager, although laws to this effect were often flouted.

p. 145   **Euclid**   Greek mathematician (third century BCE) whose writings on geometry (or adaptations of them) were widely used as an introduction to the subject for more than two thousand years.

Lucie   More correctly Lucea. Like Falmouth, it is a town on the north coast of Jamaica.

p. 146   **Custos**   In Jamaica, the chief magistrate in each parish.

muster-day   The regular day (usually once a month) when the local militia assembled for parade and drill. In Jamaica, as in other British colonies, all able-bodied free men were meant to belong to the militia, which could be called out whenever the authorities felt it necessary. While they were also supposed to help defend the island in the event of invasion by a foreign power, the main function of the militia was to suppress slave rebellions.

p. 147   Quotation from *Hudibras* (Part I, Canto II, 11, 1–4, first published 1662), satirical poem by the English writer Samuel Butler (1612–1680).

Alexander Ross   Probably the Anglican clergyman of that name (1591–1654) who was a voluminous writer on philosophical and religious subjects.

The facetious Thomas Brown   Possibly the English satirist of that name (1663–1704). Exact source of quotation unidentified.

Peter Pindar   Pen-name of John Wolcot (1738–1819), English writer of satirical verse, who spent a few years (1769–72) in Jamaica, where he was briefly rector of the parish of Vere.

Candide   Short novel, first published in 1759, by the French writer Voltaire (Francois-Marie Arouet, 1694–1778).

Mars   Classical god of war; the expression 'son of Mars' referred to a professional soldier: i.e., a member of the British regular forces (a garrison of which was stationed in Jamaica at this period) rather than of the local militia.

p. 148   **Toledo**   City in Spain, famous for the swords made there.

Penn and Venables Admiral William Penn (*c*. 1621–1670) and General Robert Venables (1612/13–1687) were the leaders of the English expedition which captured Jamaica from the Spanish in 1655. Edward D'Oyley (or Doyley, 1617–1675) was the leader of the English forces which defeated the last significant Spanish attempt to recapture the island at the Battle of Rio Nuevo (on the north coast) in 1658.

p. 149 **Bastile** Place of confinement, after the famous royal fortress in Paris (correctly Bastille), destroyed in 1789 after the outbreak of the French Revolution.

his genius was rebuked Compare Shakespeare, *The Tragedy of Macbeth*, 111, i, 54–6.

p. 150 **Asmodeus** An evil demon who appears in the apocryphal Book of Tobit in the Bible, and in later Jewish legend. The French writer Alain René Le Sage (1668–1747) made him the main character in his novel *Le Diable boiteux*, first published in 1707 and very popular in English translations in the eighteenth and nineteenth centuries.

p. 152 **According to Mr Gill** Mr. Gill was 'an eminent cook at Bath' (a fashionable English resort town in the eighteenth and early nineteenth centuries), and the quotation comes from Christopher Anstey (1724–1805), *The New Bath Guide*, a satirical poem first published in 1766 which remained popular for many years.

p. 153 Quotation from Shakespeare, *Othello*, II, iii, 378.

having adonized himself A term meaning 'made himself handsome' (after Adonis, a beautiful young man loved by Venus in classical mythology), but here used ironically.

that Fairfax who had cut such a figure in the commonwealth of England Sir Thomas Fairfax, third Baron Fairfax (1612–1671), for a time commander-in-chief of the Parliamentary forces during the English Civil War. This Fairfax died peacefully in England, but there were a number of stories about supporters of the Parliamentary cause seeking refuge in Jamaica and other Caribbean colonies after the restoration of the monarchy in 1660.

navigation laws These and the other regulations mentioned imposed a number of restrictions on trade between British colonies and Britain itself, and were intended to benefit the economy of the latter, with little regard to the consequences for the colonies.

p. 155   **The dog began to worry the cat**   Adapted from the popular nursery rhyme, *The House that Jack Built*.

fuit Ilium   'Troy was' (Latin). Used here with an ironic suggestion of vanished glory, this phrase comes, like many of Mr. Guthrie's other Latin quotations, from the epic poem the *Aeneid* (in this case, Book II, line 325), by the Roman poet Virgil (Publius Virgilius Maro, 70–19 BCE).

p. 159   Quotation from Shakespeare, *Twelfth Night, or What You Will*, V, i, 146–7.

p. 160   *Dii quibus imperium*   A not very apposite quotation from *Virgil (Aeneid*, II, 352). The original ('The gods through whose power the kingdom [stood]') refers to the abandonment of Troy by its tutelary deities. Another possibility is *Aeneid* VI, 264, where the same phrase is used to refer to the gods of the underworld.

p. 161   *Lesbia puella*   ('The girl Lesbia') is not a direct quotation, but a reference to the woman whose tempestuous relationship with the Roman poet Gaius Valerius Catullus (*c*. 84–*c*. 55 BCE) is the subject of several of the latter's best known poems.

Infelix Dido   ('unhappy Dido'; this phrase appears at Virgil, *Aeneid* IV, 68; also IV, 450, 596; VI, 456) was the Carthaginian queen who loved the Trojan hero Aeneas and killed herself when he abandoned her to continue his divinely ordained journey to Italy. She is perhaps introduced here because she was a North African, though she is usually portrayed with European features.

Sappho   Ancient Greek poetess whose love-life was the subject of much legend and invention by later writers.

Jezebel   Wicked Queen of Israel in the Bible (I and II Kings).

Rahab   The harlot mentioned in the Book of Joshua in the Bible.

Antecedentem scelestum   ('The villain who goes on ahead') is an allusion to the Roman poet Horace (Quintus Horatius Flaccus, 65–8 BCE), *Odes*, III, ii, 31–2:

    raro antecedentem scelestum
    deseruit pede Poena claudo.

'Seldom has Vengeance with her lame foot given up pursuit of the villain who flees ahead of her.'

Roland's repetition of 'scelestum' suggests that he recognises the allusion, and that it is uncomfortably applicable to himself.

p. 162   **Tamerlane**   Also known as Tamburlane ('Timur the Lame'), Mongol prince (1336–1405) and ruler from 1369, leader in many victorious campaigns, including an invasion of India in 1398. His exploits were the subject of many fanciful accounts by Western writers. He was sometimes described as being able to strike terror into onlookers by his mere gaze, which is the point of the reference here.

Vathek   Principal character in the novel of that name, originally written in French by William Beckford (1760–1844) and first published in 1787 (after an unauthorised English translation the previous year). The novel is set in an imaginary Orient, and it is said of Vathek himself that 'when he was angry, one of his eyes became so terrible, that no person could bear to behold it; and the wretch upon whom it was fixed instantly fell backward, and sometimes expired'—see Peter Fairclough, ed., *Three Gothic Novels* (London: Penguin, 1986), p. 151. Beckford was a celebrated art-collector whose enormous wealth was derived from estates in Jamaica.

basilisk   Fabulous monster, supposedly hatched by a serpent from a cock's egg, whose glance was fatal to those upon whom it fell.

Saturnia regna   The reign of the god Saturn; in classical mythology, a golden age of primeval simplicity. The phrase can be found in, e.g., Virgil, *Eclogues*, IV, 6.

p. 164   Quotation from James Thomson, *The Castle of Indolence*, Canto I, stanza LXIX (first published 1748).

Medea   In classical mythology, Medea helped Jason to win the Golden Fleece, and later married him. When he rejected her to marry another, Medea took her revenge by killing the children she had borne him.

p. 165   ***Nil habet ista sui***   Untraced; the Latin appears to mean 'She has nothing of her own', but its relevance in this context is not clear.

Nimium lubricus aspici Here used to mean 'very greasy in appearance'—but the phrase is a quotation from Horace, *Odes*, I, xix, 8, where it is applied to a woman's face and means 'very dangerous to look at' (because the beholder runs the risk of falling in love with her).

bump of philoprogenitiveness … organs of acquisitiveness A reference to the pseudo-science of phrenology, popular in the nineteenth century, which claimed that a person's character could be read by examining the bumps on his or her skull.

Cerberus The three-headed dog which was the guardian of the underworld in classical mythology.

gradatim One by one (Latin).

unpleasant salivation A reference to the side-effects of the then standard practice of treating venereal disease with mercury.

p. 165–6   **like Falstaff** See Shakespeare, *The Second Part of Henry the Fourth*, I, ii, 176–7. **Vaward** = vanguard; Mr. Fillbeer, like Falstaff, admits that he is not as young as he was, but refuses to admit that he could be described as old.

p. 166   ***locum tenens*** One holding the place of another, a deputy (Latin).

p. 169   ***sang froid*** Coolness (French: 'cold blood').

cocoes Nothing to do with the cocoa tree from which chocolate and drinking cocoa are obtained, but a root vegetable similar to eddoes or tanias.

p. 170   Quotation from Shakespeare, *Othello*, II, iii, 365–7.

p. 171   **Falstaff** and **Bardolph** appear in several of Shakespeare's plays (the *First Part* and *Second Part of Henry the Fourth*, and *The Merry Wives of Windsor*). Bardolph also appears in *Henry V*.

wight Person (a facetious archaism here).

Amine picking rice with a bodkin A reference to a story in the *Arabian Nights*.

p. 173   ***damned spots*** Compare Shakespeare, *Macbeth*, V, i, 35.

p. 174   ***Sit mihi*** It looks as though Mr. Guthrie is having trouble remembering the whole of the phrase, which should be *Sit mihi fas audita loqui* ('May I be permitted to speak those things which I have heard': Virgil, *Aeneid*, VI, 266).

p. 175   **guilty thing**   Compare Shakespeare, *The Tragedy of Hamlet, Prince of Denmark*, I, i, 148.

p. 177   Quotation from Shakespeare, *The Tempest*, III, i, 31–2.

Seven Sleepers of Ephesus   A legend popular in many medieval and later versions, of seven early Christians who had been walled up in a cave near Ephesus (in what is now Turkey) by a pagan emperor. Instead of dying, they slept for many years until they awakened to testify to the miracle. Later they returned to their cave, where they are supposed to sleep until the General Resurrection at the Day of Judgement.

p. 183   *genii loci*   Guardian spirits of the place (Latin).

p. 184   **Proteus**   A sea-god in classical mythology, who had the ability to change his shape.

p. 189   Quotation from Shakespeare, *Measure for Measure*, III, ii, 185–8.

p. 195   **two or three fathoms of mahoe rope**   The name mahoe is applied to several species of tree in Jamaica; the use of their bark for making rope was widespread at least from the middle of the eighteenth century (see *DJE* under 'Bark-Tree'). A fathom is a measure of length equivalent to six feet, or a little under two metres.

p. 196   The quotation is not, as stated, from *The whole life and death of Thomas Lord Cromwell* (1602) but from *The History of Sir John Oldcastle* (1600). Both these plays were sometimes attributed to Shakespeare, though (as with *The London Prodigal*, for which see note on p. 133 above) this attribution is rejected by most modern scholars.

canaille   Rabble (French).

Solomon ... nothing new under the sun   Compare the Book of Ecclesiastes (traditionally ascribed to King Solomon) in the Bible, especially ch. I, v. 9.

p. 197   **unfortunate Darius**   Persian king, defeated by Alexander the Great, 331 BCE, and killed by one of his own followers during his subsequent flight.

crazy Charles   Charles XII, King of Sweden (1697–1718), who was forced to seek refuge in Turkey after his defeat by the Russians at the Battle of Poltava (1709).

Napoleon   Napoleon Bonaparte, Emperor of the French (1804–1814, and again in 1815), exiled to St. Helena as a prisoner of the British after his defeat at the Battle of Waterloo (1815). His death in 1821 was still recent when *Hamel* was being written.

Where the thrush and lark ...   Source unidentified.

Santa Maria   Now usually known simply as 'santa'; the tree *Calophyllum jacquinii* (see *DJE*).

p. 198   **Where the huge axe ...**   Quotation from Milton, *Il Penseroso* (first published 1645), 11, 136–7. (Original has 'rude', rather than 'huge'.)

the Jesuit Le Comte   Louis Le Comte (1655–1728) was one of a group of Jesuit missionaries who arrived in Beijing in 1688. His *Nouveaux mémoires sur l'état présent de la Chine* was first published in Paris in 1696. An English translation appeared in 1737.

p. 201   Although the quotation is given as from an English translation of a work by the French writer Francois Rabelais (*c.* 1494–*c.* 1553; perhaps from his *Gargantua and Pantagruel*), the expression 'as good sit still, as rise to fall' was proverbial in English, and can be found in, for example, John Heywood's *The Spider and the Flie* (1556).

forged pass   See note on p. 143 above.

Quinbus Flestrin   The name (supposedly meaning 'the Great Man-Mountain') given by the Lilliputians to Gulliver in Jonathan Swift's *Gulliver's Travels* (first published 1726).

p. 203   **acquittal of the bishops**   In 1688, King James II had seven bishops of the Church of England tried for refusing to read from their pulpits his Declaration of Indulgence (an attempt to use royal power to suspend existing laws against non-Anglicans). The acquittal of the bishops was the prelude to the king's overthrow later the same year.

harness   Armour. Compare Shakespeare, *Macbeth*, V, v, 51.

Master Matthew   A character in the play *Every Man in his Humour* (1598) by the English playwright Ben Jonson (1572–1637), but the author of *Hamel* appears to be making a mistake by quoting from memory: in the play, the words 'melancholy, and gentlemanlike' are spoken not by Master

Matthew, but by one of the other characters, Master Stephen.

Mr Lambert   Daniel Lambert (1770–1809), an Englishman who became famous for his enormous size. At the time of his death he reportedly weighed 739 pounds (over 300 kilos).

p. 204   **effigies**   Likeness, resemblance (Latin).

Wesley   John Wesley (1703–1791), founder of Methodism (and an opponent of the slave trade).

interval   In the sense mentioned here goes back to the eighteenth century (see quotations in *DJE*).

vile phrase   Shakespeare, *Hamlet*, II, ii, 111 (a term there applied by Polonius to 'beautified').

p. 205   Quotation from Shakespeare, *The Winter's Tale*, V, iii, 76–7.

cheap tracts   'Margaret Blue' is unidentified (and may be fictitious), but *The History of Tom White, the Post Boy* was an actual tract by Hannah More (1745–1833), published in her series of 'Cheap Repository Tracts'. These and many similar publications were produced in large numbers at the end of the eighteenth century and the beginning of the nineteenth. Intended mainly to be bought in quantity by the respectable middle classes for free distribution to the poor, it was hoped that they would encourage the latter to become more Christian and more contented with their lot in life, and so help to prevent in Britain anything like the revolution which had occurred in France. There is some evidence that quantities of the Cheap Repository Tracts were sent to the Caribbean for distribution among the slaves, perhaps with similarly mixed motives.

Candide   Voltaire's novel (see note on p. 147 above) satirises the idea that 'all is for the best in this best of all possible worlds'.

p. 206   **Phaeton**   In classical mythology, Phaeton was a son of Apollo the Sun-god. Having persuaded his father to allow him to drive the Chariot of the Sun across the sky, he proved unable to control the Divine Horses and fell to his death. The point of the allusion here is the suddenness of the tropical sunset, and the virtual absence of twilight, in contrast to more temperate latitudes.

wands ... stout enough Compare the description of Satan's spear in Milton, *Paradise Lost,* I, 292–4: 'to equal which the tallest pine/Hewn on Norwegian hills, to be the mast/Of some great ammiral, were but a wand'. The cotton-tree, or silk-cotton tree *(Ceiba pentandra)* is widely known in the Caribbean, and traditionally regarded as the abode of spirits. It is of course quite different from the shrubs from which cotton is derived (which are species of *Gossypium).*

p. 207   **Some sable Ovid** The most famous work of the Roman poet Ovid (Publius Ovidius Naso, 43–17 BCE) was his *Metamorphoses,* a lengthy poem linking together retellings of many mythological stories, all based in some way on trans-formations of the sort suggested here.

p. 208   ***Duras immittere curas*** A quotation from Virgil *(Aeneid,* IV, 487), but it means 'to give harsh cares' not to 'soothe' them.

p. 209   **professor** A term still sometimes applied to a practitioner of obeah.

p. 212   Quotation from *The Good Natur'd Man,* a comedy by the Irish writer Oliver Goldsmith (?1728–1774), first performed and published in 1768.

            Instar montis equum 'A horse like a mountain', quoted from Virgil, *Aeneid* II, 15. ***Divina Pallas*** ('the divine Pallas', or Athene) is adapted from the same line, in which the Greeks are described as building the Trojan Horse *divina Palladis arte* ('by the divine art of Pallas'). Applying the god-dess's name to Roland in this way suggests a peculiar sense of humour on the part of Mr. Guthrie.

            jessies More usually, jesses, a word normally applied to leather or other straps employed to restrain the legs of a bird used for falconry.

p. 214   ***Dido! dux et Trojanus!*** 'Dido! and the Trojan chief!'; adapted from Virgil, *Aeneid,* IV, 124. The reference to the amorous encounter of Dido and Aeneas in a cave perhaps suggests here Mr. Guthrie's scepticism about Roland's ac-count.

p. 216   ***Humanum est errare*** 'To err is human'; in spite of the Latin form he has given the idea, Mr. Guthrie (or at least the author of *Hamel)* is probably thinking of Alexander Pope,

Essay on Criticism (first published 1711), 1, 525: 'To Err is *Humane; to* Forgive, *Divine.*' The phrase *Errare humanum est* does appear (V, 58) in the *Anti-Lucretius* of Cardinal Melchior de Polignac (first published in Paris, 1747), but while this lengthy Latin poem enjoyed a certain renown in its day, it seems unlikely to have formed part of Mr. Guthrie's reading. Variations on the idea, if not the exact words, can be found in classical authors.

p. 218   Quotation adapted from Shakespeare, *The Tragedy of King Lear*, I, ii, 75–7.

Animum rege 'Control your wrath'; quotation from Horace, *Epistles*, I, ii, 62.

p. 219   ***posse comitatus*** 'Power of the county' (Latin), i.e., men who could be summoned by local authorities to impose the rule of law (exactly like the posse in a movie Western). For the custos, see note on p. 146 above.

p. 223   Quotation from Shakespeare, Hamlet, II, ii, 549–50.

Magi   Wise Men (as in the Bible).

Delphic or Dodonian oracle   Shrines in ancient Greece, where it was believed that divinely inspired prophecies foretold the future. The temple at Delphi was dedicated to Apollo, that at Dodona to Zeus.

p. 225   **cogging, pettifogging knave**   A cheating rascal. 'Cogging' originally referred to cheating at dice, while a pettifogger was an unscrupulous lawyer.

p. 232   Quotation from Shakespeare, *The Tempest*, III, ii, 106–7.

d——n   Damnation.

p. 238   **like another Eneas**   As described by Virgil in Book II of his *Aeneid,* the hero Aeneas escaped from the burning ruins of Troy carrying his aged father Anchises on his back.

p. 239   Quotation from Butler, *Hudibras* (see note on p. 147 above), Part I, Canto I, 11, 873–4.

there is a time for all things   Paraphrase of Ecclesiastes, iii, 8, in the Bible.

p. 240   **œillades**   'Winks' (French).

p. 245   ***ruses de guerre***   'Strategems of war' (French).

p. 249   Quotation untraced, but it is a rhymed adaptation of Shakespeare, *The Tragedy of Julius Caesar*, IV, iii, 218–24.

p. 252   **halter**   Here means a hangman's noose.

p. 253   **Jael and Sisera**   in the Bible (Judges, iv), Jael, the wife of Heber the Kenite, killed Sisera, who was captain of the armies of Jabin, king of Canaan, and an enemy of the children of Israel, by driving a tent-peg through his skull while he slept.

p. 255   **Holy Dunstan**   A reference to a legend dating back to the eleventh century about Saint Dunstan (Archbishop of Canterbury; died 988). In his youth the saint, who is often associated with metalworking, had been working in his forge when he was tempted by a devil whom he drove away by seizing his nose with a pair of red-hot tongs. Some, though not all, versions of the story say that the devil had taken the form of a beautiful woman in his attempt to lead the saint from the path of virtue.

Cazotte's *Diable Amoureux*   First published in 1772, *Le Diable Amoureux* was the best known work of the French writer Jacques Cazotte (1719–1792). The hero of the story raises the devil.

Cocytus   A river in the underworld in classical mythology.

p. 257   **Tartarus**   In classical mythology, the underworld, the abode of the dead.

Jack Ketch   A common nickname for a public hangman.

p. 259   Quotation from Shakespeare, *The Tempest*, I, ii, 317–18.

p. 263   **Jonkanoo Tom Fool**   Jonkanoo (also John Canoe and various other spellings) is a Jamaican popular festival of African origin. The first written reference to it is in Long. By the later eighteenth century it had come to include a number of European elements and was characterised by parades of costumed and masked performers. Fillbeer's suggestion is that Combah looks like a Jonkanoo masquerader, though by this date Jonkanoo costumes were normally much more elaborate than the 'Osnaburgh sheet' or 'white cloth' which covers Combah at this point.

Sampson in the hands of the Philistines   See the Biblical account (Judges, xiii–xvi).

p. 266   **Barbadoes is famous for big legs**   These were the result of elephantiasis, caused by a nematode infection transmitted by mosquitoes, and apparently relatively common in

Barbados in the eighteenth and nineteenth centuries, though it was also found in other parts of the Caribbean. Today the condition is extremely rare.

macaucas   A term applied to various types of worm or grub: see *DJE* under 'macaca'.

p. 268   Quotation from Shakespeare, *Twelfth Night, or What you Will*, III, i, 118–19.

more majorum   'According to the custom of the ancestors' (Latin). The suggestion is that if Fairfax had been unable to marry Joanna, he might have been willing to take Michal as his mistress, in the way in which many white men in the slavery period lived with slaves or free coloured women as sexual partners.

p. 271   **prints of a Negro on his knees in chains**   Such an image, usually with the caption 'Am I not a man and a brother?', was one of the the most widespread emblems of the successive movements against the slave-trade and later against slavery itself. It was originally produced in 1788, in the form of a porcelain cameo by the famous English potter Josiah Wedgwood.

p. 272   *taboo*   Here used to refer to an obeah charm, but the word is of Polynesian (Tongan) origin, and strictly refers to the practice of setting something aside from ordinary use because it is invested with a sacred character. The earliest quotation given in the *Oxford English Dictionary* is from James Cook, *A Voyage to the Pacific Ocean* (1785).

p. 275   **catchpole**   A bailiff, any official whose duty it is to arrest someone.

p. 277   Quotation from Act IV, Scene ii, of *Pastor Fido: or, The Faithful Shepherd* (first published 1677), a masque by Elkanah Settle (1648–1724) based on an earlier translation (1648) by Richard Fanshawe (1608–1666) of the pastoral tragi-comedy *Il pastor fido* (first published 1589) by the Italian writer Giovanni Battista Guarini (1538–1612).

Una dies ...   The Latin means 'the same day is sometimes a parent, sometimes a stepmother' (i.e., can bring both good and bad things). It is a line of hexameter verse, and probably a quotation, but the source is unidentified.

p. 280   **gourd of Jonas**   Possibly a reference to the Book of Jonah in the Bible, where (in the King James Version) the plant which God causes to grow up to provide shade for the prophet is referred to as a gourd. The spelling Jonas may be a misprint for Jonah; while it is the usual Latin version of the name, in the Latin Vulgate translation, the plant is called *hedera*, ivy.

I'll pheeze you   Also found spelt 'feeze'; a good Shakespearian term of abuse, apparently meaning 'I'll do for you', or, more specifically, a threat to flog or beat the person addressed. See Shakespeare, *The Taming of the Shrew*, Induction, i, 1.

eat dirt   Eating dirt was apparently fairly common among slaves in the Caribbean. Contemporary white observers often interpreted it as an attempt to commit suicide, but some modern historians suggest it may have been a symptom of hookworm infestation.

p. 281   **the route of Mahomet**   The Prophet Muhammad was said to have ascended into heaven following a miraculous journey from Mecca to Jerusalem.

Lysippus   Ancient Greek sculptor of the time of Alexander the Great (fourth century BCE). The suggestion that he was responsible for the famous group of four colossal bronze horses brought in 1204 from Constantinople to Venice (where they have spent most of the last eight centuries displayed on the facade of St. Mark's Basilica) is not accepted by modern historians of art.

p. 289   **She should have died hereafter**   Quotation from Shakespeare, *The Tragedy of Macbeth*, V, v, 17 (original reference is to Lady Macbeth).

p. 299   Quotation from Shakespeare, *Othello*, II, iii, 363–4.

weeping for her children   In the Bible (Jeremiah xxxi, 15; Mathew ii, 18) it is Rahel or Rachel who weeps for her children. The original reference in Jeremiah is to the return of the children of Israel and Judah after the Exile.

p. 301   **Centaur**   In classical mythology, a creature which was half man and half horse.

p. 304   **Styx**   In classical mythology, the Styx and **Lethe** were both rivers in the underworld (**Hades**). The phrase *inamabilis* *unda* ('unlovely wave') is adapted from one or the other of two passages in Virgil referring to the underworld (*Georgics*, IV, 479; *Aeneid*, VI, 438).

p. 305 Quotation from Shakespeare, *Hamlet*, V, i, 238–40 (Laertes speaking of Ophelia).

p. 306 **disciples of Esculapius**　Doctors: Aesculapius was the ancient Greek god of medicine, a son of Apollo.

p. 307 **cocoon**　A plant traditionally valued in Jamaica for its medicinal properties; see *DJE* under 'antidote cacoon'.

p. 311 Quotation from Shakespeare, *Macbeth*, II, iii, 93–4.

vanitas vanitatum! ... omnia vanitas　'Vanity of vanities, all is vanity': from the Book of Ecclesiastes (i, 2) in the Bible. The Latin is from the Vulgate, but was so well known as to be proverbial.

from under this terrestrial ball　Quotation from Shakespeare, *The Tragedy of King Richard the Second*, III, ii, 41.

p. 312 **None but the deeply wounded ever know**　Untraced.

make a foot　*DJE* defines this as 'To make an obeisance' but cites only this passage; a creolised version of the now archaic Standard English phrase 'to make a leg', with the same meaning.

p. 316 **dunder**　The lees from a rum still. It was useful, because it could be used to start the fermentation needed to produce the next batch of rum, but it had a foul smell, which is perhaps the point of the reference here. See quotations in *DJE*.

cutacoo　A type of basket; according to *DJE*, sometimes particularly associated with an obeah-man (though this passage is not cited).

p. 317 Quotation from Shakespeare, *2 Henry VI*, III, ii, 309.

p. 318 **estafette**　A mounted courier.

one hundred doubloons　Explained below (p. 330) as equivalent to £533.6s.8d, or slightly later, 'five hundred pounds'. This accords with Long (II, 582), who gives the value of the 'Spanish doub[le] doubloon, milled' (that is, a large gold coin valued at eight escudos in the currency of Spain and its American colonies) as five pounds Jamaican currency, or £3.9s.4d sterling. See also note on p. 43 above.

the rape of Helen   That is, the carrying off of Helen, wife of Menelaus, King of Sparta, by the Trojan prince Paris—the incident which provoked the Trojan War (though of course Helen was said to have gone with Paris of her own free will).

p. 322   Quotation adapted from Settle's *Pastor Fido* (see note on p. 277 above), Act III. (Original has 'ye damn'd spirits' rather than 'all ye spirits'.)

p. 323   **immortalized by Scheherazade**   Perhaps a reference to the story of Aladdin in the *Arabian Nights*—until he accidentally summons the Genie of the Ring, Aladdin is terrified by being trapped in the darkness of the cave of treasures.

p. 324   **Malvolio's mood ... Pythagoras ... fiery abode**   See Shakespeare, *Twelfth Night, or What You Will*, IV, ii.

p. 327   *Balnea, vina, Venus ...*   'Baths, wine and love-making injure our bodies.' A line of Latin hexameter verse, but source not identified.

p. 330   **congé**   Leave, permission to depart (French).

p. 331   Quotation apparently from a translation of the works of the Greek prose satirist Lucian of Samosata (120–*c*. 180 CE), but exact source not traced.

Schedoni   Bartolomeo   Schedoni,   Italian   painter (1578–1615)—but the passage referred to (p. 36 above) mentions an artist called Schiavoni.

p. 332   **Alnaschar**   A character in the *Arabian Nights* who spent the money he had inherited from his father on buying some glass and earthenware for resale. Having piled all his stock in a basket, he waited for customers and fantasized about how he would soon make such a fortune that he would be able to marry the daughter of the Grand Vizier. He resolved that, in order to ensure that she treated him with proper respect, he would not come near her the first night after their wedding (which seems to be the point of the reference to the story here). When she came to beg him to be more attentive to her, he would kick her away—but while he was imagining this, Alnaschar kicked over his basket with such force that he broke all his goods into little pieces.

p. 336   **baron David**   Jacques Louis David (1748–1825), French
painter, famous for his paintings of subjects from classical
history and mythology, including *Leonidas at Thermopylae*.
Although he was appointed official painter to the Emperor
Napoleon, the author of *Hamel* appears to be in error in sug-
gesting David was a baron (and is perhaps confusing him
with his pupil, Baron Gros).

p. 337   Quotation from Shakespeare, *The Tragedy of Titus
Andronicus*, IV, iv, 39–40 (the speakers are Tamora, Queen
of the Goths, and a Clown, i.e., rustic). Some modern editions read 'mistress-ship'.

Wowski   A black female character in *Inkle and Yarico: An
Opera*, by George Colman the Younger, which was first
staged in 1787 and remained widely popular for half a century. A play with songs interspersed, rather than an opera in
the modern sense, it had an anti-slavery theme, though it was
far from free of racist stereotyping. See the text of the play
and the editor's comments in Frank Felsenstein, ed., *English
Trader, Indian Maid: Representing Gender, Race, and
Slavery in the New World; An Inkle and Yarico Reader* (Johns
Hopkins University Press, 1999). The character Patty in
Colman's *Inkle and Yarico* is a white maid-servant (though it
is possible that Patch here is a reference to some other work).

p. 339   **the last war**   Presumably a reference to the Second
Maroon War (1795–6), though many of the Maroons in-
volved in this were deported from Jamaica by the colonial
authorities. The obligation to help in the recapture of runaway and rebellious slaves formed part of the treaties which
ended the earlier Maroon Wars of the 1730s.

p. 342   **the bishop**   Christopher Lipscomb (1781–1843), first
Anglican Bishop of Jamaica (1824–43), who arrived in the island 11 February 1825.

p. 345   Quotation from Shakespeare, *The Tragedy of King Lear*, IV,
vi, 11–12.

p. 349   **the Aquarius or the Jupiter of the tropics**   Aquarius is
the Water-Carrier in the Zodiac, while Jupiter here is
specifically Jupiter Pluvius, the god of rainfall in classical
mythology. In other words, the group here is moving
through a fine drizzle in the mountains, which is unlike the
heavy downpours often associated with rainfall at lower
elevations in the Caribbean.

chute   Fall (French). The author of *Hamel* is simply being pretentious here, as the word is not used by Milton himself.

p. 350   **imprisoned in the viewless winds**   Quotation from the same passage of Shakespeare (*Measure for Measure*, III, i, 117–27) quoted at p. 359 below, but here with 'tost' where the original has 'blown'.

p. 352   **Curtius**   In ancient Rome, a young man called Marcus Curtius was said to have leapt on horseback into an immense gulf which had miraculously appeared in the Forum, sacrificing himself to the gods in order to secure the future of the state. The story is told in Livy's *History* (see note on p. 47 above), VII, vi, but the gulf is not there described as 'fiery'.

p. 353   Quotation from Shakespeare, *The Merchant of Venice*, II, i, 1–3. The speaker is the Prince of Morocco, who is attempting to woo Portia.

Raphael   Raffaello Sanzi or Santi (1483–1520), celebrated Italian painter.

p. 359   Quotation from Shakespeare, *Measure for Measure*, III, i, 76–7.

resembling ... one of Jacob's lambs   Either brown, or perhaps (in view of the effects of the rain on Fairfax's disguise) 'speckled and spotted', though in the Biblical story (see Genesis, xxx, in the King James Version) this description is applied to the cattle and goats rather than the lambs.

p. 363   *Instar Jovis*   Latin for 'Like Jupiter', the king of the gods in classical mythology.

p. 365   Quotation from Shakespeare, *Cymbeline*, III, iii, 10–11.

As absolute as Cromwell   Oliver Cromwell (1599–1658) dissolved the Long Parliament by force in 1653, or rather, what was left of it, the greatly reduced membership known as the 'Rump Parliament'. However, as Lord Protector of England, Scotland and Ireland from 1653 to 1658, he was far from being an absolute monarch.

p. 366   **Sierra Leone**   The Maroons deported from Jamaica in 1796 were sent first to Nova Scotia, but after two years there, were sent to Sierra Leone. Sierra Leone was also the eventual destination of a group of slaves deported from Barbados in 1817 as a punishment for their involvement in the major rebellion of the previous year.

p. 367   **colour of their jackets**   Red, the usual colour for the jackets of British soldiers and colonial militia in the period, hence the use of 'red-coats' as a description for them.

p. 368   **sudarium**   Handkerchief (Latin).

as St Paul recommended   Quotation from I Corinthians, xv, 32, in the King James Version of the Bible (but the context shows that St Paul only recommends this 'if the dead rise not', a supposition he emphatically rejects).

p. 369   **A bloody war and a sickly season**   Something of the sort was apparently a common toast among army and navy officers of the period—the death of those senior to one's self improved one's own prospects of promotion.

p. 370   **junks of beef and pork**   Cut pieces. A term probably commoner in Caribbean speech than in Standard English; the only definition given in Bailey is '(among *Sailors*) Pieces of old Cable'.

p. 371   **not ... as pot-valiant as he expected**   In other words, the drink failed to stimulate his courage.

p. 372   **the queen of Sheba bringing presents to Solomon** See the account in the Bible (I Kings, x).

p. 373   *derrière*   Buttocks (French).

p. 374   *terra firma*   Solid ground (Latin).

p. 379   Quotation from Shakespeare, *Measure for Measure*, III, i, 117–27.

p. 381   *gran' Diavol del Inferno*   Great Devil of Hell (Italian).

p. 382   **a real ... minister ... ordained by some religious bishop**   This crystallises the author's attitude to 'sectarians' or non-Anglicans; compare the references to 'white Obeah men' which are put into Hamel's mouth (below, pp. 389–90).

p. 383   *in articulo mortis*   In the moment of death (Latin).

p. 387   Quotation from John Milton, *Comus* (1634),11, 814–16.

the emperor and the president of Haiti   Presumably a reference to Jean Jacques Dessalines, Emperor of Haiti 1804–06, and Alexandre Petion, President of (southern) Haiti 1807–18, or Jean Pierre Boyer, President of Haiti 1818–43. However, the author may also be thinking of King Henri Christophe (see note on p. 96 above) who had many influential European admirers.

p. 388   **the creoles will understand this**   The implication is that she had been the mistress of a white man.

the rights which Mr Wilberforce had obtained for them   Defenders of the status quo in the Caribbean colonies often claimed that unrest among the slaves was due to misunderstandings of anti-slavery agitation in Britain and of changes in legislation which it produced. The rebellion in Barbados in 1816 was said to have been caused by the prevalence among the slaves of the belief that they had in fact been freed by the British government, and that their masters were unlawfully keeping their freedom from them. There were claims that this was a misunderstanding of proposed measures for the registration of all slaves (which became law in 1817).

p. 390   *nyam-nyam*   Food (see *DJE* under 'ninyam, nyamnyam', where this passage is cited).

the resolutions of the Wesleyans   On 7 September 1824, four of the ten Methodist missionaries present in Jamaica met in Kingston and passed a number of resolutions. These were then circulated to those not present at the meeting, and while some of these disapproved of all or part of the resolutions, a version was sent to the local press, signed only by the chairman of the meeting, but in such a manner as to suggest that the resolutions expressed the views of all the missionaries. As is stated here, the resolutions were indeed officially disavowed by the Methodist Church in Britain (though the suggestion that some of the missionaries were recalled appears to be unfounded). The main points objected to were that the resolutions stated that 'Christianity does not interfere with the civil condition of the slaves, as slavery is established by the laws of the British West Indies' (which could easily be interpreted as meaning that the Methodist Church officially supported slavery, which was far from being the case), and that they criticised the activities of the 'emancipationists and abolitionists' in Britain. The resolutions were passed at a time when the Methodist Church was facing increasing opposition in Jamaica from members of the local oligarchy, and the missionaries involved seem to have hoped that passing the resolutions would encourage planters and officials to leave them alone to get on with their work of evangelisation. There is an extended discussion of this episode in Peter Duncan, *Narrative of the Wesleyan Mission to Jamaica; with occasional remarks on the state of society in that colony* (London, 1849), pp. 160–7.

p. 392   **A sincere and tender passion ...**   Untraced.

p. 395   ***hic jacet***   Death; the Latin phrase literally means 'Here lies' and was a standard beginning for epitaphs.